Harvesting Evil

Credits:
Developmental Editor: Wanda Leske
Copy Editor: Tom Siebert
Book Cover: Book Baby Publishing
Book Formatting: Weformat

All scripture quotations are taken from New American Standard Bible

Harvesting Evil

Shari Weise

∞Laurdel Publishing∞
www.laurdelpublishing.com

This book is dedicated to
Ken, Lauren, & Delaney
I love you more than words.

Thank you, God, for placing some extraordinary people in my life! You've given me a beautiful mom, who (besides my husband) is my biggest fan and cheerleader! In addition, you blessed me with four amazing friends: Wanda Leske, Dawn Faaborg, Patti Milbourn, and Tiffani Hamstra, who offered suggestions and encouraged me to finish! But your blessings didn't stop there. When I needed technical advice, you sent Police Chief Dale Nanage. This book wouldn't be possible without the help of the many people you placed in my path!

In May 2020, I began blogging on my website (shariweise.com). In the introductory blog, I invited readers to join me on a book publishing voyage. It took a while, but we're finally ready to set sail! Thank you for climbing aboard. Our hull is seaworthy, the keel is true, and our deck is watertight. But just in case the seas get choppy, I've thrown in a few life rafts.

With a highly grateful heart,
Shari

"Thriller" is not the genre that immediately comes to mind when referring to Christian literature. However, Shari Weise has written a crackling good book that is exceedingly suspenseful and supernatural but with believable characters whom you will care about. *Harvesting Evil* is reminiscent of Alfred Hitchcock's *The Birds*. But unlike that classic film, Shari's book is decidedly Bible-based, Christ-centered, and church-themed. I give *Harvesting Evil* four E's—for entertaining, educating, edifying, and excellent!

Tom Siebert, Christian Editor Connection

Part 1

Crows are intelligent, social birds capable of communicating with one another over great distances. They perceive sound at frequencies lower than those heard by the human ear. Crows possess an uncanny ability to sense death, drawing near to those who are dying. Humankind has referred to these birds as harbingers of doom. Perhaps that is why a flock of crows is called a "murder."

CHAPTER 1

Norm Keller sat in his recliner, gazing at emerald-colored cornstalks aligned in perfect rows behind his home. A large crow flew past his window and captured his attention. It crossed back across the yard before landing on the chain-link fence.

"Well, look at that!" Mary said as she walked to the sliding glass door. "That's the largest crow I've ever seen."

Another crow swooped down from the sky. It landed on the fence line, next to the first crow. It wasn't as large, but its appearance was still formidable. "Oh, there's another one," she said and shook her head. "You know how I feel about crows, Norm. They're a bad omen."

He shrugged. He never cared much for birds. He wasn't superstitious; he just didn't like the mess they made. "Looking at the size of those birds, I doubt that farmer will have any corn left by harvest time."

She turned and peered down at him. After thirty-five years of marriage, he knew the expression on her face—disapproval, hidden behind a forced smile. She looked poised to say something. His shoulders tensed. *What's she going to do today? Quietly sulk or outright ask me to join her?* He bit his bottom lip, bracing for her comment.

"I think you'd really like Pastor Cummings. He reminds me of you when you were fresh out of seminary school."

And there she goes. Her response was the one he hated most, that backhanded way of asking someone to do something without genuinely asking. He tempered his response. "Better get a move on, Mary, or you'll be late."

She sighed heavily, then gave a slight shake of her head as she kissed his forehead.

His stomach twisted in response. *I've disappointed her again.* In the few short months since they'd moved into their new home, he'd grown weary of Sundays. When they lived in Tucson, she kissed him on the cheek before leaving for church. She never said a word. But here, in their fresh-start home outside of Phoenix, she seemed poised to get him back behind the altar at any cost.

He shrugged his shoulders, then turned his attention back to the crows. Growing up, he hunted dove and quail. And much to Mary's dismay, he'd shot pigeons off their roof with a BB gun. The two crows perched on his fence line looked ripe for the picking. He raised his finger and pointed. Bang! Bang!

The massive crow slowly turned towards him. Its beady eyes, black as coal, locked with his—challenging him. He shifted in his recliner as the crow's cold dark stare penetrated his heart. The hairs on his arms raised, and his body shuddered.

The crow had captured his soul, turning it over and over in its talons, examining every part. Then, as if finding him unworthy, it released him and turned its attention back to the field. His spirit dropped with a thud, leaving him breathless.

CHAPTER 2

As he did every seven years, Tobias Smith dressed in a dark cloak and descended the massive staircase towards the summoning room. Unlike previous summonings where fear overwhelmed all emotions, in this summoning, anger coursed through his veins.

The people living in their community, his sons, even his wife, Sarah—they'd all judge him if they ever discovered his secret. They'd never let him explain. If they only knew the sacrifice he made to keep them all safe.

With each deliberate step, the old wood of the staircase creaked beneath his feet. A rusty unlit kerosene lantern swayed gently back and forth in his free hand. It resonated a tiny squeak in perfect harmony with the aged wood. The random noise it made provided a comforting distraction, keeping his mind off the evil he'd soon bring forth.

Once he'd descended the stairs, he turned and stepped into the small, dark alcove. For nearly a hundred years, his family home stood proudly on a small hill overlooking acres and acres of farmland. Over time, the house underwent many transformations. Only the staircase and the alcove remained untouched.

He struck a match and ignited the lantern. Its light cast an eerie shadow onto the richly carved wooden panels lining the alcove walls. In twenty-one years of marriage, Sarah hadn't found the room. The intricate carving and separation between the panels created an optical illusion, hiding the door in plain sight.

He removed a large bronze-colored key from his pocket. The intricate pattern of interlocking circles covering the key's head mirrored the wooden panels' design. He kept it hidden in a small box in his closet for safekeeping.

Brushing his fingers over the delicately carved wooden panels, he searched for the keyhole, then inserted the key and turned. Click. The lock gave way. He pushed against the hidden door. Sealed shut for seven years, it didn't budge. He tried again, pushing harder this time. The door yielded, sending him crashing onto the cold, hard floor. A pulsating wave of pain erupted from his knee. He bent his leg back and forth. *Nothing broken. But I'll have a hell of a bruise.*

He returned to the alcove, picked up the lantern, then paused at the doorway. Soon he'd face evil. A trembling wave, small at first, spread through his body. With each passing second, it gained momentum, holding him firmly in place. He shook his head. There was no time to stall. With Sarah and his sons at church, he needed to get started.

He held up the lantern. Its light illuminated the plaster walls of the small room. His great-grandfather, Ansas, formed the plaster using the cactus and other elements of the family's land. Covering nearly every inch of the walls were symbols painted in black. When he was younger, the drawings on the walls intrigued him. He spent hours hidden in the barn, searching through borrowed library books, trying to decipher them.

The more he read, the more frightened he became. Finally, he stopped searching. Wishing, instead, he could erase all the knowledge he'd collected. The symbols on the wall, along with the contents of the hidden room, weren't an archeological mystery to be solved; they were satanic. Further proof his forefathers weren't the upstanding citizens they portrayed themselves to be.

He stepped into the room and closed the door behind him. A small, weathered table sat in the center of the room. On one end of the table sat a black, gnarled candle. Hardened drips of wax streaked down the candle, resembling a dark waterfall frozen in time. On the other end of the table sat a small wooden bowl with a sizeable zigzag-shaped crack extending halfway down its side. Crudely carved into the outside of the bowl were faint remnants of figures that appeared to be half-human, half-animal. In the center of the table lay a leather spell book. The bowl and spell book once belonged to Ansas.

He rested the lantern on the floor, near his feet, then pulled a leather pouch from his cloak and placed it on the table. He'd performed the ritual only a few times in his life. The kerosene lamp and the pouch weren't necessary items, but they'd been handed down to him by his father. Although impractical, if they worked, he'd keep using them.

His hand shook as he struck a match and lit the black candle. The candle's light cast a flickering shadow onto the wall. His heart fluttered, then began pounding in his chest. Tiny beads of sweat lined his forehead. He momentarily closed his eyes and ran his fingers through his thinning black hair. The gesture was comforting, soothing. Through pursed lips, he exhaled a few times. Eventually, his heartbeat slowed.

He opened his eyes and began the ritual by loosening the pouch's leather ties and slowly unrolling it. Tucked within the pouch was a sachet filled with angelica, rosemary, sage, cloves, and verbena. Next to the sachet was a large black feather of a crow and an antique silver dagger. He placed the sachet and the feather into the wooden bowl, then struck a match. The sachet burst into a small flame, sending puffs of black smoke into the air. Sounds of crackling flames resonated against the plaster walls, and the room filled with the smell of burnt herbs and spices.

He opened the spell book and thumbed through its yellowed pages. Inside were drawings of the moon in various phases, along with descriptions of corresponding spells—upside-down crosses, pentagrams, and illustrations of half-human, half-animal creatures. Many of the drawings in the book matched those on the wall. He shook his head and turned to the next page in the book. Written in what appeared to be blood, he found the incantation.

As he recited the words on the page, he pressed the dagger against the palm of his hand. His blood dripped freely into the bowl. It acted as a catalyst on the fire, sending convulsing waves of black smoke towards the ceiling. He stepped back and grabbed his hand to stifle the bleeding.

The smoke twisted and turned into one pillar. He watched as the pillar of smoke advanced towards the candle's shadow. Like a small set of lungs drawing in the smoke, the shadow rhythmically expanded and contracted, slowly growing with each passing moment.

The shadow wantonly danced against the walls of the small room. After a moment, it pulled away from the wall, twisting in mid-air like a growing tornado. As the swirling darkness moved behind him, the stench of rotten eggs filled his nostrils. *Sulfur.* His eyes burned. He blinked rapidly, sending small rivers of tears down his cheeks. Warm bile filled his mouth; he swallowed it back down.

He remained as still as a cold stone statue, allowing his breaths to come in short, stunted waves. If he didn't move, perhaps the evil he'd summoned would leave him unharmed.

The shadowy spirit encircled his body, enveloping him into an embrace. He tried to breathe deeply, but the shadow squeezed him like a giant snake encapsulates its prey. Soon his arms and legs grew numb.

A cold pressure fell upon his right shoulder. A coldness so extreme, it burned. He slowly turned his head to the left and squeezed his eyes tightly shut. The frigid pressure moved onto the right side of his neck as if someone held a freezing branding iron against it. He jerked and tried to pull away. But the shadow squeezed tighter in response, sending him a brazen warning—it was in control, not him. He must succumb to its every need. *Let me go!* He silently screamed the words in his head.

Just as the world around him faded to black, the squeezing pressure abated, and he collapsed to the floor. After a few winded breaths, the blood rushed back into his arms and legs. The cold spirit hovered briefly before moving through the hidden door and out of the room.

CHAPTER 3

After dinner, Susan Green watched rolling clouds of gray and violet become an eerie shade of black. Her stomach twisted into knots. She hadn't seen the sky this dark, so early in the evening. By the look of the clouds, the storm heading her way would be severe.

In her mind's recesses, the warning voices of her parents, Anne and Steve, rang out. "If you want a house so badly, you should move to Prescott. Are you sure you aren't trying to prove a point by living so far away?" She shook her head, pushing the naysayers aside. For over ten years, she'd been under the care of Dr. Cohen. The medications he prescribed kept the voices in her head at bay. *I can do this! I can live here alone!* Determination permeated every fiber of her being. She would succeed. And in that success, she'd prove her parents wrong.

She looked around the family room and took a long deep breath. She'd purchased a home on the outskirts of Phoenix, surrounded by farmland. The site of the house wasn't ideal. But the three-bedroom floorplan more than made up for its location. Her parents tried to dissuade her from buying. They warned that living in a cul-de-sac on the last street of the sub-division would make her feel isolated.

She wasn't sure if her actions constituted outright defiance or sound adult judgment. All she knew for certain was that she wanted to own a home. This one was the nicest in her price range, so she bought it.

The first few weeks in the home proved one thing: her parents were right. She felt isolated. Despite the impending storm brewing outside, the inside of her home remained quiet. For a moment, she missed the paper-thin walls and ceilings of her old apartment. Although annoying, the arguments of the couple living next door and the creaks and groans of footsteps traversing overhead were steady reminders she wasn't alone. A half-hearted laugh escaped her lips—*what a thing to miss.*

She beckoned Libby to the sliding glass door. "Come on, girl. You need to go potty before the storm hits." It had taken time and patience, but she'd finally potty-trained the three-month-old cocker spaniel. The backyard patio was nothing more than a small concrete slab, and there wasn't a patio cover. If Libby didn't get outside before the storm arrived, there was a good chance she'd have an accident in the house later.

Success. After heaping praises on the puppy, she changed into her pajamas and made a cup of tea. Drinking tea calmed her nerves. It was a trick she'd learned from watching her mother. She found comfort in the ritual of boiling water to the perfect temperature and steeping tea leaves for the perfect amount of time.

With the hot tea in hand, she curled up on the couch beneath a small blanket while Libby curled into a little furry ball on the carpet below. She clicked the remote, moving from one channel to the next. She planned to watch television for as long as she could, hoping the subtle distraction would take her mind off the storm.

A few hours later, a drizzling mist fell over the house. Bolts of lightning cracked across the sky, quickly followed by the sound of rolling thunder. With each crash of thunder, she glanced out the sliding glass door. As the storm grew closer, Libby whimpered and nervously paced in front of the couch. The picture on the television flickered and then rolled as the storm interrupted the satellite signal. She clicked the TV off and stretched her short, thin frame, secretly wishing she had a yoga instructor's flexibility. A gentle popping sound emanated from her back and neck. *I'm only twenty-five. Too young to have cracking joints.*

Libby followed her into the bathroom. She glanced at the mirror as she brushed her teeth; curly brown hair framed her thin face. Long lashes framed her brown eyes. After brushing her teeth, she turned out the bathroom light then stepped into her bedroom. The heavy drapes covering her bedroom window were open. Beyond her small backyard sat a narrow dirt road. Just beyond the narrow road lay a massive cornfield. All bathed in darkness under a moonless sky.

She removed a patchwork comforter from the closet and placed it over the bed. Despite being threadbare in spots, she couldn't bear to part with it. The comforter was a gift from her grandmother. The mere act of sleeping under it eased her fears. She placed Libby on the bed, then crawled under the comforter. From the safety of her bed, she watched as the storm drew closer.

Intermittent bolts of lightning ripped across the night sky. Like flashes from an old camera's flashbulb, each streak of lightning illuminated the cornfield below. A roar of thunder followed the crack of lightning. She counted the seconds between them. One, two, three, four, five, six. Boom!

Raindrops pelted the bedroom window as gusts of wind rattled the glass. The raindrops also fell onto the metal fence surrounding her yard. Over and over, a constant pinging rang out as the drops struck the metal.

Libby's body quivered, and she began to whine. "Shh," Susan whispered. Her stomach knotted. She pulled Libby closer to her chest and absentmindedly rubbed the puppy's soft coat. "I'm scared too. It's a pretty big storm. Let's hope it passes soon."

The storm settled over the cornfield. Crack! Lightning erupted across the sky. She counted the seconds. One, two, three. Boom! The thunder shook the house. *It's moving closer.* Another round of lightning lit up the sky in quick succession. Like watching an old-time movie reel, each burst of light exposed a different scene of the cornfield.

Little by little, a wispy black shadow swirled downward from the center of the storm clouds. She sat fully upright in bed. *Is that a tornado?* With each flash, the black shadow grew bigger. Mesmerized by swirling blackness, she climbed out of bed and stood at the window. Another flash of lightning lit up the sky. She squinted, trying to keep her eyes focused on the darkness.

Like a layer of rippling water, the darkness spread over the cornfield; then, it slowly sank through the cornstalks. *What the...?* Her heart raced. The way the darkness moved defied explanation. A cold pressure moved through her chest, snatching the warm air from her lungs. She gripped the windowsill to hold herself upright, then closed her eyes and took deep breaths.

After a moment, she took one long breath to gather her courage, then opened her eyes. Another bolt of lightning struck. This time it was coupled with a simultaneous thunder crash that shook the house and sent her reeling back onto the bed.

Eerily quiet darkness shrouded the house. Her eyes widened as she scanned the room. She couldn't see past the edge of the bed, and the digital alarm clock on her nightstand was dark. Libby whined. She didn't attempt to silence her; instead, she pulled the shaking puppy closer to her chest and whispered, "We'll be okay."

A chill moved through the room; goosebumps covered her arms. The last lightning strike knocked the power out. She'd experienced this before in her old apartment. She knew it could take hours before the power returned.

"Come on, Libby. We need to find the flashlight."

Timidly, she made her way out of her bedroom and into the hallway. Halfway down the hall, she passed a nightlight. She shook her head as she remembered her mother's recommendation to buy a nightlight that stayed on when the power went out. *I hate it when she's right.*

Libby's toenails scraped over the vinyl flooring as she hurried down the hall. The wayward puppy brushed against her leg, sending her bumping into the wall. She righted herself and continued to the family room and kitchen. To her right, past the kitchen, was a small formal living room and front door. With the intermittent flashes of lightning to guide her, she made it to the kitchen island. She opened the drawer and smiled. "I found it, Libby."

She clicked the button on the flashlight. A thin stream of yellow light extended a few feet in front of her. *Add batteries to the shopping list.* She gripped the flashlight tightly in her hand and began walking back to her room. She took a few steps, then bumped into Libby. The puppy stood frozen, facing the living room. A low growl resonated from her throat.

"What's wrong, girl?"

She turned and aimed the flashlight toward the living room. The faint light streaming from the end of the flashlight was too dim to break through the darkness. Libby's growling continued. Another lightning strike exposed a shadowy figure outside her front door. Her mouth fell open and a weak scream escaped her lungs. She dropped the flashlight. It crashed onto the kitchen floor with a hard thud, extinguishing the light and plunging the room back into darkness.

She ducked behind her kitchen island. Her mind raced. *Can I still call*

11

911 with the power out? Loud, rapid knocks upon the front door. Her heart leaped in her chest. She took slow deep breaths, then peeked around the island into the living room. *Criminals don't knock, right?* Slowly, she picked up the flashlight and smacked it against the palm of her hand. The light flickered on.

The knocking resumed, followed by a deep voice. "Susan, are you okay?"

She deeply exhaled as she recognized the voice. Norm. She silently nodded, then pulled herself upright and yelled, "I'm coming." She rushed to the front door, unbolted the lock, and opened it a few inches.

Norm's six-foot, four-inch body filled the doorframe. Her gaze moved from the top of his head down his body. By the time her eyes reached his feet, her mouth fell open.

Black round glasses framed his deep blue eyes. Salt and pepper gray hair lay in a tousled mess on his head. A long, dark raincoat covered his upper body. Striped pajamas and dark slippers peeked out beneath the coat.

In one hand, he held a flashlight with a fully charged battery. In the other hand, he had a tiny pink umbrella. *Is that his granddaughter's?*

She curled her lips inward, stifling the laugh, which threatened to burst from her chest. Tiny parasol, giant slippers. A warm sensation crept over her face. *Stop!* She admonished herself. *Don't laugh! He's here to check on you!* A slow exhale helped her regain her composure. She'd never seen the retired pastor look anything other than professional. By his haphazard appearance, she was sure Mary had tossed him out of bed to perform a welfare check.

"I'm okay, Norm. I can't believe this storm, though. It's crazy, right?

"One of the biggest I've seen. Thankfully, it looks like the worse part has passed."

"Do you think the power will be back on soon?"

He shrugged. "I'm guessing one of the transformers blew. I'm not sure how long it takes to get a crew here to fix it. Anyway, I'm glad you're alright. Mary insisted I check in on you. Do you need anything?"

She shook her head. "Libby and I are going to crawl straight back into bed. Thanks for checking in on us. Knowing you and Mary are right next door makes me feel safer."

Norm smiled and raised his hand. "I better get home. You let us know if you need anything, okay?"

"Will do."

She returned to her bedroom and pulled the drapes closed while averting her gaze from the window. Then she placed Libby on the bed and crawled in beside her. As she lay in total darkness, images from the storm raced through her mind. She squeezed her eyes shut and shook her head. *Think about something else!* Dwelling on the storm was similar to pulling on a stray string. If she did it, she risked becoming unraveled. So, instead, she focused on Libby's breathing. Finally, the rhythmic movement of Libby's chest lowered the nervous tension within her belly. Within a few moments, she drifted off to sleep.

✳ ✳ ✳

As he left Susan's house, Norm lowered his umbrella and looked towards the sky. The downpour of rain had weakened to a light misty drizzle. Between the new moon and loss of power to the subdivision, the cul-de-sac stood in total darkness. He slowly pointed his flashlight up and down the dark, vacant street.

Movement on the roof of his home captured his attention. He shined his flashlight upwards and froze. Black crows lined the roofline. In fifty-six years, he'd never witnessed birds outside during a storm. *Why are they sitting on the cold, damp roof, instead of seeking shelter?* He shuddered. In the daylight, the crows exuded a dark aura he found unsettling. But here, in the dead of night, the crows' unusual behavior didn't leave him unsettled; it frightened him.

His gaze moved to the largest crow. While the smaller crows turned towards the field, the large one stared down at him. Slowly, the crow turned its gaze towards the cornfield as if beckoning him to do the same. He complied. Another crash of lightning illuminated the cornfield. A fine white mist covered the ground. *Is that smoke?*

Like a group of rowdy cheerleaders, the crows on the roof cawed loudly. He glanced back in their direction. All the smaller crows flapped their wings and cawed while facing the cornfield. The large crow turned away from the field and stared down at him again. The air grew colder. He pulled his raincoat closer to his body and forced his gaze away.

He rushed back to his house. Once inside, he tossed the umbrella and raincoat into a heap against the front door. With his flashlight in hand, he ran to the family room at the back of the house and drew back the curtain covering the sliding glass door. Then he jerked the door open and stepped onto the concrete slab. The crows continued to clamor on the roof above. He aimed the flashlight at the base of the cornstalks. Thin white smoke billowed from the ground in churning waves, rising straight up as though it were boxed into the cornfield by an invisible wall.

The stench of rotten eggs filled the air. *Gas leak?* He shook his head. Although he'd never experienced one before, he was confident it wouldn't look like this. The smoke grew thicker. Within moments, the entire cornfield appeared engulfed in an invisible fire.

He shined the flashlight back and forth over the wall of smoke. Within the flashlight's beam, he saw darkness move through the smoke. Like cotton candy drawn onto a paper stick, the darkness swirled as it pulled in the white smoke. Its movement through the white haze seemed purposeful, provocative. As if spawned from dark and white procreation, the smoke turned a dull shade of gray.

Cool, pungent air gusted through his thin pajamas. He shivered, then returned to the house. As he drew the sliding glass door closed, a sensation washed over him. It felt as though there was something within the gray smoke watching him. The hairs on the back of his neck raised, and every fiber of his being went on high alert.

Timidly, he reopened the sliding glass door and extended the flashlight back through the door's opening. He pressed his forehead against the cold glass and stared onto the field. He didn't see anything, but the strange feeling washed over him again. *Something is watching me!*

His hand shook wildly, sending the flashlight crashing to the concrete slab. It ricocheted off the concrete, then fell to the lawn below. With short, studded movements, it rolled back and forth, sending eerie beams of light through the grass's blades.

He looked back at the gray wall. His gaze started at the bottom, then slowly moved upward until it rested on the glint of two red eyes. He fought to look away. But the hypnotizing red eyes held his gaze. They taunted him as if calling out, "I am here. What are you going to do about it?"

14

He felt a wave of dizziness, and then his entire body broke out in a cold sweat. His legs felt like jelly. As they began to buckle, he grasped onto the sliding glass door handle to keep from falling. He tried to scream, but the sound escaping his throat was merely a whimper. He yanked the sliding door shut with a force that shuddered the glass. With fumbling fingers, he secured the door's lock, then pulled the curtains closed. *What the hell was that?*

With his heart still pounding deep within his chest, he stumbled down the hallway, then fell against the doorframe. He glanced into the bedroom. Mary lay quietly in bed. She looked peaceful, seemingly oblivious to the sinister force behind their home.

Over time, his heartbeat slowed. *It's my imagination! A trick of the light.* Slowly, the shaking in his body faded. With a faltering gait, he entered, then crossed the bedroom, holding onto the footboard of the bed and dresser for support. When he reached the bedroom window, he held the plastic rod for a full minute, wondering if he should open the blinds or crawl into bed with Mary. After a few deep breaths, he straightened his shoulders, then slowly twisted the plastic rod, tilting the blinds open enough to peek out. After a moment, his eyes adjusted to the darkness. The churning within the fog appeared to have stopped, leaving a solid wall of gray over the corn. He continued staring, searching for any hints of red. *It's gone.*

Mary stirred in the bed. "What are you looking at?" she whispered.

"Nothing. I…I'm coming to bed."

He crawled into bed, sheltering within the bedding's warmth. Mary had returned to sleep. He focused on the blankets covering her body. They ebbed and flowed in perfect rhythm with her breathing. That gentle up and down movement settled his nerves. He placed his hand over her hand and gave a gentle squeeze.

Competing thoughts raced through his head. *Was there something out there? Something evil?* He gently shook his head. *No! It was only my imagination. If I allow myself to believe there's something evil out there, I must acknowledge there's something good to fight it. There's no darkness without light.*

He left the church nearly two years ago. Mary said he was fighting with God. In her attempts to console him, she'd sweetly whisper, "Fights end. Wounds heal." Once they moved to their Phoenix home, she stopped saying those words. He knew she prayed he'd return to his faith. Her praying didn't bother him. If Mary wanted to waste her time praying, it was her call, her choice. At least, she cared enough about him to keep him in her prayers.

What bothered him was her not-so-subtle attempts to entice him back to the church. Each attempt left him seething and her pouting. Someday, she'd have to face the fact he no longer believed in God. End of story. No trick of light or overactive imagination would change his mind.

He stared at the ceiling fan above the bed. The motor's hum, coupled with the fan blades' hypnotic spin, drowned out his racing thoughts. The deeper he sank into the mattress, the more his body relaxed. Eventually, exhaustion overtook him. He closed his eyes and fell asleep.

CHAPTER 4

Norm loved the way everything looked after a heavy rainstorm. Asphalt roads, sidewalks, even the rocks covering the front yards, all washed clean by rain. After last night's storm, instead of awakening with a sense of renewal, he awoke filled with dread. He reached out to Mary's side of the bed. Empty. Her portion of the bedding lay in a messy pile. The room was shrouded in gray light, the kind of light that occurred when storm clouds filled the daytime sky.

He glanced at the alarm clock; the red numbers on the clock face resembled the red eyes from last night. Tightness seized his chest, quickening his heart and stealing his breath. He slammed his eyes shut. *It wasn't real!*

As if restraining a bully who threatened to punch, he shoved the red eyes' image to a proverbial room in the back of his mind—that place in his psyche where he pushed all unwanted thoughts. Once he'd tucked the image away, he slammed his mind's door shut and locked it. The tightness in his chest eased.

The aroma of bacon wafted into the room, stirring his appetite. His mouth watered, and his stomach growled. *Bacon?* It was something Mary made for breakfast on a Saturday, not during the week. He climbed out of bed and headed to the kitchen.

As he approached the dining room table, Mary strolled out of the kitchen and handed him a coffee cup, saying, "Good morning."

He kissed her cheek. "Thank you. I need this."

Her blue eyes lit up, and she smiled. He studied her face. Her skin was fair and smooth, like fine ivory porcelain. Tiny lines at the corners of her

17

eyes gave a hint of her age. The navy nightgown she wore deepened the blue in her eyes. She wore her gray hair short and stylishly swept back from her face. He remembered the tears she shed on her fortieth birthday when she first noticed her hair turning gray. She worked hard that year, trying to stay a brunette.

On her forty-first birthday she stood in front of him, and using an animated voice, exclaimed, "Guess what I just read in a magazine?!" Before he could come up with a quippy response, she patted her hair with both hands and continued, "Twenty year olds are dying their hair gray! Honestly, Norm, it's a trend. And, to think, for a whole year, I've fought to cover mine!" He remembered the way she put her hands on her hips and slowly turned, like one of those fashion models he'd seen on television.

"Get one last look, Norm. I have an appointment with Tammy this afternoon. By the time I get home, this mousy brown color will be gone!"

Her feisty resolve captivated him. It was one of the reasons he'd first asked her out, and it was one of the reasons they'd stayed married all these years. A warm feeling spread over his chest as he glanced down at her and smiled. *My tiny, beautiful spitfire.*

He sat at the dining room table and glanced at the battery-powered clock on the wall: 6:42. In two hours, he'd need to leave for work. He glanced down at the breakfast plate filled with bacon, eggs, and toast.

"Bacon and eggs on a Monday?" he asked, lifting the coffee cup to his lips.

"I didn't get much sleep last night. I've been up for a while."

"The storm?"

She gazed into his eyes. She had a funny look on her face, the look people got when they wanted to say something but were afraid to hurt your feelings. After a moment's pause, she spoke, "It's a good thing I love you so much."

He leaned back. *Crap! My snoring kept her up again.*

Before he could apologize, she continued, "You tossed and turned all night. Nearly knocked me off the bed, twice!"

"I did?" How strange, he could have sworn he'd woken in the exact position he'd fallen asleep on his back with the ceiling fan slowly turning above him.

"I'm sorry, Mary. Must have been the storm."

She nodded and continued eating. A few minutes later, she pointed at his plate. "You're not hungry?"

"Huh?" He looked down. The two pieces of bacon were gone. But instead of eating the toast, he'd used it to push his scrambled eggs across the plate. The soggy and cold piece of toast was still in his hand.

She narrowed her eyes. "You don't look so good. Maybe you should call into work?"

The ease at which Mary dismissed his job at the hardware store infuriated him. He curtly shook his head. Calling in wasn't an option, especially on Mondays. They'd be busy with delivery trucks and will-call orders.

"I'll be fine. Really. I promise I'll get to bed early tonight."

"You sure?"

"Uh-huh."

After leaving the ministry, he worked a handful of odd jobs. The hardware store was one of the best jobs he'd had. It wasn't a typical hardware store. They also carried supplies for gardening, farming, animal feed, and fencing. If someone wanted something they didn't have in the store, they'd special order it.

Trading in his clergy robe for a red vest and nametag wasn't as easy as it might seem. Although he had a firm grasp of tools and home improvement techniques, he'd never worked a day on a farm and had little experience around livestock. His humbleness and ability to learn quickly won him the respect of his coworkers. The customers, many of whom he knew by their first name, often sought him out.

Mary pushed her chair back and reached for his plate. "You done?"

He nodded, tossed the piece of toast onto the eggs, and handed her his plate.

"I'll clean this up." She pointed to the sliding glass door in the family room. "Will you open the curtain and let in some light?"

"Sure."

Just before reaching the door, his stomach knotted. He swallowed uneasily. Warily, he pulled back the curtain covering the sliding door. Gray light streamed through the window. A cold sensation spread throughout his body, holding him firmly in place. His eyes widened, and his mouth fell open. The door in the recesses of his mind burst open and the image of two red eyes raced through his head.

Mary stood beside him. "Well, look at that."

Covering the cornfield was an ominous gray mist. When he went to bed last night, the gray smoke was just six feet high. It remained confined to the cornfield, but overnight had grown to a height of ten feet. It covered the entire field like a dense, ashen blanket.

"What do you think about that, Norm?"

"I–I'm not sure. I've never seen anything like it."

She reached for his hand. "You're shaking. What's wrong?"

He fought to push back the image of the glinting red eyes. *There must be a reasonable explanation for this!* He took a long, slow breath, then opened the sliding glass door and stepped outside. She followed. Minus the area directly above the cornfield, the rest of the morning sky was blue with a few white clouds. Sunlight streamed over their house. It bounced off the misty gray wall, warming the air around them.

"That's fog, right?" Mary whispered.

He glanced down at her face and forced a smile. "I think it was from the storm last night. Probably has something to do with the irrigation canals around here." He found the explanation comforting. It seemed more plausible than the alternative one running through his thoughts.

She nodded. "Makes sense."

He stood in silence while scanning the backyards bordering the cornfield. While families filled the houses in the central part of the subdivision, nearly every house on his street sat empty. They had small backyards and metal fencing instead of brick. It seemed like the houses on this street were an afterthought, an ugly stepchild to the rest of the homes in the subdivision.

Crows still accumulated on the fence line. His attempts to shoo them away had grown pointless. In the aftermath of the storm, hundreds of them spread out along the chain-link fences.

He glanced down at the narrow dirt road separating the cornfield from the homes. It lay covered in mud, an open invitation for anyone with a four-wheel-drive pickup. He glanced upward, then back towards the sky over the houses in the rest of the subdivision. Everywhere he looked, the sky appeared blue and mostly clear. The cornfield seemed to be the only piece of land covered in fog.

He glanced back down at Mary. "I need to get a closer look."

"Won't you be late for work?"

He shook his head. "I'm not going in till nine."

He looked at the back fence. Scaling it wasn't an option. Although it provided a barrier between the houses, the fence looked flimsy and unable to bear weight. He'd considered replacing the metal fence with brick when they first moved into the house, but Mary dismissed the proposal out of hand. She was right. Their backyard would have felt even smaller, and they would have lost their view of the mountains. The only way to safely get to the misty wall was to go back inside the house, through his front yard, and down the drainage wash, which led to the field.

He went inside the house to change clothes and put on a pair of tennis shoes. Mary followed close behind. "I can't go out there with you this morning. I have to get ready for work, or I'll be late. Can't this wait?"

He glanced at her and shook his head. "It can't."

He knew his response risked starting the week with an argument. But he needed to put his mind to rest. He needed to prove the previous night's storm and the morning fog were nothing out of the ordinary. Besides, he didn't have to be at work for two hours. There was no way he'd spend that time sitting around the house.

A short time later, he stepped out of the front door. His house sat at the end of the cul-de-sac, between Susan's home and a drainage wash. Across the street was a large, tall, brick wall that bordered a row of backyards in the central part of the subdivision. His and Mary's house was tucked away at the end of the cul-de-sac, offering them a sense of privacy. The only drawback was the mailbox in front of his house. He knew that as more homes on his street became occupied, the foot traffic to the mailbox would increase.

Within minutes, he'd trekked through his front yard, past the mailbox, to the wash's edge. He looked towards his right. A steep, narrow wash bordered the north side of the subdivision. It was covered in grass and had a depth of fifteen feet. He looked to his left. There, next to his home, the wash came to an abrupt stop. Rainwater from last night's storm pooled into a small lake at the bottom.

Walking along the top of the wash proved harder than it initially looked. The dew-covered grass was soggy and slippery. He carefully skirted the edge, knowing one misstep would send him tumbling down the side and into the water below. Once he'd reached the end of the wash, he paused to catch his breath. Large puddles of mud covered the dirt road separating the wash and the gray wall. He studied the ground, looking for a safe place to step.

He stepped onto the driest area of earth he could find. It gave way, and his foot slid into the mud a few inches. He paused for a moment, then fully put his weight down. He sank a little more.

Behind him, Mary's voice rang out: "Are you stuck?"

He was startled, unaware she'd stepped outside. He glanced in her direction. She was dressed for work and standing on their small concrete slab. He leaned back, pulled his foot free. Pop! The sucking sound of mud releasing his foot brought a smile to his face. "No, not stuck. But this mud is pretty thick."

"Why not wait until we get home from work? The mud will have dried up by then."

He shook his head. "The fog will evaporate soon."

"I have to leave, or I'll be late. Are you sure you'll be fine?"

Heat crept up his neck and onto his face. He deeply inhaled. *She's just worried. Let it go.* He exhaled and forced a smile. "I'm good. I'll see you this afternoon."

"Okay." She turned and strutted back into the house. The slight shake of her head didn't go unnoticed. She might have wanted him to try again later, but he wasn't a quitter. Crossing the muddy road triggered the memory of playing Frogger in his late teens. Just like his arcade hero, he was determined to maneuver himself across the muddy road.

He stepped forward onto a different spot in the road. His foot sank about an inch before the sole of his shoe pressed against a large rock. Feeling solidly grounded, he stepped out with his other foot and found another large stone under the mud. *I can do this.* He looked at the remaining distance in front of him and then glanced back. *Ugh! Barely out of the starting gate.* He shook his head, then kept moving forward, gingerly placing one foot in front of the other.

When he reached the halfway mark, the crows on the fence line cawed and excitedly flapped their wings. A small cluster flew off the fence line and landed on the road in front of him. With each step towards the gray wall, their cawing intensified. More crows flew down from the fence, landing behind him. They pecked at his pant legs. If he didn't know better, he would have sworn they were pushing him in the direction of the fog. He kicked at the onslaught of crows and shouted, "Go, get out of here!"

Undeterred, the small crows continued their assault. One crow on the fence line overshadowed the others in size. He was sure it was the same crow from last night. Its scolding caw captured the attention of the smaller ones. They lowered their wings and fell silent in response. Most flew back onto the fence; a handful remained on the ground surrounding him.

He glanced at the large crow, fighting the urge to thank it for calling off the smaller crows' attack. Its beady eyes stared back in response.

He glanced up at the foggy wall. He was nearly close enough to touch it. As he approached the wall, the air became dense and filled with the odor of rotten eggs. A fullness pressed onto his chest, stealing his breath away. The sun, fully risen, sent warm beams of light onto his back. Beads of sweat rolled down his forehead. He wiped them away with a shaking hand.

Standing on the dirt road, he couldn't shake the feeling he was in some type of purgatory, stuck somewhere between the world he knew and a world of despair behind the wall. His mind relived the events of the previous night. He needed to know if what he saw last night was real or if it was his imagination.

He took another step towards the wall. Up close, the glistening wall looked like thin strands of gray cotton candy haphazardly strung together— airy, light, yet strangely dense. The gray strands moved, swirling ever so slightly. His eyes widened as they strained to penetrate the fog's thick perimeter. *Where are those red eyes?* He couldn't see them, but he sensed they were there.

Thin wisps of gray danced in and out of the wall, like long fingers probing the other side. Timidly, he raised his hand. As though it sensed his presence, one of the wisps abruptly stopped its retreat. Instead, it expanded and slowly lifted, giving him the impression of a small cobra, poised to attack. Before he could pull his hand away, the wisp struck, sending a jolting shock up his arm. He jerked his hand back in response.

Lightheadedness overtook him. He wasn't sure whether to blame the warm humidity in the air or the throbbing tingle spreading through his hand. Whatever the cause, he took deep breaths, trying desperately not to pass out. *This was a mistake. I've got to get off this road!*

He turned and tried to walk away but his leg wouldn't budge. He glanced down, expecting to find his foot fully submerged in the mud. It wasn't. Instead, one of the wisps was wrapped around his leg, holding him firmly in place. Another wisp reached out for his free leg.

"Jesus Christ!" he yelled out as he yanked away from the wisp's grasp. He stumbled backward and fell into the muddy water. Unlike his careful approach, his retreat was haphazard. He pulled himself into a semi-upright position, then sloshed through the mud, tripping and falling few more times. At the edge of the wash, he collapsed. His chest burned with each breath. It took a moment for him to gather his thoughts. *Did that really happen? Or was it all in my head? Is this happening because I walked away from God?*

One by one, tears slowly rolled down his face. Then he glanced down at his body. His hands, shoes, and jeans were soaked and covered in mud. Slow-burning anger spread through every fiber of his being, pushing aside the sense of anguish and defeat trying to take hold.

He wiped his tears aside, then lifted his head upwards. "Screw you!" He yelled towards the sky above.

He glanced back at the wall. "Screw you, too!"

Struggling, he pushed himself upright and trudged home. Once there, he left his jeans and shoes in the garage. He didn't want to hear Mary's comments about mud mucking up the plumbing. *I'll rinse and put those in the washer later before she gets home.* Right now, he needed distance between himself and the cornfield. He quickly showered and left for work.

✳ ✳ ✳

Susan hadn't experienced a good night's sleep since moving into her new home. As a single woman living alone, she found the nights long and wrought with unease. With each passing day, she'd grown exhausted. Last night's storm added to her fatigue. She groaned, then buried her head further into the pillow in a futile attempt to delay the start of her day.

Libby's cold, wet nose buried into her curly brown hair. Susan pulled the comforter over her head. Undettered, Libby squirmed beneath the comforter. Soon, her warm, wet tongue found Susan's ear. Susan giggled. "Alright. I give up." She said as she pushed back the covers. Libby didn't retreat; instead, the young puppy eagerly began licking her face and neck. Libby's soft fur tickled her nose. She laughed fully with each playful attack until tears slid down the sides of her face. For a moment, everything felt right. She smiled and stroked Libby's soft coat.

Libby moved to the bottom of the bed and whimpered.

Using a voice filled with encouragement, she said, "Go on, Libby…use your doggy door."

Libby's small head cocked side to side. Then, in one bounding leap, she jumped off the bed and ran down the hall. The doggy door swung open and shut.

She smiled. *Good girl.*

Outside, Libby began to bark. All thoughts of praise left her head. *Bad girl!* was the prevailing thought. She wasn't sure if Mary or Norm were home. If so, Libby's barking would certainly disrupt their morning. She marched to the family room and pushed back the vertical blinds covering her family room window.

Her gaze quickly moved beyond Libby and onto the mesmerizing gray mist covering the cornfield. It was the first time she'd seen fog up close. She opened the door and stepped onto the concrete slab. Her eyes moved upward and then swept side to side. With precision, the fog ran parallel to the dirt road. It extended straight up, covering the cornfield like an ashen blanket. Except for the fog blanketing the cornfield, the rest of the sky was blue with a few white clouds.

She gazed at the crows on the fence line. She first noticed them a week ago. With each passing day, a few more arrived. She shook her head. *I'd swear there are twice as many today as there was yesterday!* Like a row of tiny sentries, the crows lined all the backyards. But compared to the other backyards, the concentration of crows was the greatest behind her home. The smaller crows on the fence line quietly cawed at each other. One crow, nearly as large as Libby, sat in the middle of her fence line. It eluded an air of authority, like a general overseeing his troops. She wasn't sure what upset Libby more: the gray wall or the black crows perched atop the chain-link fence. Libby barked in the direction of the crows. *Mystery solved.*

"Libby!"

Libby stopped barking but didn't move. She stood, body erect, in the middle of the yard as if challenging the large crow. The crow looked down at the young puppy dismissively, then turned in Susan's direction. She took a step forward and clapped her hands loudly, shouting, "Shoo! Go away!"

A few of the smaller crows scattered. But the massive crow wrapped its talons tightly around the metal fence pole, brazenly maintaining its ground. Its beady eyes held her gaze.

She clapped her hands again. "You heard me. Go! Get out of here!"

The bird didn't flinch. Instead, it continued to stare. She couldn't shake the feeling it was probing her thoughts, looking for a weakness. For a moment, doubt filled her entire being.

"This is my house, my backyard," her voice trailed off.

Was she trying to convince herself or the crow she belonged there, living on her own? She furrowed her brow, making one more attempt to stare the bird down. It didn't waver, but her feeling of doubt increased. *You're nothing more than a scared child!* The words rang out in her head. Tears welled in her eyes. *No, I'm a grown woman! I can do this!*

The crow continued to stare. With each passing second of the bizarre staring contest, she sensed her mind spinning further out of control. *Stop!* She silently screamed as she closed her eyes and broke away from the crow's scrutinizing gaze. When she opened her eyes, the crow was still staring.

A warmth crept up her face. "You win!" she yelled.

The bird lifted its head higher, then turned away. In a prideful stance, it puffed out its chest. An uneasiness consolidated in the pit of her stomach. *It knows it's won!*

She couldn't shake the feeling she'd unwittingly given the bird control over her, over her soul. That thought left her trembling. *Meds. I need my meds.* She needed to go inside and take them. It was the only thing that would calm her nerves. She glanced down, and in a shaking voice, called out to Libby, "Come on, girl!"

Libby paced back and forth. Her barking resumed.

"Libby, come!"

The sharp tone caught Libby's attention. In response, the young puppy bounced through the grass and ran into the house.

* * *

Throughout the workday, Norm glanced at the clock hanging on the wall behind the cashiers. With each passing hour, he'd grown more and more convinced the experience he had earlier in the day was all in his head. He just needed to get back home to prove it. As soon as he punched out from work, he hopped in the car and turned onto Central Avenue.

The sheriff parked an empty squad car at the corner of First Street and Central to deter speeding. To keep the deterrent useful, he'd place a deputy behind the wheel a few times a day. Speeding down Central Avenue was like playing Russian roulette. You never knew if you'd get a free pass or a ticket with a hefty fine. He glanced into the squad car as he drove past. *Deputy.* His heartbeat quickened. He glanced down at the speedometer, 27 miles per hour. He breathed a sigh of relief. As soon as the squad car was nothing more than a speck in his rearview mirror, he pushed down on the accelerator. If he drove fast enough, he'd have time to examine the fog again before Mary got home.

Fifteen minutes later, he pulled into the garage. He nearly stumbled as he made his way out of the car and into the house. Once inside the house, he ran to the family room. His heart sank as he looked out the sliding glass door. The misty gray wall had evaporated, leaving behind rows of glistening cornstalks.

A cream-colored truck, covered in dents and scratches, sat on the dirt road behind Susan's house. The driver's door stood open. A tall, thin man wearing faded jeans, a dark T-shirt, boots, and a baseball cap leaned over the truck bed, gazing at the cornfield. He held a cigarette in his hand. As he gazed upon the field, he took one long drag of the cigarette, then exhaled, sending a puff of smoke into the distance.

A farmhand checking the field? He opened the sliding glass door. A long, swooshing sound erupted from the door as it rolled along the track. He watched the man on the road visibly startle, then toss his cigarette onto the ground, rubbing it into the earth with his boot. Norm stepped through the sliding glass door and onto the small concrete slab. He raised his hand and yelled, "Hello, there!"

The man didn't acknowledge him. Instead, he jumped into the truck and slammed the door shut. He shifted the truck into drive and accelerated in a near agitated state, sending dried mud into the air.

CHAPTER 5

Saturday morning. Nearly a week had passed since the storm. Susan lay in bed, half-asleep, half-awake. The heavy curtains of her bedroom window blocked the daylight. A soft tapping sound resonated from behind the curtain. Her eyes fully opened, and she raised her head. Libby had also taken notice of the noise. The young dog stood on the bed, four legs erect, body leaning in the window's direction. The soft tapping increased in volume. Soon it sounded as though a barrage of hail was pelting the glass.

Before she could stop her, Libby bolted off the bed and ran down the hall. The doggy door swung open and shut. Libby's barking began in earnest. She jumped out of bed and ran down the hall. When she reached the sliding glass door, she yanked back the blinds and screamed.

As if being tossed out of a swirling tornado, crows bombarded her sliding glass door in rapid fire succession. Others flew haphazardly over the yard. Amidst the swirling sea of black crows, she glimpsed Libby's blonde coat.

Despite the danger, Susan threw the sliding glass door open, then held her hands up to protect her face and ran in Libby's direction.

"Caw! Caw!" The boisterous cry of the largest bird on the fence captured the attention of the others. Soon the intensity lowered as the wayward flying crows settled over the grass, fence line, and her bedroom windowsill.

She knelt on the ground near Libby. Amazingly, the young dog was unscathed. She glanced up at the large crow, confident it was the one who'd challenged her to the bizarre staring contest. As she knelt on the ground, glancing up at the crow, she sensed its power. The crow stared down at her, then spread its wings in a dominating manner and cawed again. Its icy cry chilled her blood. *Why me?* She wanted to scream. *Why have you chosen my house?* As those questions ran through her head, the crow lowered its wings, puffed out its chest, then turned its attention on the cornfield.

* * *

The sight of the crows triggered a memory of the storm. Although Susan thanked Norm for checking on her the night of the storm, she hadn't thanked him in a manner her mother would have approved, a handwritten card or baked goods. She looked through her kitchen cabinets and smiled. Everything she'd need to bake oatmeal chocolate-chip cookies was on the shelves.

A few hours later—ding! The timer on the kitchen oven rang. The aroma of fresh-baked cookies filled the air. She filled a plate with cookies, attached a leash to Libby's collar, and headed next door.

She knocked and waited. No answer. As she turned to leave, Mary opened the door. She was leaning on a walker. "Good morning, Susan. Oh, I see you brought Libby. Hello, Miss Libby. Sorry, it took so long to answer. I struggled a bit getting out of the recliner." She pointed to the black compression bandage around her ankle. "Norm's napping, and I'm a bit slow."

"Oh, no. What happened?"

"Bad sprain." She shook her head. "I tripped over an extension cord at work."

"That's terrible."

"Yeah. But my doctor said it could have been worse. Thankfully, I don't need surgery. But I can't put any weight on my leg, and I'm supposed to keep it elevated."

Norm entered the doorway. He kissed Mary on the cheek. "Sorry, honey, I didn't hear Susan knock." He spied the plate in her hand. "Cookies?"

"Uh-huh. They're for you, hot out of the oven." She handed him the plate. "I wanted to thank you again for checking in on me when the power went out. They're chocolate chip with oatmeal. It's my mom's recipe."

He looked down at her, smiled again. "They look delicious. Thank you." He removed the plastic wrap.

"Oh, no, you don't, Norm!" Mary playfully slapped his hand. "We're both watching our weight. We can wait till after lunch."

"You heard Susan…these cookies have oatmeal, good and healthy."

He snatched a cookie off the plate and popped it into his mouth before Mary uttered another word. He smiled again and winked. Mary laughed. That playful back and forth between them was something she'd witnessed with her parents. It was also something she hoped she'd experience in the future with her husband. She just needed to get out there and start looking for Mr. Right. She raised her hand. "I'd better get going."

"Are you free tonight? Mary asked.

"Uh…"

"Join us for dinner. My friends from church dropped off some meals. We've got more than enough to share."

"Are you sure?" She pointed to Mary's leg.

Norm interrupted. "That's a great idea."

A home cooked meal? Her mouth watered at the thought. She'd learned how to bake. But when it came to cooking, she could barely boil water. For weeks, she'd eaten microwaved dinners and boxed macaroni and cheese.

More important than a home-cooked meal, she missed sitting around a table engaged in conversation. A warm sensation spread through her chest, and she smiled. "If you're sure it's not an imposition, I would love to have dinner with you."

"It's not. We'd love the company," Mary said. Her eyes lit up, and she smiled.

"And I've wanted to go to town to do a little grocery shopping," Norm added.

Oh, no. This is an imposition. "Please don't go into town on my account. We can reschedule; wait until you're all …."

"No." Norm interrupted. "It's no trouble. I planned on driving to town this weekend anyway."

Before she could rebut, Mary interjected, "Honestly, he does like to grocery shop."

She paused briefly, then added: "It's settled then. Dinner tonight. Let's say at five o'clock. Will that work for you?"

People typically didn't go out of their way for her. She glanced at their faces, both filled with bright, encouraging smiles. *Perhaps they need this as much as I do.* Finally, she answered, "Yes, that would be great." Her mother's voice rang out in her head. "Susan, mind your manners. Don't show up to dinner empty-handed." *Oh, no. I'm rude.* "What can I bring?" she asked.

"You've already brought dessert. There's nothing else we need. Just bring yourself, and since Miss Libby seems to be so well mannered, why not bring her too?" Norm said.

Libby lifted her head and wagged her short tail vigorously back and forth. She knelt and stroked Libby, then adjusted her bright pink collar. A small silver heart hung from the collar. She rubbed her finger over the engraving, Libby's name, and her phone number.

"Okay...we'll see you both tonight."

✳ ✳ ✳

After saying goodbye, Norm closed the door and turned to Mary, saying, "Are you sure you feel up to entertaining? We'll have lots of opportunities to invite her over when you're feeling better."

"I'm good, and I don't mind the company. Also, did you see that girl? She's a waif of a thing. I doubt she's eating well. And the dark circles under her eyes? It looks like she's not sleeping well, either. It's a good thing we live next door to her."

Mary had a look he could only describe as quiet determination. He smiled and gave a knowing nod. He knew from past experiences she was concocting some plan to help the girl next door. "You know, the last time you had *that* look in your eye, we adopted Sunny from the pound."

Mary shook her head and laughed. "I'm not looking to adopt her, Norm. Just put some meat on her bones."

Mary was right. Although Susan appeared petite by nature, she looked too thin. And those dark circles under her eyes. It was apparent she wasn't sleeping well. Tears welled in his eyes. *Rose.* An image of his youngest daughter flashed through his head. It wasn't the image of the strong-headed girl with pigtails who'd grown into a beautiful woman. No. It was an image of Rose in the throes of an opiate and amphetamine addiction: unkempt hair, thin, with dark circles under her faded blue eyes. Something about Susan reminded him of Rose. He was sure she wasn't taking drugs. But she had an aura about her, a fragileness that gave him the impression she was barely holding herself together. She needed protection. He couldn't protect Rose, wasn't able to save her. He wouldn't make the same mistake twice.

Mary placed her hand on his arm and looked into his eyes. "You okay?"

He forced a smile. The images of Rose faded from his mind. There was a slight tremor in Mary's arms, and her face had become a dull shade of gray. "I'm okay. But you don't look so well."

"My foot is starting to throb."

"Come on. Let's get you to your recliner so you can put your leg up. Then, I'll make you something to eat."

He stepped into the kitchen and made lunch for Mary, a peanut butter and jelly sandwich with a glass of milk. He placed both on the small table next to her.

"You're not eating?"

"If it's okay with you, I thought I'd grab lunch at the diner. I haven't seen Dave or Bob in a while."

After Mary's fall, he'd taken time off from work to care for her. Her friends from church helped by bringing in meals. Lately, she moved more freely, which lessened his fear of leaving her alone. Besides, heading into town allowed him to stop at the diner.

There was a good chance he'd run into his friends at the diner. Dave and Bob grew up in the area. They'd know if the fog that blanketed the field after the storm was a normal phenomenon. He'd already attributed the encounter with the fog to an overactive imagination, exhaustion, and guilt for turning his back on God. But knowing the fog was nothing unusual would further put his mind at ease.

Mary smiled and nodded. "I don't mind. Just don't get so wrapped up with your friends you forget to stop at the grocery store."

"Is there anything else you need before I head out?"

Mary shook her head. "I'll just eat and then close my eyes for a bit."

"Sounds good. I'll be back before you miss me." He leaned down and placed a kiss on Mary's lips.

CHAPTER 6

Norm enjoyed going into town. It reminded him of the place where he'd grown up; a safe place where kids rode their bikes to the candy store and families lined sidewalks waving American flags during parades. Whenever possible, he grabbed lunch at the Desert Diner. The family-owned restaurant was on the town's main road, Central Avenue, nestled among storefronts, churches, and the grocery store.

The diner offered large portions of home-cooked meals at low prices. They also sold pies and cookies at the front counter. A vibrant hum filled the air as servers bustled about and customers shared the latest gossip. Despite the threadbare vinyl covering the seats and mismatched dishes, people were always standing around waiting for a booth.

Mary didn't share his enthusiasm for the diner. According to her, a good restaurant had matching plates and tablecloths. Since he was often alone, he could skip the line and sit at one of the barstools along the large counter. It was here, sitting at the counter, where he met some of the local farmers. It was also where he learned his subdivision was the first commercial housing development in the area.

He arrived at the diner just as the breakfast crowd thinned. Bob Marshall and Dave Franklin, two local farmers he'd befriended, sat in a booth near the entrance. Bob was a plain-speaking man who inherited his mother's Irish tendencies: red hair, pale skin, and freckles. He wore a long white T-shirt and a pair of coveralls, which hung on his lean frame. Dave was a stocky man with broad shoulders. Beneath his handlebar mustache was a kind, gentle face. Dave was the kind of man who looked as comfortable in a suit and tie as he did in a cowboy hat, jeans, and boots.

"Norm!" The sound of Bob's voice captured his attention. He looked towards the booth and spied Bob eagerly, motioning him forward with his hands.

He smiled and strolled in their direction. "Is this seat taken?"

Bob scooted across the booth seat, opening up a spot for him to sit. "Hey, buddy, were your ears burning? I just told Dave I hadn't seen you here or at the farm supply store in a while."

He shook both men's hands and sat down. "I've taken most of the week off to be with Mary. She fell at work and badly sprained her ankle."

A look of concern filled Dave's face. "Oh, no."

He nodded. "Yeah. Doc told her she's lucky. Right now, it looks like she's not going to need surgery. But he said that could change if it doesn't heal. He gave her strict orders to rest and keep the leg elevated."

Dave shook his head and gave a half-hearted laugh. "Mary? Rest? How's she handling that?"

"You know Mary…she's always on the move. She keeps pushing herself until she starts hurting. Just today, she invited our neighbor over for dinner."

"Oh, that's no good. She needs to rest," Dave responded.

"I tried to tell her that, but she thinks the girl isn't sleeping or eating well, and she wants to help. Honestly, Susan…that's the girl's name. She's lovely. I'm sure dinner will be fine. Mary's friends at church dropped off a few casseroles. I'll just warm one of those up tonight."

"Well, you tell Mary we'll keep her in our prayers," Dave said.

Bob nodded in agreement.

"I will."

Ruth, one of the diner's servers, stepped up and interrupted the conversation. "Hello, stranger. The boys here were just wondering when they'd see you again. What can I get started for you?"

Norm smiled. There was a palpable warmth radiating throughout the community. People cared about one another. Mary's friends from church had filled their refrigerator and freezer with meals. His friends seemed genuinely happy to see him. It was like slipping on a pair of comfortable shoes. Living here felt right.

"How about the French dip sandwich and a glass of iced tea? Oh, and skip the fries. I swear Mary can smell them a mile away. She'll dog me all afternoon if I eat those."

Ruth laughed. "These two ordered just before you arrived. So, let me get your sandwich order back to the kitchen. That way everybody's meal comes out around the same time. I'll be right back with your tea."

He turned his attention back to Bob and Dave. "I was hoping I'd run into you two. I wanted to ask you about the big storm we had last weekend. Was that a normal storm for the area?"

Dave spoke up: "We get some pretty big monsoon storms in the summer. I'm sure you had similar ones in Tucson. Nasty storms, like the one last weekend, aren't as common. We typically see one every few years or so. I heard your subdivision and the Smith farm took the brunt of the storm."

A look of concern spread over Bob's face. "Did your house suffer any damage?"

"No…no damage. Just a lot of wind and rain. We also lost power. The storm mainly stayed over the cornfield behind our house."

"I think I know that field. It butts up to your subdivision, right?" Dave asked.

He nodded. "Mary's bummed about the corn. She says it's blocking her views of the mountains."

Dave shook his head. "Tell Mary not to worry. After that corn is gone, the field will probably sit empty again for the next few years."

"Seriously?"

Dave nodded. "Yes, and it's a shame. All that land, yet Tobias only plants that field once in a blue moon."

"Corn. He only plants corn," Bob interjected.

Dave nodded. "That's right; they only plant corn in that field. I don't like to speak poorly of Tobias. But it's no secret his farm struggles financially. He could make some money if he'd plant the field year-round or lease the land."

He shook his head slightly back and forth. What Dave said didn't make sense. The Smith farm had large barns filled with livestock, and that the family lived in a vast, three-story Victorian-style home on the top of a small hill. Given all he'd heard, he concluded Tobias was a very wealthy man.

"Are you sure…about the finances?"

"Positive. Bob and I've lived here most of our lives. I'm telling you—Tobias has struggled for years. He's sold off considerable amounts of his family's land. I can't imagine there's much left to sell. And it's a shame. They can't afford farmhands. It's just him and his four sons running the farm, and they don't have to struggle. That piece of land behind your home? Lots of farmers have offered to lease it. I don't know what Tobias is thinking. He could have leased that land all year long, year after year. Instead, he sold off the area adjacent to it—that's the land where they built your subdivision."

He thought of the interaction with the man in the truck. "You know…I think I saw him on the road behind my house. At first, I thought maybe the guy worked on the farm. Now, I'm wondering if it was Tobias."

"What did he look like?" Dave asked.

"I only caught a glimpse of him. Tall, thin guy. Mid-forties, maybe? He wore jeans, boots, and a baseball cap. He had an older model, cream-colored truck. It looked pretty beat up."

Dave nodded. "Baseball cap? Cream-colored truck. Yeah, that could have been Tobias."

"I'm sure he heard me open the sliding glass door, and when I stepped outside to introduce myself, he bolted into his truck and sped away."

Bob nodded. "Sounds like something Tobias would do." He paused, then added, "He's cool…like the concrete beneath your feet."

Dave shook his head. "Honestly, he's not that bad. Just different."

"Growing up on *that* farm would make anyone different. I swear the farm is cursed." Bob interjected.

Images from the night of the storm flashed through his mind. He shuddered. *It was only my imagination.*

"You okay, Norm?" Bob asked.

Dave narrowed his eyes. "Don't listen to him, Norm. That farm is not cursed. It's had its share of tragedy, mind you, but I wouldn't say it was cursed."

"What kind of tragedy?"

Bob shook his head. "You sure you want to hear all this?"

He nodded, anxious to know everything about Tobias and his farm.

Dave shrugged. "Okay…well, the farm's been in Tobias' family for nearly a century. I don't know if you knew that or not."

He shook his head.

Dave continued, "All I know is what I've heard growing up. At one point, the Smith family was the wealthiest in the area. Never had many family members, mind you, but they could afford to hire seasonal help."

"Lots of money. Lots of workers. Sorry, it doesn't seem too tragic."

"Yeah, I hear you. It seems like life would be rosy for them, but they also had a lot of death."

"Death?" A cold chill moved through his body.

Dave nodded. "Uh-huh. Well, for one thing, Tobias' mother died a few days after he was born."

"That's terrible!"

Bob raised his finger and interrupted, "Yep…rumor has it, she had a seizure. Thomas, that's Tobias' father; anyway, he was a wreck. He didn't know what to do with a baby. So, he put Tobias in one of those small wooden rocking cradles and left him by the fireplace. I'm guessing to keep him warm. Early in the morning, one of the seasonal workers was near the house and heard a baby crying. So, naturally, he knocked on the front door. When no one answered, he went inside the house. Know what he found? Thomas passed out drunk in his room, and the baby was lying in the cradle downstairs. Here's the strange part…by the time the worker found Tobias, he wasn't crying anymore, and the little cradle was rocking all by itself."

"You're pulling my leg."

Dave responded, "I don't know about the 'cradle rocking by itself' part of the story. It's something most of us heard growing up—you know—a ghost story."

"Ghost story?"

"Uh-huh. Most people who've told that story say the ghost of Tobias' mom was rocking him, trying to comfort him. I believe there's a logical explanation. Tobias was crying and kicking around in the cradle. He made the cradle rock back and forth, and when the cradle started rocking, it made him stop crying. Simple as that. There's one thing I do know for sure. They found Tobias dressed only in a thin cotton gown. He'd kicked himself out of his blanket and had soaked his cloth diaper. There was nothing but smoldering embers in the fireplace, and the house had a chill. Tobias is lucky to be alive. He could have frozen to death. And, if the worker hadn't brought Tobias straight to his wife, I'm certain he most likely would have starved."

Bob interrupted to finish the story. "Yep, that little wife had given birth to a baby just a few weeks before Tobias was born. That sweet momma nursed him, just like her own. My daddy said it was a miracle the little momma was even on the farm. I don't know how many men would know how to care for a baby. If not for the worker and his little wife, my daddy said Tobias probably would have died—cold, hungry, and alone."

He slowly looked from Bob to Dave.

Dave nodded. "When Thomas sobered up and found out the worker and his wife helped Tobias, he asked them to stay at the farm after the season finished. You know they lived on that farm until Tobias was old enough to go to school. I'm guessing that's when money became tight, and Thomas couldn't afford to keep them on any longer, so he asked them to leave. How painful it must have been for Tobias. Being so young and losing the only mother and the only brother he knew. I think that's why I've felt compassion for him. Honestly, that surrogate family was a bright spot in his life. They had a grounding effect on him, offered him some sense of normalcy. There's quite a bit of folklore around here. I'm sure you'll hear lots of rumors about that farm. People can be cruel. Many families around here are envious of the amount of land the Smiths acquired through the years. But I think they forget about all the losses they've had too. Keep that in mind if you hear people talk."

He sat quietly for a moment as the image of a baby lying in a cradle, cold and hungry, flashed through his mind. In a low voice, he whispered, "Wow. I don't know what to say. It's a horrible way to start your life."

Bob nodded. "Yep…at least that's the story we all heard growing up. Thomas never remarried, so other than the surrogate brother he had when he was young, Tobias grew up as an only child."

He sat quietly for a moment. *Death.* "You said…there was a lot of death. Who else died?"

Dave nodded to Bob, encouraging him to continue. "Well, I think the worst tragedy on that farm had to be those three kids. Don't you think so, Dave?"

"Yes," Dave replied.

He took a long, slow breath and leaned back into the booth. He knew all too well the pain of losing a child. He wasn't sure if he wanted to hear Bob's story.

Bob glanced around the diner. In a hushed voice, he spoke: "This happened a long time ago…when the farm belonged to Jonas.

"Jonas?"

"Tobias' Great-uncle."

He nodded.

"Anyway… Jonas and his wife had three kids: real young. The oldest was five."

He fidgeted in his seat and leaned back. The story had started. Like it or not, he had a front-row seat to the heartbreaking tale.

Bob continued, "They all died within days of each other. Officially, they died of the flu. But no one knows for sure. It was in the spring. So maybe a late case of flu went through the house. But there were whispers those kids weren't sick at all. That something else happened to them, and they covered it up."

He gasped.

Dave shook his head. "Don't listen to his conspiracy theories, Norm. Those kids perished from the flu. They're buried in the family cemetery."

Bob narrowed his eyes and pursed his lips. "Whatever happened…I think we can all agree it was sad."

"What happened after the children died? Surely, there was an autopsy, an investigation."

Dave quickly answered, "Yes…there was an investigation…I'm telling you, it was the flu. End of story."

"That's the official word. But don't forget, Dave. It happened a long time ago, long before we were even born. And you know what they say: money talks. That family had a ton of money back then. They could have greased the palm of someone to keep a secret."

Dave slowly shook his head back and forth and extended his hands in the air, palms up. "Ugh. I give up."

He looked between the two men. Even though the children died before either Bob or Dave were born, it seemed highly improbable someone could buy off an official to cover up three childrens' deaths. Despite the intrigue of a conspiracy theory, Dave's conclusion seemed most plausible.

"What happened to the family after those children died?" he asked.

Bob motioned to Dave to continue the story. Dave nodded and spoke, "It gets worse. The wife perished a few weeks after her children."

"The wife died too?" His heart sank. The loss of three children was heartbreaking enough. Add in the mom...Bob was right; this was a tragedy.

"Yeah," Dave said. "I don't believe the conspiracy theories about the children. He looked in Bob's direction. "But the wife...that's another story."

Bob nodded. "Yep...I think we can all agree; the facts surrounding her death are a bit muddy."

A questionable death? A tiny chill washed over his body. He leaned forward. "How so?"

Bob continued, "Well...I've heard three different stories." He held three fingers up, then lowered them one at a time as he listed off the possible causes of her death. "She either died of the flu, committed suicide, or..." He paused before lowering his third finger. "There's a rumor she was killed to cover up what happened to the kids."

Dave quickly interjected, "I don't give much weight to the coverup theory, Norm. I believe those kids perished from the flu. But..." He glanced around the room, then leaned forward. In a lowered voice, he whispered, "There were all kinds of rumors about her death at the time. You'd be a fool not to wonder if something wasn't amiss. Then you add in Jonas' behavior after she passed."

"Jonas? How did he behave?"

"I think he acted strangely. I understand; you've just lost your wife and kids. Maybe you want to make a fresh start somewhere without the memories. But this guy...I don't know, Norm. He signed over his share of the farm to Lukas and left town before the authorities finished the investigation."

"Lukas?"

"His brother. That's also Tobias' grandfather. Jonas didn't just leave; he disappeared. Didn't show his face here again until he was in his seventies."

His seventies? He could understand the need to get away from the scene of the tragedy. Rose's death was one reason he and Mary had moved from

Tucson to Phoenix. But to be gone for such a long time, he had to admit, it looked suspicious.

Dave continued, "The guy disappears for decades, then one day, he just shows up on the farm. Strange, right? He passed away a few days later. They buried him in the cemetery next to his family."

"I can see how his leaving might have spurred the conspiracy theories," he said.

Both Bob and Dave nodded.

"I know you said Tobias runs the farm but is Thomas still alive?"

Dave answered, "Uh…no, he passed away years ago. Cancer. My father was certain cancer had traveled to Thomas's brain before he died." Dave pointed his finger at his head and whirled it in circles. "You know…he wasn't right in the head."

Dave paused for a moment; his mood became more serious. "You know people give Tobias a hard time. They talk about him being strange or coldhearted. But there's quite a family legacy there. I think Tobias is simply different because of his upbringing."

"How old was Tobias when Thomas died?"

Bob answered, "He was a few years out of high school." He turned to Dave to verify his facts. "What do you think, Dave? Tobias was twenty…one…two, maybe, when he took over the farm."

Dave smiled and pointed his finger back and forth between himself and Bob. "Well, he graduated a few years before us…I'm forty. You're…?"

"You know how old I am, Dave; we both graduated high school together."

"Yeah, but you repeated a few grades; so, I think you may be older."

"Smartass!"

He laughed at the exchange; grateful Dave took the opportunity to lighten the mood. It was nice to have friends who'd lived here nearly all their lives. They offered insight into the farm and Tobias. He pictured the Smith family tree. It once had the potential to be a mighty elm, but death pruned many of its branches, leaving it little more than a small bonsai.

"So, besides Jonas and Tobias, everyone else on the farm just had one baby, right? One son?"

Dave answered, "You're right. Thankfully for Tobias, he and Sarah have four strong boys. There's an excellent chance they'll be lots of grandchildren too. I'm telling you: Sarah was probably the best thing that ever happened to Tobias. She brought goodness to that farm."

Bob smiled and added, "Yep, and she's quite a beauty. She's got long, straight black hair that goes all the way down her back, and her eyes are this intense shade of green. She's tall. And she's got curves in all the right places."

"Whoa, there, Bob…she's married."

"I know…just trying to give ole' Norm here a visual. Anyway, I wish you could have seen how girls threw themselves at Tobias when we were in high school. I'm guessing they thought they'd be sitting in that big farmhouse on the hill, having servants wait on them. I laugh, just thinking about it. Nothing could be farther from the truth! Running a farm is hard work. Being a farmer's wife is a hard life. I'm guessing those delicate flowers who fawned all over Tobias would have crumbled within a few weeks with the rigors of running a farm. But not Sarah. She was different. She didn't throw herself at Tobias. Quite the opposite. Tobias did all the chasing there. He's lucky he caught her too. Sarah took to farm life like a duck takes to water."

Dave nodded. "Bob's right. Sarah is a nice Christian woman, exceedingly kind. But she's also a no-nonsense kind of gal, if you get what I mean. Did you know she bakes the pies for the diner?"

"The ones in the refrigerated case by the cashier?"

"Yep," Bob interjected. "She also cans fruit and makes jellies and jams. You might have seen some of those around town. Super tasty, I might add. My favorite's peach butter." Bob smiled, closed his eyes, and rubbed his stomach for effect. "Yum, yum. That thick, golden goodness."

He laughed. He'd already asked about the storm. But before the conversation topic moved away from Tobias and his farm, he wanted to ask Dave and Bob about the strange fog that arrived after the storm. "Hey, can I ask another question about that storm?"

"Sure, what's the question?" Dave asked.

"Well…after the storm, there was a fog that settled over the cornfield. It was strange, you know, thick. Ever seen anything like that?"

"You know it's not uncommon to get a mist over your land with a storm," Dave said.

He paused as his gaze moved back and forth between the two men. He'd only known them for a few months, mainly from the times they chatted at the diner or the store. He shifted uncomfortably in the booth. The nagging thought there was something supernatural in the field passed through his thoughts. He pushed the thought away. *I just need them to tell me the fog is normal.*

"This wasn't a mist," he began. "It was a fog. I know the difference. I don't know how to explain it. It was strange, something I've never seen before."

"I wouldn't overthink it, Norm. If you think it was a fog, it probably was, and there's nothing crazy about that." Bob said.

"You sure?"

Dave nodded. "Yeah, I'm sure."

A comforting thought passed through his head. *The fog was typical.*

"Careful, Norm. Your city's showing," Bob added.

Dave and Bob laughed. His shoulders relaxed as he joined in their laughter. Before he could utter a witty comeback to Bob's city remark, Ruth returned to the table with their meals. After Ruth's interruption, the conversation turned to other topics.

CHAPTER 7

All afternoon, Susan glanced at the clock. At 4:59 p.m., she placed the leash on Libby's collar and headed next door. Norm greeted her with a huge smile.

"Hope you're hungry!"

Excited to have a meal that didn't come frozen or out of a box, she'd avoided snacking all day. The aroma of garlic sent her stomach rumbling. "I am."

Norm led her to the dining room. In the middle of the table was a large casserole dish; filled with ground beef, pasta, and a red sauce. Next to it was a serving bowl filled with green beans and a small basket of rolls. The white porcelain plates, dark blue cloth napkins, and vase of pink flowers in the center of the table gave the impression she was dining in a fancy restaurant and not the neighbor's home.

Mary sat at the end of the table with a huge smile on her face. "Welcome. We're so happy you could join us."

"Everything looks and smells amazing, Mary. I'm embarrassed to admit it, but the only pasta I know how to make is macaroni and cheese out of a box."

Mary chuckled. "My friend Bernice made this casserole. She said it's easy to make. You can make one large batch and freeze it in portions. If you like it, I'll ask for the recipe." She motioned to the chair next to her. "Go ahead and take a seat."

She sat down and placed the napkin on her lap. Libby curled up in a ball on the floor near her feet.

Mary extended her hand out. "Would you join me in prayer?"

She looked down at Mary's hand. *I should have anticipated this.* For a brief second, her heartbeat quickened. No one had ever asked her to join them in prayer. *Hopefully, I won't have to say anything.* She forced a tiny smile and held onto Mary's hand. If her mom could see her right now, she'd commend her for being polite. She reached her other hand out towards Norm. His attention was elsewhere. She pulled her hand back and lowered it onto her lap. Mary closed her eyes and bowed her head. She did the same. As Mary spoke, a thought ran through her head. *Norm was the retired pastor. Why wasn't he saying the prayer?* She gingerly lifted her head and peeked. Norm sat quietly, looking at Mary. She closed her eyes again and focused on Mary's words.

* * *

Norm often wondered what people thought when those around him prayed, and he remained disengaged. After all, Mary kept introducing him as a "retired pastor," and he didn't correct her. It seemed less awkward to go along with the charade than try to explain the truth; after spending over thirty years in faithful ministry, he stepped away from the church, from God.

After Rose died, something inside his heart irreparably broke. For the first time in his life, he'd experienced a level of anger he didn't know he could feel. After years of addiction, his prayers seemed answered when Rose finally agreed to drug rehab. With treatment, she abstained from drugs for months. She phoned every week, and he sensed the spark of her youth returning.

Her unexpected overdose left him heartbroken. While he wallowed in stunned grief, Mary and their oldest daughter, Grace, handled all the funeral arrangements. The only clear memory he had from that day was Rose lying in the coffin at the funeral home. Everything else was a blur.

After Rose's death, church leaders urged him to take time off. Instead, he threw himself headlong into every aspect of the church. He knew it was a façade, a tough guy act. Each day, he forced a smile while feigning empathy with friends and parishioners. He was afraid if he stopped for even a second and allowed himself to grieve, the pain within his heart would take him to a dark place, a place he knew he'd never leave.

So instead of allowing grief to take hold, he became angry. Anger made him feel strong, powerful. Like a mighty ship, anger cradled him above a sea of despair. Till one day, it sent him crashing into the rocky shoreline. On that day, he found himself in front of his congregation, fighting the urge to scream, "God isn't faithful! You can't count on him to be there in your time of need!" At that moment, he knew he must walk away; otherwise, he would go down, taking the whole church with him.

So, after the service, he quietly packed his things and emailed his resignation. Mary pleaded with him to talk to someone, anyone. He refused. Time moved on. Days turned to weeks; weeks turned to months. Eventually, even his most loyal friends stopped calling. Deep inside, he knew he was hurting Mary, but he couldn't stop. He'd made his mind up. He'd never step foot inside a church again. Almost two years had passed since Rose's death. In all that time, he'd kept true to his word, avoiding church, the Bible, and any talk of faith.

After Mary finished praying, an awkward silence filled the room. He glanced in Susan's direction. She was looking towards the floor at Libby. He smiled and asked, "So, how are you and Libby settling in?"

Susan turned her attention back to the table and smiled. "We're doing okay."

"Just okay?"

"No…we're doing good. It's just quiet around here. Do you know what I mean? Almost too quiet. I guess I never realized how unnerving it could be."

"I understand. But I've got to admit I like the quietness that comes with living away from the larger cities," Mary said. She quickly added, "But Norm and I have each other…so it's never really too quiet in the house."

He interrupted, "You lived in downtown Phoenix before moving here——isn't that right?"

"Uh-huh. Near Central Avenue. It's funny. I didn't realize how much I'd miss the sounds of traffic or sirens. I even miss the sound of the light rail pulling into the station by my apartment."

"So, this is quite a change for you."

She nodded, then her lips curled up in a tiny smile. "But there's one thing the city doesn't have; living out here…I get to see all the stars at night."

"Oh, I agree. Isn't it wonderful?" Mary paused, then added, "I hope you don't mind me saying this, but I admire you."

"Me?" Susan's eyes widened as she pointed at herself. "Why?"

"Because you're such a bright woman. So young, and you already have your first home."

Susan shook her head. "Honestly…my house payment is close to the rent of my old apartment. And, compared to my old apartment, this house is huge. Plus, I get to have Libby."

"And your parents; they must be so proud of you. They both seemed very nice. They live in Payson—isn't that, right?"

"Prescott."

"Oh, now I remember."

"They moved there a few years ago. I know they struggled with the decision to move away. My mom tried to talk me into moving to Prescott instead of buying this house. But I like my independence."

"Why did they move away?"

"My mom couldn't take the summer heat anymore."

"Oh, I fear, I'm getting to be like your mom," Mary said. "I'm hoping my ankle heals by the end of the month. Norm and I plan to go to Northern California around the fourth of July weekend to see our daughter, Grace. It'll be the perfect time to get out of Phoenix."

"So…when you go…you'll be gone for a while?"

Mary smiled. "At least a week."

"That sounds…great," Susan said.

Norm glanced at Susan. Her eyes were widened, and her voice seemed unnatural. Like she'd forced the word great from her throat.

"Are you okay?" he asked.

Susan fidgeted in her chair. "I'm okay. It's just…"

"Just…?"

She shook her head and smiled, a half-smile. The kind of smile that faded before it reached the eyes. "I'll be here…alone."

Mary reached out and held onto Susan's hand. "I'm sure more people will move onto our street before we leave."

Susan nodded. Her gaze quickly fluttered away. He'd seen the look hundreds of times before, on the faces of his parishioners. Fear. He'd recently experienced the feeling himself, on the night of the storm. Was

Susan merely afraid to be alone, or did she see something in the field? Bob's comments about the farm being cursed and images of the two red eyes flashed through his thoughts. His stomach clenched. "Is there anything else, Susan? Anything bothering you?"

She slowly shook her head and gave a half-hearted laugh. "My mom would say I've watched too many scary movies. It's just the cornfield; it's so close to our houses. I guess I didn't realize how much it would bother me. I wish we had brick walls like the rest of the subdivision. If we did, I wouldn't have to see it all the time."

He nodded. The chain-link fences around their properties posed a threat to their privacy and safety. The cheap metal fencing wouldn't keep anyone from entering their yards.

Susan spoke again. "I think I'll feel better when more people move into the houses on our street." A flush crept up Susan's face. "Oh, no...that didn't come out the way I meant it. I'm super thankful you both live next door! It's just our street seems so isolated. So quiet." She paused, then added, "Honestly, having you both so close is probably the only reason I get any sleep at night."

Mary smiled and reached for Susan's hand. "No need to apologize. We understand what you meant. We're both happy to have you living next door to us."

Susan was right. Their little street was like a small island, and the three castaways sitting at the table were its only inhabitants. The small backyards and chain-link fences covered in crows were undoubtedly a deterrent to potential home buyers. The large cornfield looming just beyond the fence line didn't help. It blocked the views of the mountains and created a sense of claustrophobia.

Mary interjected herself back into the conversation. "I know one thing. That cornfield is bringing a bunch of these crows. Ugh! They make such a mess."

Susan slowly nodded. "I've never liked birds. And now I've got a backyard full of them. It's strange—isn't it? To have so many crows in one place?"

Mary shrugged. "I'm sure they're here because of the corn. But I must admit, they are a bit intimidating, hanging out on our fence lines like they own the place. I don't even try to shoo them away anymore; they keep coming back."

He thought about his encounters with the crows and shuddered. Mary said they were here for the corn. But he couldn't shake the feeling they were here for something else, something living within the cornfield.

Susan spoke again. "There's one; it's huge. Have you seen it? It seems to hang out on the fence between our houses. I think it's big enough to hurt Libby. And, those beady eyes, always staring at me. Eww!" She squeezed her eyes shut and shuddered.

"Oh, I know the one you're talking about; he acts like he's the boss of the little ones." Mary smiled and nodded. "Well, don't you worry, once the corn is gone, those crows will leave."

"Yeah, until they plant something else in the field that brings them back," Susan replied.

He thought of the conversation he'd had with Dave and Bob earlier in the day. He pointed to the cornfield. "I don't think we'll have to worry about that field any time soon. I spoke with the guys at the diner. They said the land sits empty for years at a time." He paused and then added, "That doesn't seem normal."

Mary shook her head. "Normal? How would we know what's normal on a farm? You went to seminary school, and I have a degree in business. We are not farming experts."

He'd struck a nerve. He may not have a degree in agriculture, but he could tell when something was off. Ignoring Mary's comment, he turned to Susan and continued, "The farmer who owns the land is Tobias Smith. Anyway, the guys told me he's turned down multiple offers to lease the land. I hear it sits empty most of the time."

"And?" Mary asked.

"I also heard his farm has money problems. Doesn't it seem strange that a farm with money trouble wouldn't do something that could bring them easy money?"

Susan nodded. Mary rolled her eyes.

He turned away from Mary and spoke directly to Susan. "Have you noticed how dark the soil is?"

"Yes, it's a blackish-red color."

"The guys said that soil is some of the best in the county. So why not lease it?"

He glanced over at Mary. She narrowed her eyes and frowned. "Norm, I don't know Tobias. But I've met his wife Sarah and their sons at church. They are good people. It sounds to me like your farming buddies are spreading gossip because Tobias isn't doing their bidding. Did any of you consider the soil is probably good because he doesn't plant it all the time?" She paused for a moment, then continued. "Besides, I'm happy the land will sit vacant most of the time. There'll be nothing to spoil our views of the mountains."

He opened his mouth to speak, then abruptly closed it, capitulating to Mary. He didn't wish to argue in front of Susan. Dave's comments about other farmers being jealous swirled through his head. *Mary's right. I'm spreading rumors.*

After dinner, he cleared the table. A short time later, he returned with a pot of coffee and Susan's plate of cookies. Mary and Susan were talking about Mary's sprained ankle.

"The doctor told me it could take a month to heal."

"How will you manage when Norm goes back to work?"

"I should be good. I'm moving well. Norm will make breakfast for me before he leaves, and he's bought some of those easy microwavable meals for lunch."

"I can check in on you."

"Oh no, that's okay. I hate to be a bother."

"Honestly, Mary. I don't mind. I work from home. I could stop by around lunchtime. Maybe make your lunch?"

He overheard Susan's offer of help. His shoulders relaxed. Today was the first time he'd left Mary alone since she hurt her ankle. He felt guilty, leaving her to fend for herself. Knowing Susan could check in on Mary while he worked eased his mind. "Susan, that would be wonderful! I was worried about leaving Mary alone on the days I have to work."

Mary smiled. "Okay…if you're sure it's not any trouble."

Susan shook her head. "It's not. Would you like me to come around noon?"

"That would be great. We have plenty of casseroles in the freezer. I hope you don't mind leftovers."

"If they're as good as this casserole, I don't."

CHAPTER 8

Pastor Ted Cummings pulled into the parking lot of Desert Springs Community Church and smiled. The number of cars in the parking lot each Sunday continued to grow. Sprawled out in front of him was the main church, a large one-story building with beige stucco walls and a brown tile roof. A large cross stood on top of the church; like a beacon, it welcomed newcomers inside.

He pulled into his parking space at the back of the church office. Because he sometimes spent evenings in his office, the congregation reserved a parking spot adjacent to one of the parking lot lights. In front of him was a post with a sign that read:

Theodore Cummings
Senior Pastor

In truth, he was the only pastor in the small church, a position he'd held for the past six months. He interviewed and was hired straight out of seminary school. With the church's small membership and a modest stipend, he'd wondered how many pastors had declined the position before the church settled on him.

He entered the church foyer. The physical structure of the church hadn't changed since his arrival. An overhead light illuminated the foyer. Two large tables lined the entrance to the church's main sanctuary. A large vase filled with brightly colored flowers sat in the middle of one table. Various literature about the church covered the other table. A large bulletin board, covered in flyers, hung above one of the tables. A silver-framed blackboard on the wall above the other table caught Ted's attention. Behind the glass, in white letters, the notice read:

Welcome
Desert Springs C.C.
Ted Cummings, Pastor
Sunday Service 9:00 am
Sunday School 10:15 am

He remembered the feeling of joy that spread through his chest the first time he saw his name on the board. That cheery wave soon faded, replaced by a profound sense of responsibility. During his interview, he learned the previous pastor died suddenly, leaving behind a grieving congregation. He had the knowledge to interpret biblical Scriptures, prepare sermons, and conduct worship services. He prayed God would help him find the words to comfort and counsel church members through their grief.

He glanced at the doors leading to the sanctuary. Frequently polished, they shimmered in the light of the foyer. He entered the sanctuary and strode down the center aisle. Rows of pews lined both sides of the church. They were covered in a light green fabric, threadbare in spots, but clean and tidy. Small wooden boxes at the back of each pew held Bibles, song hymnals, pencils, and offering envelopes. A sizeable wooden altar covered in a sheet of white marble sat at the front of the sanctuary. A four-foot-tall golden cross hung on the wall behind the altar. A light fixture with three spotlights hung directly over the altar. One light shone down on the altar, one shone onto the cross, and the other light shone onto the church organ. *Our church is humble in furnishings but not neglected.*

He stepped behind the altar and remembered the wave of doubt that crashed upon him during his first sermon. Forty-five members sat in the pews. *How will I learn everyone's name? Let alone know them on a personal level?* He'd recognized the destructive influence of doubt as it fought to invade his psyche. He'd fought doubt by closing his eyes and taking deep breaths. With each cleansing breath, he blew away the anxiety and replaced it with thankfulness. *God will help me remember their names. He will use me to make a difference. I am grateful for the opportunity given to me! Thank You, God!*

Each Sunday, he arrived at church early and began his day with a humble prayer. He thanked the Lord for the opportunity to lead the church. He also prayed for wisdom and the ability to help everyone who passed through the doors. Within six months, the weekly attendance increased to just over one hundred; most were official members while a handful of others were testing the waters.

As he knelt at the side of the altar and prayed, the door next to him squeaked open, capturing his attention. He finished his prayer and turned. Standing in the doorway was Bernice King, the church's secretary. She'd become his biggest ally. Watching over him like a protective mother, she helped him find a balance between the congregation's needs and the personal time he needed to settle into his new role.

She stepped forward and lowered her voice. "Sorry to disturb you, pastor. A few minutes ago, Sarah Smith showed up here, asking if she could see you before the service. She's upset. I hope you don't mind, but I put her in your office."

He glanced down at his watch: 7:56 a.m.

"I'm sorry…I should have asked you first. It's just, I've never seen her like this before. Do you want me to tell her you'll speak to her after the service? Or should I see if she wants to schedule a time during the week?"

He shook his head. "It's okay, Bernice. I've got some time. Tell her I'll be right there."

He'd met Sarah and her four sons soon after he arrived at the church. They were all active members of the congregation and well thought of in the community. One by one, he scrolled through her son's names in his head. It was a kind of game he played with himself—a way to test his memory. John, the oldest, was in his early twenties. His wife's name was Kate. No children. The youngest was Daniel, a senior in high school, just turned eighteen. Sandwiched between the oldest and youngest was a set of nineteen-year-old twins, James and Charles. James was single. Charles' girlfriend, Rachael, recently moved to Tucson to attend the University of Arizona. Members of the congregation collectively referred to the brothers as the Smith boys. They attended church regularly and were well-liked by the community. Finally, he thought of Sarah's husband, Tobias. Unlike Sarah and her sons, who were regulars every Sunday, he rarely attended church.

He entered the office. One glance at Sarah and his heart fell into his stomach. She sat, partially curled up, in the chair across from his desk. Her eyes were red and puffy. She clung to the box of tissues in her lap with a white-knuckled grip. She looked small, not the confident, strong woman he'd grown to know.

He sat next to her and leaned forward. "Good morning, Sarah."

She met his gaze and whispered, "Good morning, Pastor Cummings. I'm sorry to bother you."

"It's not a bother. What's wrong?"

"It's Tobias."

"Did something happen to him?"

She shook her head. "No." She paused briefly as if gathering her words. "He's been under a lot of stress, and he won't tell me what's wrong. He's not eating, not sleeping. I can't get him to go to the doctor. He keeps saying everything will be better in a few weeks. When I ask him what he means by that, he just shakes his head and walks away. He's hiding something from me. I can feel it. When I asked him again this morning, he lashed out at me. We had a terrible fight, the first one in years."

"I'm so sorry, Sarah. What do you think is going on?"

She shrugged her shoulders and looked away. "I guess he's worried about our finances again. I thought our money troubles were finally behind us. Now, I'm not sure. I think he's banking on a good harvest from our north field. We've got a huge crop of corn growing there, and it's due for harvest in a few weeks."

"Did you ask him…about the finances?"

She glanced up and curtly shook her head. "When we were struggling a few years ago, I pushed him to sell off our last piece of available land." She paused as tears filled her eyes. "Did you know the land under the subdivision used to be ours?"

He nodded.

"I don't think he's fully forgiven me for insisting we sell that parcel. He refuses to see all the good it did. That subdivision brought a lot of young families here. All the businesses are now booming. I believe selling the land didn't just save our farm; it saved our town."

While the land's sale preceded his arrival at Desert Springs, he'd heard about the pushback Tobias and Sarah initially received from the community. Locals feared there'd be an increase in crime and a strain on the county resources. But once families moved into the subdivision, the cynics put aside their concerns.

"I've only heard people mention the subdivision in a positive light, for the very reason you stated: more families, more business. I know I wasn't here when all of this happened. But rest assured, Sarah, it sounds like you and Tobias did a good thing."

For a moment, she sat perfectly still. The only movement was that of tears escaping her eyes and slowly rolling down her face. He wasn't sure if she was quietly praying or thinking. He waited. Finally, she blinked her eyes open and gave a slight nod. Her lips curled up in a partial smile. "Thank you, pastor. You don't know how much I needed to hear that."

He glanced at his watch. She must have noticed. "I'm so sorry. I should have asked Bernice if I could see you after the service."

"Don't apologize, Sarah. I was just checking the time. I'm not running late, but I do need to start getting ready. Do you think Tobias would talk with me? I could come out to the farm, or he could come to the office, whatever works best for him."

A look of relief washed over her face. "I hoped you'd offer to come to our house. I doubt Tobias would come here, pastor. But he might be willing to speak with you if you went to the farm."

He smiled and nodded. "Ask him if he's willing to talk and then call Bernice to set up a time. In the meantime, I will keep him and your whole family in my prayers." He glanced down at his watch again. If he didn't end the conversation in a few minutes, he'd be late. "Let's say a prayer for Tobias before you leave."

CHAPTER 9

Susan awoke with the sunrise. A sense of joy filled her entire being. She glanced over at Libby. She, too, seemed less skittish and more disciplined. She also offered a sense of protection, helping Susan sleep more soundly.

Susan was sure Mary had something to do with her newfound sense of joy. For over a week, she'd spent her lunch breaks next door. The lunchtime visit was a brief reprieve from the loneliness of her day. She knew Mary appreciated the help and surmised she also enjoyed her company. Even on Norm's day off, Mary still invited her to stop by for lunch. The days when Norm joined them were filled with laughter as he entertained them with his adventures at the hardware store.

With her hair pulled haphazardly into a ponytail, she washed her face and brushed her teeth. What would her mom say if she found out lunchtimes spent with Mary alone included listening to Bible stories?

Her parents didn't believe in organized religion and often commented negatively about attending church. They also didn't pass up an opportunity to point out the potential flaws of the pastors they'd seen on television. So what would they think of Norm? He seemed nothing like the pastors she'd seen on television. He didn't talk about God at all.

She pulled her medicine bottles from the cabinet and lined them on the counter. Although she loved her parents, she couldn't help wondering how different her life might have been if she were Norm and Mary's child. They didn't judge her. They didn't question her ability to live independently. Mary even told her how proud she was of her.

She glanced down at the bottles lining the counter. *If Norm and Mary were my parents, I wouldn't need all these.* She shook her head, then placed half the bottles into the cabinet without opening them. *I don't need all these to feel normal.*

She strolled to the kitchen. Rising early gave her a chance to walk Libby before she logged into work. The mere rattle of the leash made the young dog's body quiver with excitement. She pulled the leash from the wall and attached it to Libby's collar.

Instead of walking through the subdivision, they ventured along the irrigation ditch separating the subdivision from the farm. At the southernmost end of the ditch, a small bridge led to the farmer's property. She crossed it and continued walking.

A sizeable three-story home stood in the distance. Its white and gray exterior was in stark contrast to the dark green grass blanketing the surrounding grounds. Like a fanciful skirt, a wide porch wrapped around the house's back and side. The home, sprawling lawn, and large trees reminded her of estates she'd seen on the east coast. It looked out of place in the middle of the desert. Nestled within an area of the tree line was a small cemetery. If Libby hadn't been with her, she would have ventured closer.

* * *

The following morning, Susan returned. She wasn't sure what drew her to the cemetery on the farmer's land. The only cemetery she'd ever visited was Arlington National Cemetery with her mother and father. Despite being fourteen, she was too fascinated by the cemetery's history and grandeur to be frightened.

She prepared for her clandestine adventure, filling a water bottle, packing a light snack, and applying sunscreen on her fair skin. Libby recognized the routine of the walk and eagerly ran around her feet. "Sorry, girl. It's just me this time."

Walking to the border of the subdivision took less time than she remembered. Soon, she found herself at the small bridge over the irrigation canal. As she stood there, contemplating her next move, her mother's voice rang out in her head. *You're trespassing. They'll call the sheriff.*

She glanced around, weighing her options one last time. Moving ahead felt right. She wanted to see the cemetery. Walking back home without even trying seemed dumb. She stepped onto the bridge, fully committed. Within a few steps, she was in the center of the bridge. She'd crossed it so fast the last time she vaguely remembered how dangerous it was. The bridge was four-foot-wide and roughly six-foot-long. There were no railings to keep people from falling over the edge. She glanced down and shuddered. *Six-foot drop.* One misstep, and she'd fall into the shallow water below.

After crossing the irrigation canal, she stopped. Her eyes scanned the lawns and area around the large home. Fifty yards of open ground lay between the canal and the tree line. She sprinted towards the tree line and dashed behind a large tree. Then she glanced at the main house. The home had a majestic feel from far away, like a giant white castle in the middle of the desert. But the vision of the home at a distance proved merely a mirage. Upon closer scrutiny, the home's paint was faded and worn, and the wooden poles holding up the porch roof were dry and cracked as if the Arizona heat had sucked every bit of water from the wood. She glanced at the beautifully arched windows above the porch: so *many windows—so many ways to get caught.*

Her eyes gazed upon the landscape extending away from the home. The deep green lawn remained lush and well-manicured, and the flowerbeds were more beautiful up close. To the right of the house stood a twenty-foot-tall tree. The largest branch housed a handmade swing made of two large ropes cradling a wooden seat.

She remained hidden in the tree line. Deep green canopies provided the cover she needed to avoid detection while shading her from the summer heat. She glanced back at the house. Quiet. She stepped out of the tree line. The knot in her stomach tightened. She shook her head. Should she stay hidden in the tree line or move forward? If she continued, staying low to the ground, there was a chance she could move through the cemetery without being seen.

In front of her were two rows of graves, each further apart than she initially thought. Small trees were strategically placed within the cemetery grounds. *I can hide behind those.* She took a few deep breaths, crouched low, and then briskly moved to the closest grave marker. She glanced down the row of graves, each bordered by railroad ties or stones. The headstones consisted of bricks painted white and held together by cement. She remained crouched as she moved from one gravesite to the next. A layer of gravel covered the hardpacked earth. Like finely ground glass, it was sharp and painful to the touch.

Beads of sweat rolled down her forehead. She wiped them away with the back of her hand. The names on the headstones were all Spanish. Only a few of the graves had dates. Were they the graves of migrant workers who'd died on the farm?

She continued onward until she reached the trees at the end of the row of graves. The shade offered a reprieve from the heat of the day. The ground around the tree was dry and cool, and it lacked the fine gravel she'd encountered over the graves.

She sat and took a few sips from her water bottle, then leaned back against the tree. The fragrant aroma of the flowering beds filled the air. She found comfort in the peaceful silence. After a few moments, she looked around and planned her next move. From this vantage point, the cemetery appeared divided into three sections. She'd have to cross a small clearing before moving into the next section. But once there, she'd easily be hidden by the largest headstone in the cemetery.

She crouched and made her way through the clearing, then dashed behind the large headstone. She knelt in front of it and read the names engraved there. Three children, siblings. John died at age five. Helen was three when she died. Gertrude died at two months old. All died within days of each other. She shuddered. *The death of one child would be devastating. To lose three children around the same time was unimaginable!* She glanced at the next grave marker. Elizabeth. The inscription read: *Died of a broken heart.* The death date was just a few weeks after the death of her last child. On the other side of Elizabeth's grave marker, she found one with the name "Jonas." He died in his seventies. Elizabeth and Jonas' deaths were decades apart. Was Jonas Elizabeth's husband?

The quiet peace of the cemetery evaporated. Despite the heat of the morning sun, a cold pressure gripped her chest. A feeling coupled with the sensation of being watched. She glanced around the cemetery, then up at the house. A woman with long straight black hair stared down upon her. By the look on the woman's face, she knew she'd spotted her.

Susan quickly scanned the cemetery, looking for a way out or a place to hide. An area at the far end of the graveyard was shrouded in darkness. If she ran fast, she might be able to hide among the tombstones there. She bolted towards the dark area of the graveyard, then dove behind the largest grave marker she could find. A cold, damp layer of green clover covered the ground. She laid there, motionless, for a few moments until her heart rate slowed.

Gingerly, she peeked past the grave marker. The woman from the window now stood on the area of grass behind the house. Her hand was raised to block the sunlight, and it looked as though she was intently scanning the cemetery with her eyes. Susan jerked her head back and pressed herself further into the moist earth. *Please don't see me!*

After a few moments, she peeked out again, catching a glimpse of the woman walking back towards the house. *That was close.* Susan slowly rolled onto her side, pushing herself upright onto one elbow. This area of the cemetery differed from the rest. The trees lining this corner of the graveyard were closer together, providing full shade, and the air smelled musty and old.

Nearly hidden from view by the shade, she sat upright and glanced down at her clothes. The front of her shirt and shorts were damp and stained by the green clover covering the ground. Moist earth covered both hands. She wiped her hands on her legs, took a few deep breaths, and regained her composure.

She turned and glanced up at the headstone she'd hidden behind. The two-foot-tall headstone was made of white painted bricks cemented together. Scrawled on the bricks in black paint was the name—Rex. *A dog's name.* She shuddered as her thoughts drifted to Libby.

She glanced at the ground bordering Rex's grave. Instead of another headstone, there were two large flat stones, one on each graveside. Both lacked date and names, nothing to identify the remains buried below. She scooted along the ground, moving further into the tree line. Nestled in the tree line, she could see all the ground in the shaded area of the cemetery at once. The appearance of flat unmarked stones sandwiched between random headstones repeated over the area. Since the flat stones aligned with the headstones, she felt confident they were also grave markers. But grave markers for what?

She couldn't shake the feeling she'd stumbled onto a forbidden section of the cemetery, purposefully hidden from view. She leaned upon the nearest tree and took some deep breaths. Thick, musty air filled her lungs. A wave of nausea passed through her body, sending bile into her mouth. Slowly, she lowered herself to a seated position, opened her water bottle, and swallowed the bile down with a few sips of water. With the remaining water, she rinsed her hands. Once her dizziness and nausea passed, she glanced one more time at the farmhouse and the barn. Seeing no sign of the woman, she exited the tree line and raced home.

* * *

Later in the afternoon, Susan stopped by Mary's house. She wanted to tell her about the cemetery and the discovery of the graveyard section, which seemed forbidden. But she couldn't. Based on Mary's previous descriptions, the woman who spotted her in the cemetery was Sarah Smith. Mary spoke highly of Sarah. And if Sarah accused her of trespassing, Mary would be disappointed.

CHAPTER 10

Although Susan knew taking Libby to the cemetery would have been a mistake, she still felt guilty leaving her home. The following day, she rose early and headed out the door with Libby in tow. As she stepped onto the driveway, her carefree mood disappeared.

Lying on the ground was her trashcan. Its contents were strewn over the street and sidewalk. *Who did this? Why?* She shook her head. It didn't matter who knocked it over. She'd be the one who'd have to clean it up. She felt a wave of anger slowly rising within her chest.

"Coyotes," a man's deep voice echoed in the background.

She startled, and her heartbeat quickened. She turned towards the voice. A handsome young man strolled in her direction. Solidly built and of average height, the young man wore a pair of denim jeans and a white T-shirt, which enhanced the look of his golden brown, muscular arms. Wavy black hair covered his head. Even at a distance, she could see the strong features of his face.

A flush crept up her neck and face. She looked down. *Holy crap! I'm a mess.* Hair pulled back, no makeup. She felt sure the black pair of shorts made her fair skin look opaque. She was grateful she wore a pair of large dark sunglasses. They made her feel less exposed.

The young man continued to approach; his walk was purposeful, determined. Libby wagged her tail and moved towards him. She jerked on Libby's leash, bringing her to a stop.

The young man abruptly halted and smiled, showing a mouthful of pearly white teeth. The smile lit up his green eyes. When she first heard his voice, she thought the guy might be close to her age. But once he stood directly in front of her, she realized she was wrong. Way wrong. The handsome man looked as though he was barely out of high school. Oh, how she wanted to walk away. It was a good thing she was wearing dark glasses. Otherwise, he'd probably figure out how embarrassed she was. Instead, she closed her eyes and gently shook her head. *He's a baby! I'm such an idiot.*

She glanced up and down the street. A few houses away, parked alongside the curb, was an older, orange and white pick-up truck. A large trashcan sat upright in the truck bed. *He's delivering a trashcan. Someone else is finally moving into a house on our street!*

Her shoulders relaxed, and she loosened the grip on Libby's leash.

The young man smiled and took another step forward. In one hand, he held a shredded microwave food container.

"It looks like coyotes raided your trash," the young man said. He leaned over and righted her trashcan, then placed the shredded container inside.

"Coyotes?" With the summer heat approaching, she ran a fan in her room at night. She thought she heard coyotes howling over the sound of the fan blades but wasn't sure. She looked at Libby. *I'm glad I kept the doggy door closed last night.*

The young man spoke again: "I'm sorry, ma'am. I forgot to introduce myself." The young man's smile widened. "I'm Daniel Smith."

Ma'am? His friendly salutation delivered a momentary blow to her ego. *How old do I look?*

She took a step forward. "I'm Susan Green, and this is Libby."

Libby's tail wiggled back and forth with such force her whole backside shook. She tugged on the leash, pulling Susan closer to Daniel.

Daniel squatted on the ground in front of them. He wiped his hand on his pant leg. "May I pet her?"

She nodded and loosened her grip on the leash. Libby ran to Daniel. He began brushing her coat. "She's got a sweet disposition."

She smiled. "Thank you." *Something about his name sounded familiar.* "Are you related to the farmer down the road?" She pointed to the southern end of the subdivision.

"Yes, that's our farm. It's been in my dad's family for generations." Daniel replied, "This is my second job…delivering a trash can when one of these houses sells. Your street is the only street with empty houses. Once these houses sell, this job goes away."

"This is your second job?"

"Yes, ma'am." He chuckled. "It's not as bad as it sounds. My other job is delivering newspapers for *Valley News* on the weekend. "I just graduated. So, I now have time to work a real job with a regular paycheck. I have an interview this afternoon at Kroger's. Working nights, stocking the shelves."

"Don't you work on your family's farm?"

"Absolutely, ma'am. That's a given. We're a family. We all pitch in." He smiled and pointed in the direction of the old orange and white truck. "But I'm saving up for a new truck."

Something about his easygoing manner put her immediately at ease. He was kind, so willing to help a total stranger. With his help, it only took a few minutes to clean up the trash.

"Thank you for helping me clean up this mess."

Daniel nodded and pointed at the trashcan. "I'm sure the coyotes were just looking for food scraps. I don't want to worry you, but I've seen quite a few flyers on the light poles and mailboxes in this subdivision. With those coyotes out on the loose, I'd keep a good eye on your dog."

"I will. Honestly, I don't know what I'd do if anything ever happened to her." Acknowledging out loud how much Libby meant to her brought tears to her eyes. She was grateful she was wearing sunglasses.

"Well, I should head out," Daniel said. "It was nice to meet you."

She watched Daniel walk to his truck. He removed a large trashcan in one quick motion and placed it on the ground in front of her neighbor's house. In all the commotion, she'd forgotten someone was finally moving into one of the houses. A calmness washed over her, and she smiled.

"Come on, girl, let's go for our walk," Susan said as she tugged Libby's leash.

When they returned home, she showered, brought her breakfast into her office, and opened the laptop. As a medical coder, she could work from home. While she worked, Libby lay at her feet. Mary informed her Norm had the day off and planned to mow her grass. By mid-morning, the familiar drone of the lawnmower caught her attention.

* * *

As Norm pushed the lawnmower, he focused his eyes on the grass in front of him. Tim McGraw's song "I like it, I love it" blasted through the set of headphones covering his ears. *I used to love mowing the lawn. Maybe someday, after the corn is gone, I'll at least like it again.*

He sang along with Tim, belting out the lyrics. If Mary were standing there, she'd likely make some comment about his singing. But, despite his unease, knowing Mary and Susan were safe within their homes brought him comfort.

Weeks earlier, from the anonymity of their home, Mary waved him over to the window. "Norm, come look at this!" she insisted. "She's struggling with her lawnmower. We should help her."

He glanced through the window and watched as Susan struggled to push her lawnmower over the grass. He glanced down at Mary. "And by 'we'…you mean me… right, honey?" He asked, pointing at his chest.

"Well, since you are the expert at grass mowing. Yes, *you* should go and help that poor girl. Look at those lines. That lawnmower is bouncing her all over the place. Seriously, Norm, she's going to hurt herself!"

The following day he was at Susan's door offering his free lawn care services.

* * *

Susan glanced up from her computer. *I bet Norm would like some fresh lemonade.* She stopped at the sliding glass door in the family room on her way to the kitchen. Norm was mowing the last row of grass. His head was down; his eyes appeared focused on the ground. A pair of headphones covered his ears. In bounding strides, he crisscrossed the small backyard at a rapid pace. *He's racing across the lawn; must be in a hurry to finish.*

She stepped outside and walked in his direction. He appeared oblivious to her approach. Then, just as he mowed the last few blades of grass, he glanced at her and startled. "Oh, I didn't see you!" He shut off the lawn mower's engine.

Once she saw Norm up close, her heart sank. Beads of sweat streamed down his ashen face. His arms and legs visibly shook. "Are you okay?"

He removed the headphones. Loud country music streamed through the speakers. He lowered the headphone's volume and shook his head. "I'm sorry, Susan. I didn't hear you. I like playing music. It helps me focus on the grass and not on..." He haphazardly waved his headphones in the direction of the cornfield. "...all this."

"I asked if you were okay. You look like you're overheated. Can I get you something to drink?"

"I'm okay. I'll just get this lawnmower put away and get back home. I can rest and get a cool drink there." He steered the lawnmower towards the small side gate at the side of her house and took a few steps. His legs wobbled.

"Stop, Norm! You're not okay. I can put this lawnmower away myself. Come on. I'm getting you inside the house."

He quietly nodded and released the push bar on the mower. Worriedly, she watched him stagger into the house. Once inside, she rushed to the refrigerator and pulled out a pitcher of lemonade. He leaned against the kitchen island as she filled a cup with ice. "You need to sit down, Norm. Even if it's only for a minute." She pulled a chair back from the island. She noticed his knees buckle as he plopped into the chair. *At least he made it inside without passing out.*

She filled the cup with lemonade and thrust it in front of him. "Drink."

He nodded, and in a whispering voice, he thanked her and raised the cup to his lip with both hands.

"Once you feel steady on your feet, I'm walking you home."

"You don't have to do that."

"Oh...yes, I do. I'm going to tell Mary you got overheated. That way she can keep an eye on you."

He shook his head. "It's a little warm today, but I'm sure this has more to do with me being a little out of shape."

She thought about his comment. Being out of shape and mowing grass in the heat was the perfect combination for a heart attack or stroke. She'd never forgive herself if something happened to him. "Maybe, I should mow my own—."

"No!" He interrupted.

She drew back at his abrupt response.

His voice softened. "I'm sorry. I didn't mean you couldn't mow your lawn. I know you can. I'm just saying I don't want you to mow your lawn on my account. I promise I'll slow down next time." He smiled, then raised the cup again, finishing the lemonade in a few quick gulps.

She breathed a sigh of relief. "You look a little better now. There's some color coming back into your face."

He smiled. "I'm feeling better. You don't have to walk me home."

"You'll tell Mary what happened…right? You know she invited me over for lunch."

He nodded curtly. "I'm pretty sure if I don't tell her, you will."

She smiled and nodded.

* * *

Later, after dinner, Susan plucked a light green tennis ball from Libby's basket of toys. She stepped onto the small concrete slab outside her sliding glass door. The newly mowed grass looked inviting. The evening sky's beauty captured her attention: warm colors of gold, orange, and magenta layered the sky and reflected off the nearby mountains. As the sun lowered behind the cornfield, it backlit the cornstalks, sending long shadows across the small dirt road towards her backyard. *Those shadows look like long crooked fingers, reaching out for me.* A shudder went through her body.

A gentle breeze stirred, drawing her attention to the cornstalks themselves. The warm breeze cradled the cornfield, moving the stalks of corn slowly back and forth in rustling, rhythmic waves. The aroma of the fields filled the air. She took off her sandals and stepped onto the grass. Freshly cut, the blades of grass squished between her toes. Despite the warmth of the air, her feet felt cool and refreshed.

Libby bounced up and down, nipping at the tennis ball in her hand. With each day of play, Libby became more skillful at chasing the ball and bringing it back. Susan gave a small laugh, then tossed the ball across the lawn. Libby dashed after it. She tackled the ball with her mouth, then rushed back, dropping the ball at Susan's feet. She smiled, knowing they'd repeat this process over and over until Libby was exhausted.

Susan remembered the day when she first laid eyes on Libby. Despite being the littlest puppy in the litter, Libby seemed to have bounds of courage, a trait she desperately wished she, herself, possessed. Although the litter's runt, Libby bested the other puppies. She'd sneak up on them, jump on their back, and then wrestle them to the ground. Susan remembered the first time she looked into the puppy's tiny face and noticed she had different colored eyes, blue and brown. She remembered the owner of the litter's voice behind her. "Hey…don't let those eyes bother you. We'll sell you the little runt for half price." The owner had treated Libby as if she were some kind of throwaway dog. She was sure if Libby hadn't been as feisty as she was, the owner probably would have allowed her to die. So, she took the discount, knowing in her heart she would have paid full price to have her.

Libby bumped Susan's leg, drawing her attention back to the game of fetch. She looked down at her tiny sidekick and smiled. "Are you looking for this?" She threw the ball across the yard. Libby gave chase, pouncing on the ball as it rolled to a stop on the other side of the yard. Above Libby, perched along the fence line, the crows quietly stirred. Libby appeared immune to their presence. She ran back with the ball and dropped it at Susan's feet. She then stood in a crouched position with her tail wagging feverishly. Susan threw the ball again. Libby gave chase. She captured the ball in her mouth and began walking back. Halfway across the yard, Libby abruptly stopped and turned towards the cornfield. She stood there, frozen in place; the tennis ball dropped from her mouth.

"Libby."

Libby began walking towards the back fence.

"Libby!" She forcefully clapped her hands to get Libby's attention.

Libby continued walking, seemingly oblivious to her voice.

She narrowed her eyes as she scanned the thick stalks of corn. *The movement of the cornstalks is distracting her.* She walked towards Libby. Instead of acknowledging her presence, Libby eagerly paced along the fence line.

The birds, perched on the fence line, began cawing and flapping their wings. On the ground, a few feet below the crows, Libby's agitation grew as she whimpered and increased her pace back and forth. *She wants out.*

Susan felt a sense of urgency all around her. Like a wave of electricity, the ball of nervous energy grew and spread throughout her body. She scanned the rows of corn. The outside row of stalks gently swayed in the breeze. While a section of stalks in the center of the field moved in the opposite direction. A loud rustle emanated from within the corn. *It's moving towards us.* Her body trembled, and her eyes widened as she urgently scanned the corn again.

The crows on the fence line became raucous. With a fevered upsurge, they aggressively flapped their wings and bowed up and down. A thought flashed through her mind. *Coyotes.* They knocked over her trashcan last night. Perhaps they found Libby's scent and were moving in her direction.

Her heart raced, and her palms became sweaty as her gaze shifted between Libby, the crows, and the cornstalks. Whatever was out there, moving towards them wasn't just hungry, it sought to devour everything in its path.

A cold sweat broke out across her forehead. She haphazardly scooped Libby into her arms and bolted towards the house. Once inside, she placed Libby on the floor and abruptly pulled the sliding glass door shut. With a shaking hand, she secured the lock, then closed the vertical blinds. All the while, diverting her gaze from the cornfield.

Libby moved towards the doggy door. Susan pulled her back and slid the plastic cover over the opening. Libby bumped against the plastic cover twice, then whined. "Sorry, girl, but you're not going outside."

Then Libby paced back and forth in front of the sliding glass door. The vertical blinds rippled in her wake. She paced a few more times, then suddenly stopped. Her tail started wagging, and she turned away from the window.

Susan sat on the edge of her couch. Libby followed and sat next to her feet. She reached out with a trembling hand and stroked Libby's soft coat. Libby's short tail vigorously wagged back and forth. With each stroke on Libby's coat, the tension in her shoulders lessened. Once her heartbeat and breathing slowed, and the trembling of her hand stopped, she walked to the sliding glass door and pushed back the vertical blinds. The cornstalks gently swayed back and forth. A half-hearted laugh escaped her lungs, brushing aside her lingering fear. *It was nothing—just the wind.*

* * *

Susan rarely remembered her dreams, but she never forgot her nightmares. She hated the loss of control she felt when mired in one. The only sensation she could equate it to was falling over a cliff, unable to stop the descent. That night, after playing with Libby, a vivid and horrific dream interrupted her sleep.

In her dream, she and Libby stood on the dirt road behind her home, staring into the cornfield. The sound of rustling cornstalks captured her attention. In the distance, she detected their movement. Stagnant and warm, the air hung thick over the dirt road. *No breeze.* In horror, she realized something was moving through the stalks. The rustling grew louder.

Between the cornstalks, she spied a pair of coyotes. Slowly, they emerged out from the stalks and onto the road. Their shoulders hunched forward, bodies crouched, and heads hung low. Her gaze rapidly moved from one coyote to the other. Their ears were pinned down, and their lips curled back, exposing long sharp teeth. Their yellow eyes focused on Libby. A low growl resonated from the coyotes as they slowly and methodically encircled her and Libby.

Inexplicable panic silenced her scream. She awoke with her mouth open, unable to make a sound. For a moment, she was unable to move her arms and legs. Her heart continued to race as beads of sweat ran down her face. *It was just a dream!* She repeated the comforting phrase over and over in her head. She reached out and found Libby whimpering in the bed. Her legs were in motion like she was running in her dream. *She's dreaming too!* She gently stroked Libby's coat. The whimpering stopped, and Libby's legs stopped moving. Despite Libby's presence, Susan spent the remainder of the night being startled awake by each innocuous sound inside the house.

CHAPTER 11

Tobias stepped into the kitchen. Breakfast was on the table, and the aroma of coffee and bacon filled the air. Sarah stood at the sink, washing dishes. His heart fluttered in his chest. He'd been on pins and needles for the past few days, trying to make up for the argument they'd had over the weekend.

Most of their twenty-one years had passed with a sense of normalcy. She loved him. But would she have married him knowing his family's dark secret? What if she found out now? Would she love him enough to stay?

He learned of his family's dark side soon after discovering Sarah was pregnant with his child. Within a few short days, he'd experienced both the greatest joy and greatest sorrow in his life.

His first instinct was to take Sarah as far away from the farm as possible. But what then? How would he support her and a baby? He'd worked the farm his entire life, knowing one day it would be his. Could he just walk away and give it all up?

And, if he walked away, what would become of his father? The man who once worked nonstop from dusk to dawn could barely make it past noon. His thin, muscular frame had grown skeleton-like, and his behavior had become increasingly erratic. For months, he'd stood by helpless as his father slowly deteriorated before his eyes. Despite his pleas, the man forcefully refused help. Leaving the farm, leaving his father, wasn't an option.

So instead, he'd decided he'd tell Sarah everything. Then together, they'd decide where to raise their family. But when his father learned of his plan to talk with Sarah, he frantically pleaded with him to reconsider. "You can't risk telling anyone, Tobias! I mean it. You know the rumors about Jonas and Lukas. We can't draw any more attention to this farm or our family!" He'd never seen his father so out of control. Eyes widened, brow furrowed, pacing the floor; he looked like a man teetering on the brink of insanity.

Twenty-one years ago, he convinced himself keeping his father's secret was the only thing that could ease his father's troubled mind. But, in truth, he also held the secret because he wasn't sure Sarah would stay. What if she found out now? Would she forgive his deceit?

Throughout the years, her love was the one constant, which kept him sane. He wrapped his arms around her and placed his head on her shoulder, hopeful she'd fully forgiven him. He whispered into her neck, "Good morning, beautiful."

She leaned back against his chest. "You sound like you're in a good mood this morning. Did you finally get some sleep?"

He smiled. His heartbeat steadied. *We're back to normal.* "I did. I'm pretty sure I fell asleep as soon as my head hit the pillow. How about you?"

"Same."

Sarah's rolling cart was in the kitchen. A few years ago, he found it at the Goodwill store for twenty dollars. It was in a sad state when he purchased it; one of the caster wheels and half of the middle shelf slats were missing. He brought it home and gave it to the boys to restore. They cleaned the cart and removed the middle row of slats, replacing them with a shelf. They added a towel rack on the side. It was her Mother's Day present. Sarah loved it. She lined the shelves with plastic containers filled with flour, sugar, and spices. One shelf held her electric mixing bowl and spatulas. Although they'd remodeled the kitchen, there was no room for an island. She stored the baking cart in one of the downstairs closets, rolling it to the kitchen whenever she baked.

"You're baking today?"

"Uh-huh, fresh bread for dinner."

"Are you going to join me for breakfast?"

Sarah shook her head. "I've already had some bacon and toast. I want to get started on baking before the sun warms the kitchen." She paused, then asked, "What are your plans for the day?"

"Usual. Check the fields, then head to the barn. I thought we'd invite

74

the boys for dinner?"

"Of course."

Despite the large home, his sons all lived in smaller homes on the property. During the week, they'd all gather in his kitchen for lunch. Getting them to show up for dinner took an invitation.

"I haven't seen Daniel. Do you know how his interview went?"

"No. I haven't spoken to him, either. I know he's been busy all weekend delivering papers. Oh, and he delivered another trashcan to the subdivision."

Her comment left him feeling like someone punched him in the gut. The acid in his stomach churned, stealing away his appetite. His shoulders sank, and he fought to keep his voice from cracking. "Another trashcan? So, another house sold? Did he mention when they're moving in?"

"No." She turned from the sink. "You okay? You don't look well?"

"Huh?" He shook his head to clear his thoughts. "Yes...yes. I'm okay. I'd better get going."

"But you didn't touch your breakfast."

"Not hungry."

"Tobias, I don't want to start another fight. But I wish you'd go to the doctor. I know you slept last night, but you're hardly sleeping, and you're losing weight."

"You know how I feel about doctors."

"I'm serious. I can set up the appointment."

"Don't waste your time. I won't go."

She shrugged her shoulders and gave a heavy sigh. "I know you said you didn't want to talk with Pastor Cummings. Are you sure it wouldn't help?"

He shook his head. "Can we just let this go?"

She nodded softly. "Will you at least come home for lunch?"

"I'll try."

* * *

Tobias jumped into his truck and pulled out a plastic container of antacids from the glove box. He shook a few into his hand and popped them in his mouth; with any luck, the pain in his belly would subside.

Like insidious cancer, his family's secrets festered, then spread through his soul. It also raged havoc on him physically. He felt pressure within his chest, his heart raced all the time, and he'd developed a slight tremor in both hands. With his whole body in a heightened state, he felt as though he'd shake himself out of his skin at any moment.

He put the truck into drive and headed north towards the cornfield. He felt sure the evil spirit he'd summoned a few weeks earlier lay somewhere within the field. He'd come to think of it as his dark scarecrow. But instead of keeping animals out of the cornfield, it beckoned them in. It sought only one thing...to feed.

He remembered the last summoning seven years ago. Sarah shook him awake in the middle of the night.

"Tobias, wake up!"

He was in a deep sleep, having succumbed to exhaustion from working in the fields all day. "What's wrong?" he whispered, barely awake.

"I hear something howling outside. It sounds like a hurt animal."

He pushed himself upright in bed, leaning against his pillow. The cry, off in the distance, filled the room again. His forehead broke out in a cold sweat.

"That's it," Sarah said, pointing out the window. "You heard that, right?"

He recognized the cry. He'd lived on the farm his entire life. It was a sound he'd grown to know. *It's hungry!* A chill passed through his body.

"It's probably a coyote. I'll get my rifle and put it out of its misery."

I must feed it. Maybe one of the small goats? He'd wrestled with the thought as he jumped from the bed and dressed. When he was a young boy, his prize goat escaped from its pen and went missing one night. Once he learned about his family's secret, he was sure his prize goat ended up in the cornfield. He never asked his father about it. So, he never really knew for sure. As he dressed, trying to decide which animal to take to the cornfield, he felt certain his father wrestled with the same question. Chickens laid eggs, and goats gave milk. Nearly every animal on their farm had value.

He remembered stepping from his bedroom and finding Rex in the hallway. The dog followed him down the stairs and out the front door. Tobias looked at the young dog at his feet. Rex was a great dog, and even though he was another mouth to feed, he also had value. Rex was loyal and protective of his young sons. *I can't take their dog! I'll grab a goat!* The evil in the field howled again. Tobias stood on his front porch weighing the stray dog's value against the value of the goat.

"Come on, Rex." He tearfully placed the dog in the cab of the truck. When he arrived at the cornfield, he opened the door and stepped outside of the truck. He quickly changed his mind. *I can't do this to the boys!* He turned back to close the door but was too late. Rex was already out of the truck, walking towards the field.

"Rex!" he called out as he chased the dog. "Come back!" The dog quickened its pace to a run, seemingly oblivious to his cries.

"Rex! Stop!" He yelled as the dog disappeared into the cornfield. He sobbed until his whole body ached. *What have I done?*

The anguished look on each son's face when he broke the news was forever edged into his mind. "Rex got out of the house last night. I'm sorry, boys; the coyotes got him."

"No!" cried, John. "He was in my bed last night. How could he get out?"

He shook his head. "I don't know how he got out." It was the truth; he didn't know how Rex ended up in the hallway. All he knew for sure was the dog was gone, and his children were in pain.

All four boys fell into his lap, crying. He cried, too. "I'm so sorry."

He'd made a makeshift grave in the cemetery, knowing he couldn't retrieve what was left of Rex's body until he'd harvested the corn. After his sons said their goodbyes to Rex, he took them to the animal shelter to pick another dog. It was another mouth to feed, but he didn't care.

He drove until he reached the dirt road next to the long metal fence line. *So many crows!* Like clockwork, they arrived before each summoning ritual. He knew they'd leave as soon as the harvest was complete. Over the years, he'd noticed a pattern. Like spectators cheering on their team, the small ones stayed on the fence line, cawing and bobbing up and down while the massive crows flew in and out of the cornfield.

He'd been born into a family that embraced darkness. Of his forefather's many transgressions, the worst was conjuring the evil spirit. His forefathers worshipped and interacted with the spirit through ritual sacrifices. With each return to the farm, the evil's appetite grew more ferocious. He'd seen the flyers plastered on the mailboxes and light poles in the subdivision. Each described a missing dog or cat. A pang of guilt struck. He pushed it aside as quickly as it came. Although he hated to admit it, those unwitting sacrifices kept the evil's hunger at bay.

The pain in his belly returned, spreading up over his chest. His fist tightened in response. This time his pain was fueled by outrage, not anxiety. Little by little, he'd sold off parcels of his farm until all he had left to sell was the ground beneath the subdivision. If the developers had kept their word, the people living in those homes might be safe.

But they didn't. Fueled by greed, as the project neared completion, they reached out to their friends on the county board asking for changes. The area between the subdivision and his farm should have contained a series of small washes, deep enough to detract people from coming onto his farm. As an added measure, the original design included a solid brick wall along the back of the subdivision. He didn't know the developer added an additional row of houses until he saw the concrete foundations where the washes should be. By then, it was too late.

He thought about the fight he'd had with Sarah on Sunday. He knew she worried about his health and that she was disappointed he hadn't joined the family at church in weeks. But how could he explain that while she and their sons were at church, he needed to stay home to patrol the cornfield?

As he sat in the truck, he made a promise to himself. This would be the last time he summoned the evil spirit. Over the next seven years, he'd find a way to keep the evil from returning, or he'd die trying.

CHAPTER 12

Susan stared intently at her bathroom mirror. Disheveled hair. Dark circles under her eyes. She hardly recognized the face staring back. Exhaustion became a driving force that sent her crashing into bed night after night. She'd fall asleep as soon as her head hit the pillow, then awake a few hours later in the middle of a nightmare with her heart racing and sheets soaked in sweat. Once awake, her mind fixated on every creak and groan of her home's settling wood.

In all her nightmares, she and Libby stood frozen on the narrow dirt road behind her home. The sound of loud rustling filled the air as the cornstalks in front of her pushed aside. Night after night, the dream ended with a hungry pack of coyotes emerging from the cornfield.

But last night, her dream changed. Just like every night, she stood frozen on the dirt road with Libby by her side. But instead of coyotes, what emerged from the cornstalks was a dark shadowy creature with piercing red eyes. While she found the coyotes frightening, the dark shadowy creature was terrorizing.

She thought she'd overcome her childhood fears of monsters. But they'd come back full force. Mary seemed to be healing fast. Soon, she and Norm would spend most of their days at work, leaving her alone on the street throughout the day. Were her nightmares a result of the anxiety she felt about being alone?

Watching Daniel drop off a trashcan at the house next door reassured her that she wouldn't be alone for much longer. But unfortunately, the sense of comfort she felt was only fleeting. A few days after seeing the trashcan delivered, Norm informed her the house was purchased as a rental investment. He thought it would take a while before the owner found someone to rent the house.

She opened the medicine cabinet with a shaking hand. Her pill organizer sat empty, and the pill bottles were in disarray. She searched through the bottles until she found the bottle of anti-anxiety medications. *I've got to pull myself together. I see Dr. Cohen soon.*

The kitchen phone rang. She opened the medication bottle and shook one of the pills into her hand. She washed it down with a handful of water. The phone rang again. Every Sunday, without fail, her parents called. Reluctantly, she crept towards the kitchen. The phone rang a third time. She glanced at the caller ID: Mom. She didn't feel like talking. But she had to answer, otherwise her mother would worry. She took a deep breath and answered on the fourth ring, "Hi, Mom."

"You took so long to answer. Is everything okay?"

She sat at the island and held the kitchen phone with both hands. "I'm fine."

"I was starting to get worried."

She shook her head. Even though her mother vehemently denied it, she knew the woman was looking for any excuse to petition the courts. If her mother received guardianship over her, she'd force her to sell her house and move to Prescott. She needed to change the trajectory of the conversation and fast. "I'm giving Libby a bath today."

After a brief pause on the line, her mother responded, "Oh, a bath. How nice. Make sure the water's not too hot. And don't use your shampoo; use the one we bought at the pet store."

She took another deep breath and smiled, having successfully changed the subject to Libby. One topic on which she and her mother could find common ground. Her thoughts drifted back to the time she first moved into the house. Her parents worried she'd struggle with the transition. So, they arrived on moving day and spent a week helping her unpack boxes and put together furniture.

She bought Libby a few days after they returned to Prescott. She wouldn't have told them about the puppy, but her mother heard barking over the phone the following weekend. She remembered the line of questioning: "What's that noise, Susan?" She also remembered her lame reply. "Oh, a dog is barking on television." Finally, after the barking continued, she had no choice but to confess to buying Libby.

She heard the heavy sigh of disappointment before her mother started in. "It's a huge responsibility. You've never had a dog. It's harder than it looks. You should have discussed this with us when we were at your house." The tirade went on for a few minutes. Her mother rebutted every point she made. When she'd reach the point where her entire body trembled, she asked to speak with her father. Instead of talking, he calmly asked one question: "Would you like me to come back to install a doggy door?" She remembered the comfort of her father's words. "Yes, thank you," she whispered as tears of relief streamed down her face.

She was on pins and needles all week as she awaited her parent's arrival. The angst she'd felt was unnecessary. She never knew if her father said something to her mother or if her mother had a change of heart. But instead of chastising, her mom commented on how good a companion and protector Libby would be. She arrived with a handful of articles on how to train a puppy, and while her father installed a doggy door, her mother took her shopping for puppy supplies.

She knew her parents meant well, but their weekly calling and nonstop advice left her feeling like a smothered child. That realization triggered a memory from her teenage years. After all these years, only flashes of the memory remained: oxygen mask pressing down on her face, a pinch of the IV as it entered her arm, followed by a blaring siren and sway of the ambulance as it sped down the road. The ambulance movement left her feeling claustrophobic and nauseous, a feeling briefly relieved by the draft of cold air as the gurney rushed through the hospital's sliding glass doors. In the emergency room, she was surrounded by bright lights and the blur of doctors and nurses.

The following morning, lying in a hospital bed, she overheard her mother tell the nurses it was a miracle her father found her before it was too late. He'd forgotten a piece of equipment and had unexpectedly returned home. She quietly seethed when her mother sat alone at her bedside and expressed her disappointment in a lowered voice. "I still can't believe you took my bottle of sleeping pills. I've never been so embarrassed in my life. This isn't the way we handle things, Susan. What do I tell my friends when they ask why you're here?"

Unable to express her anger towards her mother, she verbally struck out at the nurses and doctors. But her rage melted each time she looked at her father's blank face. In the days following her unsuccessful attempt, she realized she wasn't the only one in her family who was unhappy.

Once her condition stabilized, she transferred to an inpatient psychiatric hospital. There she met Dr. Cohen, a steadfast rock upon whom she threw herself against until her anger broke. Within a short time, he'd successfully petitioned both of her parents into therapy—a move that helped her father find his voice. After years of counseling and medications, it was Dr. Cohen's recommendation that finally convinced her parents to allow her to live on her own.

Lost in thought, it was a moment before she realized her mom had finished talking about Libby. "Are you still there?"

"Sorry...yes, I'm here."

"Did you hear me? I said we could add you to our family plan."

"Family plan?"

"Cell phone, Susan. I said we could add you to the family plan on our cell phone."

"That's a nice offer...but I..."

"You need a phone, especially when you're driving on those country roads. What would you do if your car broke down?"

She shook her head. Fearful her mother could reach her anywhere, anytime, she'd politely refused all offers for a cell phone. But her mother was in one of her moods. She wouldn't let the subject go until she'd gotten her way. Only one thing could end the conversation. "Okay."

"Okay? That means you'll get one?" The relief in her mother's voice was palpable.

Her mother was right about one thing: having a cell phone would come in handy if she were ever stranded on the side of the road. "Yes. I'll get one."

"Well then, we'll pick one out the next time we see you. I'd better run. Your dad says, 'hi'. We're heading into town in a bit to do some shopping."

"Tell dad I said hi and that I'll talk with him next week."

✳ ✳ ✳

In the afternoon, she took a long nap, awakening with her mind clearer and more focused. The mental clarity offered her the opportunity to determine the cause of her ever-increasing anxiety. Knowing she'd be the only person on her street during the day frightened her, but why?

She pondered the question. Surely, it wasn't a fear of living alone. She'd lived on her own for five years before moving into her home. It had to be the home's location. That, combined with the large cornfield looming just outside her backyard. Something about the cornfield didn't feel right. It seemed silly, but she struggled to shake the feeling someone or something was watching her from within the corn. That sense of unease was exacerbated by the barrage of crows and the nightmares.

To steady her nerves, she searched the internet for information on corn. *How fast does it grow? When is it harvested?* The cornstalks stood eight feet tall with silky brown tops. *They'll harvest it soon!* That small nugget of knowledge alone was enough to lower the tension in her body and cause her shoulders to relax.

CHAPTER 13

A few days later, she was in Dr. Cohen's lobby, waiting for her monthly appointment. The doctor provided an objective sounding board upon which she often worked out her problems. She typically looked forward to the appointment because she always felt better after talking with him. But after experiencing ongoing nightmares, she worried he'd notice how shaky she felt inside.

Soon after arriving, the door next to the receptionist opened, and Dr. Cohen summoned her inside. Over the years, she realized he was the only doctor at the clinic who personally came out for his patients, another in the long list of reasons she liked him.

Dr. Cohen's office radiated a cozy warmth. She nestled within the confines of a soft, leather recliner, then briefly closed her eyes. She took a few deep breaths, deeply inhaling the smell of leather and lavender. Once settled, she scanned the room. The walls were a deep golden color. Books lined the bookcases of one wall. Behind his desk was a credenza covered in a stack of patient charts. A small bobblehead figure stood on top of the pile. *Something new.*

She pointed at the figure. "What's that?"

He smiled. "You like that, huh? It's a Sigmund Freud bobblehead, a gag gift from one of my internal medicine friends."

Dr. Cohen leaned back in his office chair. He was in his late sixties, short in stature and thin. An array of small gray curls messily covered his head, and a pair of reading glasses sat on the tip of his long narrow nose. She was convinced both sides of his brain functioned independently. One side focused on what she said. The other made lists of notes to add to the stack of charts on the desk. Just as soon as she thought one side of his brain had wandered off with the other, he made a comment that reassured her he hadn't missed a word she said.

He looked over the glasses. "How have you been?"

She wrapped her arms around her body and pulled herself further into the recliner. "I'm doing...good."

"Good? So, the new house, Libby? Everything is still going well?"

She nodded. Technically, she wasn't lying. The house was in working order; Libby was doing well. The only thing falling apart was her sense of well-being.

"I know you had hoped to meet new people."

"Do you remember me talking about Mary, my next-door neighbor?"

He nodded.

"She's home with a sprained ankle. So she and I have lunch together during the week. She'll be going back to church soon, and she's asked me to come with her. She thinks it'll be a good way for me to meet some people my age."

"Sounds wonderful, Susan."

She thought about Mary going back to church. A slight tremor went through her body, and her eyes welled with tears. She pursed her lips, looked away, and slowly nodded. Mary's return to church also meant she'd return to work. And, even though Mary said the chance was slim, if the doctor allowed her to return to work, he might allow her to travel to California to see Grace.

"Is everything okay?"

She took a deep breath to hold back the tears, then looked into his face. "I'm okay. I was just thinking of Mary. She sees the doctor on Friday. She says he'll let her go back to work if she's healed."

He adjusted in his chair. "That upsets you."

"I'm happy for her; really, I am. But it means I'll be all alone on our street whenever the two of them are at work."

"You still have empty houses on your street?" he asked in disbelief.

She nodded. "Norm doesn't think any more houses will sell until the cornfield and all the crows are gone."

He held his pen close to his face, then tapped it against his lip. "We talked about the differences between living in your old apartment and living in your own home." He held out his hand, palm facing up, and raised it to the height of his head. "The activity and noise levels of your old apartment were here." He lowered his hand to his lap. "The noise and activity in your house are down here. Last month, you told me you felt you were adjusting to the quiet. Do you still feel that way?"

Damn! He was like a skilled dentist probing and finding a painful, sensitive nerve. She was amazed at how quickly he could get to the root of what was bothering her. Silence. Quiet. Most people are comforted by those words. But to her, they were terrifying. It reinforced how alone she was. In the dead calm of silence, there was nothing to distract her mind, nothing to keep it from playing tricks on her. Mary's presence had filled the void of silence momentarily. She wasn't looking forward to being alone again. She thought about her last appointment. At that time, she told Dr. Cohen she was adjusting to the silence. It wasn't entirely a lie. She'd taken up the mantra: fake it till you make it. She glanced up at Dr. Cohen. *Fake it till...*" I'm still adjusting. But I know eventually, I'll make it".

He smiled and nodded. "How about your medications? Any concerns? You're still taking everything as prescribed?"

She nodded and tried to smile. "Uh-huh. My meds are fine." In all the years under Dr. Cohen's care, she'd never lied to him about her medications. *I can't tell him I felt good and stopped taking them.* The corners of her lips awkwardly curled up as she tried to widen her smile. He leaned forward and looked over the top of his glasses. His forehead furrowed. After a moment, he spoke. "I have a feeling something is bothering you. I won't push, but if you want to talk about it."

The conversation needed to change course before he realized she was lying about her medications. *Tell him about the nightmares.* She felt confident stopping her medications hadn't caused them. Perhaps Dr. Cohen would have a rational explanation for why they began in the first place.

She leaned forward. Then, in a lowered voice, she whispered, "You're right; something is bothering me."

A look of concern flashed over his face. "Tell me about it."

"Okay…it's about the cornfield behind my house."

"Is there something about it that upsets you?"

She slowly nodded. "I have dreams, nightmares actually, about it."

86

"How long has this been going on?"

"Every night for over a week."

He looked over his glasses again. His lips pursed together to one side of his mouth. "I know you said you're taking your medications. And, I believe you, Susan. I do." He paused again. "It's just that sometimes people feel good and stop taking their meds. Unfortunately, doing that can cause sleep disruptions."

He was probing. There was no way she'd admit to missing doses. She forced a smile. "I remember you telling me that. It's one of the reasons I make sure to take everything, just like you told me to."

He leaned back, then smiled and nodded. "Okay. What about these nightmares you're having. Do you want to talk about them?"

She closed her eyes for a moment. The soft leather recliner cradled her body. She was in a safe place, speaking to the only person who might be able to help her break the cycle of recurring nightmares. She took a deep breath, opened her eyes, and began speaking. "The nightmares started one night after Libby, and I played ball in the backyard."

Dr. Cohen nodded, encouraging her to continue.

"Well, we were playing—just like normal, and then Libby started acting strange."

"What do you mean by strange?"

"I think she heard something in the field. Something I couldn't hear. I don't know. She kept walking back and forth along the fence like she was looking for a way out of the yard." She paused for a moment, then continued. "I think the crows heard something too. They started cawing loudly and flapping their wings. You know, like they were all riled up. I don't know how to say this, but it felt like someone, or something was coming towards us."

"Did you see anyone in the field?"

She shook her head.

"Maybe, an animal?"

She shrugged her shoulders, "I'm not sure, but the cornstalks moved like something was out there." Her voice lowered. "All I know for sure is that I've had nightmares ever since."

"What happens? In your nightmare, what happens that frightens you?"

She paused for a moment, summoning the courage to put her nightmares into words. After a moment, she continued. "My nightmare is a little different than what happened. It takes place on the small dirt road between the cornfield and my backyard. Libby and I are standing on the road. I can hear the rustling of the corn, and I can see it move. I want to run back into my house. But I'm stuck on the road, unable to move. After a minute or so, coyotes start coming out of the corn. They circle us, waiting to attack. That's when I wake up."

A look of concern spread over his face; one she hadn't seen since she was a teenager. "Okay…let's try to drill down to why you have bad dreams about coyotes. Have you seen one? I'm sure they're out in your area."

"I haven't seen any. But I've heard them howling at night. And they knocked over my trashcan the night before I started having the nightmares."

He smiled. "So, maybe…when the coyotes knocked over your trashcan, that worried you. Maybe deep down, you're worried they might come after Libby. Oh, I see how traumatizing that could be. So, this is the only nightmare you're having?"

She looked into his eyes and nodded. Just by talking with him, he'd discovered the reason she dreamt about coyotes. It all made sense. He seemed worried but not overly concerned.

She glanced down and paused for a moment. What would he think if she told him a dark shadowy creature with red eyes had replaced the coyotes? There was no way he'd be able to rationalize the dark creature. Just the thought of its two red eyes sent a chill through her body. The monster felt so real. The only solace was that in her nightmare, the dark shadow stayed within the corn. She hated holding anything back from Dr. Cohen. But there was no way she'd tell him about it, knowing it was his support that finally convinced her parents she should buy her home.

Dr. Cohen pressed his fingers against his lips. He took a long slow breath before he spoke. "Okay, so we think we know the source of your nightmares. I also believe there's a reasonable explanation for the moving stalks. Isn't it possible an animal moved the stalks? Or perhaps the wind?"

She curtly nodded.

"I want you to think about all of the changes you've made in just a few short months: new home, new dog, and working from home instead of going into an office. Honestly, Susan, I believe you are adjusting to all of these changes."

She thoughtfully listened to Dr. Cohen. *What he's saying makes sense.* She offered a weak smile. "You're right. Just talking with you helps put it into perspective."

"You know the mind is pretty powerful, and our imaginations can sometimes get the best of us." He pointed at her face. "Especially if we aren't getting enough sleep." Despite her attempts, she struggled to cover the dark circles under her eyes. "I hesitate to prescribe a sleeping aid for obvious reasons." He pulled a small brochure from one of the files and handed it to her. "I want you to read this. It offers tips on getting to sleep. He paused and ruffled through the files again. "Here's another one...on anxiety. I believe I've given these to you before. Even so, please read both brochures today. I'd also like you to start incorporating some relaxation techniques tonight. If this doesn't work, or if you feel you need another appointment before next month, please don't hesitate to call."

On the way home, she stopped by the store. Along with some groceries, she purchased a bottle of melatonin. She knew neither Dr. Cohen nor her parents would approve of the purchase, but she'd read online it might help her sleep. So that night, she put some of the brochures' recommendations into practice and took a dose of melatonin before crawling into bed with Libby. Within minutes her eyes flickered shut, and her body relaxed. And for the first time in over a week, she didn't dream.

CHAPTER 14

Pastor Ted Cummings could readily identify emotions in other people just by being close to them. He knew it was discernment. Something many Christians have when they walk with God. He viewed it as a gift, something that grew with his faith. He found it most helpful in situations where he counseled parishioners.

He glanced down at the note in his hand. Scrawled onto the paper in Bernice's fine handwriting were Mary Keller's address and phone number. He'd driven past Cherry, Oak, and Aspen streets. Only one street lay ahead, and it was beyond the brick wall borders of the subdivision, Pecan. *Found it.* As he left the main subdivision and turned onto Pecan Street, a tingling sensation spread through his body. It was followed by pressure, deep enough to steal his breath away. He shuddered. *There's something terrible here.*

Bernice placed Mary on his list of homebound parishioners. Apparently, she was upset. She'd taken a fall a few weeks back and was unable to drive. He tested his memory: petite woman with striking gray hair and a gregarious personality. According to Bernice, Mary's husband was a former pastor who'd turned his back on his faith. Bernice felt confident Mary would have returned to church weeks earlier if only her husband had tried to get her there. *How sad.* What would make a pastor turn his back on the church? Maybe he'd get a chance to meet the man. Perhaps he'd be able to help the former pastor see a path back to his faith.

He parked and silently prayed before approaching the house. A scholarly looking man, tall, solidly built, with graying hair and glasses, opened the door.

"Pastor Cummings?"

"Yes, that's right. You must be Mary's husband, Norm." He smiled and offered his hand.

Norm shook his hand curtly and feigned a smile. "It's nice to meet you. Mary's been talking about it all morning. Unfortunately, I won't be able to stay. But I've left some cookies and iced tea on the table."

As he shook Norm's hand, he sensed confliction, the desire to stay and talk overshadowed by fear and an overwhelming compulsion to flee. He wasn't sure what demons the former pastor faced. But he knew the man needed help. So he offered a prayer on his behalf as he entered the house.

He found his way to the dining room. Mary sat at one of the dining room chairs. Her Bible stood open on the table in front of her. A huge smile lit up her face as he approached the table. "Good morning, pastor!"

"Good morning, Mary. I apologize for not getting here earlier in the week. We have several parishioners who are homebound."

She looked down and gave a slight shake of her head. "I'm so sorry. I should have canceled. I've been feeling much better, and I'm fairly certain the doctor will release me tomorrow during my appointment."

Bernice told him Mary was on the mend, and she'd be back to the church within a few weeks. She also told him she felt Mary needed to talk with him sooner than later. He leaned forward and smiled. "I've seen everyone on my list this week. I'm happy to be here."

She nodded. "Honestly, I'm happy you're here. There is something I wanted to discuss with you."

"Is it about your husband? Bernice said he's a pastor. She also mentioned he no longer attends church."

Tears welled up in Mary's eyes. She opened her mouth, then closed it again. Tears gently flowed down her face. "He's…a …good…man." She nodded as she spoke, and he couldn't help thinking she was trying to convince herself as much as him. "Honestly…he's good. He'd give you the shirt off his back if he knew it would keep you warm, give you his last scrap of food if you were hungry. And when he practiced his faith, he was the Godliest man I'd ever met."

A box of tissues sat in the middle of the dining room table. He moved the box in front of her and sat down. "Are you okay?"

She dapped her face with the tissue and nodded. "I was hoping Norm would stay and maybe talk with you too."

"You're sad because he didn't stay."

Mary lowered her eyes and nodded again.

"Okay. We can talk about that if you'd like. But first, let's start with a little prayer."

They both closed their eyes.

"Dear heavenly Father, we ask you to be with us today. We ask that your humble servant Mary will find comfort in your word. In Jesus' name, we pray."

She whispered, "Amen."

He sensed the words filled her with peace. So he smiled and quietly thanked God for comforting Mary.

"I hope you don't mind. Before visiting, I asked Bernice to tell me a bit about you and Norm."

"I don't mind. Bernice is one of my best friends. She's a trustful sounding board."

He chuckled. He was also grateful for the guidance Bernice offered him as he acclimated to his new role.

"Bernice said your husband led a church in Tucson. Is that right?"

"Yes. He did an amazing job. He helped many people find their faith."

He smiled. "That's wonderful."

"I'm sorry he ran off like that. I wish he would have stayed and spoken with you. He's been having nightmares every night this week. He denies it, but he's waking up in the middle of the night in a cold sweat, shaking with fear. I think talking to you would have done him some good."

"Do you think these dreams have anything to do with his loss of faith?"

"I don't know. But something has changed since the nightmares started. When he's home, he just sits and stares out the window at the cornfield. Something is on his mind. He just won't talk about it."

"I can see it hurts you."

She nodded.

"Does Norm have friends here? Someone to whom he could talk?"

She smiled and nodded. "Oh, my. Norm so many friends. He makes them easily. But in Tucson, they were our friends. So we'd have them over to our house. He knows I like hosting." She pointed to her ankle. "Obviously, not so easy to do right now."

"Those friends in Tucson...I'm guessing they were friends from church?"

She nodded, then quickly offered, "I'm okay with him making friends outside of the church. And, once I'm all healed up, I'll ask him to invite them to our house. Right now, we have a neighbor, a sweet young girl, who comes over for lunch and sometimes dinner. You'd like her, pastor. She's never attended church. But once I can drive again, she said she'd start coming to church with me."

"Oh, that's great news, Mary. I look forward to meeting her. What's her name?"

"Susan Green."

He made a mental note of her name for future reference. Then his thoughts turned to Norm. Ever since Bernice told him Mary's husband was a former pastor, he'd wanted to meet him. He couldn't imagine walking away from his faith. What happened in Norm's life to turn him away from God? "Maybe you could tell me a little bit more about you and Norm. Would that be alright?"

She nodded and smiled.

"How long have you been married?"

"Thirty-five years. We met when Norm was in seminary school. You know they say 'love at first sight.' Well, it's true. Such a strikingly handsome man and a Christian." Her face lit up. "He swept me off my feet."

"Do you have any children?"

"We have...had...two grown daughters, Grace and Rose."

She'd spoken of her daughters in the past tense. His stomach churned in response. "You said...had. Did something happen to one or both of your daughters?"

She nodded again. Her lower lip quivered, and her tears returned, flowing unabashed down her face. It took her a few moments to regain her composure. Finally, she spoke, "Grace is alive and well. She lives outside of Modesto with her husband and two young daughters." She shook her head. "But Rose...she died a few years ago. Norm blames himself and God for her death. If he gave you the cold shoulder when he let you into the house, I'm sorry. You're an extension of God, church, all the things he turned his back on."

"So, that's why he left the church?"

She looked down and curtly nodded.

"May I ask how she died?"

She looked into his eyes for a moment before speaking. "She died of an opiate overdose. She'd gone through rehab. We thought she was managing well until the police showed up to notify us she died. Norm blames himself for her addiction. He also thinks he could have stopped her from overdosing. But after everything I've read about opiate addiction, I don't believe there's anything either of us could have done to stop it."

His heart sank. "That's tragic. And, you said Norm blames himself? I don't understand."

"He blames his family genetics. I know how it sounds, but sometimes I wonder if he's on to something. Norm told me his mom suffered from horrible depression. She'd struggle to get out of bed for days on end. It was hard on him as a teenager. His mom relied on him to get his brother and sister ready for school, make sure there was food on the table. You know Norm practically raised his brother and sister."

"And, Norm's father? Was he part of his life?"

Her face skewed awkwardly. "He was an alcoholic who left his family when Norm was just starting high school." She shook her head and continued. "I know he contacted Norm when Norm was in seminary school. Norm never told me what his father said. I just know it wasn't good. It was the last time he and Norm spoke. We heard he died a few years later."

"That's very sad."

"Norm feels his family's history of addiction and depression might have something to do with Rose's addiction and her death. He thinks somehow she was genetically predisposed to become an addict." She paused for a moment. "I'm sorry. I'm sure you have better things to do with your time than listen to this."

He shook his head. "Please, don't apologize. The more I know about you and Norm, the better I can support you as your pastor. I'm wondering what brought you here? To Phoenix?"

"After Rose died, Norm changed. At first, he threw himself into work. Everyone asked him to take time off, but he wouldn't listen. Then, after a few months, his energy ran out. I'd come home from work and find him sitting alone in the house with all the lights off, crying. His emotions were all over the place, and he refused to get help. Finally, one Sunday afternoon, he comes home from his office with a box of his belongings and tells me he's resigned from his position. I was dumbfounded. If I'd only known what he was thinking, I might have been able to talk some sense into him. Soon after that, I realized he'd started drinking."

"Alcoholism?"

She gave a slight shake of her head. "To Norm's credit…he stopped drinking before it became a habit. Honestly, I think he was frightened he'd turn into his father. So, drinking, yes, but no alcoholism."

"It was Norm's idea to move here?"

"No…it was mine."

That comment took him by surprise. He'd assumed Norm pushed for the move.

She continued, explaining, "We thought about moving to Modesto to live near Grace, but we couldn't afford it. And, honestly, I wasn't ready to quit working for the state. I'll have a pension when I retire. So, I started looking for positions in other field offices and came across one in Phoenix. We started looking for a house after I accepted the position. That's when we came across our little subdivision. The homes on this street are all spec homes. I was able to pick out the flooring and countertops. The house is a bit smaller than we'd like. But it's just the two of us. We don't need a lot of space. So, I thought, new home, new job, new start."

"How's it going? So far?"

"Nice. I love the church. Everyone's been great! The day after my fall, people started showing up with meals. I know Bernice had something to do with all that. I truly feel I've found my church home. I pray every day Norm will put his anger and his pride aside and join me at church. I won't give up on him. He's a good man. I believe in my heart; he'll come back!"

She grimaced and squirmed in the chair as if looking for a more comfortable position.

He noticed the look of discomfort. "Are you feeling okay?"

"Just getting a bit stiff. Would you mind helping me walk over to my recliner? I've been sitting for a while with my leg down. It's starting to ache."

"Absolutely. Tell me how I can help."

After escorting her to the recliner, he placed her iced tea on a nearby table.

She pointed at the curtain covering the sliding glass door. "Could you let some light in?"

He pulled back the curtain. "So, that's the cornfield I've heard so much about."

"You've heard about our cornfield?"

"I've heard some farmers talk about the field. I know Sarah and Tobias Smith own it."

"Norm said Tobias only plants corn in that field."

"I heard the same thing." He thought about the conversation he'd had with Sarah in the office. "I believe they'll harvest it soon."

"Oh…that would be nice. I miss the views of the mountains."

His gaze moved to the crows lining the fence line. "I don't think I've ever seen so many crows in one place at the same time."

"I know. You get used to them after a while."

The crows fluttered on the fence line and cawed.

"You know, Mary, it looks like those birds are talking to each other."

With that comment, their cawing rose to a frenzied crescendo. Then, they spread their wings, showing their abundant plumage, and began bobbing wildly up and down.

"I don't think those crows like me looking at them." He gave a half-hearted laugh. As soon as the words left his mouth, he instinctively felt he was wrong. The crows on the fence line weren't looking in his direction at all. Instead, they appeared focused on the cornstalks behind the house. His gaze moved from the crows and onto the corn. The stalks stood upright. Yet, he noticed a section of the stalks gently moving in the distance as if being pushed aside. Whatever was in the field was headed in his direction.

A dizzying feeling swept over him. He reached for sliding glass door handle to keep from falling. Then, somewhere in the back of his mind, a voice screamed out. *Danger!* He could feel the emotions of whatever was moving towards him. *Hatred! Hunger!* The pressure he'd first felt as he pulled onto Mary's street returned stronger this time. He broke out in a cold sweat, and his legs trembled.

Mary's voice broke through his thoughts. "Pastor, are you alright?"

He startled and turned in her direction. He feebly forced a smile and nodded.

"You don't look so good. Your face is pale. I think you should get another glass of tea. It's a pretty warm day."

He nodded and slowly made his way to the table. He grabbed onto the back of one of the dining room chairs, willing his legs to hold him upright. With a shaking hand, he raised the glass of tea to his lips and took a sip. Slowly, the pressure in his chest eased. He closed his eyes and prayed for the Lord's guidance before walking back into the family room.

He forced a reassuring smile at Mary, then glanced out the window. The birds, which were so vocal just a moment earlier, had calmed. The cornstalks stood fully upright and still. *What just happened?* He thought about what Mary said about Norm. She said he sat in the chair, looking out at the cornfield. Had he seen or felt something? Was it the reason he was having nightmares? He felt confident what he'd just experienced would trigger a nightmare tonight. He glanced down at Mary. She seemed perfectly at ease.

She smiled. "Your color is coming back. You had me worried for a moment. You looked like you might pass out."

"I think you're right. It's probably the heat. I think I should head home. Can I get you anything before I leave?"

"If it's not too much trouble, could you hand me the small blanket there," she asked as she pointed to the blanket lying haphazardly on the opposite recliner. "I think I'd like to take a nap.

He placed the blanket over her. "I enjoyed talking with you today, Mary. I look forward to seeing you in church real soon."

"Thank you, pastor. Talking with you has been helpful. Emotional but helpful. It feels like you took a weight off my shoulders. Oh...one more thing, before I forget. I spoke with Bernice, and she said there isn't a women's Bible study in our subdivision yet. I ran the women's Bible study at our church in Tucson. If it's alright, I would love the opportunity to start another group here once I'm up and moving again."

"Sounds like a wonderful idea, Mary. Let's talk about it after you've healed."

He left the house and staggered to the car. With a trembling hand, he placed the key in the ignition and started the engine. His mind tried to make sense of what his whole body felt. Mary didn't seem to sense it. But he was sure what he'd felt was real. He'd never felt evil so close throughout his years of schooling and during his short tenure as an ordained pastor. He held onto the steering wheel with a white-knuckled grip, trying to stop shaking. His primitive urge was to put the car into drive and push the accelerator down to the floorboard.

Instead, he closed his eyes and prayed out loud. He prayed angels would descend upon Mary and Norm's house to protect them from the evil in the field. He prayed angels would surround him and protect him as well. Then, a sense of calm washed over him. His mind cleared.

CHAPTER 15

For Susan, Fridays were met with equal amounts of joy and dread. Although they brought an end to the work week, it also meant she'd spend the weekend eating meals on her own. This Friday proved especially dreadful. Mary had a doctor's appointment later in the afternoon. Once the doctor cleared her for work, their routine of week-day lunches would end.

Still waiting for Mary and Norm to return home, Susan took Libby for a walk after dinner. Crossing over in the main subdivision was like walking into a new world. A friendly world, bustling with commotion.

The fragrant aroma of summer barbeques filled the air. Children rode their bikes on the street or played in small groups on the sidewalk. They were overseen by parents, sitting in lawn chairs on their driveways. Laughter and conversations intermingled with the cheers of those watching baseball games in their garages.

They arrived at the small park in the middle of the subdivision. Filled with a basketball court and playground equipment, it seemed to be a magnet for many families. She sat on the edge of a short wall and marveled at the beautiful chaos of a healthy neighborhood. Then a pang of jealousy struck—what a stark contrast to the homes lining her outcast street.

A young boy approached, stocky build and a head covered in thick dark curls. Susan guessed he wasn't much older than ten. "Hey lady, what's your dog's name?"

"Libby."

Libby immediately stood at the sound of her name. Her small tail vigorously wagged back and forth. She began pulling on the leash as she moved towards the boy. The boy knelt and reached for her. He glanced at Susan. "She won't bite me." His comment was meant as a question. But he didn't wait for the answer. Instead, he began stroking Libby's head.

She laughed as she watched Libby's tiny tail wag so hard; it shook her whole body. "Be careful. She's very sweet. She just hasn't spent a lot of time around other people. She needs to get to know you." The boy continued stroking Libby's coat. "She's so soft."

She smiled. It was nice to see Libby getting attention.

"Our dog ran away."

"It did? Oh, I'm so sorry. Did it come back?"

He gazed at the ground and sadly shook his head. "No."

A voice called out in the distance. "Connor! Time to come home."

The boy turned in the direction of the voice. "I'll be right there." He turned back. "That's my mom. I've got to go. Thank you for letting me pet your dog. She's nice."

She remained at the park for nearly an hour, sitting, walking, then sitting again. The sunset stole daylight as it sank behind the mountains in the distance. A warm breeze began to blow. One by one, the families disappeared inside their homes. Once the last family left the park, she headed home.

Taped to one of the light poles were two flyers, each with a picture of a dog. Both dogs disappeared on the same day. She bent down and stroked Libby's head, then glanced at the metal heart hanging from Libby's collar. Libby's name and her phone number remained easy to read. *Just in case.*

The street light overhead went out, and a large portion of the street became dark. High overhead, a faint stream of moonlight lit her path home. She pulled Libby's leash and quickened her pace. "Come on, Libby. Let's go home." Random porch lights offered a momentary reprieve from the darkness. She moved past one long expanse of the brick wall and then rounded the corner onto her street. She took another fifteen steps before she nearly tripped over Libby. The dog had stopped dead in her tracks.

She sensed the danger before she saw it. Her gaze moved from Libby to the end of the cul-de-sac. There, in the shadows beneath the street light, she spied a pair of coyotes meandering around the community mailbox. Libby's body became erect. Her short tail, which generally lived in a state of perpetual motion, lay flat and tense between her back legs. A deep guttural growl followed her muffled bark. The coyotes turned their heads in unison and began moving in their direction.

She reached down for Libby, scooping the dog up in one quick motion. Libby's underside was wet. *Don't worry, girl, I'm afraid too!* Running home wasn't an option. The coyotes had traveled past Norm and Mary's house, towards the end of her driveway. She took a few steps back. *There's a family watching television just a few houses away. I might be able to get there.*

She continued her slow retreat. But each backward step she took, was matched with two advancing steps of the coyotes. A tear escaped her eye and slid down her cheek. *I won't be able to outrun them.* The coyotes moved into a crouched position, head low, ears pinned back. Despite all the missing animals, they looked thin and unfed.

Her racing heart pounded in her chest. With every sense heightened, she wildly scanned the ground, searching for anything she could use as a weapon. Rocks littered the ground next to her, but none were lethal enough to stop an attack. The only weapon she had was her voice. She screamed, "Get out of here! Leave us alone!"

The coyotes stopped, and for a moment, it looked like they might leave. But their reprieve didn't last. Once one of the coyotes took a step in their direction, the other followed suit. Their guttural growls, low at first, echoed through the cul-de-sac, growing louder as they advanced. Their lips curled back, exposing sharp teeth that glistened in the faint light. Libby began to whimper and shake within her arms. She held her tighter and took another step back. Soon she'd be back on the adjacent street. At that point, she'd turn and run.

Coming up from behind was the sound of an approaching car. Afraid to turn her back on the coyotes in front of her, she continued listening to the car. *Keep coming. Keep coming. Please don't stop!* A few seconds later, Norm and Mary's large blue sedan turned into the cul-de-sac and pulled up alongside her. The car's headlights shone brightly on the pair of coyotes. They stopped. The blast of the car's horn took her breath away. It also startled the coyotes, who turned and bolted towards the end of the cul-de-sac, past the mailbox. Seconds later, they disappeared into the wash.

She sighed heavily. Her body trembled so violently; she nearly dropped Libby as, sat her onto the ground.

Norm parked the car in the middle of the road and ran to her side. "Are you okay?"

She opened and then closed her mouth, unable to speak. Instead, she tersely nodded. Tears flowed from her eyes, running down her cheeks. After a moment, she found her voice. "I don't know what would have happened if you two hadn't come home at that very moment! I couldn't have stopped them."

Norm shook his head. "I don't want to think about what could have happened. Those coyotes looked like they hadn't eaten in weeks."

She nodded. "I know, but how can that be? Flyers are hanging everywhere with pictures of missing dogs and cats! They're the ones taking them—right?"

"That's what I thought too. But you saw those coyotes; they look malnourished. I'm sure they'll find some rabbits out in the wash or in the cornfield. They're moving in that direction. Hopefully, it's the last time we see them."

"I hope so! In the meantime, no more nighttime walks for us!"

She thanked Norm and waved to Mary, who was in the car. As soon as she came home, she placed the cover over the doggy door. *Sorry girl. No more trips outside alone.* She found a package of potty-training sheets she'd used when Libby was a puppy. As a precaution, she spread them out over the living and family room floors.

CHAPTER 16

Saturday morning. The nightly doses of melatonin left Susan feeling groggy and stiff. She rose from the bed, put on her robe, and headed towards the family room. Libby anxiously paced back and forth at the back sliding-glass door. As soon as she opened the door, Libby sprinted through the door and squatted on the grass.

The doorbell rang as Libby reentered the house. She followed Susan through the kitchen towards the front door. The pungent odor of urine filled Susan's nose as she entered the living room. *Libby found the sheets.*

She pulled back the blinds on the small window next to the front door. Norm. He stood on the front porch holding a carton of vincas. She glanced at the scattered, dirty potty sheets covering the living room floor and shook her head. She cracked the door slightly. *Hopefully, those flowers will camouflage the smell.*

"Hi, Norm."

He handed her the carton. "Good morning, Susan. In all the commotion last night, I forgot to give these to you. Mary and I picked them up last night after dinner. She said you wanted to plant some flowers in your backyard pots. It's a thank you for all that you've done for Mary when she was laid up at home."

It had been weeks since she mentioned wanting to plant flowers. She didn't have the heart to tell Norm her growing fear of the cornfield overshadowed the joy of planting flowers. Once the corn was gone, she'd enjoy spending time in her backyard again. "They're beautiful. Thank you! I've enjoyed spending time with her. How was the doctor's appointment? What did he say?"

His face lit up. "Doc says she's healed perfectly."

"I'm happy for her, for you both." A thought flashed through her mind, causing her stomach to flip. "So, she'll go back to work soon?"

"Even better. The doctor said she's well enough to travel. So, we can still spend the fourth of July week with Grace as we'd hoped. We're heading to Modesto in the morning."

Her knees suddenly felt weak as the blood drained from her face. It was one thing to be alone for a few hours during the day. Another to hear, she'd be alone day and night for a week. "You're leaving tomorrow?" she whispered.

A puzzled look crossed his face. "I thought we'd mentioned it. I know neither of us wanted to get our hopes up in case Mary couldn't travel. But we kept our fourth of July vacations in place, just in case."

Her heartbeat increased. They had mentioned it. Weeks ago. But Mary told her she didn't think the doctor would allow her to travel. As her mind drifted, Norm's voice interrupted her thoughts.

"Will that be okay? We'd be home Saturday night."

"Huh? I'm sorry. What did you say?"

"Oh…I was asking if you wouldn't mind looking after our house while we're gone. Maybe turn some lights on and off, so people think we're home."

Certain she'd lose her composure if she spoke, she curled her lips inward and nodded.

"That's great. We'd appreciate it."

The look of excitement on his face was palpable. She'd seen a similar look on Mary's face each time she spoke about her daughter and grandkids. "Mary wanted me to invite you to dinner tonight. That way, we can give you a key and show you which lights to turn on. Would that be okay? Say, six o'clock?"

The thought of spending the evening with Mary and Norm sent a comforting warmth through her chest. She offered a weak smile. "I'd like that very much."

After Norm turned to walk away, she closed, then rested her head on the door. Silent tears streamed from her eyes. The tenuous strand of security she'd experienced for the past few weeks broke apart once Norm shared their travel plans. After a few minutes, she straightened up and wiped away the tears. *I can do this. It's just for the week.*

* * *

Susan spent the late afternoon baking cookies. The mere act of measuring and mixing ingredients offered a distraction from her fears. She placed the warm cookies onto a dessert plate, then put the rest in a container so Norm and Mary would have cookies for their trip. She headed next door. Mary answered her knock.

She fought to relax throughout dinner, but she felt her shoulders tighten each time the conversation shifted to the impending trip. There was no way around it. She had to face the fact they were leaving. Nothing would change that. All she could do now was learn everything she could about the house to feel comfortable while they were gone. "Could you show me the lights you want me to turn on and off? Do you have a schedule?"

Mary nodded. "I'll show you the lights. There's no schedule, though. Just turn them on and off as you see fit."

She felt a nervous tension throughout her body. "I'd feel better if you gave me some kind of schedule."

Norm interjected, "I'm sure we can write something down for you, Susan. Right, Mary?"

Mary smiled and nodded. "Of course, I'll leave it on the kitchen counter."

The tension in her body lowered. She followed Mary into the kitchen. Mary pointed to the light switch on the wall. "This is a good light to put on at night. It's one of those floodlights. Norm put it up a few weeks ago. It'll light up the whole backyard and the first few rows of corn. It's a good deterrent to thieves."

She shuddered.

Mary curtly shook her head. "I'm sorry. That didn't come out the way I meant it. I was trying to say keeping the lights on would give the illusion we're home."

She forced a smile and nodded. Keeping criminals away from their homes was Mary's plan. And it was a good one. As she listened to Mary talk about keeping criminals away from the house, she realized her own fears ran deeper. Random criminals weren't nearly as scary as someone or something roaming through the cornfield behind her home.

After Mary showed her the lights, she poured three glasses of milk and set out the cookies. "I can't believe you baked extra for our trip. That was so nice."

Norm leaned forward. His entire face lit up, and he smiled. "You baked some cookies for our trip?"

She nodded.

He continued, "You know those are my favorite cookies."

Norm and Mary never hesitated to give her compliments. It had taken her a while, but she was finally getting used to their words of encouragement. She glanced at Norm and smiled broadly. "Thank you. What time do you think you'll leave tomorrow?"

Norm looked at Mary. "What do you think? Nine o'clock? I'm taking the car to McAdams early in the morning for a quick oil change and tire check. But I think we could be on the road by nine."

"That sounds about right," Mary answered.

"And you'll be home next Saturday?"

"Yes. We both work Monday. So that gives us a day off between the trip and work."

After dessert, Norm and Mary walked her to the door and said their goodbyes. Before walking away, Mary hugged her. "You'll be okay with us gone…right?"

The question took her off guard. She forced a smile and nodded. "Of course. Be safe, and don't worry about anything. I'll see you on Saturday."

The door closed shut behind her, signaling an eerie finality. She stood, frozen in place. Under the dim porch light, she glanced down at the set of house keys and the piece of paper with Grace's phone number. *This is it! I'll be alone here for a week!*

Her stomach twisted, sending a burning sensation towards her heart, and filling her eyes with tears. She turned and raised her trembling fist, fighting the urge to knock on Norm and Mary's door. What would she say? *I've had bad dreams about the cornfield. I can't shake the feeling there's something terrible out there.* She lowered her fist and shook her head. She'd had so many opportunities to broach the subject during dinner. Had they seen anything strange? Did they think an animal was living out there? Did they see the

106

larger crows move in and out of the field? She had. It was an observation; she'd made just a few days earlier.

A small wave of anger washed over her as she walked away. She aimed the anger at herself. *Why couldn't I have just asked them?* They would have listened to her concerns and offered a rational explanation.

Deep down, she knew why she didn't bring it up. Norm and Mary accepted her, treated her like a daughter. They complimented her on living alone, owning her home. If she walked straight back and knocked on their door, she'd likely cry and shake through the whole conversation. And that would cause them to question her sanity—something she couldn't bear.

On the other hand, if she waited until morning, she'd have plenty of time to pull herself together. It was settled. She'd stop by their house before they left town, casually bring up the cornfield, and see how they responded.

* * *

Susan awoke to the familiar sounds of crows outside her bedroom window. She glanced at the clock on her nightstand: 8:02 a.m. Afraid she would oversleep, she'd skipped last night's dose of melatonin, and as a result, spent the night tossing and turning within her cornfield nightmares.

She sprang out of bed, dressed, and headed to Norm and Mary's house. Her knocks went unanswered. *Norm said he was taking their car in for an oil change. Did Mary go with him? Were they leaving town from there?* She took a few deep breaths to steady the nervous tension rising in her chest. Hopefully, she hadn't missed the opportunity to talk with them before they left for California.

She returned home and dialed their number. The answering machine's sterile voice asked her to leave a message. She tried to remember the short speech she'd practiced on her way home from their house, but her mind drew a blank. While most of her message was rambling, in the end, she managed to ask the most critical question: Had they seen anything unusual in the cornfield?

* * *

Norm rose early and drove into town. He dropped the car off at

McAdams Tire Shop, then ran across the street to grab breakfast. He returned home at 9 a.m. and joined Mary, who was in the kitchen, removing ham and cheese packages from the refrigerator.

"Perfect timing. Mustard or mayo?" Mary asked as she held up the two condiments.

He smiled and pointed to the jar in her hand. "Mayo." Despite Mary's multiple attempts, she still hadn't convinced him to try mustard on his ham sandwiches.

He glanced at the counter. A small light on the answering machine was blinking.

"We've got a message."

"We do? Someone must have called when I was in the shower."

He hit the play message button on the answering machine. Susan's meek voice filled the room. Her last line captured his attention. "Have you seen anything unusual in the cornfield?"

"Unusual? What does she mean by that?" Mary asked. "The only thing unusual about the field is all the crows. But that's not strange. It's just annoying and dirty."

He stared at the answering machine. *Why is she asking? Did she see something?* Like a crudely made horror film, the stormy night played out in his mind. He shuddered as he remembered the red glowing eyes staring at him through the foggy mist. Then his thoughts turned to Mary. She'd spent weeks alone in the house resting her ankle. "So you haven't seen anything besides the crows?"

Mary shook her head as she placed layers of ham onto the pieces of bread. "Have you?"

This was the opening he would have welcomed soon after the storm. But now, so far removed from that night, he questioned what he saw. *Mary's been here day after day, and she hasn't seen anything. On the night of the storm, the power was out, and everything was dark. There was no moonlight, no streetlights, only my flashlight. Can I say for sure there was something in the field?* For weeks, he'd picked up extra shifts at work or spent time at the diner. *I left Mary home, alone, when she was injured and needed me the most. All because of my imagination. I'll make it up to her on this trip. Whatever she wants to do, we'll do it.*

Mary looked in his direction. "Well? Have you seen anything?"

He curtly shook his head. "No."

He reached for the phone. He wasn't sure what he'd say when Susan answered, but he wanted to make sure everything was okay.

Mary's voice grabbed his attention. "You're calling her back?"

"Uh-huh."

Mary placed the sandwiches into little baggies. "If you call, you'll risk getting into a long conversation. So why not leave her a note instead. That way, we can get on the road."

He nodded, then pulled a pad and pen from the kitchen drawer. He tapped the pen on the counter as he considered what to write. Mary stepped out of the kitchen. She returned with an insulated cooler bag and began filling it with sandwiches and cookies. "I'll get the car started."

He looked down at the pad of paper. *Hello, Susan. Thanks again for watching the house.* Those were the only words he'd written. He didn't want to cause her undue fear, but he also didn't want her to wander into the field. He continued writing. *I've checked with Mary. She hasn't seen anything other than the crows. There's always a chance those coyotes are out there, so maybe you and Libby should stay away from it. We'll see you on Saturday. If you need anything, don't hesitate to call. Norm.*

* * *

Through her living room window, Susan spied Norm and Mary's car as it left the cul-de-sac. *They didn't get the message.* She grabbed their house keys and headed next door. Next to the kitchen phone was a note from Norm. Her heart sank, and tears welled in her eyes. *I did call; you chose not to call me back.* Slowly her sorrow gave way to anger. She crumpled the note and tossed it into the trashcan.

* * *

Wednesday afternoon. For Susan, the last few days had passed in a blur. First, she took melatonin each night to keep the nightmares away. Then coffee and Xanax in the morning to push aside the groggy disorientation. The remainder of her medications lay untouched on a shelf in her medicine cabinet.

Her life had become a vicious cycle, slowly spiraling down and out of control. *Frightened little girl, you can't do this alone!* She heard those words playing over and over in her mind. Focusing on work was the only thing that drove the negative voices from her head.

Catching a glimpse of herself in the mirror brought her back to reality. She'd worn the same pair of pajamas for the past two days. Her hair was a tangled mess. *When did I last shower? Brush my teeth?*

She shook her head. She hadn't felt this out of control since high school. Being alone on the street while Norm and Mary were on vacation had affected her more profoundly than she imagined. Her fears were fueled by the eerie silence that filled the street day and night. Only the calming voices of others could fill the quiet void. She went into the kitchen, picked up the phone, and dialed. Her mom answered on the second ring.

"Hello."

"Mom?"

"Susan, it's good to hear your voice. You're calling in the middle of the week. Is everything okay?"

The palpable worry in her mother's voice stole the breath from her lungs. Her lips trembled as she fought back the tears. *Pull yourself together.* She took a few deep breaths before answering, then forced a smile. "I'm good. I can't call during the week just to say hi?"

"Of course, you can. How's work? Libby?"

"Good. But I'd rather talk about you and dad. What are you guys doing today?"

"We're both getting ready for the Fourth of July party tomorrow at the clubhouse. Your dad is operating the grill, and I'm working at the dessert table. I know how you hate the drive up north, but why not come up and spend the holiday weekend here. I know you'd have fun."

The Fourth of July holiday fell on Thursday. As a result, her office was closed on Friday. So, she'd have four days without work, the one thing that kept the negative voices out of her head. Perhaps, visiting her parents would be the distraction she needed.

Her thoughts turned to Mary and Norm. They were counting on her to watch over their house. What if something terrible happened to their home while she was out of town? *I must have done something wrong before they left. Otherwise, they would have called instead of leaving me a note.* If she did a good job watching their house, maybe she'd regain their support. "I promised Mary and Norm I'd watch their house this week."

"Oh, Susan, they should never have asked such a favor of you! That's way too much stress. I can hear it in your voice. So don't feel obligated—okay?"

The remark didn't surprise her. Her mother's overprotective interferences sounded more like a way to gain control than an offer of sound advice. How could she make her mother understand? It wasn't a matter of feeling obligated; she didn't want to disappoint them.

"I do feel obligated, mom. I told them I'd watch their house."

Despite her overwhelming desire to prove herself to Mary and Norm, she found herself wavering. She wasn't sure she could stay alone on the street much longer. *If I leave tomorrow that's only two nights away. I could drive home early Saturday. If I get home before they do and nothing has happened to their house, they'll never know I left.*

That's it. Her mind was made up. "You're right. It would be nice to get away. I still have work to finish today, but I could leave in the morning by ten o'clock."

"Oh, that's wonderful! I know your dad will be so happy. I'll head to the store and pick up some of your favorite snacks. And, if you leave that early, we'll be here in time for lunch. How about chicken salad sandwiches with homemade bread?"

She knew those "favorite" dishes were among the ways her mother hoped to persuade her to move to Prescott. She wasn't sure if it was Xanax or relief, but she didn't experience the quiet anger she typically felt with her mother's blatant manipulation. "Sounds great. I can't wait."

"Okay, it's settled. Did you want to talk about anything else?"

She paused briefly before answering, "No...not right now. We'll have plenty of time to talk once I get there."

"Sounds good. Be careful. With the holiday, there'll be lots of cars on the road."

"I will. Love you."

"I love you too, sweetheart."

*** * ***

She hung up the phone with renewed energy. In less than twenty-four hours, she'd be asleep on her parent's front porch hammock, inhaling pine-scented air. The gentle vibration of hummingbirds around her parent's hummingbird feeder would soon replace the raucous near-continuous cawing of the crows. And, based on what she'd read on the internet, there was a chance the cornfield would be gone by the time she returned home.

After dinner, she placed a leash around Libby's neck and led her to the front yard to relieve herself. She then packed her suitcase and treated herself to a long bath. An hour later, she stood back in front of the mirror. Body clean. Teeth brushed. She'd even taken time to shave her legs. *I almost look normal.* She dressed in comfy pajamas, curled up on her family room couch, and painted her fingernails and toenails. Libby lay on the floor beneath her. As her toes dried, her shoulders relaxed. A few moments later, her eyes grew heavy. She yawned and glanced at the clock on the stove: 9:42 p.m. She planned to skip the dose of melatonin, then stay up as late as she could. That way, she wouldn't be in a melatonin haze in the morning.

Libby strode to the sliding glass door, then began pacing in front of the window. The vertical blinds covering the glass door swooshed in her wake. Then she slammed against the doggy door and whimpered.

Susan stepped toward the front door. "Come on, girl. We're going out the front door instead."

Libby didn't come. Bump. Bump. She repeatedly pushed against the closed doggy door. Her whimpering increased.

"Libby!" Susan cried out again.

She tipped her head back and closed her eyes. *She's stressed.* Maybe it would be okay to go into the backyard this one time. She pushed the blinds aside and glanced at the ever-present crows lining the fence. She glanced at the cornfield. Mary was right. Against the night sky, the floodlights from Norm and Mary's house lit up the dirt road and the first few rows of corn. The dry withering silk on the stalks rustled in the night's warm breeze.

She opened the sliding glass door. Libby bolted past her and onto the grass. But instead of relieving herself, she dashed to the back of the fence line and started to pace.

As soon as Susan stepped outside, she sensed it again, an uneasy feeling of being watched. Goosebumps covered her arms, and a smothering wave of heaviness crashed upon her. The crows began to chatter and flap their wings excitedly. The pounding of her heart as it slammed against her chest drowned out their frantic caws.

"Libby!" She raced across the grass and scooped the dog into her arms. Movement within the cornstalks captured her attention. Her eyes widened as she nervously scanned the field.

At last, she saw it. A dark shadow was moving in her direction. It had a density strong enough to push the cornstalks aside. Within the shadow, she spied two red eyes. They locked onto hers, holding her gaze.

Every fear, every anxiety—they all paled in comparison to the horror standing before her. *It's real!* Her mind screamed. The monster of her ongoing nightmares stood on the opposite side of the road within the corn.

She screamed and tried to run. But there was a disconnect between her brain and legs. She twisted and stumbled backward, falling hard against the grass. Libby fell at her side. She scooped Libby against her chest with one arm and then frantically pushed herself up. She ran towards the house, tripping and slamming onto the small concrete slab outside her sliding glass door. Leveraging her weight against the slab, she stood upright and then ran inside the house. With a roaring thud, she pulled the glass door shut then locked it. Instead of following her, the shadowy figure retreated into the corn. Just as quickly as it approached, it slipped out of sight. With shaking hands, she pulled the blinds shut.

Call someone! Her brain screamed in a horrified panic. But who? Norm and Mary were gone. The sheriff? Her parents? What would she tell them? There's a monster in the field? She hadn't felt this out of control since she was a teenager. The adrenaline coursing through her veins left her body violently shaking. Her breath came in short, stuttering waves. She stumbled, then fell onto the couch. A constricting tightness wrapped around her chest. *Breathe! Breathe!* It felt like an eternity before her lungs opened, and her breathing slowed. Once the shaking of her body lowered to a tremble, she grabbed a large kitchen knife from a drawer in the island. Then, room by room, she moved through the house, turning on lights and rechecking the locks.

For the next few moments, a long, deep silence filled the house. Finally, an overwhelming compulsion drove her back to the sliding glass door. She stood in front of the door, closed her eyes, and with a shaking hand, slightly pulled back the blinds. Gingerly, she opened her eyes and peeked outside. *Nothing but corn.* The crows sat quietly on the fence line.

She contemplated putting Libby into the car and leaving for Prescott that very moment but dismissed the thought as quickly as it came. She was in no condition to drive through the mountain passes. Besides, showing up at her parents' house in an agitated state would give them the ammunition they needed to deem her incapable of living independently.

I must sleep here tonight. She took a pill to calm her nerves, then stood at the foot of her bed. *There's no way I'm sleeping in this room. It's at the back of the house, close to the field.* She walked into the guestroom, a room sparsely furnished with a queen-size bed and a small nightstand. She stepped into her office and retrieved her office chair. Libby stayed close by her feet, following her from room to room. She brought her office chair into the guest room, then closed and locked the door. The chair fit nicely under the doorknob, creating a barricade. She crawled into the guest bed. Libby jumped onto the bed and nestled on the pillow next to her head.

Huddled beneath the covers like a scared child, she longed for the arrival of daylight. Although her eyelids were heavy and her body was physically exhausted, her mind was on high alert.

She closed her eyes and tried to sleep, but every creak and groan of the house startled her awake. *Is it in the house?* She'd wonder as she reached for the knife in response. Once she rationalized the sound, she'd place the knife back on the nightstand and close her eyes again. This pattern of being startled awake happened a few times until exhaustion enveloped her body.

Eventually, her mind relaxed, and she dreamed of the drive to Prescott. Comforting images of pulling into her parent's driveway and running into their arms filled her mind. She dreamt of lying on the hammock on their porch, eyes closed and surrounded by the fresh smell of pine trees.

Then, in the middle of the night, darkness invaded her dream. She fought to stay inside the calming dream, the one where she was at her parent's home. But the harder she fought to remain in her calm place, the stronger the force tried to pull her back to her own home, to the cornfield. She was caught in a tug-of-war of the mind. *Something is playing with my thoughts.*

She wasn't strong enough to fight it. Eventually, darkness fell over her, like a curtain being lowered in the middle of a play. When the curtain rose, her dream had placed her back at home.

In her new dream, it was morning. She rose out of bed, opened the sliding glass door, and stepped into the backyard. There was a small gate in the back of her fence. She opened the gate and stood in the middle of the dirt road between the field and her backyard. *This isn't real. There isn't a gate in my backyard fence.* A voice in her head screamed. She willed herself to wake up but couldn't.

Movement within the cornstalks captured her attention. Her heart began pounding in her chest. The dark creature moved to the edge of the corn. Its red eyes burrowed into her eyes. *Come!* A deep, raspy voice hissed. Still dreaming, she violently shook her head.

In the dream, she felt something furry brush past her leg. *The gate is open!* She stood paralyzed on the dirt road watching as Libby ran into the cornfield. *Follow!* The deep raspy voice taunted.

She awoke, crying out "No!" to her empty bedroom. Her heart raced within her chest and her entire body violently shook. The sheets were soaked with perspiration. *It's a bad dream!* She looked at the clock on the nightstand: 3:10 a.m. *I can sleep for a few more hours.* She glanced down at Libby, who lay on the bed beside her. Libby's paws twitched, her body shuddered, and she quietly whimpered. *She's dreaming too.* She reached down and gently stroked Libby's side until the young dog quieted.

Stay away from the cornfield! Norm's warning flashed through her head. She had no intention of going anywhere near it! She buried herself within the covers and closed her eyes. This time she didn't dream. Driven by exhaustion, once her eyes closed, she fell into the depths of deep sleep. She was leaving first thing in the morning for her parent's house. All she needed to do was make it through the rest of the night.

CHAPTER 17

Fourth of July. Tobias awoke before dawn. He sat up in bed, watching the sun slowly rise through his bedroom window. Like most nights, he'd tossed and turned all night, receiving little sleep. Despite the lack of sleep, nervous energy ran through his veins. *Harvest day! We made it! We just need to get through today; we just need to clear the field.*

As he contemplated the significance of the day, he felt Sarah stirring in the bed next to him. She moved closer and gently placed her hand on his arm. He turned and looked into her eyes, then gently stroked her cheek. He then ran his fingers over her long black hair, which laid on her pillow like thick strands of black silk. *So soft. So beautiful.*

"Are you taking John with you?" Sarah asked.

A pang of guilt. During the last harvest, John was only fourteen. Worried for their safety, he'd sent his family away while he harvested the corn. His sons were grown men now; sending them away or refusing their help would raise suspicion. Besides, John insisted he'd help with the harvest. Thankfully, the farm had only one corn picker, an older model John Deere with a wagon attached at the back. He had no intention of letting John ride it. Instead, John would alternate wagons and move corn from the wagons into the cribs. He nodded. "I told him I only needed him for a few hours. He can spend the rest of his day with Kate."

"Don't work too late; we're going to John and Kate's for a barbeque and then to the high school to watch fireworks."

"I won't." He leaned over and kissed Sarah's forehead. She smelled of lavender. A warmth filled his heart, and he smiled. "I love you."

CHAPTER 18

Susan awoke and looked at the clock on her nightstand, 9:15 a.m. Despite falling into a deep sleep after her nightmare, she awoke with an excruciating headache. Last night's fall in the backyard combined with restless sleep, left every muscle in her body tense and sore. She forced herself out of bed, eventually walking to the family room. With a trembling hand, she pulled back the blinds covering the sliding glass door. The cornfield looked benign. Even the ever-boisterous crows perched silently on the fence.

She took a few ibuprofens to stifle the pounding in her head, then dressed and placed her suitcase in the trunk of her car. She quickly ran to Mary and Norm's house and turned on all the lights in the main rooms. Their home might be lit up like a Christmas tree for the next few nights, but she didn't care. At least their home was secure. She'd done her job. Hopefully, she'd arrive home before Mary and Norm on Saturday to turn the lights back off. And, if she were lucky, they'd never know the difference.

She ran home, tossed snacks and water bottles into a cooler, then secured Libby's carrier into the car. All she had left to do was put Libby into the dog carrier and leave.

She marched into the kitchen, grabbed her car keys, and tossed her purse over her shoulder. "Libby?" She called out as she scanned the family room.

She was here just a few moments ago.

She turned towards the living room. The front door was slightly ajar.

She got out! But how? I closed and locked that door! She ran out the front door, closing it as she left the house. There was no sign of Libby in the front yard.

"Libby!" She ran to the end of the driveway and quickly glanced left and right. The street stood empty and silent, the way it did every day. She glanced towards the end of the cul-de-sac and caught a glimpse of something small on the sidewalk beneath the mailbox. *Libby!* Her heart pounded within her chest as she ran towards the mailbox. As she moved closer, Libby disappeared into the wash.

"No, no. no," she whispered. In her mind, she replayed coming home from Mary and Norm's house. *I'm positive I closed and locked the front door when I came home.* She continued running towards the wash as her nightmare replayed in her mind. *That thing in the field invaded my dreams last night! Did it play a trick on my mind, making me believe I closed and locked the front door when I didn't?*

She reached the mailbox and looked up. Libby, running along the edge of the wash, was headed for the cornfield. She picked up her pace. The straps from her purse slid down her shoulder as it bobbed up and down against her side. She adjusted the straps on her shoulder, pulling it closer. She also increased the grip on her car keys. Biting her lower lip, she fought back the flood of tears, threatening to escape.

So close! We were so close to getting out of here! She blinked, clearing her sight and sending tears down her cheeks. She yelled Libby's name, but the young dog didn't respond. Like tiny pistons of an engine, Libby's legs propelled her furry body forward.

"Libby, stop!" She screamed as she continued running along the top of the wash in Libby's direction. Her heart sank. *It's like she can't hear me.* She was living out her worst nightmare and felt powerless to stop it.

Up ahead, Libby stepped onto the dirt road just outside of the corn. "Libby, no...!" she screamed one last time. A surge of adrenaline coursed through her veins, pushing her forward.

The birds began to caw. Then they flew down from the fences and covered the small dirt road between the fence line and the cornfield. The crows spread their feathers outward, increasing the size of their chest. Their "cawing" neared hysteria; their agitation was palpable. She watched in horror as they pecked at Libby. One after another, they pecked and then flew back—cawing and clawing at her. Their attack seemed aimed at pushing her into the corn.

"Libby, stop!" She screamed as she reached the dirt road.

A small group of frenzied crows stopped their assault on Libby and flew in her direction. Their razor-sharp beaks pierced her skin. Sharp jolts of pain went through her body. Trickles of blood streamed down her legs. She kicked, trying to push the aggressive crows away.

She glanced up as Libby took her first step into the cornfield. "No!" She screamed. She stood frozen for a few seconds with her mouth gaped open and her mind in a state of disbelief. *How could this happen?* Finally, the crows' painful jabs jarred her out of the near daydream state. She feebly kicked at the crows, brushing them aside. In the distance, Libby moved further into the cornfield, out of view.

Unconditional love brought her to the edge of the field, despite her ongoing anxiety and fear. She lingered for a split second while her mind contemplated the two choices: turn back and save herself or move forward and rescue Libby. In the battle between heart and mind, love triumphed over fear. Without another thought, she ran into the cornfield.

Throughout her life, she'd avoided being in enclosed spaces because they made her feel claustrophobic. Despite the distance between the rows of corn, the stalks towered over her and encircled her on all sides. They slapped against her arms, face, and legs. As she advanced further amid the cornstalks, the air became warmer. Her palms became sticky with sweat. Beads of sweat ran down her face, between her breasts, and down the small of her back. The thick smell of earth and corn slowly filled her lungs, stealing her breath. She tried calling out for Libby again, but her mouth was dry. The words stuck in her throat.

A mechanical, chugging sound reverberated through the field. *They're harvesting the corn!* She moved towards the sound. *I must find Libby and get out of here!* She continued pushing through the cornstalks until she reached a circular clearing in the middle of the cornfield. She took deep breaths, allowing the cooler air to fill her lungs. Then she glanced at the ground and screamed.

The clearing was a trap; a makeshift snare meant to draw in prey. Animal collars, pieces of fur, and bones littered the crimson-colored dirt. In the middle of the carnage stood Libby.

"Libby!"

The young dog didn't acknowledge her at all. Instead, she stood frozen within the clearing.

With her purse dangling from her forearm and keys clasped tightly within her hand, she ran to Libby and scooped the young dog into her arms. Then, she frantically scanned the stalks. *Which direction do I run?*

In the distance, a mechanical, chugging sound reverberated through the field again. *The farmer! Run to the sound! He'll see you!*

She ran a few steps, then tripped over the carcass of a small dog. She fell to the ground in a loud thud, landing hard onto her side. A jolt of pain cascaded through her body. In the fall, she dropped her car keys and purse. The contents of the purse strewn over the ground. She also dropped Libby. The young dog rolled in the dirt and then bounced up on all fours. As if shaken from a trance, Libby acknowledged her presence and ran toward her, pressing her shaking body against Susan's chest.

Susan jumped up and grabbed her purse. She frantically tried to scoop its contents back inside. She scanned the ground for her car keys. *Where are they?* Libby, tense and shaking, pressed against her leg. The young dog began to whimper.

"Shh."

The cornstalks behind her rustled as if being angrily shoved aside. The horrific monster from her dreams was closing in. *Forget the keys and purse! Run!* Her mind screamed out. She scooped Libby into her arms as the rustling sound closed in behind her. An eerie silence followed.

Every hair on her body raised as the evil pressed against her back. Sulfur filled the air, burning her throat and lungs. She opened her mouth to scream, but she couldn't produce a sound. Instead, she stood, paralyzed by fear. Her legs, which adeptly had moved through the corn, now shook violently and threatened to buckle.

She closed her eyes and buried her face into the back of Libby's head. "I love you, Libby." She whispered. Tears silently streamed from her eyes. In a steady flow, they rolled down her face and onto Libby's furry coat.

The dark shadowy figure blocked out the sunlight overhead. She felt its hot, rancid breath on the back of her neck. She squeezed her eyes tightly shut as the darkness enveloped her.

CHAPTER 19

Tobias' father assured him the summoning incantation combined with his blood would protect him from the evil spirit. Despite his father's assurances, he didn't believe in the blood spell's protective nature, so he never entered the field before harvest time. Instead, he ventured along the edges of the corn at harvest time, methodically working his way to the clearing.

By the time he arrived at the barn, John had everything ready to go. He saw the visible look of disappointment on John's face when he told him he couldn't run the corn picker. He noticed John shake his head as he drove towards the field. He didn't care if his son was angry or not. All that mattered was keeping him safe.

The corn picker bounced as it moved over the ground. It was an older model without a cab. Sitting on the seat left him feeling exposed and vulnerable. Slow and methodically, he drove each row, expecting to see the beast's dark shadow behind every cornstalk. To steady his nerves, he desperately focused on the sounds of the picker's sputtering motor and corn falling into the wagon. Finally, with just a few rows left before reaching the clearing, he returned to the barn to take a break.

"I can finish the rest of the harvest, Dad." John offered.

He shook his head. "I think you should run home and spend some time with Kate."

"We're nearly done. I don't mind staying."

"No…I'm good. I can get the rest of this myself. Your mom and I will be over tonight for the barbeque."

"Kate suggested we go to the high school to see fireworks tonight."

"Mom told me. It sounds nice. You go on and head on out."

"You sure?"

"Yes. Thanks for all your help. I've got the rest."

He returned to the cornfield. *I'm almost done!* As he neared the center of the field, his apprehension increased. One by one, the cornstalks fell. By mid-afternoon, he'd harvested the last stalk. After returning the corn picker to the barn, he drove his truck to the field's center; a circular area purposefully left unplanted. It was the place where the evil fed.

He told himself he gathered and buried the remains in the field out of reverence. But in truth, he buried the remains to hide the evidence of death. In the past, he'd meticulously walk the clearing picking up bones, scraps of fur, and a handful of collars from dogs or cats who'd wandered into the cornfield from neighboring farms.

Every summoning, the number of animals increased. But this year, he couldn't believe the carnage. *So Many.* Littering the ground in front of him were hundreds of pieces of small animals; some remained in their collars. Flies and ants covered most of the animal corpses. Warm bile filled his mouth. He swallowed it back down.

He opened the truck bed and took out a shovel. One by one, he shoveled the remains onto a tarp in the bed of his truck. Then, near the clearing edge, he spotted what appeared to be a large brown bag. He walked over and picked it up. *Purse.* He gasped as his hand recoiled in horror. The purse fell back onto the ground with a soft thud.

He stood, frozen in place, as his blood ran cold within his veins. His eyes searched the soil around the purse. Finally, a shiny object caught his eye—*car keys.* The realization that a human, a woman, wandered into the clearing hit him like a ton of bricks falling from the sky. He felt the sensation of blood draining from his face. The world around him spun wildly out of control, leaving him lightheaded. He broke into a cold sweat and fell to his knees. Warm bile filled his mouth again. This time he didn't hold it back. He leaned over and violently threw up.

Once nausea and lightheadedness passed, he clutched the purse and keys in his arms and stumbled to the cab of the truck. *What have I done!* In a panic, he opened the door and placed the purse and car keys on the floorboard. His eyes studied the backyards of the homes lining the cornfield. *They're too far away to see what I'm doing.* Tears streamed from his eyes as he made his way back into the field. Slowly and methodically, he scooped up the rest of the remains, then raked the blood and smaller pieces of bone into the dirt. Once finished, he jumped into the truck and sped in the direction of the cemetery.

CHAPTER 20

Anne woke early and began baking a loaf of bread. While it was in the oven, she chopped chicken, walnuts, celery, apples, and grapes—then tossed them into a bowl of freshly whisked mayonnaise dressing. Fresh chicken salad was one of Susan's favorite lunch time meals. She covered the kitchen table in a light blue tablecloth and set the table with her lovely white porcelain dishes. Steve approached as she placed a small vase filled with flowers from their garden onto the table's center.

"What's all the fuss?" he jokingly asked.

She looked in his direction and narrowed her eyes.

He held up his hand and laughed. "You know I'm only kidding, right?" He wrapped his arms around her and whispered in her ear, "I'm excited to see her too. Everything looks perfect, and the smell of baking bread—it's making my mouth water. She'll notice all the things you're doing." He placed a kiss on her cheek.

"Do you think she'll like it enough to change her mind and move up here?"

He pulled away and looked into her eyes. "We can't force her, Anne. One of these days, when she's good and ready, she'll move here. I'm sure of it. If you bring it up, I'm telling you—she'll just dig her heels in harder. Okay?"

She nodded. There was no understanding of the compulsion she'd felt, a need to turn every visit into some twisted production aimed at showing Susan what she was missing, family and a sense of security. As much as she hated to admit it, Steve was right. She couldn't risk pushing Susan further away. The hint of sadness in Susan's voice and the way she'd accepted the invitation so willingly. Perhaps, there was a chance she might come around on her own. *I just need to make her feel welcomed.*

Steve glanced down at this watch. "What time did she say she was coming?"

"She said she'd be on the road by ten o'clock. It's a little past noon. She should be here any minute."

"I'm taking my book outside. Do you want to join me?"

She shook her head. "I'm going to double-check everything before she gets here."

An hour later, she stepped onto the porch. "It's after one o'clock. She should've arrived by now."

He glanced up from his book. "I'm sure she just got a late start."

"I don't know, Steve. Something in her voice seemed off yesterday."

"What do you mean…off?"

"Maybe 'off' isn't the right word. Honestly, she sounded lonely. I was thinking the excitement of the new house might be finally wearing off. I know it's not just me. I know you'd feel more comfortable if she lived closer?"

He smiled and quietly nodded.

"I hate that we can't reach her; I've begged her to let us get her a cell phone."

"You called the house?"

She nodded. "No answer. She would have called if she were running this late. Right? Do you think something might have happened to her car?" She shuddered as she pictured Susan stranded on the side of the road.

"Let's give her fifteen more minutes. If she's not here by then, I'll phone the highway patrol, see if anyone's reported a stranded driver on the highway. At a minimum, I can ask them to be on the lookout for her car."

Fifteen minutes later, he stepped back into the house and sat at the kitchen table. She paced the kitchen while he dialed the phone. When there was a pause in the phone conversation, she asked, "Should I start calling hospitals?"

He shook his head. "I don't think it's come to that, Anne. But let's see what the dispatcher says. She's got me on hold right now."

By three o'clock, his calm demeanor vanished. "Even if she got a late start, she would have arrived by now. I'm going to phone the highway patrol again."

She sat across from him as he spoke to the dispatcher. Her stomach clenched as the look on his face grew more worried. *What is the dispatcher saying?* He gave the dispatcher his phone number and hung up the phone.

"They haven't come across any stranded drivers meeting her description, no reported accidents. They'll call if they do."

She felt the tension in her shoulders loosen. "No accidents; that's good. But what do we do now?"

"We'll give her till four o'clock. If we don't hear anything by then, we'll head to Phoenix."

She closed her eyes and nodded. "I'm going to pack a suitcase. If we drive to her house, I'm assuming we won't drive back home tonight."

"Good idea. I'll pack some things too."

After packing, they sat together, staring at the clock as the minutes slowly ticked by. Finally, at 3:40 p.m., Steve jumped up and shook his head. "I can't wait any longer. Let's go."

They pulled in front of the neighbor's house. She watched as Steve ran and knocked on the front door. The neighbor answered promptly. A few minutes later, Steve jumped back into the car.

"Fred's going to keep an eye out for Susan. He'll call us if she shows up."

She nodded, then turned away, and looked out her car window as tears rolled down her face. *She didn't sound right yesterday. I should have said something. I should have done something. Please, let her be alright!*

CHAPTER 21

Sarah glanced at the clock on the kitchen wall and shook her head. *Where is he? We need to be at John and Kate's house in fifteen minutes.* She stepped onto the back porch, looking out in the distance for any sign of Tobias or John. The floorboard of the porch creaked. She turned towards the sound. Tobias sat in one of the rocking chairs. She smiled and walked towards him. "I didn't realize you were home!"

No response.

He must be exhausted. She stopped a few feet away, examining him from a distance. Her smile faded, and her heartbeat began to race. He was slumped in his wooden rocking chair, disheveled, with perspiration-soaked clothes and a layer of dirt covering his arms and face. His head awkwardly rested on the back of the chair. In one hand, he held a lit cigarette; the paper burnt into a long string of ash. In his other hand, he held a beer. Propped against the wall next to him was a shovel; fresh dirt covered the blade. He gently rocked back and forth in the chair. The wooden floorboards beneath the rocking chair creaked with each sway of the chair. There was an empty, vacant look in his eyes as he stared in the direction of the cemetery. Shakingly, he brought the cigarette to his mouth, dropping the ashes onto his jeans.

Her stomach clenched. Something was wrong, terribly wrong.

She knelt beside him and placed her hand on his knee. "Tobias, are you alright?"

He continued to rock slowly back and forth, seemingly oblivious to her presence. Finally, a tear escaped from his eye. It rolled down his cheek.

"Tobias!" She shook his arm. Still no response. She stood and leaned in close enough to smell the beer on his breath. He glanced into her eyes. A moment later, his face registered a look of recognition.

"Tobias, what's wrong? Are you sick?"

He shook his head.

Her heart pounded within her chest. "You're scaring me! Did something happen?"

In all the years she knew him, she'd only seen him act this strangely a few times before, and those times corresponded with either planting or harvesting of the cornfield. Of all the times he acted strangely, this by far was the worst. Something about the cornfield wasn't right, and she knew it. He welcomed his son's help with every field except the cornfield. Regardless of whether corn was planted or not, that field was off limits to everyone, even her. The way he guarded and tended to it was unnatural. She sensed something terrible happened. Her palms became sweaty. "It's the cornfield—isn't it? Something's happened with the field?"

He held her gaze for a moment, then whispered, "Yes."

A wave of panic washed over her. *John.* He helped with the harvest, and she hadn't seen either of them all day. "Did something happen to John?"

He shook his head.

She breathed a sigh of relief as she sat in an adjacent rocker.

The back door of the house swung open. Daniel bounded onto the back porch dramatically, "John sent me over to find you guys. The ribs are done."

She held her hand up in a halting manner. *He shouldn't see his father like this.* Daniel stopped. His gaze moved back and forth between her and Tobias. A look of worry crept upon his face. He took another step towards them. Tobias turned away and shook his head.

"Your dad's not feeling well, too much sun. Could you grab the potato salad from the fridge and bring it to John and Kate's house? I'm going to stay with him."

He took another step closer. "Do you need help getting Dad inside the house?"

She raised her hand and shook her head. "No, honey. We're okay. Just let John know we're sorry we can't make it."

He nodded. "Okay, if you're sure…call me if you need anything." He turned and went back inside the house. The screen door swung shut.

She turned her attention back to Tobias. "What happened?"

He tossed his cigarette butt onto the porch, extinguishing it with his boot. Then he covered his face with his hand. "I don't know where to start!"

She felt a knot in the pit of her stomach. This discussion was long overdue. "Start at the beginning. Tell me everything about the cornfield. Why does it have you so worked up?"

He remained silent for a moment; then, in a monotone cadence, he spoke: "There's a room in the alcove by the staircase."

That wasn't the response she'd expected. *He's talking nonsense about a room to change the subject.* She shook her head. "I've lived in this house for over twenty-one years, Tobias. There's no room there."

"There is...you just haven't found it yet."

She remembered the last time she dusted the panels. It was spring. She hadn't seen anything resembling a door. No door. No room. Period. Could the heat have caused him to hallucinate? She stared into his deadpan eyes. *He's not lying.*

They'd had a rough start to their marriage. At nearly six months pregnant, she and Tobias were unceremoniously married by the Justice of the Peace. Their first year of marriage was strained. Tobias was tense all the time. At first, she wondered if he felt tricked into marriage. But once she learned his father was dying, she assumed his anxiety stemmed from the burdens of providing for his soon-to-be young family while fully running the farm.

The past few months felt like the early days of their marriage. Tobias was continuously on edge. His face looked pale and drawn most days, and his hands shook nearly all the time.

Everything about the cornfield felt unnatural, and now she'd just found out there was a connection between the cornfield and a secret room in her house. She took a deep breath, closed her eyes, and braced herself for the worse. "So, there's a room by the staircase. What does it have to do with the cornfield?"

He paused for a long minute, then answered, "There's a book in the room."

Another unexpected answer. "Book? What kind of book?"

He looked away and whispered, "A book of spells."

She felt a wave of nausea. "Spells? Like witch–?"

His forehead furrowed. "I'm not a witch!"

A warm sensation crept up her neck and onto her cheeks. She narrowed her eyes and leaned forward. "When you say...a book of spells, I think witchcraft. It's all I know. If it's not witchcraft, what is it?"

He quickly reached for her hand. "I'm sorry. I shouldn't have raised my voice. Please let me try to explain."

She looked at his hand as it wrapped gently around hers, calloused yet gentle. She loved his hands. They toiled the fields during the day, then caressed her body at night. She glanced into his fear-covered face. *He's afraid I'll leave him.* Her rising anger faded; compassion took its place. She slowly nodded.

He looked down at his lap. Then, after a moment, he spoke. "My ancestors used spells. And, when my great-grandfather, Ansas, settled here, he brought a book of spells with him."

"What kind of spells?"

"I'm not exactly sure. The book is written in a language I don't know. My father only knew about one of the spells. He taught it to me. It was more like a spell of protection."

"Protection?"

He nodded. "Ansas put every penny into buying a small farm. And, when he struggled to grow a strong crop, he performed the spell to bring rain and make the soil fertile."

Rain? Good soil? Ordinary people would pray for these things, not perform spells. Growing up in the area, she knew the Smith family's reputation for being eccentric. So, it was no surprise that when her parents found out she was dating Tobias, they objected, worried she'd walk away from her beliefs. But she knew Tobias' heart. She sensed his desire to do good. While he never fully embraced the church, he did attend services. And he seemed genuinely happy their sons shared her faith.

"It sounds like you're defending Ansas' actions."

"I'm not. I'm just trying to explain what happened."

"You're saying Ansas performed a spell to save his small farm. Then what, Tobias? His greed took over? At some point your family, owned most of the land in the area. How did they get all that land? Did they perform other spells in the book?"

He shook his head and looked down. "My father told me it was Ansas' sons, Jonas and Lukas, who acquired most of our land. They were the ones who acquired wealth."

Wealth? Are you kidding me? She wanted to scream. She closed her eyes and took a deep breath. It was easy to envision the lifestyle of Jonas and Lukas. She'd heard about the lavish parties held in their home. First-time guests were undoubtedly impressed by the elaborately carved wooden panels lining the grand staircase walls and alcove next to the bottom of the stairs. Each hand-carved panel must have cost a small fortune.

But any wealth the farm acquired was short-lived. Despite their best efforts, she and Tobias could barely keep the farm afloat. So they sold off large parcels of land, along with many of the home's paintings and furnishings, to pay their debts.

She returned to the conversation. "The spell. How does it work?"

He paused for a moment as he glanced past her, looking onto the cemetery. *He's hiding something.* Her shoulders tensed, and warmth crept up over her neck and face. She moved closer, putting her face directly in front of his. "How does it work, Tobias?"

Slowly, he looked into her eyes. "It summons something."

"Something?"

"A spirit. I don't know what else to call it."

"You said it was a spell of protection. Now you're saying it's a spirit. You're twisting your words."

"I'm sorry...that wasn't my intention." He paused for a moment, then continued. "Our ancestors believed spirits could control nature or change a person's luck. Ansas summoned a spirit meant to bring rain and protect his crops."

"Does it have a name?"

He nodded. "Atvaras."

"Atvaras?"

"Yes. But I want you to know Ansas only used the spell because he struggled to get the farm up and running. It was Jonas and Lukas who summoned it out of greed. I think their greed made it grow stronger."

"Stronger?"

"Yes."

"And the corn? What does our cornfield have to do with any of this?" He looked away.

She fought to keep her voice steady. "Tobias, what does the cornfield have to do with any of this?"

"It's where the spirit feeds."

Her forehead broke out in a cold sweat as a wave of nausea struck. "It feeds? On what?" Before he could answer, another thought went through her head. "It's out there? Right now?"

He quickly shook his head. "It was. It leaves with the harvest."

"Have you seen it?"

His eyes widened, and the color drained from his face as he slowly nodded.

The nervous ball of tension in her stomach grew into a small wave of panic. *He's afraid of it!*

"You went into the cornfield knowing it was out there? And you took John with you?"

His cadence quickened. "I didn't allow John anywhere near the corn. Instead, I kept him busy at the barn."

A wave of anger washed over her. She pointed her finger directly at his chest. "You should have told me this years ago. Our sons could have wandered into that field when they were younger. You put them into danger!"

He leaned back in the chair and closed his eyes. For a moment, he looked small, defeated. His voice was low, barely over a whisper. "You're right. I should have said something. Now you know why I've asked you to keep the boys away from the field, especially when there's corn growing in it." He leaned forward, looking into her eyes. "I need you to understand...why I've continued performing that spell...even though I knew it was wrong. I need you to know I only did it to protect our family."

"Protect our family? What do you mean?"

He pointed towards the cemetery. "Remember a long time ago you asked me about the graves out there, the one with the three children?"

She remembered. *The children died of the flu.* She also remembered the wording on the grave of their mother. It was so powerful. She knew she'd never forget it. *Died of a broken heart.*

132

"I told you those kids died of the flu. But they didn't."

"What do you mean…they didn't die from the flu, Tobias? You told me they did. So, if they didn't die that way, then how did they die?" She covered her face with her hands and shook her head in disbelief. Then, in a low voice, she whispered, "They wandered into the field. Didn't they?"

He shook his head. "No."

Feeling a small wave of relief, she lowered her hands. *If they didn't wander into the field, what happened?*

Before she could ask the question in her head, he spoke. "My family has performed the summoning ritual every seven years."

She began counting back the years and soon realized he wasn't lying. The seven-year timeline aligned with planting corn in the field.

He continued, "I don't know if Jonas and Lukas became afraid of the spirit or if they didn't feel they needed it anymore. Whatever the reason, on a summoning year, they chose not to perform the spell. I think they believed the spirit wouldn't come. But it did. That year, a storm came, just like it does every night after I perform that spell. After the storm, a thick fog covered the field. You know, the kind of fog we get over the cornfield after a storm?"

"You've always told me the fog over the field was normal. It had something to do with the corn and how the field was situated near the irrigation canals." *You lied about that too.*

"There's no reason to hide this anymore. I know neither you nor the boys have seen it happen. But that fog seeps up from the ground. It stays over the field until it evaporates."

She nodded, encouraging him to continue. Yet, deep inside, a voice cried out, *Can I bear to hear anything else?*

"Anyway, the year they didn't summon the spirit, the storm still came, so did the fog. But it left the field and moved towards the house. Everyone was asleep. Jonas and Lukas didn't even know the fog was here until they woke up and found it covering the house, inside and out. They couldn't see more than a few inches in front of them. When the fog dissipated, they realized the children were gone."

She felt the color drain from her face. She shook her head slowly. "Are you saying that spirit took those children!"

He slowly nodded. "It's horrible, and I know it's hard to hear. But the fog came, and yes, the spirit came with it. It took Jonas' children."

"If the children were taken…how do you explain their graves?"

"Those graves are filled with their toys and other mementos."

"No bodies?"

He nodded.

"How did your family get away with that? How could people believe those children died without seeing their bodies?"

"I don't know, Sarah. It was a different time back then. My family had a lot of money and a lot of influence. I'm not sure how they did it. I only know what my father told me."

"And…their mother? Did it take her?"

"No."

"How did she die?"

Tears flowed down his face as he pointed to the large tree next to the house. The tree directly overlooked the cemetery. Hanging from one of the largest branches was a makeshift swing. When the weather was nice, she'd sit on that swing and relax.

In a voice just above a whisper, he answered, "She hung herself… right there on that tree…a few weeks later."

She burst into tears, burying her face into her hands. Even the swing, which she'd always found comforting and peaceful, was also a lie. With each revelation, he slowly shattered one reality after another. Everything they'd built for the past twenty-one years was slowly slipping through her fingers, and she was powerless to stop it.

"No, Tobias! No!"

"Sarah, I'm so sorry." He reached for her hand.

She pulled away as if touched by a red-hot poker, then slapped his face and yelled. "Don't touch me! Don't say you're sorry!"

He stepped back, and in a rushed voice, said, "Please, Sarah, I'm trying to explain. This is why I've always planted the cornfield and performed the damn spell. I couldn't risk anything happening to you or the boys!"

Her whole body felt numb. All her energy was spent. She desperately wanted to crawl into bed and fall asleep. *Maybe, just maybe. I'll wake up and find this was all a bad dream!*

"I don't know what else to say, other than…I'm truly sorry."

She closed her eyes and nodded. She stood and began to walk away. She needed to go upstairs, fill their bathtub with warm water, and wash away the wickedness surrounding her. She took a few steps, and then her mind began to clear. *Wait a minute. Something happened today. Something that sent him over the edge.* A thought passed through her head. She turned and looked at him. "What happens if something goes into the field?"

His eyes locked on hers. "I've tried to do the right thing by you and our family. I worked hard my whole life, knowing I'd eventually take over the farm." He waved his hands in the air. "If I'd known all of this, I would have moved away right out of high school, taking you with me." He closed his eyes and whispered, "I made the wrong decision. Instead, I stayed, and worse, I brought you and the boys into this. I'm so sorry, Sarah!"

She knew from experience changing the subject was one of the ways he avoided answering hard questions. A horrendous thought passed through her mind. *Someone went into the field!* Her entire body shook as her legs struggled to keep her body upright. "That spirit in the field hurt someone— didn't it? That's why you're acting so strange."

He looked her in the eye but didn't answer. She watched the color drain from his face.

"Oh, my God! This can't be happening." She began to pace back and forth. Her heart ached. She began to cry. He approached her as if trying to comfort her. She quickly stumbled backward, away from his touch. For the first time in her marriage, she was frightened of the man standing in front of her.

He took a step away from her as if to ease her fear. "I didn't find a body, Sarah. I swear!"

She glanced at the shovel propped against the wall, pointing to it in disgust. "Then why is that sitting there?"

After a moment's pause, he spoke. "After the harvest, I bury anything I find in the back of the cemetery."

"What do you mean? Anything you find?"

"Animal collars, pieces of bone, and fur."

She shuddered, then shook her head. "So, you didn't find a body?"

"No, but I did find something."

"What? What did you find?"

In a voice barely above a whisper, he answered, "I found a woman's purse and a set of car keys."

"No!" Her entire body went numb. Then, in a dizzying wave, she stumbled and fell back into the chair. She stared off into the distance, unable to look at his face. *Someone went into our field!* But when? Last month? Today? As far as she knew, no one had been reported missing.

He paced the porch. "The name on the driver's license is Susan Green. She lives on Pecan in one of those smaller houses, bordering the field."

"If you found her purse, but not her body, where is she?"

"I don't know. Maybe she saw the spirit and ran away?"

She slowly nodded, filled with a tiny bit of hope. "Should we drive to her house? Make sure she's there, safe?"

He shook his head. "Let's wait a few days…you know, just to see if she's reported missing. I think she made it out of the field. Honestly, I do, Sarah."

In her heart, she knew something wasn't right about the cornfield. The amount of anxiety he displayed whenever he planted the corn was unnatural. She addressed his lack of sleep and stress throughout their marriage, but she never directly confronted him about the field. She was complacent—a quiet bystander who was willing to stay in the dark. *I turned a blind eye. I'm just as guilty as he is!* She looked him in the eyes and, in a faint whisper, said, "I hope you're right, Tobias."

CHAPTER 22

Anne's eyes widened as she scanned oncoming traffic looking for any sign of Susan's car. Nothing. They arrived at the house shortly after six o'clock. The sun lay low in the sky behind Susan's home, leaving the front of her home fully shaded. From what she could tell, all the lights were out in the house. The nervous ball of tension in her belly began to grow. *She knows to leave lights on when she's going away.* As they treaded to the front door, nothing looked out of place. An eerie stillness shrouded the house and the street. *It's too quiet.* Steve took out his key and placed it in the deadbolt. He reached for the handle; it turned easily in his hands. He turned towards her, his brow line wrinkled, his eyes full of worry. "The door is unlocked. Stay here."

Steve pushed the door open and advanced into the home. Within a few seconds, he retreated. Pausing briefly on the porch, he took a few long, slow breaths, then stepped back inside.

She followed. Darkness shrouded the foyer. She groped the wall. When her fingers reached the light switches, she flipped them up, simultaneously turning on the porch and foyer lights. She looked out into the living room; light-blue puppy-training sheets littered the floor. *Steve installed a doggy door months ago.*

"Why is Libby using training sheets?"

"I told you to stay back, Anne." He turned in her direction. "I'm not sure what's going on here."

Despite his pleas, she couldn't stay outside. The smell of urine and feces permeated the air. Seeing the training sheets filled her with dread. Something was wrong. Her fastidious daughter wouldn't have left soiled training sheets lying around.

Steve led the way into the kitchen. At the doorway, he abruptly stopped and shook his head. *What does he see?* She pushed her way past him, expecting to find Susan on the kitchen floor. *She's not here.* The tiny wave of relief she felt vanished the second she scanned the kitchen. The counters' canisters were out of place, dishes with remnants of food overfilled the sink, and a layer of flour and sugar covered the kitchen island.

Tears filled her eyes. "She's baking again."

She watched the color drain from Steve's face. *He realizes it too.* After Susan's hospitalization, Anne tried desperately to find ways to support Susan's wellbeing. When she learned measuring and mixing ingredients decreased Susan's anxiety, she encouraged her to make different recipes. Susan settled on just one recipe, oatmeal chocolate chip. They'd discussed the topic in therapy. Dr. Cohen surmised Susan baked to keep herself in control. She looked at the dishes piled high in the sink and shook her head. Susan also kept things under control through obsessive cleaning. *Something's very wrong.*

Steve picked up a set of keys lying on the counter. "Norm and Mary's?" He asked as he held them in the air.

"I think so."

He moved to the other side of the kitchen island. "The knife drawer is open."

Her eyes filled with tears and her lips began to tremble. "Knife? Should we call the police?" she asked.

He shook his head. "We don't know what we're dealing with here, Anne. I'll check the bedrooms." He plodded down the hall. She followed close behind. He abruptly turned and raised his hand. "Stay here. I'm not letting you go any farther until I've checked the bedrooms by myself."

A surreal feeling, like a thick vine, reached up from the ground, wrapped itself around her, and now threatened to smother the breath from her lungs. *It's been ten years since he found her lying on the bed, barely alive, with a suicide note at her side.*

She watched as he gingerly moved toward her bedroom door. He placed his hand on the handle and slowly turned.

She was overcome with a saddened certainty they'd find Susan lying on the bed. She closed her eyes, fighting back the tears, and swallowed hard.

Maybe they wouldn't be too late. Perhaps they could save her. She opened her eyes and took a few steps forward. He turned again in her direction. His eyes pleaded for her to stop. "Anne...please...I'm begging you...please don't come any closer. I've been through this before. Once that image is in your head, you can't erase it."

She knew he was right. She curtly nodded her head in agreement, wiping away a tear in the process. Her palms were clammy, and her heartbeat rapidly in her chest. She took a step back as he opened the door. The room was completely dark. *She has blackout curtains.* She closed her eyes as soon as he turned the light on in the room. *Stay calm.* Her mind screamed.

"She's not in her bed." His voice cracked with emotion.

She fell against the wall in relief. Her hand covered her lower face, and she nodded. Tears of relief streamed down her face.

"Her bed is unmade. But I don't see any sign of Susan in this room. I'm going to check her bathroom and closet. Stay here. Okay? I'll be right back."

She knew there was still a chance they could find her around any corner of the house. But she was grateful Steve hadn't seen her lying in her bed. Finding her before had a profound effect on him; she wasn't sure he'd be able to handle it again.

A moment later he reappeared in the hallway. "Her room and bathroom are clear." She thrust herself into his shaking arms.

"She'll be alright." He whispered as he stroked her back.

They moved down the hall towards the office, guestroom, and garage. The door on the left was the guest bathroom. Across the hallway from the bathroom were two rooms. Steve opened the door to the office and turned on the light switch.

Anne glanced in the room. Nothing except a small wooden desk. "The office chair is missing."

"What?"

"Where's the office chair?"

"Don't know. But her computer is still here."

A moment of comfort. *She hasn't been burglarized.*

Steve moved to the guest bedroom, the room they shared whenever they spent the night. Again, he turned around and held his hand up, signaling her to stay in the hallway. She nodded. He opened the door and leaned into the room. "She's not here."

She breathed a sigh of relief and moved to the doorway.

The mini-blinds of the windows were cracked open. Outside, the sun was low in the sky, bathing the room in dim light. The office chair was in the middle of the room, and the bed was unmade."

"Why is she sleeping in here?"

He crossed the room in bounding steps, then turned on the lamp. "Not sure." He pointed down at the nightstand. "But I'd like to know why there's a knife next to the bed."

Knife? Her heart sank. She glanced at the nightstand. Next to the alarm clock and lamp was a large kitchen knife. A wave of dizziness overtook her, sending her crashing against the doorframe. He rushed to her side, quickly grabbing and holding her upright. Beads of cool perspiration dotted her forehead. It was the closest she'd ever come to passing out.

"Are you okay?" His eyes filled with worry.

She slowly shook her head. *No! I'm not okay!* She wanted to scream at the top of her lungs. Every stop on this makeshift tour of Susan's home filled her heart with dread and her mind with questions. *Why were potty-training sheets left all over the living room? Why was Susan sleeping in the guestroom? Why the knife? And the most heartbreaking of all, where was Susan?*

She looked into his eyes. "Can we call the police now?"

"Let's check the garage first. I want to see if her car is there."

She nodded and followed him through the laundry room and out to the garage. The fluorescent garage light shined down on Susan's late model dark blue compact. The passenger side door was open. The overhead light in the car was off. Finding Susan's car in the garage was the worst-case scenario. She never left Phoenix. The tenuous strand of hope Susan would be found safe but stranded on the side of the road disappeared. She covered her mouth with her hands to stifle the scream.

"She never left the house." His voice trailed off.

He stepped to the driver's side of the car and opened the door. With a faltering gait, she moved to the passenger side of the car and looked inside. Libby's small carrier was on the front passenger seat. On the floor of the passenger's side of the car was a plastic grocery bag. She picked it up and glanced inside: small bags of chips and cookies. Next to the bag was a little cooler filled with grapes, water bottles, and an ice pack. She placed her hand inside the cooler. "Not cold. This has been sitting here for a while."

He pointed to the overhead car light. "It looks like the battery is dead." He pushed the button to unlatch the trunk. They both walked to the back of the vehicle. Susan's suitcase lay neatly in the trunk.

"It looks like everything is here, ready to go," he said. "All she needed to do was put Libby in the car and go. I know she would have called if her battery was dead, or the car wouldn't start."

The heat inside the garage overtook her, causing her legs to shake violently. She grabbed onto the trunk's lip, closed her eyes, and took a few deep breaths. It didn't help. Warm bile crept up the back of her throat. She turned and violently threw up on the garage floor.

He placed his arm around the small of her back. "Come on, Anne. Let's get inside and call the police."

* * *

After speaking to the dispatcher, he hung up the phone abruptly. "This is bullshit."

"Why…what did they say?"

"She said their officers are busy managing traffic and answering calls about illegal fireworks. It'll take a while before someone can respond."

"But she's missing! That's more important than traffic and fireworks."

"I know. But she's also a grown woman. She said they'd send someone as soon as they can." He grabbed Norm and Mary's house keys. "There's one thing we didn't consider. She might be next door. I'm going to check their house."

She nodded and started walking towards him.

He shook his head and held up his hand. "You're staying here this time."

"But–"

"I'm serious, Anne. Stay here. I'll be right back."

It could be a while before an officer arrived. She needed to keep busy while she waited. Fighting back tears, she cleared the training sheets from the living room floor, then began cleaning the kitchen.

As she wiped down the countertop, she played the messages on Susan's answering machine, confident she'd left each one. She was startled when the unfamiliar voice of a woman filled the room. "Hello, my name is Jackie. My son, Connor, found your dog, Libby. Please call me back at…"

Her heart skipped a beat. *Someone found Libby!* A wave of hope washed over her. Her hand shook as she dialed Jackie's number. Jackie answered on the first ring. "Hello?"

"Jackie?"

"Yes."

"My name is Anne. Your son found my daughter's dog."

"Libby…yes, she was wandering down our street."

"Did he see a young woman with her? My daughter, Susan, is missing. This is the first lead we've had."

"Oh, no. Hold on for a moment, and I'll ask him." She heard a muffled conversation on the other end of the phone. Jackie returned to the call. "I just checked with my son. He didn't see anyone, just the dog." After a short pause, she continued, "I don't want to alarm you, but there was some dried blood on Libby's coat. It wasn't a lot. I checked her skin and noticed scratches on her back. It looks like she might have gotten tangled up in a bush. I'm not sure. But we bathed her to keep the scratches from becoming infected."

Her heart sank. They hadn't seen Susan, and Libby was found with scratches on her back. In a broken voice, she asked for Jackie's address. "My husband is checking the house next door. As soon as he comes back, we'll stop by to pick up Libby."

✳ ✳ ✳

Anne met Steve at the front door. "One of the neighbors found Libby!"

"Did they see Susan?"

She shook her head. "No. But let's talk with them. They live on Oak Street. I have the address."

They both ran to the car. Oak was just a few blocks away. They spotted a woman, a young boy, and Libby standing on the driveway as they approached the house. Libby ran to them as soon as they stepped out of the car. She glanced up at Jackie and Connor. "Thank you! Thank you so much for finding her!"

Connor ran towards her. "That leash belonged to our dog. But she ran away. My mom said you could keep it."

She smiled. "Thank you!"

Jackie walked over. "Your daughter? Was she at the house next door?"

She frowned and shook her head. "No, she's still missing."

"I'm so sorry. If you give us a description, we'll keep an eye out for her."

After giving Jackie a description, she and Steve took Libby home.

* * *

Sergeant David Brown pulled in front of Susan's house and glanced down at the time on his computer: 10:54 p.m. He'd worked for the sheriff's department for over fifteen years. During his tenure, he'd issued multiple citations and responded to numerous burglaries and bar fights. Missing person calls weren't uncommon; most people who disappeared were found within the first day or two. Those who'd gone missing were teenagers running away from home or a senior citizen who wandered off.

In some cases, the individual wasn't even missing. This was the first missing person report he'd heard of in the subdivision. According to the dispatcher, the missing person's parents drove down from Prescott when she didn't arrive at their home as expected. They found her car parked in the garage.

He stepped out of the car, making mental notes as he approached the front door. There were no broken windows or outward signs of foul play. He also looked up and down the street. He'd patrolled the subdivision long enough to know, all but two homes on the road were vacant. At the front door, he knocked twice on the door in quick succession. A man and woman briskly opened the door. A look of relief crossed their faces.

"Good evening. Sorry, it's so late. I'm Sergeant Brown. We received a call about a missing person?"

He nodded. "Thank you for coming. My name is Steve." He pointed to the woman. "This is my wife, Anne. The missing person is our daughter, Susan. We expected her at our house this morning."

"And you both live–?"

"In Prescott. Susan's car is in the garage. She never left."

His attention was fully captured. "May I come in?"

Steve opened the door widely and stepped aside.

As he entered the front door, he stopped and carefully looked at the knob, latch, and deadbolt. *No sign of forced entry*. He looked at Steve and asked, "The front door…was it open or closed when you arrived?"

"Closed but unlocked. We've checked the entire house. She's not here, and we don't see anything missing."

Steve and Anne led the way to the family room at the back of the house. He followed willingly. The faint odor of urine hung in the living room, filling his nostrils. The smell seemed out of place for the home, which otherwise seemed clean and tidy. "Does your daughter own a dog or a cat?"

Steve answered, "A cocker spaniel…Libby. A neighbor found her a few streets away. She had scratches on her back and blood on her coat."

"Blood?" His heartbeat quickened. This might be something more than a missing person. "May I see the dog?"

"The people who found her gave her a bath while they were waiting for someone to call them back." His stomach fell. *They might have washed away evidence.*

Libby was lying on the family room floor near the couch. As soon as they entered the room, the young dog stood and bounded in his direction. Her entire backend shimmied back and forth, sending her tiny tail wagging side to side. He could tell just by looking at her she had a sweet disposition. He bent down and patted her head. Steve held Libby still while he examined the scratches on her back. Most of the scratches were superficial, and a few looked like small punctures.

He glanced up at Steve. "See these tiny punctures? It wouldn't hurt to have a vet look at those. Sometimes, these little puncture wounds can get infected."

"What do you think happened to her?"

"I'm not sure. It kinda looks like she got tangled up in a bush."

"That's what Anne and I thought."

He gave Libby one last pat on the head, then stood. Although superficial, the dog was injured, and at one time, there was blood on her coat. *Had some of the blood belonged to the missing person?* He needed to secure the scene and gather as much information as he could. He pulled a small notepad and pen from his pocket. "Your daughter's full name?"

"Susan Marie Green."

"S...u...s...a...n?"

Steve nodded.

"How old is Susan?"

"Twenty-six."

"Here's a picture of her," Anne said, stepping forward. Her eyes were swollen and red. This was the most challenging aspect of his job, seeing painful expressions on the faces of those he was sworn to protect.

He studied the picture in his hand. Long, curly brown hair, brown eyes, bright smile. Overall, a beautiful girl who looked like she belonged in high school. "When was this picture taken?"

"Last year," Steve answered.

He smiled as he looked at Steve and Anne. "Beautiful young lady."

They both smiled and nodded.

"The dispatcher said you found Susan's car in the garage. Is that right?"

"All packed up and ready to go. But, the battery in the car is dead, and she didn't call to tell us she was having car trouble. We've checked everywhere in the house, even under the beds. She's not here. It's like she vanished."

"There's no answer on her cell phone?"

Both parents looked at each other and then in his direction. Anne spoke up. "We've offered her a cell phone for years. She won't take it." Tears filled her eyes. One by one, they slowly slid down her face. "We just wanted her to have a way to reach out for help if she needed it."

A stabbing pain went through his chest. He forced a smile to reassure the parents. "Okay. Let's get as much information as we can."

Steve motioned to the couch in the family room. "Would you like to sit down?"

He nodded. "Let's start with the last time you physically saw Susan?"

Anne answered, "Early April."

Steve added, "But, we talk to her every week."

He nodded, mentally ticking through the questions he needed to ask. "Has she ever run away?"

"No, never," Anne said.

"Have you phoned her friends?"

"She doesn't have any here," Steve said.

Anne interjected, "Well, she's friendly with the people she works with, but I don't think she goes out with them."

"Have you called her employer?"

"They're closed for the holiday weekend," Anne said.

Steve interrupted, "I don't think calling her employer will do any good. I'm fairly sure she didn't go out with anyone from work."

"We'll still need the name of her employer and their phone number."

Steve nodded. "We'll get it for you."

"Did your daughter have a boyfriend?"

"No," Steve and Anne stated in unison.

He knew from experience parents were sometimes the last to know their children were romantically involved with someone. "As far as you know, she doesn't have a boyfriend. Maybe she met someone on the internet? Someone she's been talking to?"

Steve and Anne looked at each other. He'd seen the look before; this line of questioning seemed to take them off guard. *They're probably wondering how much of their daughter's private life they don't know.*

Anne changed the subject. "She's friends with the neighbors next door."

He pointed his pen in the direction of the house next door. He knew the house on the other side of Susan's was still empty.

Anne interjected, "They aren't home right now. They left a few days ago to visit their daughter in California. So Susan's watching their home."

"Did you check their house?"

Steve nodded. "Once we didn't find her here, I checked next door."

"May I have the key?"

Anne nodded. "I'll go get it."

As he waited for Anne, he looked around the simply furnished room, then glanced at Steve. He had a puzzled look on his face like he was trying to understand something. Finally, he leaned forward to capture his attention. "You look like you're mulling something over."

Steve startled, then nodded. "When we first came inside the house, there were training sheets all over the front room. Our daughter had the plastic cover over the doggy door. I checked, and it's in perfect working order. I'm just trying to figure out why."

"Do you mind if I check?"

Steve shook his head. "Go right ahead."

He examined the doggy door by pushing the transparent soft plastic doors open and releasing them. The magnets at the bottom of each door clicked into place. Steve was correct; the door worked fine. The fact it was blocked didn't surprise him. Susan likely did it to keep her dog from going outside. "We've had several pets go missing in the subdivision, probably taken by coyotes."

"The people who found Libby said their dog ran away."

Inwardly, he smiled. *Blocking the doggy door was probably her way of keeping Libby safe—one mystery solved.*

A rapid knock on the door echoed through the house. Anne, who was walking back into the room, quickly changed direction and moved excitedly towards the front door.

"I'm sure it's one of my deputies." He called out.

Her shoulders visibly slumped. But she continued walking through the kitchen into the living room. The front door opened, and a brief muffled conversation ensued. Anne returned. Following close behind her was one of his deputies. *Russell. Young, eager, and proficient.* He made eye contact with Deputy Russell, who nodded in response.

Anne handed him a key. He pointed in the direction of the neighbor's house while looking at the deputy. "Let's have a look next door. Our missing person was watching their house."

Together he and the deputy searched every room of the neighbor's house. The home was clean and tidy, with no evidence of foul play. Once the search was concluded, they returned to Susan's home.

As they approached the front door, he pointed to the side of the house. "Could you look around the outside of the house? I'll finish here."

Deputy Russell nodded.

He knocked on the front door. Anne and Steve both answered. "Did you find anything we missed?" Steve asked.

He shook his head. "Everything seems in order over there. I want to look at the rest of the house. May I come back inside?"

"Yes…of course," Anne said. She opened the door wider and allowed him to pass.

He stopped in the living room, trying to get a mental picture of what the parents saw when they first arrived at their daughter's home. "Can you both walk me through everything you saw as you went through the house?"

They nodded in unison.

He smiled, grateful for their cooperation. "Okay…so, you entered the house. You found the front door unlocked but closed."

Steve nodded.

"And…you found dirty training sheets on the living room floor and the doggy door blocked. But with all the missing pets in the neighborhood, Susan was probably trying to keep…" He flipped through his notes. *What's the dog's name?* "Libby. She was probably trying to keep Libby from going outside?" He looked at both parents. They nodded in unison.

Anne interjected, "We're just trying to understand why she left dirty sheets on the floor. She always keeps her house spotless."

"Maybe…she cleans the house well before you visit…yes?"

A look of doubt filled Anne's face. *They're cooperative, but I can't shake the feeling they're holding something back. Try a different tactic.* "Okay…the dirty sheets on the living room floor—I take it—that's out of character for her? Was there anything else that seemed out of character?"

Anne's eyes widened. She glanced up into Steve's face. He nodded. Although they didn't speak out loud, they appeared to have an entire conversation. Anne quickly moved to the kitchen. Both he and Steve followed closely behind. Once in the kitchen, Anne started pointing to the sink and counters. "Her kitchen was filthy: dishes piled in the sink, canisters out of place, and flour on the kitchen island."

This is what they're holding back? A messy kitchen? Before he could probe further, she burst out in tears and raised her voice. "And…she's baking!"

Baking. What does that mean?

Anne fell against Steve's chest and continued crying. Tears welled up in Steve's eyes. Then, in a cracked voice, he began to explain: "Susan has anxiety. She's coped well for years. But you can imagine how worried we were about this move. We thought it might be too much for her; so, we stayed with her for the first week. Once we felt she was settled, we went back home. We came back down from Prescott when she bought Libby. We talk every weekend. But we haven't physically seen her in months. For the most part, she seemed to be adjusting well."

"But now you're here…back in her house…and, you're not so sure?"

Steve nodded. "Keeping everything clean and in its place is one of the ways she manages her anxiety. When she's under a lot of stress, she bakes. It's like a reset button. So, when we saw the potty sheets and the dirty kitchen and realized she'd also been baking, well, we put two and two together. Then, on top of all that, there was the knife."

"Knife?" The hairs on his arms raised. *The dispatcher hadn't mentioned a knife.* "What do you mean…what knife?"

Steve pointed to the drawer in the kitchen island. "That's her knife drawer. It was open when we arrived. When we searched the house, we found one of the knives on the nightstand in the guestroom. It matches the other ones here in the kitchen."

"Show me." He followed Steve down the hallway. Laying on the nightstand was a large kitchen knife. The sight of the knife gave him a sinking feeling. *Did the missing person place it on the nightstand to protect herself? If so, from whom? Or did someone else leave it on the nightstand?* He stepped back and scanned the bed, no sign of struggle, no sign of any violence. "It was unmade when you arrived?" he asked.

"We've left this room exactly as we found it, and we didn't touch the knife."

That's good. He glanced around the room. There was a chair in the middle of the room which looked out of place. "This chair?"

"It's from her office next door. We don't have any idea why it's in here," Anne said.

"We also don't understand why she's sleeping in the guestroom."

"Can you show me her bedroom?"

The master bedroom was clean, but the bed was unmade. He opened the closet door; half of the clothes hung a perfect distance from each other and appeared to be arranged by color. The other half were haphazardly placed on hangers, giving him the impression his missing person might be spiraling downward.

He moved to the bathroom, also clean. He opened the medicine cabinet and pulled out a handful of prescription bottles and a bottle of melatonin. He recognized one of the medications by name, a drug prescribed for anxiety. He opened the bottle, nearly empty. He showed the bottle to Anne and Steve. "This was filled recently, but it's almost gone. I think this bolsters your concerns about her current level of anxiety."

Anne quickly looked at Steve. "She didn't pack her meds."

A bewildered look crossed Steve's face. He took a step forward and reached out his hand. "Can I have a look at those?"

He nodded and handed the pill bottles to Steve.

Steve read the labels, opened the bottles, and shook his head. "You're right, sheriff. She's not taking any of these as prescribed."

Tears slid down Anne's face. "But why? She's done so well for so long. It's my fault. Something in her voice sounded off yesterday. I should have known. I'm her mother. I should have known, and I should have done something."

Steve shook his head and wrapped his arm around her shoulder. "Stop blaming yourself, Anne. There was no way to know."

He looked at the name of the prescribing doctor on the bottles. "I'd like to take the information off these bottles and give her doctor a call."

Anne and Steve nodded in agreement.

"I need to finish taking a look at the rest of the house." As he entered the hallway, he ran into Deputy Russell. "How does the outside of the house look?"

"Undisturbed, sir. No footprints outside of the windows. Screens are all intact."

"Okay..." He turned to Steve and Anne. "I'd like to show Deputy Russell what I've found so far and have him finish the search with me. May I ask you two to wait for us in the family room?"

They nodded and proceeded back to the family room. When they were out of earshot, he turned to Deputy Russell. "I'm not quite sure what we've got here. Based on the medications I've found, our missing person has a psychiatric history. There's a mismatch between the number of pills prescribed and the amount she's taken. Based on the missing doses of anti-anxiety pills and her parent's remarks about her behavior, it appears her anxiety isn't well-controlled at this time. So, that could be a factor. Her parents state she's never run away before, but…"

"You think that might be what happened."

"Exactly. But something is bothering me."

"What?"

He pointed to the second door on the right. "One of the kitchen knives is on the nightstand where our missing person was sleeping. A neighbor found our missing person's dog. There were some superficial scratches and punctures on the dog's back and blood on her coat."

Deputy Russell's eyes widened.

"I know…that's bothering me. We need some technicians to go through the house. Unfortunately, her parents have already cleaned up the place. But I'd hate to miss something. According to the dispatcher, her parents found her car in the garage. I'll check the garage. Can you call this in?"

Deputy Russell nodded and walked away.

Before going into the garage, he briefly glanced in the office. There was a computer on the desk. *Her television is undisturbed in the family room. It doesn't appear to be a burglary.* He continued to the garage. Despite being close to midnight, the garage's air was stifling and filled with the stench of vomit. He made a cursory walk around the car. Both the driver and passenger doors were open. *Did the parents open the doors? I'll have to ask.* The dome light in the car was off. *The battery is dead. Was it dead when she started the car? Or is it dead because the doors were left open?* The trunk lid was up, and her suitcase was there. He glanced at the ignition switch, no key. Did her parents remove the key? Did they put the key in the house?

He returned to the family room. The parents were slumped in one corner of the couch. They both had the same vacant look on their faces and bloodshot eyes. His heart sank. He had children of his own and couldn't imagine what they were going through. "When was the last time either of you slept?"

"We've been up since early this morning," Steve answered.

"You both look exhausted. Are you able to answer just a few more questions?"

They nodded.

"It's about Susan's car. Is her car exactly as you found it?"

"The passenger side door was open. The driver's side door and the trunk were closed."

"Everything else was the same?"

"Yes, except for the food. We threw that away."

"Food?"

"She packed some snacks for the trip. But the food in the cooler wasn't cold when we checked. So, we threw it away."

"That's fine. I was wondering about her car key. I didn't see it in the ignition switch."

"Oh…we couldn't find it. We also can't find her purse."

The sinking feeling in his stomach returned. *There was a good chance the purse and car keys were with Susan. He couldn't rule out a robbery. He also couldn't rule out a kidnapping.* "I'm going to issue an alert and send out Susan's picture. That way, if any other agency finds her, they'll contact us."

He sensed their relief. Although they both looked exhausted, he needed them to leave the house. This was now an investigation. He needed to secure everything. "I think it'll be best if you spend the night in a motel. My deputy is checking availability. He's also calling the dispatcher, asking them to send out a detective. The detective will want to go over everything with you. With the holiday, we've had a busy night. So, I'm not sure how long it will take to bring a detective on-site."

Steve nodded.

"There's one more thing. I'm wondering if you know any of the numbers to Susan's credit cards. The detective will want to see if and where they are being used."

"We have access to all of Susan's accounts. The information is in Prescott. But I can get it for the detective," Steve said.

Deputy Russell approached. "I've secured a room at the Cactus Inn. They allow pets. I've also spoken with dispatch. They're sending Hargrove."

He nodded. "Thank you." He then turned to Steve and Anne. "The hotel is downtown on Central. Deputy Russell could give you a ride. We could make arrangements to bring you back here in the morning."

Steve shook his head. "It's not too far to drive. We'll be fine, but thank you, and thank you for getting us a room."

There was a look of defeat on their faces. Finally, Anne looked up and quietly whispered, "You think something happened to her—don't you?"

A string of rapid thoughts flashed through his mind—*a history of anxiety and atypical behavior. Perhaps she suffered an anxiety-related psychosis and wandered off. On the other hand, there was a knife, a scratched and bloody dog, missing keys and purse. They had to consider she was taken against her will.* Although the parents didn't think she had a boyfriend—maybe she did—or perhaps she'd recently met someone online.

He shook his head. "I honestly don't know. I just don't want to miss anything. People leave home for all kinds of reasons. Nearly all of the time, the missing person is found, and there's a simple explanation for why they've gone missing. Your daughter is a grown woman. I'm hoping she'll come back within a few days on her own." He knew the detective would likely want to look through her computer and contact car services and cab companies to see if anyone picked up a fare in the neighborhood. He'd also track down her credit card activity. He wished he could take away their pain. All he could do was offer his sympathy. He leaned forward and looked at their faces. "No matter what happens…I want you to know how sorry I am you are going through this right now. It doesn't matter how old Susan is; she's still your child."

✳ ✳ ✳

From what she could tell, the Cactus Inn had only eight rooms. One large office at the end, which likely doubled as a residence for the motel manager. A small row of rooms followed, numbered 1–8. Steve checked them into the motel. She walked Libby through the parking lot as she phoned Dr. Cohen's office. The call went to an after-hours receptionist who told her a different physician was on-call for the holiday weekend. All the receptionist could do was pass the message to the on-call doctor. It wasn't ideal. But it was better than nothing. There were no guarantees the on-call doctor would pass the message to Dr. Cohen.

Once Steve had the key, he waved her over to room number three. The room was small, and the furniture was worn and outdated. *At least it looks clean.* She found that thought comforting. After moving their belongings in the room, Steve pulled her close to his chest. "I love you, Anne. They'll find her. Just wait and see; they'll find her, safe and sound."

She wished she shared Steve's optimism. She didn't. She didn't know how to explain it, but she couldn't sense Susan's presence anymore. It felt like a dark curtain covered Susan, separating her from the rest of the world. At least, that was the image that kept coming to the forefront of her mind. She kept trying to push the picture of Susan shrouded in darkness away from her thoughts. All she could do was wait: wait for the detective to give them some answers, wait for Dr. Cohen to return their call.

She didn't bother unpacking. In the morning, they'd head back to Susan's house. By the time she dressed into pajamas and brushed her teeth, Steve and Libby were already asleep on the bed. She crawled in next to them and closed her eyes.

She woke at sunrise. Her neck was stiff, and her head ached. She looked around the room. *It wasn't a bad dream. Susan is missing!* With that realization, another wave of sadness washed over her. Her stomach turned in response. *When was the last time we ate?* Steve stirred in the bed and opened his eyes.

"Are you hungry?" He asked.

She nodded, knowing she needed to eat to keep up her strength.

"I'll run over to the diner across the street and pick up some food."

"Okay."

Soon after Steve arrived back at the motel, Detective Hargrove phoned and asked them to return to the house. There, they rehashed the events from the previous day.

* * *

Dr. Cohen's partner phoned him Friday morning and told him the sheriff's office needed to speak with him about a missing person. His heart sank. A list of likely patients scrolled through his mind. When he further learned Susan's parents were trying to reach him, he wasn't surprised. Her name was at the top of his list.

He went into the office, reviewed his notes, and phoned Susan's pharmacy. Her medications were on a schedule for monthly refills. His stomach clenched when the pharmacist told him she hadn't picked up her last prescription. He'd sensed Susan was lying about her medications during their previous session. That's why he'd probed. Was there something else he missed? It was late morning by the time he returned the detective's call. He took a deep breath as he dialed the number.

"Detective Hargrove," the voice on the phone answered.

"Good afternoon, detective. This is Dr. Cohen. I'm returning your call."

"Thanks for returning my call, doc. I wanted to talk to you about one of your patients; she's missing."

"Susan Green."

"That's right." He could sense a bit of surprise in the detective's voice.

"Her parents called our answering service. I'll give them a call after speaking with you."

"They're pretty shaken up. I'm sure they'd appreciate hearing from you. Could you hold for a moment? Need to get my notes." For a moment, he heard the rustle of papers. When the detective returned, he read off each of Susan's medications. "I wanted you to know there's a mismatch between her prescriptions and the number of pills in the bottles."

"I can't say that I'm surprised. When I phoned the pharmacy this morning, I learned she hadn't picked up her last refill."

"Her parents said there hadn't been a problem with her taking her medications before, so this is a behavior change—yes?"

"Yes, it's completely out of Susan's character."

"I got the impression from her parents that she's a pretty disciplined person. But in situations like these, it makes you wonder; if she's doing one thing against her nature, could she do other things?"

"Like what?"

"Runaway? Hitchhike?"

"I'm concerned about the discrepancies in her medications; so, I can't say for certain she wouldn't run away. But would she hitchhike? I don't know why she'd need to; she has a car."

"That's the thing, doc. Her car was found in her garage. The key is missing. I went through the house with her parents. It looks like the only thing missing is her purse."

His mind raced. Was she anxious enough to run away? And if so, why not take her car? Would she walk away without taking her belongings? A sinking feeling spread through the middle of his stomach. He couldn't shake the feeling the detective was going down the wrong path.

"Are you certain someone didn't take her?" he asked.

"We are considering that possibility. But–." The detective abruptly paused.

"But what?" he asked.

"Nothing. I'm just trying to get a handle on your patient's mental state," the detective continued.

He sensed the evasiveness in the detective's voice. He was holding something back. For a moment, he felt like a dog with a bone, fixated on every word the detective had said.

"You asked me if Susan would hitchhike? Why did you ask that?"

After a moment's long pause, the detective finally spoke: "We have a possible lead. I was just heading out to investigate it when you called. I can't have it repeated to her parents because I don't know for certain it'll pan out."

"I wouldn't say anything."

The detective sighed, then continued, "It might help me to run it by you. It's why I asked about hitchhiking. Susan's parents said hitchhiking would be completely out of her nature. But, given the inconsistencies with her medications, I was just wondering-."

"If it were something she'd do?"

"Exactly. One of our technicians saw a woman matching Susan's description hitchhiking alongside the highway. When you consider the time her dog was found, the timeframe matches up."

A wave of hope washed over him. "He's certain it was Susan?"

"Here's the thing. Folks living around here know that's a pretty sketchy area. You don't typically stop unless you're picking up a hitchhiker, looking for drugs, or a prostitute. Our technician said he probably wouldn't have noticed the woman if it weren't for the bloody scratches on her lower legs. He thought the woman might be hurt, so he pulled off the side of the road. As he got out of his car, a truck pulled up alongside the woman. He figured the person in the truck was stopping to help her, so he went on his way. He's pretty upset; he wishes he would have stopped. But I told him we don't even know if it was Susan. It could have been someone else, someone who knew the person in the truck. Given the notoriety of the place, it doesn't sound like somewhere she'd run off to unless..."

"Unless she wasn't in her right mind? That's what you're trying to say—
—isn't it?"

"Well, we know she wasn't taking her medications as prescribed. So,
I'm just wondering if you think it's a possibility?"

His stomach clenched again. Everything kept coming back to her
medications. If only he could go back to his last appointment with Susan.
Would she still be missing if he'd done something differently? All he could
do now was try to help the detective. "Given the fact she wasn't taking her
medications as prescribed, I think anything might be possible. I will keep
what you told me in confidence. I don't want to give Susan's parents false
hope, especially if your lead doesn't pan out. Do you have any other
questions for me?"

"Not right now. But I'll call you if I think of something."

"Will you call me if you find her?"

"Well, we'd call her parents. But I'm sure they'd call you. I've got to
run, doc."

"Thank you, detective. Goodbye." He laid down the phone and wiped
a tear from his eye. A sinking feeling moved through his body. *I failed her! I
should have realized she wasn't taking her meds. Detective Hargrove knows it too.*

* * *

Once he'd given the detective the information he needed, he made a
call to Susan's parents.

Anne answered on the first ring. "Thank you for calling us back, Dr.
Cohen. I'm putting you on speakerphone. Steve's right here."

He needed to let them know about her medications. "Before I phoned
you, I called the pharmacy." He paused for a moment. "Susan didn't pick
up her last refill."

Steve's voice interrupted the brief silence. "We know. We found her
prescription bottles in the medicine cabinet. The counts were all off. She
hadn't even packed them for her trip to see us. We know she saw you a few
weeks back. Did she give you any indication she wasn't taking them?"

He closed his eyes and hung his head. He suspected she wasn't taking them as prescribed. He'd asked her twice. She'd taken her medications faithfully for ten years. There was no reason to think she'd lie about something so important. "I asked her about her medications. It's a question I ask her every time I see her. She told me she was taking them as prescribed. I had no reason to doubt her."

"I'm sorry, Dr. Cohen. I didn't mean to imply anything."

"No apology needed. I know you're just covering all the bases."

Anne spoke up. "I talked to her the day before she went missing." Her voice cracked, then trailed off.

Steve interjected, "Anne thinks she sounded stressed when she spoke with her. Apparently, the neighbors left for a trip and asked her to watch their home. We think that would have put too much pressure on her. What do you think?"

"Well, when Susan and I last spoke, she mentioned most of the houses on her street were still vacant. I know that bothered her." He glanced down at the notes. "From what I recall, Susan was spending a lot of time with the neighbor, Mary. Apparently, she was home with a sprained ankle. I got the impression Susan didn't want Mary to go back to work. At least, not until more people moved onto the street. If they left town and she was home by herself—."

"I should have insisted she come up on Wednesday!" Anne cried out.

The anguish in her voice crushed his heart. *I'm the professional. I should have seen this coming.* "Anne, please…you can't blame yourself. None of us knew how out of control she'd become." He called out, desperate to apply the words to his own feelings of despair.

"We talked with the detective this morning. He asked us if Susan had ever run away or if she'd ever hitchhiked. He explained how irrational her thoughts could become if she didn't take her meds right. He thinks her anxiety might have been out of control. What do you think, Dr. Cohen?" Steve asked.

He paused for a moment, running through his thoughts. Finally, he spoke: "The detective is right about her medication. Any fears would likely be exaggerated if she'd stopped her medications. Then there's the stress and anxiety of being alone on the street, watching the neighbor's house. When I last saw Susan, I had the impression she wasn't sleeping well. A lack of sleep can also increase anxiety. We talked about things she could do to get rest. I gave her a handout, and I told her she could call me for any concerns. I also offered to see her between appointments if needed."

"You've taken such good care of her through the years," Anne said.

Although there was nothing he could do for Susan, he could help her parents. "Anne, Steve…I want you to know you can reach out to me at any time. My office manager is trying to set us up with virtual counseling. I've been vehemently opposed to doing it. But I'll make an exception for you, if you feel it would help."

"Thank you, Dr. Cohen. I think we might take you up on that offer. We'll call your office to set something up. We'll also call you if we hear anything about Susan."

"Oh, thank you. I would appreciate it if you would. Goodbye."

"Goodbye."

Part II - Repentance

1 Corinthians 10:12
No, but the sacrifices of pagans are offered to demons,
not to God, and I do not want you to be participants with demons.

CHAPTER 23

Saturday evening. After a day's long drive from Modesto, Norm pulled into the cul-de-sac. Anne and Steve's car was parked in Susan's driveway. "Looks like Susan's parents are visiting."

"She never mentioned it. But that's nice," Mary replied.

After unpacking the car, he held up the small bag of souvenirs and chocolate they'd gathered as a thank you for Susan. "I'm heading next door to drop this off and pick up the key. Do you want to come?"

"Yes."

Together, he and Mary walked to Susan's house. Anne answered their knock.

"You're finally home."

Norm sensed a coldness in her voice. *Finally home?* They'd told Susan they were coming home on Saturday. It was a full-day drive from Modesto. Was there a miscommunication? Didn't she realize they'd be driving most of the day? As his mind pondered the reason for the strange statement, Mary took the bag from his hand.

"Yes, after that long drive, it's nice to be home. We picked up some souvenirs for Susan to thank her for watching the house. Could we see her?"

Anne's lips quivered, and tears welled in her eyes. At that moment, Steve approached, holding Libby in his arms.

"Susan's missing," he said.

Missing! Norm felt as though the breath had been knocked from his lungs. A wave of dizziness crashed down on him. He reached for the wall to hold himself upright.

"Missing?" He whispered as he gazed into Steve's eyes. He knew what it was like to have a missing daughter. There were periods when Rose disappeared. Only to return later, looking for money or food. Susan's life was on a different path than Rose's. He couldn't shake the feeling something terrible happened. *Did she confront someone trying to break into our home?*

Mary's voice interrupted his thoughts. "What do you mean— Susan's missing?"

Steve opened the door wider. "Please come in. We can talk about this in the family room."

As they passed the kitchen, he noticed open cabinets and newspapers and boxes littering the kitchen island. "You're packing up the kitchen?" Mary asked.

Anne sighed heavily, then shook her head.

Steve waved them over to the couch. "Please sit down," he said. He placed Libby on the floor. The young dog curled up at his feet. "We spoke with Detective Hargrove a few hours ago. He's the lead detective on the case. He says they have a credible lead. If he's right, it sounds like Susan ran away."

"Ran away?" Mary asked.

Steve nodded.

"I don't understand," Mary said.

Mary voiced the same thoughts running through his mind. Running away seemed entirely out of Susan's character. *There has to be a mistake.*

"We're struggling to understand it ourselves. We both thought everything was going well. Susan's been so disciplined for years. We never fathomed she'd stop taking her meds."

Mary interjected, "Meds?"

Anne nodded. "She's been on them since she was a teenager." She looked off in the distance. "It's just so strange. She's never had a problem taking them." She turned back. "What's worse is that she lied to her doctor about it."

As he thought about Anne's words, he remembered the cold reception they received at the front door. *You're finally home*—a phrase delivered with a tone of accusation, not relief. "Is there something else bothering you? Something you want to say?"

After a moment, she looked up and nodded.

Steve held onto her arm. "I think we're good."

Anne turned towards Steve, then gently pulled her arm from his grasp. "He asked," she said as she turned back to Norm. "I don't know how to say this, so I'll just say it. I'm trying not to be angry with you."

Mary reeled back. "Angry with us? Why?"

Anne took a deep breath before responding, "Asking Susan to watch your house while you went on vacation put too much stress on her."

Anne's words pierced his heart. *Did he and Mary inadvertently cause Susan's disappearance?*

Steve interrupted, "Anne, we've been through this. There were likely a million things weighing on Susan. Watching Norm and Mary's home was just one of those things, a small one. Besides, there was no way Mary or Norm could have known about Susan's history unless she said something to them."

Mary slowly shook her head. "She never said a word. She visited me almost every day. I had no way of knowing she was on medications."

"If only we'd seen her in person, I know we would have realized something was wrong with her. You saw her every day. You didn't notice anything that concerned you?" Anne asked.

He replayed the interaction he had with Susan when he asked her to watch their home. Was Anne right to be angry? Was he so consumed with excitement about the trip he'd glossed over Susan's outward anxiety? *I should have protected her, but I let her down, just like I let Rose down.* Tears welled in his eyes as he looked into Anne's eyes. "Susan seemed nervous about being here on the street alone. I sensed that, and I'm sorry. We could have asked more questions. And, in hindsight, we should have asked someone else to watch our house."

One by one, tears slid down Anne's face. "Thank you," she whispered. She paused for a moment as the look on her face softened. "I shouldn't have said anything. Steve's right. There was no way you could have known about her history."

He wanted to know what evidence the detective uncovered that made him think she'd run away. "You said there's a credible lead. What is it?" he asked.

Steve leaned forward. "They now have two witnesses who saw a woman matching Susan's description hitchhiking by the highway."

"Hitchhiking?" he leaned back and began shaking his head.

Steve nodded. "The woman was wearing blue shorts, a blue-and- white-striped long-sleeved shirt, and tennis shoes. Susan has a shirt like that; it's one of her favorites. It's missing from her closet, and she didn't pack it. So there's a good chance she was wearing it when she disappeared."

"Oh, I know the shirt you're talking about," Mary interjected.

So what if the clothing matched something Susan liked to wear? There were likely hundreds of people who had a blue-and-white- striped shirt in their closet. "But are they sure it's Susan? I can't imagine she'd be out by the highway, let alone hitchhike."

"Both witnesses said the woman had scratches on her lower legs. It's one of the reasons they remembered her."

"Scratches?" he asked.

Steve shook his head. We're still trying to figure that out. Libby had scratches and small puncture wounds on her back. Thankfully, the neighbor who found Libby bathed her and cleaned the wounds right away. The vet thinks a small animal attacked Libby or that she got tangled up in a thorny bush. He gave us an antibiotic cream to put on the wounds. I think Susan might have stepped in to help Libby. At least, if she were the woman on the road, it would account for the scratches on her legs."

Someone found Libby? Wasn't she in the house? He knew there was no way Susan would take Libby outside without a leash.

Before he could ask anything further, Steve continued, "There's also video footage from a gas station near the highway. It's grainy. But it shows a woman walking past the gas station. She's coming from the direction of the subdivision. Detective Hargrove said the woman was alone. So he thinks she walked to the highway willingly. She isn't carrying anything. So he's wondering if she dropped her purse along the way. He had a small search party combing the stretch of land between here and the highway looking for it today."

"It sounds like they're pretty sure it's her," Mary whispered.

Steve shook his head. "As I said, the footage is grainy." He reached for

Anne's hand. Tears welled in his eyes, and in a cracked voice, he whispered, "But we're hoping it's her."

"But you're packing her things. I don't understand," Mary said.

Steve had regained his composure. He spoke again in a voice filled with conviction: "I know how strange this looks. Susan's only been gone a few days, and we've already decided she needs to sell this house. But the truth is, she can't be alone, no matter what's happened. She stopped taking her meds. Both the detective and Dr. Cohen think it played a role in her disappearance. She needs to be back under our roof, under our supervision. We're hopeful a judge will grant us guardianship over Susan. We're certain Dr. Cohen will support us in this decision."

If he were in Steve's shoes, he'd do the same thing. Although there was a difference between Susan's situation and Rose's, he knew the risk of relapse. Rose overdosed. It was likely Susan would run away again.

For the next hour, Anne and Steve shared details of Susan's life. He gasped when Steve spoke of the time he'd discovered Susan after her failed teenage suicide attempt. With each revelation, it seemed more probable she'd runoff. But why? What was the breaking point? What happened while they were away? As he listened to Steve relive the house tour with the sheriff, the message Susan left on their answering machine played in his head. *Have you seen anything unusual in the cornfield?* An overwhelming sense of guilt washed over him. Instead of leaving a note, he should have called Susan the morning he and Mary left for California. *Did she see those red eyes? Is that why she ran away? Or did she wander into the field despite his warnings?*

Once Anne and Steve finished speaking, Mary held onto Anne's hand. "I will pray for her safe return. I understand why you want to move Susan home. We aren't going anywhere. We'll always keep an eye out for her, and when she does come back, I'm hoping she'll knock on our door."

Anne gave a small smile. "Thank you."

✳ ✳ ✳

"The nerve of that woman!" Mary's voice raised as she slammed their front door. "She's blaming us for Susan's disappearance."

"I don't think she's blaming us, necessarily. She's worried."

"You heard her, Norm!" Mary shook her head side to side, and in a mocking voice, asked, "Didn't you notice anything?" She paused briefly before continuing, "She's acting as though we should have known Susan was off her medicine. How could we know she was off her medicine when we didn't know she was taking it in the first place?"

He closed his eyes and took a few deep breaths. In truth, their vacation had done little more than place a Band-Aid over the gushing wound of their marriage. He was at a crossroads. Agree with Mary, and the rest of the night would be pleasant, or confront her and face the potential wrath that would follow. He chose to go straight down the middle of the argument. "You're right; we didn't know about Susan's history. It isn't fair of Anne to blame us for asking Susan to watch the house." He paused, then continued, "But we both sensed something wasn't right. We sensed she wasn't sleeping well. And, the message she left on the answering machine, asking us if we'd seen anything in the cornfield. I think she was afraid."

"Afraid of what? Corn?"

For the past week, he'd convinced himself any fears of the cornfield were all in his head. But with Susan missing, he had to face the reality he might have been right all along. Mary appeared adamant she never saw anything unusual in the field. He was confident she'd change her mind once he told her what he'd seen.

"Do you remember that terrible storm we had in early June?"

"The one that knocked out the power?"

He nodded. "You asked me to check on Susan."

"I remember."

"Well, something happened that night."

Her eyes widened. "What do you mean 'something happened'?"

He walked over to his recliner. If he were going to relive that night, he'd have to do it sitting down. Mary sat and then leaned forward in her recliner. A puzzled look covered her face.

"Okay. You remember sending me to Susan's house."

"I do."

"On the way home, I noticed a mist in the field."

"I remember the fog."

"Exactly, Mary. By the time you saw it the next morning, it had consolidated into a thick fog. But the night of the storm, when it first came up from the ground, it was a mist." He pointed to the sliding glass door. "I stood right there, watching it."

"I'm not sure where this is going?"

He paused for a moment. *Slow down and breathe.* The more he steadied his voice, the greater the chance she'd listen.

"I sensed there was something out there in the corn, watching me." He shuddered. "Then I glanced up and saw it."

Mary leaned forward. "What did you see?"

"Red eyes."

She leaned back, then glanced up and down his frame as if doing a quick assessment of his mental status. After a moment, she pursed her lips together and gently shook her head. "I'm sure you saw something. But, if I had to guess, I'd say you saw a coyote. You heard what Steve said. Susan blocked Libby's doggy door to keep her safe from coyotes."

A warmth crept up his neck and face. She was belittling a terrifying experience. "It wasn't a coyote. You don't understand. I've tried for weeks to get that image out of my head, Mary! Don't you see what I'm getting at? It had red eyes, and whatever was out in the field was as tall as me. If I saw it, maybe Susan did too! Maybe that's the reason she ran away!"

"Do you hear how crazy that sounds?"

His shoulders sank. He took a deep breath and shook his head. How could he make her understand? For weeks, he pretended the night of the storm never happened and would have continued to do so if Susan hadn't vanished.

Mary's voice interrupted his thoughts. "Did you say anything to Susan that would make her think something was in that field?"

He shook his head.

"And, the note you wrote, just before we left, you're sure you didn't write anything that might have frightened her?"

He knew where the conversation was headed. The blame was slowly shifting in his direction.

"The note was fine. I wrote that you hadn't seen anything other than the crows in the field."

Mary nodded, seemingly satisfied with his response. Then turned and looked out the sliding glass door, onto the field. A flicker of hope filled his being. *She's thinking about what I said. She's thinking about those red eyes.*

The small glimmer of hope faded when she looked back.

"I have to call Bernice. We need to activate the prayer chain at church. We need to pray for Susan's safe return. Will you join me in prayer for Susan?"

Another crossroad. If he prayed, Mary would be happy. But he knew if he did, it would be a charade. Susan's disappearance hadn't brought him back to his faith; if anything, it had strengthened the divide. Another way God let him down. He glanced down and shook his head.

"Seriously, Norm! You aren't going to pray for Susan's safe return." She leaped from the recliner and stormed down the hallway. "I'm calling Bernice."

He hung his head, feeling physically and emotionally depleted. The one person whom he'd counted on to believe him had scoffed at his revelation. If Mary didn't believe him, who would? Bob? Dave? They teased him when he asked about the fog. Maybe one of his co-workers? Would anyone believe him if he told them about the night of the storm? Tears welled in his eyes. For the first time in months, he felt truly alone.

* * *

The next morning, Norm awoke in his recliner. Minus the fitful naps, he'd spent most of the night gazing at the freshly harvested land behind his home. Mary stood over him, dressed and ready for church.

"You never made it to bed."

"I'm sorry. I fell asleep out here."

"I wish you'd go with me to church. It's not too late to get ready. I sent Bernice pictures of Susan from my phone. She's printing flyers and is organizing a group of members to hand them out at the businesses downtown. The more people handing out flyers the better."

"You heard what Anne and Steve said; the detective thinks she ran away."

"It doesn't hurt to spread the word. Maybe the detective is wrong. Even if he's isn't wrong, and Susan was on the highway, maybe someone will remember seeing her. We have to do something, Norm. We can't just sit here."

He pointed out the sliding glass door. "I won't be sitting here. I'll be out there, combing that field."

Mary's brow furrowed. For a moment, it looked as though they'd fully rehash the fight from last night. Thankfully, Mary didn't have time for an all-out brawl. Instead, she curtly shook her head and delivered a parting blow.

"You won't find Susan in that field. If you truly wanted to find her, you'd pass out flyers with the rest of us."

She turned and walked away. As she left the house, she yelled out, "I'm going to Bernice's house for lunch after we hand out the flyers! I won't be home until later this afternoon!"

He closed his eyes and took a few deep breaths. It was official. Any goodwill he'd gained on their vacation evaporated as soon as they returned home from Susan's house last night. Judging from the tone in Mary's voice this morning, it wasn't coming back anytime soon.

CHAPTER 24

Weeks passed since Susan's disappearance. Each morning, Tobias woke with a sense of guilt. Dozens of missing person flyers hung in storefronts around town. The sight of Susan's face staring at him through the windows of businesses deepened his remorse.

Sarah told him she worried the guilt he felt would take an irreparable toll on his mental and physical health. As they sat together on the back porch, she voiced her concern again. "I'm worried. Please let me make an appointment for you. Maybe with a psychologist? You need to talk to someone."

He angrily shook his head. *A psychologist!* "What would I say, Sarah? I feel responsible for the girl who went missing on the Fourth of July. Then what?"

"I don't know what you'd say...I just think talking to someone may help you feel better."

He paused for a moment, then in a lowered voice, he said, "Have you ever once considered I deserve to feel this way? Because I have. I feel like I should be in jail, and I know I'm going to hell."

"Please don't say that," she pleaded as tears filled her eyes. "All we know for sure was that she was in the field at some point, and now she's gone. The sheriff seems confident she was the hitchhiker spotted near the highway on the Fourth of July." She paused, then leaned forward and grabbed his hand. "Maybe, you could talk with Pastor Cummings. If you don't feel comfortable talking to him, come to church with the boys and me. Even if you don't talk to anyone right now, I think just being in the

171

church will help you heal. It's where we all belong, as a family."

He thought about telling Pastor Cummings his family's secret. But he knew, deep down, he couldn't do it. *He'll think I'm crazy. Or, if he's heard the rumors about my grandfather and great-uncle, he'll know they're all true!* Talking to someone wasn't an option. But one thing Sarah said rang true: going to church. He knew deep inside that the only thing that could heal his heart was God. He gently raised her hand to his lips, kissing her fingertips. He kept her hand close to his lips as he looked her in the eye. "I'm going to turn my life around, Sarah. I am. I don't know how or even why you've put up with me for all these years. But I'm grateful you've stayed."

"You're a good man. Inside here." She placed her other hand on his chest. "In here...you're good, and you're kind."

Tears welled up in his eyes. Sarah and his sons displayed a palpable devotion to God. He'd been a spectator, watching them come and go to church on Sundays. It was time to start a new family legacy, a legacy that put faith in God at the heart of their family. It was time to repent, turn away from the life he was born into, and instead devote the rest of his life to God.

"We have to tell the boys what happened," he said.

She nodded. "Soon, but not now. We need to get rid of the items in that room first."

* * *

After telling Sarah about the summoning ritual and the evil spirit, Tobias gave her the key to the room. The sheer act of giving away the key made his body feel lighter. Sarah didn't talk about the room. He surmised she worried the conversation would deepen his remorse. Despite not saying a word, he noticed she spent more time in the alcove than all the years of their marriage combined. He suspected she was quietly searching for the room. *It's hard to find, even when you know where to look. But she's tenacious; I'm sure she'll eventually find it.*

Labor Day was approaching. Daniel, James, and Charles made plans to drive to Payson for a long holiday weekend. John and Kate planned to visit Kate's parents in Texas. Although Tobias hated the thought of going into the room under the stairs, he knew the timing couldn't have been better. He wasn't sure if Sarah had found the secret room already or if she even wanted to see it. But with everyone headed out of town, he thought it would be a good time to broach the subject with Sarah. "I thought this weekend might be a good time to clear out…"

"Yes," she interrupted.

"Yes?"

"You're talking about the room. Right?"

He nodded.

"I was hoping you'd feel up to it. Ever since I found out about that room, I've wanted to clear it out. I'm sorry, Tobias, but I hate knowing those things are in our home."

✳ ✳ ✳

As soon as everyone left the house, Sarah followed Tobias into the alcove. He held a battery-operated lantern. The lantern's bright light fully illuminated the wooden panels. She scanned the walls. Even under the intensity of the lantern, all the panels looked the same. Carved into the center was a geometrical design that reminded her of a Chinese puzzle box. A floral pattern bordered the geometrical design. She held out the key. "I haven't found the door yet."

He nodded and took the key. She watched as he moved to an unexpected area of the wall. *It's purposefully placed off-center.* He ran his fingers over the panels, stopping lower on the wall than she expected. He put the key into one of the gaps in the geometrical shapes. A loud click filled the alcove.

"I can't believe I never noticed it before," she whispered.

He pushed the door open and entered the room. She followed. The lingering smell of burnt spices hung thick in the cool air. She wrinkled her nose in response. He raised the lantern, lighting up strange symbols on the wall. "What do those symbols represent?"

He shook his head. "I honestly don't know." He pointed to the book on the desk. "They're also drawn in the book." He looked around the room. "All I know for certain is that I want to paint over them."

She glanced at the rest of the room: a small table, a black candle, book, and bowl. A wave of relief washed over her, clearing out the room would be easier than she thought.

He moved to one side of the table and lifted it. "It's not too heavy. Can you help me take it to the backyard?"

She nodded and moved closer. He removed the candle and bowl from the table and set them on the floor. Gingerly, she reached for the spell book and placed it on the ground. Knowing it held a spell powerful enough to summon a spirit simultaneously filled her with fear and awe. *What other secrets lie within the pages of this book?*

Together, they carried the table through the kitchen, setting it down on the back porch. While he brought the paint and supplies into the room, she placed the book, candle, and bowl outside onto the wooden table. In the sunlight, the spell book appeared smaller but no less powerful. She examined the outside of the book, deciding whether to open it. After a moment's hesitation, curiosity overtook her. She picked up the book and carefully thumbed through the pages. Tobias was right. The symbols in the book resembled those painted on the wall. The entire book was written in a language she'd never seen. One section appeared to contain recipes. Written above and below each list of ingredients was a paragraph. *Are these instructions or spells?* In honesty, it didn't matter. As she stood there, studying each page, she was struck with a reality she couldn't escape. The small book was filled with unspeakable evil. She shuddered. The book fell onto the table in an audible thud.

Next, she turned her attention to the weathered bowl. The center was charred, and the insides were streaked with dried blood. She shook her head in disgust. *So much evil in my home! How could I be so blind!*

She returned to the room. Tobias had placed a drop cloth on the floor and poured the paint into the rolling pan. The room was small, and the ceiling wasn't too high. They'd be finished in no time.

He held up two rolling brushes. "Which one do you want?"

One roller was the typical one you'd find at any hardware store. The second one had a long wooden pole allowing it to reach the top of the wall.

She took the smaller one and began rolling the thick white paint over the wall's bottom sections. Some of the drawings on the wall resembled distorted letters and geometric shapes. Others looked like common everyday things: moon, ladder, and eye. She found the tiny whirl of the roller moving up and down the wall soothing. After finishing the first coat, they held hands and looked around the room. The symbols were entirely hidden beneath the paint, making the room look larger. "This is our clean slate," he whispered.

She smiled and nodded. Never again would evil enter their home.

"Are you okay doing the second coat yourself?" he asked. "I don't even think we need it, but it would be nice to know everything is fully covered. If you can do that, I'll start chopping up the table.

"I've got this. I'll put the paint away when I'm done."

* * *

While Sarah finished painting, Tobias chopped the table and wooden bowl into small pieces. The way the axe reverberated in his hands was cathartic. Each time the axe blade struck wood, his spirit became lighter. Bit by bit, he erased a tiny piece of his family's evil, bringing him closer to goodness, closer to God.

Sarah approached just as he placed the last piece of wood into the firepit. "I've just finished. How's the room?" he asked.

"I've put away the supplies. The walls look fresh and clean."

He smiled and nodded, then threw the spell book on top of the wood. *Soon this will be nothing but ash.* He picked up a can of lighter fluid and held it over the firepit. As he began to squeeze the can, a heaviness enveloped him, squeezing his chest and stealing his breath. His hand shook wildly in response.

She put her hand on his arm. "Tobias…are you okay?"

He shook his head and looked away. *What's wrong with me?* His mind, his heart—they cried out for him to set the firepit ablaze. But as he doused the items from the summoning room, the rest of his body screamed for him to stop! Was it the remnants of his ancestor's evil blood coursing through his veins that kept him from lighting the fire? Or was he fearful, knowing the evil would come for his family if it returned? He had no way to comprehend what would happen if he burned the book? Would it keep the evil away or cause it to return sooner? Maybe even tonight? In truth, he hadn't fully contemplated the ramifications of his plan.

"Tobias, what's wrong?"

He took a deep breath and curtly shook his head. "Nothing. I have to do this!" he said it with force meant to convince himself.

Her voice softened. "You know we're doing the right thing."

He looked into her eyes and saw her determination and inner strength. He smiled. "I'm glad you are right here, beside me." He felt his strength return and his panic fade. Jonas and Lukas may have been taken off guard, but he knew better. He'd be ready to fight if the spirit returned. He raised the can, dousing the book and the wood in lighter fluid. He pulled out a book of matches, struck one, and threw it into the firepit.

Whoosh! Flames engulfed the leather binding of the spell book. The pages eerily curled up as if trying to escape the heat. Then, like a small animal trying to break free from a trap, the book twisted within the fire. The ear-piercing shrill the book made as it burned sent them reeling backward. His heart pounded within his chest.

He didn't know what burning flesh smelled like, but he couldn't help thinking it probably smelled like the book. Between the smell and the sound, it seemed as though the book was being burnt alive. And the thick smoke erupting from the firepit far exceeded the amount that should have come from the pages. The black smoke churned and rose, drifting back towards the house. The shrieking sound lowered once the entire book was fully ablaze. It was replaced with the sounds of whirling flames and intermittent popping as the fire moved through the wooden bowl and table.

Sarah reached out and held onto his arm. "Tobias, the sound the book made! I've never heard anything like that in my life!"

He nodded, glancing from her ashen face to the fire pit. The book lay on top of the wood, transformed into nothing more than a pile of ashes.

⁂ ⁂ ⁂

Once the fire lowered to smoldering embers, Sarah wrapped her arm around his waist and placed her head on his shoulder. "You did it."

He wrapped his arm around her and pulled her closer, "We did it. I mean it, Sarah. I couldn't have done this without you."

She smiled and kissed him on the cheek. "I'll make us something to eat."

"I'll be inside soon. Let me clean all this up first."

The events of the morning had stimmed their appetite. Instead of making a large meal, she whipped up a pan of scrambled eggs, serving it with toast. Once everything was on the table, she called out to Tobias. A few moments later, he entered the kitchen.

She'd sensed an immediate difference in him. Finally shaken from the melancholy fog he had wallowed in all summer, his mood seemed lighter and more carefree. Her heart leaped when he smiled, then laughed at something she said. She'd missed the sound of his laughter. After lunch, they stood at the sink, washing dishes together. His hand brushed, then lingered, against hers as she handed him dish after dish. She sensed the passion growing inside him. His desire for her was something she hadn't felt in months. After the last plate was put away, he pulled her into his arms. Softly, he twirled the hair framing her face around his finger. Then he leaned forward and passionately kissed her mouth. Her heart fluttered as she pressed her body against his. His lips moved onto her neck. She closed her eyes and savored the warm sensation spreading through her body. He placed his lips against her ear and whispered, "Let's go upstairs."

Consumed with a passion they hadn't experienced in months, they spent the rest of the morning making love. In the afterglow, she lay against him, softly twirling her fingers through the hair on his chest. She wanted to stay there, falling asleep by his side, but her thirst drove her out of bed. She tossed a robe around her body. "I need a glass of water. Can I bring you back anything?"

He shook his head, then closed his eyes. "I'm good. I just want to close my eyes for a little while and rest."

She stood there for a few moments, studying his face. He seemed at peace. She hadn't seen that look since high school. At the time, neither of them knew about his family's dark secret. They were both innocents, young and in love. Her heart leaped at the thought of a fresh start. Not just for Tobias, but their marriage, their family. She smiled and kissed him on the forehead. "I'll be right back."

* * *

In the kitchen, Sarah took a glass from the cabinet and filled it with water. As she approached the staircase, she noticed the lantern's light covering the walls of the alcove. *I forgot to shut off the lantern.* As she entered the alcove, she glanced into the small room. The glass of water fell from her hand, shattering onto the wooden floor below. A blood-curling scream escaped her throat.

✳ ✳ ✳

Tobias lay beneath a thin sheet with his eyes closed. The pillow and bed beneath him cradled him in comfort. It wasn't just physical comfort. Despite all the darkness, Sarah still loved him. She hadn't only stayed; she helped rid their home of evil. For the first time in his adult life, he felt truly at ease.

Relaxed, he allowed his mind to drift into the foggy state between wakefulness and dreams. A few moments later, the sound of shattering glass, coupled with Sarah's scream, sent him bolting from the bed and down the stairs.

At the bottom of the stairs, he turned and saw Sarah in the alcove. Her eyes were wide and filled with fear. She pointed a shaking finger towards the small room. "They came back!"

Cold fear gripped his heart. He sprinted to the doorway and looked inside of the room. "You're sure you fully painted over these?" He knew the answer. He'd only asked the question because he couldn't believe his eyes.

"You saw it yourself, Tobias. One coat covered everything. We added a second coat to be sure. I'm telling you—those symbols were gone!"

Slowly, he sank to the floor, placed his head into his hands, and sobbed. He'd assumed burning the book and other items from the summoning room would put an end to the evil. He was wrong. The symbols had returned, darker and seemingly more powerful. The way they clung to the walls, like thick dark mold, confirmed his worse fears—the evil wouldn't go quietly.

"I don't know what to do," he whispered.

Sarah clasped her hands together and brought them to her lips. In trembling steps, she paced the small alcove. "I think we should call Pastor

Cummings."

Sarah was right. They could'nt do this alone. To rid themselves of the evil, they needed the Pastor's help. He looked into her eyes and nodded.

"I'll call him and ask him to come right away," Sarah said.

CHAPTER 25

In the weeks following Susan's disappearance, Norm combed the field behind their home while Mary joined search parties and hung flyers. His search of the area yielded nothing more than a handful of animal bones. Mary's search party teams fared no better.

When Susan disappeared, Mary and her friends hung flyers on light poles and most storefronts along Central Avenue. A missing person flyer also hung in the front of the hardware store. Each time Norm entered the hardware store, he glanced at the flyer with Susan's smiling face and felt a pang of guilt and sadness.

Over time, Arizona's summer monsoon storms faded, then washed away the flyers. One by one, they were taken down from the storefronts. Norm knew it wouldn't be long before someone removed the one hanging in the hardware store window.

Despite this certainty, when he glanced at the section of window where the flyer once hung and saw it had been replaced, his heart sank. He stood outside the store, unable to move forward. His body shook, lips trembled, then one by one, tears fell unabashed from his eyes. *She's gone!*

He took deep breaths, trying to regain his composure. It didn't help. He shook his head and stumbled to his car. He watched as people entered and left the store; many were laughing and smiling. A wave of anger crashed over him. It was like the whole community had given up on Susan, abandoned her memory.

Tap. Tap. He startled, then turned toward the passenger side window. Brody, a young employee of the store, stood at his window. His face was full of worry. "You okay, Norm?"

His mouth fell open, but no words escaped his lips. He glanced at his watch. *I've been sitting here for almost thirty minutes.* Then he realized the car was off, and it was the end of summer. Beads of sweat slid down his face. He wiped the back of his hand over his forehead, closed his eyes, and leaned back in his seat. He'd never missed a day of work without calling in. *What will Mike think?* He knew he was in no shape to engage customers. Still, he had to speak with Mike, offer some excuse for not showing up. He opened his eyes and looked out the car window. Brody was in a full sprint, running through the parking lot and into the hardware store. A few moments later, he ran out of the store, headed in Norm's direction. Mike followed closely behind, carrying a bottle of water.

Mike opened the passenger side door. "Hey, Norm, are you feeling okay?"

He stiffly nodded. "I'm sorry. I didn't come in today."

A look of compassion filled Mike's face. He sat on the passenger seat and handed him the bottle of water. "Do you want me to call someone? Your wife, maybe?"

He shook his head.

Mike grabbed at his tie and collar, loosening it. "Norm, it's hotter than Hades in here. Can you make it inside?"

Norm shook his head. "I'd rather stay here."

"Okay, but drink that water, and maybe start the car and run the A/C."

He nodded and started the car.

"Hey, Brody, could you run inside and let Margaret know I'll be out here for a while with Norm?"

"Sure."

Brody ran towards the store. Mike turned and looked at Norm again. "Do you want to talk?"

Another nod. After a moment, he spoke. "Do you remember the flyer in the window?"

"The one with the missing girl—she was your neighbor, right?"

"Uh-huh."

"Such a sad story, having a breakdown and running away."

Mike's words crushed him. Was it the way Susan would be forever remembered in this community? The broken girl who ran away. He looked around the parking lot for a moment, then continued. "Every time I saw the flyer hanging by the front door, it hurt my heart."

"But your wife asked us to put it up in the window?"

"Yes. I'm not saying this right. It hurt because I felt we'd never see her again. But on the flip side, seeing the flyer kept her memory alive. I don't know how to explain it."

"You didn't want people to forget she was still missing."

He nodded. "Yes. Every time I saw the flyer, I thought people were still thinking about her, cared about what happened to her."

Mike nodded his head in agreement. "And Margaret took the flyer down yesterday and put up the Labor Day flyer, so you feel like we've stopped thinking about her...is that what you're trying to say?"

A crushing pain radiated through his chest. Tears flowed freely. He nodded and buried his head in his hands.

Mike placed his hand on Norm's shoulder. "Oh, Norm, I'm so sorry. I didn't think about the impact that might have had on you. Go home. We'll look at this as a bereavement day. Alright? You're okay to drive?"

His red, swollen eyes locked with Mike's eyes, and he nodded.

"Okay, call me first thing in the morning and let me know if you need more time away?"

"Thank you," Norm whispered.

"Not a problem at all. When Brody first ran into the store, he told me he thought you had heatstroke. Honestly, I'm relieved you're physically okay."

He stayed within the speed limit, careful not to get a speeding ticket on Central Avenue. Then, as he passed Coldwater Liquors, an overwhelming craving hit him. Like a pebble dropped into a lake, the rippling effect of temptation spread through his entire body. Knowing how out of control his life had become in the aftermath of Rose's death, anytime, the craving lifted its ugly head; he'd stomp it down quickly —killing it before it could raise havoc in his life.

Don't stop! Drive home! The words rang out loudly in his head. Those words were soon drowned out. *You need it! Turn back!* He made it a few more blocks before the gnawing craving consumed him, sending him into the ever-constant line of patrons at the liquor store's drive-through window.

Knowing Mary would see the charge on their bank statement, he searched the car's compartments, looking for loose change. Between what he found in the car and the few bucks lining his wallet, he had just enough money to buy a small bottle of cheap vodka. And, by the time Mary returned from work that afternoon, he was numb.

CHAPTER 26

As they waited for Pastor Cummings, Sarah pleaded with Tobias. "Pastor Cummings needs to know everything so he can help us." He knew Sarah was right; the more the pastor knew the better. He nodded. "We'll tell him everything about the spell book and the spirit. We'll tell him about the animals who've wandered into the field." He thought about Susan. Telling the pastor he'd found Susan's purse and keys in the field wouldn't bring her back. And if reported to the sheriff, it might keep him from following up the lead on the young women spotted near the highway. "We'll tell him everything. Everything except finding Susan's purse and keys."

"But—"

"Listen, to me, Sarah. You said it yourself; the sheriff thinks someone picked Susan up along the highway. And since I didn't find her body, I believe she's alive and still out there. Telling anyone I found her purse and keys might change their investigation, keeping them from following up on that lead. It would also cast suspicion over our family and hurt you and the boys."

She began to say something but stopped and slowly nodded. "You're right."

* * *

Pastor Ted Cummings was eating his lunch and reviewing his upcoming sermon when Bernice sent a call from Sarah to his office. Sarah said there was an emergency at the farm but became evasive when he

184

pressed further. All he could ascertain was no one had been hurt. He packed up his sermon and left, passing Bernice's desk as he left the building. "I'm heading out for the rest of the day."

"Going out to the Smith farm?" she asked. "Sarah sounded pretty upset."

Over the past few months, he'd come to know a few things about living in a small town. Although the people were kind and generous to a fault, they also made a point of knowing each other's business. There was no way he would fuel any gossip. He turned away and raised his hand. "Enjoy the rest of the afternoon, Bernice. I'll see you Sunday morning."

The cryptic nature of Sarah's call sent his mind running through possible scenarios he'd find once he arrived at the farm. He remembered Sarah's visit to the church and her concerns over Tobias. Despite his willingness to come to the farm, Tobias never agreed to meet with him. Perhaps he'd had a change of heart.

The moment he pulled onto the farm, he sensed a heaviness in the air, as if someone placed a leaden blanket over his shoulders. *There's an evil here, weighing down this farm.* In that instant, he knew, whatever reason Sarah and Tobias summoned him to the house wasn't good. Before getting out of his car, he bowed his head and prayed for God's guidance.

Sarah answered the door before he knocked. "Pastor, thank God you're here. Please come inside."

"Your call sounded urgent. I came as quickly as I could."

He crossed the front door threshold and gazed at the immense wooden staircase. The heaviness he'd experienced outside paled in comparison to what he felt at the base of the stairs. In contrast to others who might be distracted by the staircase's beauty, he sensed it was a decoy, meant to draw eyes away from the home's evilness. He glanced at the room and alcove to the right of the stairs. Both were shrouded in a spiritual veil of darkness. The hairs on his neck stood up.

He turned back to Sarah. "You said you needed my help."

"We do. Please come. Tobias is in the kitchen."

He followed Sarah to the back of the house and into the kitchen. Unlike the heaviness he'd experienced upon entering the house, the kitchen radiated warmth—providing a small area of refuge to the home's inhabitants.

The aroma of fresh coffee filled the air. Tobias sat at one end of the large kitchen table. He looked visibly shaken.

"Tobias," he said as he extended his hand.

"Thank you for coming here on such short notice, pastor."

"Of course, I'm here to help you in any way I can."

✳ ✳ ✳

For the next hour, Tobias showed Pastor Cumming the summoning room, firepit, and cemetery as he shared his family's secret. The pastor remained silent, asking a few clarifying questions along the way. After they'd finished walking around the house, they sat down at the kitchen table.

Pastor Cummings leaned forward. "Tobias, Sarah, thank you for sharing this with me. I can only imagine how frightened you were when you discovered the symbols had returned to the room."

"We're still terrified," Sarah whispered. "Why did they come back? What do you think it means?"

The pastor sat quietly for a moment as if gathering his thoughts. Finally, he spoke: "Tobias, your forefathers brought a generational curse upon your family, one that's passed from father to son for decades."

"Curse?" Tobias whispered. "How do we break it?"

"You've taken the first steps. You've decided not to participate in this evil any longer, and you've rid your home of the Satanic abominations."

Satanic abominations? The pastor's description of his family's objects sent a searing pain through his heart. Tears welled in his eyes. He'd spent his entire adult life minimizing his family's dark secret. Between summoning years, he pretended the evil didn't exist. Yet every time he glanced at the alcove or the north field, he was reminded of the wickedness he summoned. He went through the motions of going to church with his family, but he didn't fully embrace any biblical teachings. If he had, he would have shared everything with Sarah years ago. He knew her strength, her devotion to God. She wouldn't have left him. He'd used the fear of losing Sarah and his sons as a crutch, an excuse that allowed him to continue perpetrating sin.

Pastor Cummings continued. "Changing your heart and removing those objects from your life is only the beginning. Tobias, you have to repent fully. You must accept the Lord into your heart and ask for his forgiveness. You must ask the Holy Spirit to guide your steps, to show you what it is like to live a life like Christ. You can only rid yourself of this evil through true repentance and acceptance of Christ in your life."

He saw the look of compassion on the pastor's face. The words he spoke filled him with hope. For the first time in his life, he saw a bright path ahead. He smiled and then closed his eyes as Pastor Cummings led him and Sarah through prayer. He accepted the Lord into his heart, then asked for forgiveness and guidance. Each word of prayer left an imprint on his heart. Pastor Cummings also included a prayer for the house. He specifically requested any evil spirits bound to the spell book or the summoning room be cleansed from their home.

After the prayer, he led Pastor Cummings and Sarah back to the summoning room. He squeezed his eyes tightly shut, then pushed open the door and held up a lantern with a shaking hand. He didn't open his eyes until he heard Sarah's words: "They're gone. All of the symbols—they're gone."

A wave of relief washed over him. He opened his eyes, looked at the walls then smiled. Slowly his smile faded. At first glance, the walls looked clean and white. But as he looked closer, he could see the symbols on the wall, significantly faded, but still there. *Am I the only one who sees them? Or are those symbols seared into my brain. Will I continue to see them because I feel guilty for not telling Pastor Cummings about Susan? He told me I needed to repent fully. But I didn't.*

He glanced at both Pastor Cummings and Sarah; they both appeared convinced the walls were white. He joined in them as they outwardly thanked God for answering their prayers.

* * *

After the pastor left, Tobias spent the rest of the weekend reading his Bible and going through the house, making sure he'd removed anything his grandfather or great-uncle might have used in their occult practices. The dark cloak, the kerosine lantern, the leather pouch—he destroyed them all. After he was finished, he buried the firepit's remnants in the cemetery.

He and Sarah also dusted and cleaned the house from top to bottom. They opened the windows, allowing a gentle breeze of fresh air to blow through the home. Late Saturday afternoon, they stood at the bottom of the staircase and looked around.

"I know I still have to repair or replace some of the fixtures, but doesn't our home seem different?" he asked.

Sarah smiled and nodded. "Yes, for the first time since I moved into this house, it feels good, Tobias. I don't know how else to explain it. It feels like a dark shadow has been lifted off the house. Everything about our home feels different, even the walls and this staircase seem brighter."

Her words described how he felt. Gone was the image of a great house on the hill where rich and powerful men worshipped darkness. In its place was a humble home filled with God's love and goodness.

✳ ✳ ✳

The following morning, after church, Tobias worked on small projects around the barn, waiting for his sons to return. After dinner, he would tell his sons everything that transpired over the weekend.

The mood around the dinner table was elevated. *Maybe I should wait a few days before saying anything.* As he contemplated this, Sarah leaned across the table in John and Kate's direction. "Okay, what's up with you two?"

He watched as John grabbed Kate's hand and raised it to his lips. He looked into her eyes as if waiting for permission to speak. She smiled and nodded.

"We have some news," John said.

"We're having a baby," Kate quickly added.

Daniel, James, and Charles clapped and congratulated the couple.

Sarah jumped from her chair and hugged them both. "That's wonderful news. Do you know your due date?"

"Early March. We were waiting until we made it through the first trimester before we said anything," John said.

Sarah smiled, then turned and looked at Tobias. The look on her face was one of quiet pleading. *She doesn't want me to say anything tonight.* He looked her in the eyes, smiled, and quietly nodded. Then he joined everyone in congratulating the young couple.

CHAPTER 27

L ike a small windmill spinning wildly in the garden, the days following Susan's disappearance ticked off the calendar. Norm worked as many days as possible. While Mary seemingly thrived, wrapped up in church, work, and friends. With each passing day, he felt the sense of purpose he'd found in his fresh-start life slip through his fingers.

Susan was still missing. Her parents worked through the court system to sell her home and move her belongings to Prescott. The move happened quickly and without formality. Meanwhile, the unofficial word around town was that the sheriff deemed Susan a runaway. He couldn't help but feel the folks living around town had closed the book on Susan's young life while he remained mired in the story, searching for a happier ending.

Soon after Susan's house was sold, a couple with two young boys moved in. He couldn't understand the ease at which Mary befriended the new neighbors.

"How can you dismiss Susan so easily?" he asked.

"Dismiss her?" Mary's voice rang out. "I think about that girl every day."

"But you made friends so easily with the couple next door."

"That's right, Norm, and I'd do it all over again. I wish we'd known Susan better. If we knew about her history of mental illness, we might have been able to stop her from running away. And we wouldn't have asked her to watch the house. We put a burden on someone who was struggling. You might think it's a betrayal for befriending them. But I'm just trying to make up for not knowing Susan well enough!"

That comment silenced him. All he could do was quietly nod and walk away.

✳ ✳ ✳

Fall arrived, bringing cooler weather outside and a downright chill inside the house. For the first time in thirty-six years, he'd forgotten their October wedding anniversary. Mary went through the day without acknowledging the occasion. Then, at bedtime, she left a card on his pillow and moved into the guest room. Although she smiled when he brought flowers home the next day, he knew it would take a while before she genuinely forgave him.

Despite his objections, Mary invited the neighbors, their two sons, and Bernice for Thanksgiving dinner. As soon as the dishes were cleared from the table, he excused himself and went out to the garage.

The following night, as they ate dinner, Mary leaned forward and placed both elbows on the table. "I'm worried what happened after Rose died might be happening again."

He narrowed his eyes and curled his lips inward. *She's afraid I'm drinking again.* He didn't feel up to playing word games with her. *If she thinks I'm drinking, she can say it out loud.* "What do you mean?"

She paused for a moment, then pointed at the glass he held in his hand. "You know what I mean. I'm worried you'll start drinking again."

He felt a pang of guilt, then a wave of anger. *How does she know?*

For months, he spent his free time in the garage working on projects. He had a bottle of vodka hidden in the back of one of the cabinets. Whenever he could, he'd sneak a little vodka into whatever he was drinking. *Did she find the bottle?*

"Well, I'm not drinking…so you can change the subject."

"It's just…"

"It's just what, Mary?"

"You're doing that thing you do with your hands…you did it when you started drinking after Rose died."

He thrust both hands in front of him and turned them palm up, then palm down. "What do I do with my hands?"

191

"You roll your glass between your hands, and you rub the glass with your thumb."

He picked up the glass. *She's right.* A warm sensation moved up from his chest, spreading over his face. *I'm craving a drink and can't wait to get back into the garage.* "I told you I'm not drinking. This conversation is over." He pushed his chair away from the table. "I've got work to do in the garage."

* * *

A few nights later, Norm showed up at the dinner table with bloodshot eyes, reddened face, and slurred speech. A wave of sadness and anger quickly rose within Mary's chest. *He's drinking again.* She wanted to comfort him, but she was too tired to fight. She'd watched for weeks as he transitioned from sadness into a realm of anger. Barbed words, filled with venom, took the place of the kind, gentle words he once used.

She quietly picked up her plate and moved to her recliner. Eating dinner in silence was slowly becoming a habit. Even after Rose died, dinner time was the one time of day when they'd sit and talk about their day. She wasn't a fan of "quiet dinner time," the nickname she'd given this new routine.

She turned on the television and pressed the remote until she found a singing competition. The judges appeared to have a great time discovering new talent. The show was something she and Norm would have enjoyed watching together before he began shutting her out of his life.

She wasn't sure how much she could take. He'd ruined their anniversary and Thanksgiving. Tears flowed from her eyes. She wiped them away with the napkin in her hand, then shook her head. There was no way she'd wallow in self-pity. With Christmas just a few weeks away, if she didn't comfort him soon, he'd destroy that holiday, too.

She kept her back towards him, closed her eyes, and quietly prayed. She prayed he'd find comfort, prayed he'd stop drinking, and prayed he'd make his way back to God.

* * *

The following day, after Norm left for work, Mary searched the garage looking for alcohol bottles. Buried under painting cloths, behind gallons of old paint, and sandwiched between the old camping stove and propane bottles, she pulled out three partially full vodka bottles in various sizes.

Later that night, over dinner, she welcomed the silence. It gave her space to practice what she wanted to say and time to gather the courage needed to say it.

He took the last bite of food and pushed his dinner plate away.

It's now or never. Say it! She took a deep breath and closed her eyes. "We need to talk."

He leaned back, crossed his arms, and narrowed his eyes. "Okay…talk."

She felt a warmth creeping up from her chest, warming her face. She despised it when he used a defensive tone. She took another deep breath. *Stay calm.*

"I know you're hurting, Norm. Susan's disappearance has stirred up many memories of Rose, at least for me it has, and I'm sure it's the same for you. We've gone for weeks without hardly saying anything to each other. Now, we're eating dinners in silence, like two strangers." She paused for a moment and took another deep breath. "I know you think it will help, but drinking isn't the solution. I thought we could call Pastor Cummings. I'm sure he would take the time to come here to speak with you and to pray with you." *There, I've said it!*

"What do you mean we can call Pastor Cummings? You told him you think I'm drinking? You have no right!"

"I know you're drinking again. But no, I haven't told him about it. I was just saying if you want someone to talk with other than me, I believe he would come."

"I told you I'm not drinking again!"

She'd gone over and over in her mind what she'd say if he denied it. She'd hoped to remain calm, but something inside her snapped. She pushed herself up from the table, nearly knocking over the dining room chair, and in great strides, she marched to the garage. The door slammed shut behind her, sending a tremor through the house. One by one, she opened the garage cabinets, scooped the vodka bottles into her arms, and stormed back into the house. The garage door slammed shut again. She approached the dining room table. He sat still in his chair, looking at his dinner plate. She slammed the first bottle onto the dining room table with enough force to leave a mark on the tabletop—*Oh, calm down, Mary. There's no reason to mar a perfect table.* With more restraint, she placed the other two bottles next to the first. "This is what I'm talking about!"

* * *

A warm flushing sensation rose from throughout Norm's body, settling on his face. His face skewed inward, and his lips trembled. He rose from his chair and pounded his fist on the table. "I won't have you checking up on me…treating me like I'm a child!"

Like a receding tsunami wave, Mary stepped back and crossed her arms, tucking her fisted hands against her shaking body. Her lip curled inward. She narrowed her eyes until they resembled two sharp darts, ready to strike.

A heavy silence filled the air. He crossed his arms and took a deep breath, bracing for her next inundating wave of anger.

A flush crept up her neck and face. She blinked rapidly. One by one, tears slowly fell from her eyes. She curtly wiped them away with the back of her hand. In a halted voice, she said, "I can't do this anymore!"

She turned on her heel, headed to the guest bedroom, and slammed the door shut.

* * *

I can't do this anymore. Mary's words played over and over in his head through the night. By morning, he'd come to a decision. *I can't hurt Mary anymore. I need to stop drinking.* He rose early, and for the first time in months, he made breakfast. As he set the plates of bacon and eggs on the table, Mary stepped into the dining room, fully dressed and ready to leave the house.

He offered a smile. "I'm sorry about the fight we had last night. I made you breakfast this morning. I was hoping we could talk."

She curled in her bottom lip as tears welled in her eyes. Then a look of determination crossed her face. She curtly shook her head. "I'm sorry,

Norm. I'm leaving."

A gut punch. *What did she say?* His body went numb. He stumbled and sat in the chair. He expected a fight and the typical silent treatment that followed. He'd buy flowers, say he was sorry, and eventually, everything worked out. They'd been through a similar struggle after Rose died. Back then, despite his drinking, she didn't walk out on their marriage. She stayed by his side. It was her love, which gave him the strength to stop. He looked into her face and whispered, "What do you mean...leaving?"

She looked down at the floor. "I was on the phone with Grace last night. She booked a flight for me to California. Bernice is on her way over to take me to the airport. Once I'm with Grace and away from all of this..." She waved her arms wildly in the air. "...I can think more clearly about what I want."

An icy chill flowed through his body, and he shuddered. *I can't do this alone!* "I love you, Mary. Please don't let me lose you, too!"

He watched as she looked off into the distance. *The jury is out for deliberation.* After a moment, she looked into his face. She didn't have to say anything. He already knew. *She's reached a verdict: guilty.* His stomach lurched.

In a voice no higher than a whisper, she spoke: "I honestly believe you love me. I love you too. But right now, I don't think you love yourself. You're obviously in pain. You know in your heart where to find your strength. It's here, in the word of God." She pointed to her Bible, ever-present on the dining room table. A moment passed before she spoke again. This time, her voice was filled with compassion. "You're grieving; you've been grieving for a long time. First Rose and now, Susan. I believe somehow you blame yourself for Susan running away. You know what the Bible says, Norm; you studied it! The Lord is your strength! You know I'm right! It's time you start leaning on God again. You have to trust he will heal your heart."

He looked into her eyes. "Tell me what I need to do to get you to stay." His voice lowered. "I'll do anything you want."

She slowly shook her head. "I'm sorry. We both need space. I've spoken with my boss, and I've already packed. Bernice will be here any minute. I know you think it would be better if I stayed, but honestly, the time away would do us both some good." She took a few steps towards their bedroom, then turned back and looked him in the eye. "I love you. The ball's in your court. One of these days, you'll have to accept the fact Rose was sick, and her death was a tragic accident. There was nothing we could have done to stop it! You also need to accept the fact Susan was sick too. That's why she ran away. That's not our fault! There was nothing we could have done to stop that either! Once you begin to accept the fact you aren't to blame for Susan's disappearance, I believe you'll start to heal." The bedroom door closed.

She planned this! She knew I'd deny drinking last night, giving her the excuse she needed to leave. He sat at the table, quietly seething. Slowly, his anger faded as he realized he'd left her no choice.

Nearly ten minutes passed before the front doorbell rang. Mary re-emerged from the bedroom. She'd packed two large suitcases and had another bag over her shoulder. *She plans to be gone for a while.* She paused at the end of the hallway and looked in his direction. Her shoulders slumped forward, and her eyes were puffy and red. She raised her hand, then turned and shuffled towards the front door.

His heart sank. He leaned forward in his chair, placing his elbows onto the table. The voices at the front door were inaudible. A moment later, the front door closed. *She's gone.* He closed his eyes and buried his face in his hands. Tears flowed unabashed, and his shoulders heaved up and down as his breath came in stunted waves.

Muffled footsteps. He raised his head and brushed the tears from his eyes. *Mary.* A look of concern covered her face. Without saying a word, she threw her arms around his shoulders and pressed her face, wet with tears, against his chest. He wrapped his arms around her and held her close, deeply inhaling the flowery aroma of her shampoo. A moment later, she gently pulled away. She kissed his cheek and whispered, "I promise to call tomorrow." She paused, then added, "I love you. I want—no—I need my old Norm back."

For the second time, he watched her walk away. His heart fell against his stomach. Soon, the front door closed again, followed by the sound of Bernice's car. He shook his head. *I blew it! I've pushed her away!* He sat at the dining room table, staring at the vodka bottles, losing track of time. After a while, his hands began to shake. He steadied his hands by grabbing onto his drinking glass, slowly stroking the glass with his thumb. His mouth was dry.

He reached for one of the vodka bottles. His hand stopped mid-way through the air. *Stop! I must stop! But I can't do this alone. I need help.* He pulled out his cell phone. Dave answered the phone on the first ring.

Twenty minutes later, the front doorbell rang. The look of surprise on Dave's face reinforced how out of control his life had become.

"I hate to say it, Norm...but you look like hell."

A warm sensation crept up and over Norm's face. He took a deep breath, straightening his tall frame, then ran his shaking hands through his messy hair. He forced a smile. "Thanks for coming."

Dave nodded. "What happened?"

A sting of disbelief. "It's Mary...she left me."

"Norm, that's terrible! I'm so sorry," Dave said as he entered the house.

He led the way to the dining room table, turned, and beckoned Dave to sit at the table. Dave's eyes were focused on the vodka bottles, methodically moving from one bottle to the next. A puzzled expression filled his face as he looked up into Norm's eyes.

"It's the reason she left. One of the reasons she left." He said as he fell into his chair.

Dave sat down and slowly shook his head. "I've never seen you drink."

He leaned forward and studied Dave's face, a look of disbelief and genuine concern. *He's my friend. He won't judge me.* He took a deep breath and began speaking. "I did this before...after my daughter, Rose, died. I didn't want to stay at home, and I didn't want to spend time with my old friends. Most days, I just drove around. Then one day, I stumbled onto this little bar by our house. It didn't bother me that the place was dirty and filled with smoke. It felt like home. The bartender, Tim, was a nice guy. Talking to him was easy. He didn't judge. I ended up spending the afternoon talking with him. That little bar became my safe place. And Tim was good. I'm not kidding, I'd walk in, and by the time I was at the bar, there'd be a vodka tonic in front of me."

He felt his thoughts drifting as he remembered the past. He turned back to Dave and continued, "I'd come home, and Mary would confront me. She'd tell me I smelled like smoke, or my face was flushed, or that I slurred my words. Eventually, we had one big blowout. She told me she couldn't stay married to me if I continued drinking. It was a wake-up call for me. I loved her and didn't want to lose her; so, I stopped drinking. We worked it out together. The next thing I know, she's put in a transfer at work, and we're moving from Tucson to Phoenix. She said it was a way for us to get a fresh start. But looking back now, I wonder if she wanted to get me away from the bar. It was too close to our home. One slip up, you know, and bam, I might go back."

"Makes sense. But you both seem happy here."

"We were…are…but I blew it this time. I started drinking again around Labor Day. Now Mary's walked out. I'm pretty sure she won't come back until I've stopped drinking for good."

Dave nodded. "I'm here for you. How can I help?"

"I know you said you had some experience with alcoholism in your family."

"My brother is an AA sponsor. When he stopped drinking, he was admitted to a treatment center. Would you like me to give him a call?"

He nodded.

"Okay, did you want to talk with him?"

"I trust you to talk with him. I'd like to take a shower."

✳ ✳ ✳

The gentle caress of lukewarm water steadied his craving for a drink—a clean body, a clean slate. *I can do this! I can stop drinking!* Thirty minutes later, he returned to the dining room, showered, freshly shaven, and holding a small duffle bag.

"Now, that's the Norm I recognize." Dave smiled and placed his hand on Norm's shoulder. "I've spoken with my brother. He made some calls. We need to go to the facility by Mercy Hospital. They'll be expecting us."

Finally, he had a plan, a way to move towards the future.

"Yes, but I have to do something first." He pointed in the direction of the dining room table. "The bottles on the table…where are they?"

A puzzled look spread over Dave's face. *He must think I've changed my mind and want a drink.*

"I'm sorry. I poured the alcohol down the drain. I thought that's what you would've wanted. I tossed the empty bottles into the little recycle bin under the sink."

He nodded. "There's no need to apologize." He plucked the three bottles out of the recycle bin and walked into the backyard. Dave followed close behind.

A knot of anger grew in the middle of his stomach. He tossed the first bottle into the field with all his might. "I hate you!" *Evil presence in the field. I'm positive you're the reason Susan is gone!*

Dave stood quietly behind him.

He threw the second bottle as he yelled out again, "I hate you!" *Opiates! For killing my sweet Rose!* He fell against the fence, grabbing onto the metal support.

"You okay, buddy?" Dave asked as he stood beside him, placing his hand on his shoulder.

He turned and looked into Dave's widened eyes. *I'm sure I'm scaring him.* He turned back toward the field and flung the last bottle. He yelled again. This time his voice sounded sad and defeated. "I hate you!" *Alcohol for numbing my pain!*

Another thought flashed through his mind. *I hate...no...that's not true. I don't hate God. I've gone down a path of hatred for so long. I know my pride keeps me from admitting I was wrong. I turned my back on God instead of leaning on him.* As he glanced at Dave again, a thought passed through his mind. *God put him in my life for a reason.* He quietly wept.

"You okay?" Dave asked.

He nodded. "I'm ready to go now."

CHAPTER 28

S econd thoughts set in on the way to the airport. Mary phoned Grace. "I don't know if I should come. Your father was quite a wreck when I left. I shouldn't leave him like this."

"You aren't leaving him for good—right? You're just coming here to clear your head. I've already bought your ticket, Mom. Please come. We're all looking forward to seeing you. Besides, I think the break will do you both some good."

A wave of guilt crashed upon her. Her phone call to Grace last night had set this whole plan in motion.

"I want to see you guys too."

Her manager graciously authorized the time off from work, and Grace paid for the airplane ticket. She couldn't back out without reimbursing Grace, and honestly, paying her back for the ticket would stretch her already-tight budget. She nodded her head, mind made up. "Okay, I'm on my way. I'll see you in a few hours."

"Good. You're doing the right thing, mom. Have a safe flight. We'll be at the airport when you land."

She checked her bags at the terminal kiosk, found her boarding gate, then marched into the closest airport giftshop. She perused the rows of magazine covers on the wall: 'Ring in the New Year in Style," "No surgery Facelift—look ten years younger with foods found in your refrigerator," "Find the right haircut to match the shape of your face." After a moment of reading covers, she settled on one. In truth, it didn't matter which one she bought. It was more likely the magazine would be used for hiding tears rather than reading.

After her purchase, she found a seat near the gate and glanced at her boarding pass. She knew Grace paid a premium to get her on board early. She smiled and closed her eyes. *Thank you, Grace.*

She boarded and found her seat. It was near the window. She fastened her seatbelt and covered herself with her coat. If she were lucky, the flight wouldn't be full, and the middle seat on her row would stay empty.

No such luck. As the flight filled up, a young woman with a radiant smile, leaned into the row. "I think this is my seat."

The young man occupying the aisle seat, unbuckled his seatbelt and stood. "Here, let me help you."

The young man fumbled over himself, as he helped the young woman settle in her seat. Young love. She felt a knot in the center of her chest. At least the two love birds will keep themselves company during the flight. As she faced the window, a tear slid down her face.

"Are you okay?" the young woman asked in a voice barely above a whisper.

She turned and offered a weak smile, to convince herself as much as the woman sitting next to her that she'd be okay. "I'll be alright."

The young woman reached into her purse and removed a travel-size package of unopened tissues. "I always keep some on hand." She smiled. It was a sweet smile. The kind of smile that lit up her eyes. She'd seen the same smile on Rose's face before the drugs took hold and wrecked her body.

She pulled out her package of tissues. "Thank you. I brought some."

The woman leaned towards her. "It's none of my business. But if you'd like to talk, I've been told I'm a good listener."

She wasn't sure if she could speak to the woman without losing her composure. She'd pictured flying to San Jose curled up under her coat, head pressed against the window, eyes closed, not engaged in conversation. She glanced at the young woman, then at the young man sitting on the other side. He was looking at them both. He smiled a sheepish, hopeful grin. She felt sure he was thinking, *Leave grandma alone. I'll talk to you.*

He's handsome, and he's right. You should leave this grandma alone. People meet and fall in love on airplanes. The two of you would make great-looking babies. I'm not standing in the way of that.

She slowly started to shake her head, searching for the words. *Wouldn't you enjoy talking to someone your age? Oh, and newsflash, he's handsome and seems interested in you.* Before she could speak, the young woman quietly said, "Be strong and courageous."

She recognized this biblical passage from Joshua. Being one of her favorites, she'd often recite it during times of stress. The rest of the verse brought immense comfort: "Do not be afraid, for the Lord your God is with you wherever you go."

Did the Lord place this woman on the plane to bring her comfort? She looked past the woman to the young man. He'd turned his attention to another young woman sitting across the aisle. *He seems fickle. Maybe it's a good thing she didn't strike up a conversation.*

She looked into the woman's kind eyes and sensed overwhelming compassion. She also felt this woman knew her, knew everything about her. How strange. Yet how reassuring. She smiled. "You're right. The Lord is with me…us. I am on my way to spend time with my daughter."

Mary spent most of the flight talking. It was cathartic. As promised, the young woman with the sweet smile and kind eyes was a good listener. She sat, seemingly mesmerized listening to the troubles with Norm. When the conversation turned to the topics of Rose and Susan, the young woman asked probing questions and nodded words of encouragement to keep the conversation moving.

As the flight approached San Jose, the attendants made one last pass through the cabin, and the young woman spoke up again. "You said your husband started drinking after your daughter died. But was able to stop. He started drinking again after the young woman living next door to you disappeared. Is that right?"

She nodded.

"From what you said, your husband sounds like he's a good man, a very protective man. Isn't it possible he feels he's failed to protect two people he cared about? That's a huge burden for anyone. He must be in terrible pain."

Acknowledging Norm was in pain sent a searing ache through her own heart. She left him when he was at the lowest point she'd ever seen him. *You left him when he needed you the most.*

As the plane touched down, she closed her eyes and thanked God for putting the young woman next to her. Then she turned to the young woman. "Thank you for listening. I feel God placed you in this seat for a reason. You've helped me see my situation from a different point of view."

"I'm glad you found our talk helpful. I wish you and your husband all the best."

CHAPTER 29

O nce Mary unpacked and settled in at Grace's house, she looked at her phone. One missed call. She sat on the bed and listened to Norm's phone message. The sound of Dave's voice caught her off-guard.

"Hey Mary, it's Dave. Norm is okay. He called me after you left this morning. Well…um…the bottom line is that he wants to stop drinking, which is great. I made some calls, and he's here at Mercy Hospital's Behavioral Health Unit. He asked me to give you a call. They're admitting him. Could you call the facility when you get this message? The number is…"

She replayed the message, and with a shaking hand, wrote down all the details. A repeating thought ran through her mind. *I shouldn't have left!*

She prayed God would protect and heal Norm as she dashed down the stairs to the kitchen. There, she found Grace and her husband sitting, drinking a cup of coffee. Her grandchildren were out of earshot. Grace looked up, and her eyes widened. "What's wrong?"

Her lip began to tremble as she fought to hold back the tears. "It's your dad."

"Is he okay?"

"I never should have left him. I just listened to the message on my phone. It wasn't from your father. It was from his friend, Dave."

The color left Grace's face. "Oh no! What happened?"

"He's checked himself into a behavioral health unit. He wants to stop drinking."

A wave of relief spread over Grace's face, and she gave a heavy sigh.

"Mom, this is good news! I know you weren't sure if you should come here, but honestly, I don't know if dad would have tried to get help if you hadn't left."

It didn't feel like good news. Being admitted to a healthcare facility sounded serious. "I'm so sorry, Grace. I should be with your dad."

Grace held up her hand, then motioned to the chair across the table. "Sit down, Mom. I know you want to be there. Let's see what's going on first. Okay? Did dad's friend say where he's at?"

She sat down and then handed Grace the small piece of paper where she'd jotted down the phone number to the unit.

"This is good. Why not call and see how he's doing."

She dialed the phone number. After a few minutes, she heard Norm's voice on the line. "Hello, honey. It's good to hear your voice."

"How are you?"

"I'm doing okay. The people here are nice, top-notch. I believe they are going to help me, Mary."

"I'll come back, Norm. I mean it. If you want me there, I'll take the first flight home."

From the corner of her eyes, she saw Grace and her husband look at each other. She no longer cared about the cost of the flight. She'd book and pay for the return trip to Phoenix on her own, in addition to paying back Grace and her husband.

"I figured you'd say something like that, Mary. But I want you to listen to me. Okay? I want you to stay with Grace. Spend some time with her and our grandkids. I know how much you miss them. I'm serious; stay and enjoy time with them. You and I can talk over the phone. I'm in good hands. If you come home right now, it'll be another way I've let you down, and I can't let you down anymore."

Tears slowly streamed down her face. She wiped them away with her fingertips. She knew he was speaking from his heart, and she knew staying with Grace would be the right thing to do.

"You still there, honey?"

"Yes," she answered in a barely audible voice.

"You okay?"

She nodded as tears continued to flow. She whispered again, "Yes...I love you, Norm."

"I love you too, honey. I've got to go now. I'll talk with you tomorrow."

"Okay…bye."

"Bye."

The following morning, she phoned the hospital again; this time, she asked to speak with Norm's doctor. The receptionist put her on hold for five minutes before coming back onto the line. "Doctor Pierce is in rounds right now. He's asked if he could call you back in an hour or so."

"That will be fine. Do you have my cell phone number?"

"Is that the phone number you are calling from right now?"

"Yes."

"Then…yes, I have it, and I've just checked to make sure it's in your husband's chart."

"Thank you for your help. I'll wait for the doctor's call."

Dr. Pierce phoned her a few hours later. "Sorry, I hoped to call you sooner. We had a bit of an emergency here."

Emergency. She gasped, and her knees buckled.

"No…oh my. I'm so sorry the emergency had nothing to do with your husband. Norm's stable."

Stable? What does she mean by that? She hadn't expected the doctor to characterize Norm in that manner.

"So…he's stable. That's good, right?"

"Yes, sorry…yes, he's doing well."

"I don't know if Norm told you, but I'm visiting our daughter in Modesto. I'm wondering if I should come back home?"

"That's admirable, Mrs. Keller. Norm permitted me to share his medical information with you. So I'm going to tell you what he said this morning. He told me he thinks you need time with your daughter and that he'd feel guilty if you came home because of him."

"So, I should stay here."

"If you need someone to tell you to stay in California, then I will be that person. Don't add to your husband's guilt. You can call and offer support over the phone. His friend Dave is here right now. He said he's available and willing to stop in to see Norm anytime he's needed."

A wave of relief passed over her. *He's in good hands, mentally and physically.*

"So, you think you'll be able to help him stop drinking?"

"Yes, I think there's a good chance. He seems committed to abstaining from alcohol. Right now, my main concern is his depression."

Depression! She felt like someone just dropped a load of bricks on her. "I thought he was in the hospital to stop drinking."

"We know about the drinking, and we are watching for signs of withdrawal. But based on the admission intake, it sounds like Norm has been depressed for a few years. We have a treatment plan that includes medications and psychotherapy."

"He's agreed to this?"

"Yes. You didn't think he would?"

"Honestly, no...I am surprised. When our daughter Rose died, Norm was a mess. I asked him to get professional help. I don't know if he was too prideful or didn't believe it would help. But he kept telling me no! When we moved to Phoenix, I thought he was getting better. And he was for a while until..."

"Your other daughter died."

"What? No, Susan wasn't our daughter. She was our neighbor, and she didn't die; she ran away! Did Norm tell you Susan was his daughter and that she died?"

"I'm sorry. I must have misunderstood. Perhaps he viewed her as a daughter figure. He's blaming himself for her disappearance; he seems convinced himself he could have done more to protect her."

"To be honest, Dr. Pierce, we both let Susan down. I'm sure Norm told you she had mental health issues. We didn't know it, and we put her in charge of taking care of our house. It sounded like she was already under a huge strain. We both feel responsible for adding to her stress. But the sheriff's office did an investigation. They are convinced she ran away."

"Thank you for clarifying this...this gives me more insight into your husband. I believe he should stay here for at least a week. It might take a bit to get him stable on these new medications. He said he doesn't take any other medications. Is that correct?"

"That's right. He's been in great health our whole marriage."

"That's what I was hoping to hear. We've got your husband. You spend time with your daughter and grandkids."

"Thank you, Dr. Pierce. I appreciate you calling and letting me know what's going on."

"Have a safe flight home. Goodbye."

She closed her eyes and prayed God would heal Norm's mind and body.

CHAPTER 30

The hospitalization proved to be a turning point for Norm. Through his counseling sessions, he realized he'd created an outward persona of a seemingly happy man, going through life's motions without any joy in his heart. For the first time in years, he didn't have to pretend anymore. Happiness coursed through his veins, providing him with renewed energy and a sense of purpose.

Even Mary had commented on how much clearer his thoughts appeared. In the morning, she'd be on a plane headed back home. When she'd left for California, their marriage was on shaky ground. With the success of treatment, he felt new hope they would get back to the way they were years ago. He couldn't wait to see her again, and by the way their conversations had gone over the past week, he believed she felt the same way.

He phoned. After the first ring, she answered, "Hi honey, I'm just checking to see when your plane arrives tomorrow."

"Looks like I'll be arriving just before noon. I can't wait to see you."

"Me too."

"I want you to know how much I love you. I'm willing to keep working on our marriage."

Ouch. There was a little flip in his stomach. He'd stopped drinking, and with the medications, he felt like the old Norm, the man she'd fallen in love with nearly thirty-seven years ago. *Willing to work on our marriage?* He shook his head. *What else does she need me to do to prove that I've changed?* He took a deep breath. Whatever she needed, he'd do it. *She's coming home, and that's all that matters!*

"I love you too, Mary. I want to make things right between us."

"Okay…I didn't want to talk about this until I was home. But I think maybe I'll say it now. That way, you can think about it tonight without me there. I just need to know you and I are on the same page."

"I feel we are…what do you need me to think about?"

There was a long pause on the phone, so long he thought he'd lost the connection. "Mary?"

"I'm here."

"Honey…just tell me –."

"I feel like the man I fell in love with is coming back."

"I do too…for the first time in years; I'm hopeful for the future."

"Alright…please don't be mad. But I miss talking about God in our home. I need to know if you would be willing to come to church with me?"

After Rose's death, he ran from the pain instead of grieving her loss. He traveled so far down a path of self-destruction it became easier to feign being hurt and stay angry with God than to admit he was wrong. With counseling, he understood how depression played a significant role in the upheaval of his life. In less than three years, he'd tossed aside God, his congregation, and his marriage, all for the sake of his pride. A thought flashed through his head. She's right. *It's time to repent, time to change!*

"I'm willing to try."

"Well, that's the first time in years you've said you'd considered it, so that's something! I'd like you to talk with Pastor Cummings. Maybe, not right away. We can wait until you're ready to talk. But Norm, he reminds me of you and how you counseled our congregation in Tucson."

"I'll consider it…not alone. I would want you there."

"Of course, I'll be there. Oh, I love you, Norm. You've made me so happy!" Her voice cracked. A slight pause, then she added, "I can't wait to see you tomorrow."

"Goodnight, honey. I love you."

When he was a pastor, he gave sermons about repentance. Such a simple concept: turn away from the destructive things in your life and turn towards God. It was a change of heart and a change of mind. For him, it meant moving past the anger and the pride that caused him to walk away from God in the first place. He'd clung to the anger like a life raft. He now had to let go and trust God would be there to save him. Instead of blaming

God for Rose's death and Susan's disappearance, he needed to lean on him to heal, just as Mary had done. He knew saving his marriage would entail joining Mary at church, opening the Bible again, and speaking with Pastor Cummings.

He wasn't sure of all the things his future held. But he trusted God had a plan for him. After hanging up the phone, he closed his eyes and bowed his head. "I don't know what plans you have for me, Lord," he said out loud in the empty house. "I accept the fact I may never know why Rose died or why Susan disappeared. But I do know this: I've decided I'm going to trust you to guide me moving forward. I surrender wholeheartedly to you. Thank you for Mary; she's my rock and for Dave, such a wonderful friend. Thank you for the wonderful doctors and nurses at Mercy. Thank you for giving me a second chance with Mary. Please bring her home safely."

As he sat there, a comforting warmth washed over him. Then, he heard God's voice in his head. *You were meant to live in this house. You were meant to know Susan. Stay vigilant. For I know the plans I have for you!*

CHAPTER 31

Friday night, early January. Months passed since their home was cleansed. Despite Tobias' desire to tell his sons about his family's dark secret—he allowed one excuse after another to keep him from doing so.

First was the news of Kate and John's pregnancy. Then Charles announced he and Rachael were engaged and planned to marry in early December. With the holidays, pregnancy, and wedding, a perpetual sense of happiness hung in the air. Telling his sons would have shattered everyone's joy.

With Charles moving into Rachael's Tucson apartment in a few weeks, this would be one of the last weekends all four sons would be on the farm together. In just a few short weeks, Charles would begin a new job with a large manufacturing plant, and Rachael would start another college semester. Knowing Charles and Rachael would embark on their marriage journey miles away from the farm filled Tobias with a tremendous sense of peace.

Tobias glanced at the faces of his family as they sat around the backyard firepit laughing and joking. He felt blessed to be surrounded by his children. Then his thoughts turned to Susan. Months had passed since she disappeared. The sheriff's only lead, a hitchhiker, looking for a ride to Las Vegas, fizzled out. In every practical sense, the investigation had grown cold. He looked off in the distance and wondered about Susan's parents. What were they doing tonight? A pang of guilt washed over him.

Sarah gently rubbed his leg. "Hey there. You okay?"

He looked into her loving face, forced a half-smile, and nodded. "I'm okay, just thinking."

"Thinking about what?"

He raised his hand and shook his head. He didn't want to talk about Susan or the sadness he felt.

He glanced at his family again, grateful they were all safe and together. There were no more excuses. Tomorrow, he and his sons would finally have the conversation he'd put off for so long.

✳ ✳ ✳

Saturday morning. Telling his sons about their family's dark legacy proved harder than Tobias imagined. Sarah told him she wanted to be by his side when he broke the news to his sons. That way, they could offer a united front, but he declined. He didn't want the boys to associate her with the darkness. Sarah and his sons were innocent victims. He hoped that the relationship she had with her sons would remain intact by keeping her out of the conversation.

As Tobias gathered his sons in the kitchen, he remembered the initial shock he felt when his father told him about the darkness. His father's confession expressed no remorse. Instead, it focused on one thing, teaching Tobias how to use the summoning spell. Unlike his father, who offered no alternatives, no way out, he'd strived to break their family's curse. He hoped that knowledge would lessen the blow.

He told his sons about the spell book, hidden room, and summoning spell. He explained that he continued summoning the spirit every seven years out of fear it would come for his sons if he didn't. He told them the spirit's appetite seemed to grow stronger with each summoning. And his concerns about the spirit's hunger were the reason he drove around the field every day, trying to keep people away. Lastly, he explained how, with Sarah and Pastor Cumming's help, he'd turned his back on the darkness.

As he spoke, he looked around the table. All of his sons had a look on their faces of quiet disbelief. One by one, he answered questions about the summoning ritual and the spirit itself. While answering questions about the evil reignited his fears, John's question about the spirit's origin filled him with shame.

"I'm trying to understand. One of our ancestors summoned a spirit to save his farm?"

Over the past few months, he'd had multiple conversations with Pastor Cummings. The pastor used biblical Scriptures to explain the concept of generational curses. Through these conversations, Tobias realized his great-grandfather condemned his bloodline once he'd invoked the spirit. A condemnation he would have passed to his sons and grandchildren if he hadn't changed his heart.

"My great-grandfather came to this country believing rituals and spells could change a person's fate or fortune. I used to defend him, thinking he was merely misguided. But Pastor Cummings helped me understand; my great-grandfather performed a satanic act. He summoned a demon."

His sons shuddered in unison.

Daniel's face went pale. "Demon?" he whispered.

"Yes. And even worse, he passed the spell book and those rituals onto my grandfather and great-uncle. My father told me stories about those two men, stories I won't share with you. All you need to know is that they were vile, corrupt men, truly evil. They used the spell book to gain tremendous power and wealth."

"Did you perform other spells in the book?" James asked.

He shook his head.

"But your grandfather and great-uncle did," John interrupted.

"Yes, my father told me they did."

"You and mom did the right thing by burning that book," John said.

He smiled and nodded. Then he described how he and Sarah removed everything from the hidden room, burned it, and painted the walls. When he explained how the symbols returned to the room after he and Sarah burned the book, they gasped and shook their head.

"That's when your mom called Pastor Cummings. He came here right away. He knew what to do. By the time he left, he'd purified our house, and the symbols disappeared from the wall."

A thought passed through his mind. *I'm the only one who saw the symbols on the walls after the cleansing. But was that all in my head?* Whether it was in his head or not, fear of finding the marking still on the walls had kept him out of the summoning room since Pastor Cummings cleansed it.

John stepped forward. "I want to see the room."

"I'd prefer not to go in there again," he said.

John glanced at his brothers, then looked into his eyes. "I think we'd all like to see it."

Daniel, James, and Charles all nodded.

He knew his sons wouldn't stop asking until they saw the room for themselves. So, he shrugged his shoulders. "Okay."

He removed the key from one of the kitchen drawers, then turned towards Daniel. "Could you grab a few flashlights?"

He led them to the alcove, opened the door, then stepped back. He kept his eyes averted from the room while John and Daniel stepped forward and shined the flashlights onto the walls. He listened carefully, waiting for one of his sons to tell him they could see the symbols. After hearing no comments, he stepped forward and asked Daniel for his flashlight. He shined it on the wall. A wave of relief washed over him. A tsunami of doubt quickly followed that. The room was still quite dark, and he only had a flashlight. When he saw the symbols, it was under the light of a powerful lantern.

"Do you think the demon will come back in another seven years?" Daniel asked.

"I don't know," he replied.

Charles spoke up. "Even if it does, you heard dad, this house has been purified. So that means the demon can't enter it, right?"

A sinking feeling moved through his body. Although he couldn't see the symbols, he knew he hadn't fully repented. Only Sarah knew he'd found Susan's belongings in the field. He indirectly answered Charles' question. "We will never summon the demon again. But if it does return in seven years, we'll have one thing my great-uncle didn't have, our faith."

After they re-locked the room, he took his sons to the cemetery. They stood at the empty grave of the three children, and he reiterated it was out of fear the evil would come for one of them that he'd continued performing the summoning spell. He led them to the back of the cemetery—explaining it was where he buried the remnants of animals he'd found in the field.

John knelt at Rex's grave. "Hi, Rex. I'm sorry. I haven't seen you in a while." He glanced up at Tobias with tears in his eyes. "I can't believe it. It's been years since I've been out here, but it still hurts when I remember him. He was such a great dog."

A pang of guilt filled his chest. He quietly prayed none of his sons would ask if Rex had succumbed to the evil in the cornfield. His prayer was answered; they didn't ask about Rex. That brief sense of relief was shattered with Charles' remark: "Something is bothering me. The girl who went missing on the Fourth of July. She lived in the subdivision. Did you ever find any sign of her in the field?"

His stomach churned, and he felt the color drain from his face. Then, before he could answer, Daniel spoke up. "Charles, we all know what happened to her. Sheriff said she was hitchhiking along the highway."

John stood and approached them. "I'd like an answer to that question myself. She lived in one of those houses right next to the cornfield, and she disappeared on the day we harvested the corn."

He closed his eyes and took a few deep breaths. There was no way he'd lie to his sons. He had to tell them about her purse and keys. He opened his eyes and looked at the four faces staring back at him. He could tell by the look on their faces they knew he was holding something back.

James' eyes widened, and he vigorously shook his head. "Please tell us you didn't find her body in that field."

"I…didn't!" he sputtered.

A look of relief washed over James' face.

John's furrowed his forehead and narrowed his eyes. Then, he took a step forward. "But, you know something, don't you…about that girl?"

He closed his tear-filled eyes and hung his head. Until this point in the conversation, he'd felt a sense of camaraderie with his sons. He knew they didn't approve of him performing the ritual, but they didn't blame him either. Instead, they blamed their ancestors for setting all of this in motion. They told him they'd noticed the change in his demeanor once he began regularly attending church. And how they would fight alongside him if the evil returned.

Realizing a possible connection between Susan and the cornfield threatened to sever their support. The fragile unity he'd sensed broke apart in his hand, then like grains of fine sand, it slipped through his fingers. He opened his eyes and, in a cracked voice, spoke: "You're right. I did find something when I cleared the field."

John, James, and Charles gasped. While Daniel quickly covered his mouth as if to stifle a scream.

He quickly continued, "I didn't find Susan's body! But I did find her purse and keys."

Daniel lowered his hand and whispered, "No body?"

He nodded. "Just the purse and keys."

"If you didn't find her body, what happened to her?" John asked.

"I think we know what happened to her...she ran away, just like the sheriff said," he answered.

The silence that followed was deafening. He realized each of his sons was processing what he'd just told them. Finally, John spoke: "Let's assume she ran away as the sheriff said. The question I'd ask is why. Why did she run? I think we all know the answer to that question. She saw that thing in the field, and it scared her out of her mind. Isn't that what the sheriff said? She had a mental breakdown and ran away?" He angrily shook his head and paced. "Just because you didn't find a body doesn't mean we aren't responsible for her disappearance."

"You're right," he replied. "It's a guilt I live with every day. I can't help thinking how differently our lives would have been if I'd told you and your mother about the evil, instead of summoning it. We would have fought this together."

John stepped forward and placed his hand on Tobias' arm. "You have to turn her belongings over to the sheriff. You understand that—don't you? Her family needs closure."

He quietly nodded. For months he'd debated whether to hand Susan's belongings over to the sheriff. He'd made excuses that in doing so, he'd bring attention to his family and away from the sheriff's investigation. But, with the Las Vegas lead having gone cold, he knew stepping forward and telling the truth was the right thing to do.

"Absolutely not!" Daniel shouted. "Think about what you're asking dad to do."

James interjected, "I'm with Daniel. Turning her purse and keys over to the sheriff isn't going to help anything." Then he glanced at Tobias. "You're positive she wasn't attacked in the field—right?"

He nodded. "I only found her purse and keys, nothing else."

James looked at John. "I understand you want to bring closure to her family. Honestly, I do, too. But at what cost? What good will it do? It doesn't change the fact she ran away."

John crossed his arms and stared at the faces of his brothers, then turned his attention directly at him. "Let me get this straight. We spent weeks searching for that girl last summer, and all this time, you've had evidence the sheriff's department could have used in their investigation. But instead of turning it in, you buried it; you tampered with evidence." He turned to Daniel and James. "And, you two…you're defending him!"

Daniel pleaded, "All I'm saying is that if you're asking me to choose between dad's freedom and closure for her family. I'm choosing dad. I believe him when he says she ran away. Reporting dad to the sheriff isn't going to bring her back. The only thing it will do is tear our family apart."

John shook his head. "I'm sorry. I can't go along with this." He walked over the makeshift graves and pointed. "In which of these graves did you bury her purse and keys."

"Are you seriously going to dig them up and turn them over to the sheriff?" James asked.

John nodded.

There was no use in arguing. John's mind was made up. And, since Charles remained silent throughout the whole exchange, he assumed he was on John's side. He couldn't bear to see his sons at odds. The only way to move forward was to show Daniel and James it was the right thing to do. For months, he'd been given a reprieve of sorts. While he struggled with his guilt every day, he hadn't faced any questions from outsiders. Speaking to the sheriff and fully confessing, fully repenting was a long time coming. A sense of relief washed over him. Come what may, he was ready to make things right. He pointed to the grave where he'd buried Susan's belongings. "You'll find what you're looking for there."

Part III - Deliverance

Thessalonians 3:3
The Lord is faithful.
He will strengthen and protect you from the evil one.

CHAPTER 32

Pastor Ted Cummings parked his car and headed into the sanctuary. The sting of January's cold air was a reminder of a new year, a new beginning for those who confessed their sins and turned to God.

Today's service was about forgiveness. It wasn't the sermon topic he'd initially planned. The congregation was transitioning into a series of sermons on the Wonder and Majesty of God. He'd worked with the praise band and the Sunday school to find music and lessons that aligned with the sermon series. Today's service was supposed to be the kick-off to the series. Everything would have continued as planned if not for the dream he had last night.

In his dream, he'd just finished the first sermon when the lights in his church office rose to a blinding level. He squeezed his eyes shut to block out the radiating light. Once the lights lowered, he opened his eyes and gasped. Standing in front of him was an angel of the Lord. A peaceful wave washed over him as the angel took a step forward and slowly looked around the room. "God's word is spoken here."

Although it was a statement instead of a question, Ted felt compelled to answer, "Yes, we speak God's word here."

The angel pointed to the sermon on his desk.

A bubbling excitement rose in his chest. "This is tomorrow's sermon on the Lord's wonder and majesty."

The angel smiled and resoundingly stated, "Oh Lord, my God, you are very great. You are clothed with splendor and majesty."

"Yes, exactly!"

"This is a good sermon, but it must wait. There are those in your congregation who are hurting. Tomorrow they need to hear God's words about forgiveness."

"Forgiveness?"

"Yes."

He slowly shook his head as a tirade of excuses ran through his head. *We've picked out Sunday school lessons to match the sermon. Bernice made flyers. I don't have time to write a new sermon by morning.* But, as the naysaying thoughts coursed through his mind, one resounding thought overshadowed them all. *This angel is a messenger of God!* That realization was quickly followed by another: members of his congregation were hurting.

"How can I help them?"

The angel spoke again. His words were straightforward and eloquent. Within a few short sentences, Ted realized the angel had recited a sermon. He opened his eyes and sprang up in bed, expecting to find the angel standing there. *I'm in bed, not my office.*

He glanced at the alarm clock: 10:20 p.m. When he crawled into bed an hour ago, he was exhausted. Now he felt fully refreshed, as though he'd slept through the whole night.

With each passing second, he became more alert. His heart excitedly fluttered as he thought of the many saints who received visits by angels. *God sent this angel to me! Therefore, I will heed his words.* He leapt out of bed and sprinted down the hallway to his home office. His fingers moved effortlessly on the keyboard as he transcribed the angel's sermon word for word. After finishing, he prayed, thanking God for his mercy and grace.

The following morning, he gathered the church staff and shared his dream. The church was a family. In his team's eyes, if a family member was struggling, they wanted to help. He thanked his team for support, then led them in prayer, asking God to help anyone in the congregation struggling with the concept of forgiveness.

He glanced at the Smith family from behind the altar and knew they were why he needed to change the sermon. John, who always sat at Tobias' right side, was sitting at the end of the aisle with Kate. The look on John's face fluctuated between anger and sadness. Finally, he looked at Tobias seated in the pew. He looked defeated but relieved. Had he finally confessed to his sons? Did the family need his help in healing? Before he gave his sermon, he knelt at the altar and asked God for his help in delivering the sermon.

After the service ended, he stood at the door, shaking hands and offering well wishes to his parishioners as they departed. Tobias approached. There was a pensive look on his face. Tobias reached for his hand, then pulled him in slightly. "Thank you for that sermon today. You don't know how much we needed to hear it."

A warmth spread throughout his chest. Inwardly, he thanked God again for sending him the angel. Then, outwardly, he looked into Tobias' eyes and smiled. "If you need to talk, I can come out to the farm today."

Sarah leaned forward and nodded curtly. He could tell by the tears welling in her eyes and the forced smile on her face; she was struggling to keep her composure. Finally, in a low voice, she whispered, "Thank you, Pastor. We might take you up on that offer."

He nodded. "Call me. I'm here to help you in any way I can."

✳ ✳ ✳

A nervous tension spread through Tobias's body all morning. He knew Sarah noticed it too. She'd placed her hand on his knee throughout the church service to stop his bouncing leg and tapping foot. As he approached the barn, his stomach twisted in knots. John had asked if they could all meet in the barn after the service. He didn't know what John had to say, but he felt sure it had something to do with calling the sheriff. He stopped just outside the barn door, closed his eyes, and prayed God would guide their conversation.

Once he was inside the barn, he gazed into the faces of his sons and offered another apology. "I want to say again how sorry I am for everything I've put our family through. You are all grown men. I should have told you and your mother what was happening. I know now we would have found a way to break our family's curse together. If I'd only had the courage to say something, that girl wouldn't have gone missing."

"Her name was Susan—Susan Green," John said.

An awful pain spread through his chest. He raised his voice. "I know her name!" He closed his eyes and took a deep breath. *Stay calm.* He tried again in a lowered voice. "I'm sorry. I know her name. It's just hard to say it—that's all."

Charles reached out and gently grabbed his arm. "It's okay, Dad." He looked at the faces of his brothers. "We're all having a hard time saying her name."

Charles's comment was met with nods; even John nodded in agreement.

John stepped forward, saying, "I have something I want to say, and I thought it would be best to say it to everyone at once." He turned and looked directly at Tobias. "I've decided not to turn you into the sheriff. Don't get the wrong idea. It's just that I think you should be the one to do it. Not your wife, not your sons."

He quietly nodded. He fully agreed with John. He'd stayed up late trying to convince Sarah it was the right thing to do. He felt confident; in time, she'd agree.

"There's something else. Kate and I are moving to Texas this month. Her dad offered me a job when we were there in September. So I called him last night. The offer is still good. If we leave soon, we'll have some time to get settled before the baby comes."

John's words sent a crushing blow to his heart. He closed his eyes and slowly shook his head. Both he and Sarah were anxious to meet and spend time with their first grandbaby. *This will crush Sarah!*

"Why leave now? Are you trying to punish Mom and Dad?" Daniel exploded.

John shook his head. "No, it's not that. Kate's wanted to live near her mom ever since she found out she was pregnant. And, you heard what dad said yesterday. That demon took three children from this farm. I have to protect Kate and our baby."

James shook his head. "Mom and Dad burned the book. So, there's a chance they've stopped this whole thing."

He thought back to the time when he and Sarah were first married. She was pregnant with John. Once he learned of his family's dark secret, his first instinct was to leave the farm to protect Sarah and their baby. In hindsight, he realized how different their lives would have been if he'd had the strength to walk away. Despite the heartache their move would bring, he supported John's decision.

"Your brother is making the right choice," he said.

All four sons turned in his direction. Even John had a stunned look on his face.

"He needs to protect his family. Besides, that job offer won't be there forever. I'll talk with your mom. It'll take a while, but in the end, I know she'll understand."

"Thank you. I want you to know I'm not trying to hurt anyone," John said.

"I know."

Charles glanced up at him. "With both of us leaving, how will you manage the farm?"

He looked over to Daniel and James. "We'll manage."

"Rachael and I still plan to move here once she's done with school," Charles continued.

Outwardly, he smiled and nodded. Inwardly, he wondered if Charles would still feel the same way a few years from now, especially if he had children.

Charles must have had a similar thought because a few seconds later he offered a caveat to his prior statement. "I know my place is here, alongside my family. But, if I'm not living here and something happens, all you'll need to do is call me, and I'll get here as soon as I can."

He saw a look of concern pass between Daniel and James. He knew what they were thinking. John would be living in Texas, and the odds of Charles residing on the farm again were slim.

James turned to John. "What about you? Will you come back?"

John looked at the ground and shrugged. "I don't know."

James continued in a voice full of condemnation. "Just what I thought. You and your family will be safe in Texas. Charles will be God knows where. But Mom, Dad, Daniel, and me—we'll still be here when that thing comes back. We'll be the only ones here to fight it."

"I said I'd come back, and I meant it. If I'm not already living on the farm, all you'll have to do is call me," Charles said.

John looked into James's face. "You can call me too. Alright?"

He took a deep breath and then thought about how different things might have been if he told Sarah about his family's secret sooner. Maybe that girl. *Say her name!* Susan. Maybe Susan might still be here if he had. One thing was sure: his family wouldn't have been emotionally torn apart.

He looked at each of their faces. Just a few nights earlier, they were all huddled around the fire pit, laughing and joking. Images of the boys throughout the years flashed through his mind. First, as young children running and playing, then as grown men, working together. His eyes filled with tears. Then, in a cracked voice, he said, "With both of you leaving, this might be the last time we're all standing together in this barn. We have so many good memories here. Couldn't we set aside our differences and come together?"

One by one, each of his sons nodded. Then Daniel stepped forward and hugged him, something none of his sons had done since he told them about his family's dark secret. When Daniel pulled away, there were tears in his eyes. "You're right, Dad. Besides, our enemy is Satan, not each other."

James hugged him next, then Charles. They were all crying. Finally, John stepped forward and hugged him as well. He cherished the loving gesture from his sons. But knowing John had forgiven him at some level warmed his heart the most.

CHAPTER 33

When Norm and Mary first moved into their new home, he hadn't imagined the friends he'd make and the sense of community he'd experience. But, after Susan disappeared, he lost his sense of contentment. He couldn't understand why God would put another young woman within his care, only to take her away.

Two things brought him comfort: Mary's safe return and the sound of God's voice in his head. *You were meant to live in this house. You were meant to know Susan. Stay vigilant, for I know the plans I have for you!*

Knowing God placed him in this subdivision next door to Susan brought him immense comfort. Although her disappearance saddened him, he understood with complete certainty that God knew Susan's whereabouts. So, he vigilantly prayed God would protect her and bring her home safely.

After Mary returned from Grace's house, he told her about the feeling of comfort and of hearing God's voice.

"Perhaps your purpose is to help Pastor Cummings at the church. Maybe even preach again?"

Preach? He hadn't stepped foot inside a church for years. He glanced down at her, then stifled a laugh. While he was ready to dip his toes back into the proverbial church water, Mary already had him swimming laps in the deep end of the pool.

* * *

A few weeks had passed since he'd heard God's words. Perhaps Mary was right. Maybe God wanted him to preach again. But he couldn't shake the feeling God's message referred to something different. *You were meant to know Susan.* He took a long deep breath and relaxed his shoulders. He needed to trust that God had a plan for him. *Stay vigilant.* God would show him the path he needed to follow.

✳ ✳ ✳

Norm was prone to having vivid dreams, and when he did, he often heard about it from Mary the following day. She'd start by telling him how he squirmed all over the bed and talked in his sleep. She'd finish by telling him how nice it would be to have separate beds, something he vehemently opposed.

That night, as he crawled into bed next to Mary, he thought about God's comforting words. Then, within minutes of laying his head down on the pillow, his eyes closed, and he began to dream. This dream was different and more vivid than any dream he'd ever had.

In his dream, he'd lost his way and found himself wandering aimlessly through a gray, misty fog. The ground below him was dirt covered in a thin layer of pebbles and small rocks. His feet were bare. In the distance, he saw a patch of light. He headed toward the light and eventually wandered into a small clearing. The fog was thinner here. In the middle of the clearing, a tall man sat on a large boulder. He was dressed in a flowing white robe. A golden rope was tied around his waist. "Are you ready for battle?" the man asked.

"Yes," he replied.

The man looked him up and down. "Where is your sword?"

Norm shook his head. "I don't know. I've lost it."

"Don't you remember? You dropped your sword and ran after she died." The man paused for a moment, then continued. "Here, walk with me, and I will help you find it."

He followed the man out of the clearing. Everywhere the man went, the fog grew thinner, and the ground lit up. The dirt beneath his feet became smooth. Norm glanced to his right. A few feet away, a hint of gold shimmered from the ground. He moved closer and found a sword half-buried in the dirt. The hilt, made of fine gold and adorned in jewels, was exposed. He pulled on the sword, moving it up and down, trying to remove it from the dirt. The blade was heavy. He tugged with all his might. Eventually, it broke free from the ground. "I don't remember it being this heavy."

"You haven't wielded it in years."

Norm remembered, yes, it was a long time since he held the sword. He remembered the ease at which he once wielded it. He knew every inch of the blade. Suddenly, the sword became lighter. It felt right, and he felt stronger, just holding it in his hand.

"You have your sword, yet you are still not ready for battle," the man said. "Where is your shield?"

"I dropped it with my sword."

He searched the ground. A few feet from where he found his sword, he spied the golden shield, partially covered in a thick layer of dried mud. He clawed at the ground, freeing his shield. He stood upright with his sword in one hand and his shield in the other.

"You have your sword and shield again."

"I need my helmet?"

"It is on your head. You have your salvation. It pained me to see you walk away from me. But I will never leave nor forsake you."

Acknowledging the Lord's unfailing grace and mercy filled him with joy. He closed his eyes and smiled, savoring the moment. "Thank you for never leaving me. Please forgive me, Father, for turning my back on you, thinking I didn't need you."

The man turned and, with long strides, continued moving through the fog. Norm followed closely behind. This area of the fog was thicker and darker. Still, the man exuded a warm glow.

Norm held a sword and shield, and his head was covered in a helmet. Yet, he felt safest walking behind the man.

The man stopped and pointed at a large boulder. Leaning against the boulder was a breastplate.

"Put this on," he said, pointing to the breastplate.

Norm obliged.

"You are ready for battle. But you can't do this alone. Trust in me with all your heart, and do not turn away from the faith again. I will strengthen and uphold you. I will bring others to fight alongside you. You will succeed."

The Lord will send others. But who? As if in response to his question, an image passed through his head. The farmer, his sons, and Pastor Cummings. They would help him.

The man untied the rope from around his waist and placed it around Norm. "The ground you stand on is tainted with evil. Stand on truth and take back what is mine."

The man disappeared, taking the light with him. Norm stood in the middle of the gray mist. Slowly the mist thinned. He looked around and realized he stood in the middle of the field behind his home. He gazed upon his reflection in the window at the back of his house. He wore a breastplate and belt. The helmet on his head was gold. In his right hand, the sword. In his left hand, the shield. Both radiated a warm golden glow.

Behind him, at a distance, was a dark shadow. Slowly, the shadow slithered across the field, moving in his direction. He turned to face it. The closer it came, the larger it grew. Its blackness was dense, a void he felt could swallow him whole. He trembled. Then knowing the darkness couldn't hurt him, he firmly planted his feet and continued staring ahead.

At last, the dark shadow slithered directly in front of him. Its height matched his own. It had pitted skin, gnashing teeth, and red eyes. Its yellow rotten breath mixed with the layer of filth loitering over it.

The demon stood motionless while its eyes slowly scanned his body, moving from his helmet to his feet. Then he sensed an emotion growing within the demon, *fear!*

In the distance, a beeping sound captured his attention. He continued staring into the eyes of the demon. He had no intentions of turning his back on evil. Instead, he'd face it head-on, confront it.

But the beeping grew louder and louder. With each beep, the demon's eyes grew brighter while the rest of its body receded. Then, something pushed against his back. He blinked, then rubbed his eyes. Finally, the fogginess of his dream cleared, and he realized he was staring at the alarm clock.

Mary nudged him again with her elbow. "Norm, can you turn off the alarm?"

"Sorry, yes." He fully awoke, remembering every detail of his dream. A sense of resolve enveloped him. He knew what he had to do. As he sprung out of bed, Mary asked him if he would start a pot of coffee. She told him she'd be up to make breakfast soon.

He strode to the closet. In a wooden box, hidden beneath cufflinks and watches, was the cross he once wore around his neck. He picked up the cross. It felt lighter in his hand than he remembered. He pressed it against his lips, holding it there for a moment. Then he placed the chain around his neck. *Thank you, God, for showing me your plans!*

He went to the dining room table. Lying there was Mary's Bible. Before he'd turned his back on God, he'd start each day by reading his Bible. *The Bible was my sword, and the shield was my faith. I cast them aside after Rose died.* He thought about the past few years and how he avoided touching the Bible. He remembered the many times he didn't move it out of the way to set the dinner table. And, as shameful as it was to admit, he wouldn't bring it to Mary after she hurt her ankle.

Stay vigilant! God showed him his purpose through the dream. *Evil is coming! God has already given me everything I need to fight it!* He opened Mary's Bible to Ephesians, eager to read about the Armor of God.

"Norm, you didn't start the coffee—" Mary stopped mid-sentence and gasped. "You're reading the Bible."

He glanced at Mary, who stood in the doorway with both hands covering her mouth. She closed her tear-filled eyes and whispered, "Thank you, God, for answering my prayers."

He smiled in response to her joy. Then glanced down at the Bible in front of him. It was Mary's, not his. His Bible was filled with highlighted passages and verses. And in the margins of the tear-stained pages, he'd journaled both the hardships and blessings of his life. A wave of sadness washed over him. The last time he held his Bible, he'd thrown it into a box along with personal items from his old church office.

"I wish I could remember what I did with the box of things from my office. My Bible was in there," he whispered.

Mary smiled, then ran back to their bedroom. A moment later, she returned with his Bible. "Don't you remember? You took the pictures out of the box when you came home, then told me to donate everything else. I did what you asked, but I couldn't give away your Bible. Instead, I stashed it away, praying someday you'd want it back."

CHAPTER 34

Over breakfast, Norm relived the details of his dream. He told Mary about the man who exuded a warm glow and how the man helped him find his lost armor.

Mary leaned forward, sipping her coffee, appearing to cling to his every word. A smile crossed her face when he talked about picking up his sword.

"Your Bible," she whispered.

"Yes."

When he told her a demon with red eyes approached him at the end of the dream, *ready for battle,* she visibly trembled, and her face paled. "A demon?" she whispered.

He nodded. "I'm positive, Mary. This is what God meant when he told me he had a plan for me." He needed her to understand; it was his duty to act. "Do you remember the fight we had when we first found out Susan was missing?"

"I remember fighting, not what we fought about."

"I told you what happened on the night of the storm. Do you remember? The power went out, and you sent me to check on Susan. I told you I saw something was in the field, something with red eyes."

She gasped and reached for his hand. "I do remember. But what you said that night didn't make sense. I thought—"

"That I made it up?"

"Not intentionally. I thought you were distraught. You never said anything about that field until Susan ran away. I'm sorry if you felt you couldn't tell me sooner."

He brought her hand to his lips and gently kissed it. "This isn't your fault, Mary. I'm the one who saw something that night. I kept trying to convince myself it was all in my head. Because if I allowed myself to believe there was something evil out there—"

"You would have had to acknowledge God…that's what you're trying to say—isn't it?"

He slowly nodded as tears welled in his eyes. "I wasn't ready to let go of my anger. I can't help thinking that if I had, things would be different. Susan might still be here." Images of Susan flashed through his mind. He remembered the message she left on their answer machine. "Do you remember the call she made, right before we left?"

"Yes. She asked if we'd seen anything unusual in the cornfield?"

A pang of guilt squeezed his heart. "I've played that message so many times in my head." His voice trailed off.

"This is making sense to me, now. You think she saw something out in the field—don't you? Something scary enough to frighten her away. That's the reason you kept walking through that field after we came home. You were looking for something. After all these months, you still blame yourself for her disappearance."

One by one, the tears escaped his eyes. "I don't know if she saw something or if something happened to her in the field. All I know is that I've searched every inch of that field, looking for any clues to her disappearance. I believe she sensed something and was reaching out to us for help. I know I asked you back then, but I must ask you again. When you were home with your ankle, did you ever see anything strange in the field?"

She slowly shook her head. "I thought the fog was strange, and those crows gave me the willies. But as for seeing or feeling anything evil? No, I didn't. But—"

"But what?"

"I think Pastor Cummings might have."

"Pastor Cummings?"

"Don't you remember the time he came to visit me when I couldn't get to church?" She looked off in the distance. "I remember…he was standing at the window and then looked sickly all of a sudden. He told me he needed to leave. I never thought…oh, my. Do you think he saw something?"

"I'm not sure. But I'd like to sit down and ask him about it."

"I'll call Bernice today and ask her to put us on his calendar. We can invite him here for dinner. I'm sure he'd enjoy a home-cooked meal."

"That's a great idea, Mary. Maybe being here will trigger a memory."

* * *

A week later, Norm kissed Mary's cheek. "I'm meeting Bob and Dave at the diner. Too much estrogen at your women's Bible study for me to stick around."

She playfully rolled her eyes and gave a small laugh. "Very funny. Enjoy your friends. Oh, and don't forget—Pastor Cummings is coming over for dinner."

Forget Pastor was coming? Not a chance. While they'd spoken briefly over the past few weeks, this was the first opportunity the two men had to sit down and talk. A small bundle of nervous tension spread through his stomach. *Will Pastor Cummings believe I saw a pair of glowing red eyes in the field, or will he question my mental state?*

He glanced at Mary. "Do you need me to pick anything up from the store?"

"Nope. I've got everything. By the way, I'm making a roast."

His mouth watered, and his smile widened.

"I thought that would make you happy," Mary said.

Happy? He was ecstatic! Mary's pot roast was one of his favorite meals. And the roast beef sandwich he'd make with the leftovers. Yum! His stomach rumbled at the thought of two pieces of bread, covered in a layer of mayonnaise, with chunks of roast stacked in the middle. Those roast beef sandwiches always seemed tastier than the original roast dinner. "Are you making enough for me to have a few roast beef sandwiches this week?"

"Don't I always make enough?" she asked with a smile. As if to further reassure him, she added, "I bought a *huge* roast. Don't worry. They'll be plenty for dinner and leftover sandwiches."

"Thank you, honey. That's one of the many reasons I love you."

He leaned down, kissed Mary on the cheek, and then picked up his wallet and car keys from the kitchen counter. From the corner of his eye, he noticed a dark object pass by the kitchen window. He ran to the family room and flung back the curtains covering the sliding glass door.

"What's all the commotion?" Mary called out.

He didn't answer. Instead, his gaze was laser-focused on the yard. A moment later, the dark object swooped past the sliding glass door from the other direction. His heartbeat quickened. *Was that a...?*

Like a fighter pilot coming in for a strike, the large crow crisscrossed the backyard a few times, then landed on the fence that once belonged to Susan. His blood ran cold. Once settled, it slowly turned its head in his direction. Its eyes locked with his, holding his gaze for what seemed like minutes. Then slowly, the bird turned away and focused its attention on the field.

Mary was now at his side. "What are you looking at?"

He raised a shaky hand. "A crow just landed on the fence."

"Oh, not again. Remember the pigeons we had on the roof in Tucson? They're so hard to get rid of once they make your house their home. I hope this doesn't mean they're coming back. The pigeons were dirty. But the crows weren't just dirty; they gave me the creeps. I'll never forget how they covered Susan's whole yard. It was some kind of omen. I'm sure of it."

Whether their presence last summer was an omen or not. He was sure of one thing: the crows were connected to the ominous presence in the field. He opened the sliding glass door, stepped outside, then glanced up and down the row of backyards. *Calm down; there's only one.*

As that thought passed through his head, another crow landed on the fence line next to the first. He felt the Lord quicken his spirit, telling him this was the premonition of what was to come. *The crows are returning, and this time they aren't here because of the corn.*

235

CHAPTER 35

D inner with Pastor Cummings couldn't have been more timely. Throughout the day, Norm watched as more crows arrived along the fence lines of the neighbor's backyards. All the while, his and Mary's fence line remained untouched. Instead, crows clustered in small groups on the ground behind and next to his yard.

His and Mary's faith in Christ was strong. He was rereading his Bible, and he and Mary both prayed that God would protect their house through angels. He knew it was those prayers of protection which kept any crows associated with the evil presence at bay.

Promptly at five p.m., the doorbell rang.

"He's here!" Norm yelled out as he quickly headed to the front door.

The young pastor was as engaging in person as he appeared standing behind the pulpit.

"Hello, Pastor. Please come in," Norm said as he shook the pastor's hand.

"Please call me Ted. Mary told me you're a retired pastor. I've been looking forward to sitting down and talking with you."

He smiled and nodded. Having returned to the church, he no longer felt like a fraud when he heard himself referenced in this manner.

Mary stepped out of the kitchen and smiled. "Oh Pastor, we're so excited you were able to join us tonight. Dinner's almost ready."

"Thank you for inviting me. It's so nice of you to share your evening with me. I'm not sure what you're making, Mary. But it smells amazing."

Mary's face lit up. He loved to see her happy. He turned to Ted. "She's made a pot roast tonight. It's one of her specialties."

Mary wrapped her arms around his chest, squeezing him tightly, then she glanced over to Ted and motioned to the dining table. "Please have a seat. I hope you're hungry."

*** *** ***

After dinner, Norm began clearing the dinner plates. Mary took the dishes from his hands. "I've got this. You two go talk."

He kissed her on the cheek, then led Ted outside, motioning him to the pair of lawn chairs in the grass. Ten crows lined the neighboring fence line, quietly cawing and moving back and forth.

Before he could say anything, Ted pointed to the field behind the house. "The last time I was here, that field was full of corn."

The comment was a perfect segue to the conversation he'd hope to have with Ted. If Mary was right, the young pastor either saw or sensed something in the corn on his prior visit.

"That field is one of the reasons I asked you here tonight."

Ted's eyes widened. "It is?"

He took a deep breath, then spoke: "I've thought about what I'd say tonight. Now, you're here, and I'm not sure where to start."

Ted's offered a smile. "Perhaps, at the beginning?"

He nodded. Ted exuded a calmness that put him at ease.

"Do you remember that storm we had last June? The one that knocked out power to the subdivision."

"Gosh, Norm, we get so many storms around here, especially during monsoon. I can't say I remember one in particular."

"Yeah, I can understand how they might all blend together." He pointed towards the field. "Anyway, that night, after the power went out, Mary asked me to check on our neighbor, Susan."

"Isn't she the one who ran away on the Fourth of July?"

His shoulders slumped. He glanced into the field and nodded. Each time someone mentioned Susan running away, it caused him pain. If she did run away, he and Mary missed the warning signs of her mental instability. If she fell victim to the evil presence in the cornfield, he hadn't warned her. Either way, he felt culpable in her disappearance.

Ted continued, "I'm sorry, Norm. Mary said you two had taken her under your wing. I can only imagine how difficult it must be to talk about her."

He gave a short nod and said further, "Susan was a bit shook by the storm. But otherwise, okay. Once I knew she was safe, I turned and started back home. That's when I saw the crows on my roof."

A puzzled look crossed Ted's face. He pointed to the crows along the top neighbor's fence line and on the ground. "Crows on your roof during a storm?"

"Odd, right?"

Ted nodded.

"That's not all that was odd. There was also smoke in the field."

"Smoke? Like smoke from a fire?" Ted's eyes widened as he leaned closer.

"Uh-huh. The way it rose…" He shuddered as he remembered back to that night. "I don't know how else to describe it. It was like the smoke hit some kind of invisible wall and then shot straight up. It covered all the corn. I'm over six feet tall, and that smoke rose taller than me."

"And it wasn't anywhere else? Just the corn?" He pointed to the road and the backyards of the other houses.

He nodded. "I know it sounds strange…but it's true…and, there's something else…." He paused and looked down.

Ted leaned forward with his elbows on his knees and hands clasped together. "You want to tell me something. But you're struggling to find the words. You know you can speak freely in front of me."

He glanced into Ted's empathetic eyes. He knew that no matter what he said, the young pastor wouldn't judge him or break his trust.

"I believe something happened to you the night of the storm. Something that scared you."

"Yes, how did you know?" He whispered.

"I discerned your fear."

Tears welled up in his eyes. He swallowed hard and took a deep breath. "You're right. Something did happen that night. Something I couldn't explain."

"What did you see?"

He looked around the yard. They were alone. Still, he sensed he was being watched. Then he glanced at the crows. They stood perfectly still, facing their direction, no cawing, no movement. *Is it possible those crows are listening in on our conversation?* That thought would have been laughable if the conversation weren't so grave. He looked away from the crows and leaned closer to Ted. In a voice no higher than a whisper, he said, "I saw two red glowing eyes in that smoke."

"What?" A look of bewilderment washed over Ted's face. He shook his head and leaned back. Then, after a moment, he asked, "Some kind of animal?"

He vigorously shook his head. "No, Ted. Those eyes were level with mine." He pointed to the area of the field directly behind his home. "It stood right there, directly behind our home."

Ted's eyes widened. After a moment, he appeared to regain his composure. "I believe you."

"You do?" A wave of relief washed over him. For months, he'd held onto that secret. Unwilling, then too afraid to share it with others.

Ted nodded, lowered his hands, and said: "Now, there's something I need to tell you."

"Okay."

"Do you remember when I came to your house to visit Mary? She was home with a sprained ankle."

"Yes, I let you into the house."

Ted paused for a moment. "After Mary and I talked, she sat in her recliner and asked me if I could open the curtain so she could look outside. The first thing I saw were crows on the fence. There must have been over a hundred of them on these fences. They were all riled up. At first, I thought maybe an animal was coming. But then I sensed something. I don't know how else to describe it other than it felt like something evil was moving through the cornfield, headed straight for me."

A sense of relief washed over him. *It wasn't my imagination. Ted sensed it too!*

"Did you see anything?"

Ted shook his head.

"There's something else I want to tell you." Images of Susan flashed through his head. His voice cracked, and he fought back the tears. "I don't know how to say this…so, I'm just going to say it."

"Are you okay?" Ted placed a hand on his shoulder.

He leaned forward, clasped his hands together, and rested them under his chin. "It's about Susan."

"The neighbor who ran away?"

He closed his eyes and slumped his shoulders. *Am I the only person who thinks there might be another explanation for her disappearance?* He sighed. "Mary and I didn't know about her history. So, I'll admit it was quite a shock for us. We were out of town when she went missing, and by the time we came home, rumors about her having a breakdown and running away had already taken hold. But people didn't know Susan the way we did. She might have been young, but she had a good head on her shoulders. So, I guess what I'm trying to say is that I don't think she ran away."

"But the sheriff's office…they concluded she did. If she didn't run away—" Ted's eyes widened, and the color drained from his face. He pointed to the field. "Are you trying to tell me you think she went into the field?"

He paused for a moment, then inched closer to Ted and nodded. After Mary dismissed his suspicions once they'd found out Susan was missing, he'd kept quiet, worried that no one would believe him. Then, finally, there was a chance someone would. He anxiously scanned Ted's face, looking for a response.

Ted held his gaze for a moment before he spoke. "What makes you think she went into the field? Did you come across something? Some piece of evidence?"

He slowly shook his head. "I searched the whole field. The only thing I found was a handful of animal bones. So, no proof…just a gut feeling."

Ted looked down. After a moment, he answered, "I do believe there was something in that field. I felt it. You saw it." He wrung his hands together, "But…I don't know, Norm. If you're asking me to believe it took your neighbor?" He shook his head. "That's a pretty big leap for me to take. Especially when the sheriff has evidence she ran away."

A pang of disappointment filled his chest. Perhaps the pastor would see things differently once he explained his dream.

Just as he opened his mouth to speak, Mary's upper body extended out through the opening.

"Are you two ready for dessert?" she asked.

He held up his hand. "Could you give us a few more minutes, honey. We're almost done."

"Sure…I'll set out the coffee and cake," Mary said as she slid the door shut.

He turned back to Ted. "I understand what you're saying. Honestly, I do. If a member of my old congregation brought this claim to me, I'd likely counsel them away from this train of thought. But two things happened to me recently. I think when you hear it, you might change your mind."

"What happened?"

"Well, first off, God told me I was meant to know Susan. I believe that means that I was supposed to know what happened to her. He also told me I needed to be vigilant. He had plans for me."

"God has plans for all of us. We just need to put our trust in him," Ted interrupted.

"Yes, I know that's true. But I believe God's plans for me involve Susan. Or at least, what happened to Susan. I've kept myself open, waiting for God to either tell or show me what he meant. That's when I had a dream."

"Dream—that's the second thing that happened to you?"

He nodded. "That dream connected all the dots. I now understand that the red eyes I saw in the cornfield last June belonged to a demon. Through the dream, God showed me the demon. I know my purpose is to fight it."

A knowing look crossed Ted's face. "I know Mary is waiting on us. We need to finish this conversation. Do you think you could come into my office this week?"

"I don't think we have much time. I believe the demon is coming back soon."

"Is that what you ascertained from your dream?"

"No. It's the crows."

"I don't understand."

He pointed to the crows. "I think you feel it too. The crows are connected to the demon. They started arriving last weekend. But there's no corn in the field. So, why did they come back?"

Ted glanced at the crows on the fence again and nodded. "Let's get together within the next few days. Maybe you could come to my office. There's something I have to do before we meet. But I'll call you once that's done."

* * *

On the drive home, he replayed Norm's words in his mind. *The crows are coming back.* There was something strange about the crows when he visited Mary. The excitement they displayed when he sensed something evil was palpable. Regardless of what Tobias said, his family conjured the demon out of greed. The crows could be lesser demons, extensions of that main demon—demons of anger, unforgiveness, jealousy, and hatred.

The fact they weren't on Norm and Mary's fence line was further proof they were connected. Norm and Mary were strong in their faith and knowledge. They were reading God's word and praying for protection over their house. That's the reason the crows wouldn't cross over their fence line. Even though they weren't able to get physically close, he knew they were intently listening to every word of his and Norm's conversation. It was the reason he invited Norm to his office.

He hadn't settled on a meeting time because he needed to first speak with Tobias and Sarah. He had no intentions of breaking their trust. But he hoped, once they learned of Norm's dream, they'd permit him to share the secret of the summoning spell and room.

There was a farewell potluck planned for John and Kate after tomorrow's service. Between the service and potluck, he hoped Tobias would find time to speak with him. Besides garnering his permission to share information with Norm, he also wanted to make sure Tobias had shared everything he knew about the demon.

The meeting with Norm had left him unsettled. Something Norm said bothered him, like an annoying itch he needed to scratch. Norm said he was *meant* to know Susan. He also seemed confident the phrase had dual meaning. He was meant to know her *and* know what happened to her.

The sheriff seemed confident she'd run away. But Norm seemed equally sure she'd wandered into the field. *What if Norm's right?* Tobias told him the cornfield was designed as a snare. A place where the demon could lure in small animals then feed on them. He knew it wasn't improbable that a human could be drawn into its trap. He shuddered as he visualized Susan stepping into the rows of corn.

Tobias cleared the area after the harvest, removing and burying all evidence of the demon's devastation. Was he sure only animals met their ending in the field? If the demon attacked Susan and Tobias knew, then covered it up, he hadn't fully repented. He'd left an open door for this and other demons to walk through. Neither his life nor home was safeguarded.

CHAPTER 36

Ted waited anxiously for the opportunity to shake Tobias's hand after the service. When Tobias stood before him, he pulled him in slightly and looked him in the eye. "Good morning, Tobias. I was hoping we could talk today, either before or after the potluck."

Tobias shook his head. "I'm sorry, Pastor. Today's not good. John and Kate are leaving this afternoon."

"Oh, I didn't realize they were leaving so soon."

He nodded. "John thinks it'll be better for Kate if they spread out the trip. They'll get in a few hours of driving today, stay in a motel, then finish the drive tomorrow. Sarah and I want to spend as much time with them as we can before they leave."

"I completely understand. How about tomorrow? Perhaps I could stop by the farm?"

Tobias nodded. "Sure, just give me a call in the morning."

✳ ✳ ✳

After the potluck, as Tobias drove onto the farm, a fullness pressed upon his chest. He took a few deep breaths, trying to shrug the feeling aside. *I'm feeling this way because John and Kate are leaving.*

By three o'clock, John and Kate were on the road. Charles and Rachael left soon after. For the first time he, Sarah, James, and Daniel were alone. The fullness in his chest returned. Although he was sure it was related to his sadness, he couldn't shake the feeling. *Something's wrong.*

After burning the book and cleansing their home, he'd pushed aside thoughts of the demon. Why let worries of the evil's return consume him when there was a chance they'd prevented it from coming back to the farm?

He kissed Sarah on the cheek, then jumped into his truck and headed for the north field, the same place where he'd planted corn every summoning year. A sad reminder of Susan's fate, he'd avoided it since the last harvest. He couldn't avoid it anymore. If something were amiss on the farm, he'd most likely find evidence of it there.

From a distance, tiny black dots lined the fence line. Once he drew closer, his heart sank. Crows! There were hundreds of them lining the fence lines of all but one of the homes that butted up against his field.

The appearance of crows preceded every summoning spell. *Not again!* His mind screamed out. Then his thoughts turned to John and Kate. *John did the right thing for his family.* As much as it pained him that they'd chosen to live in Texas, he was grateful they were making a new life for themselves away from the farm.

* * *

Later, over dinner, Sarah glanced in his direction. "You're quiet tonight."

He glanced at Daniel and James. Both men stopped eating and turned their attention to the exchange between himself and Sarah.

He forced a smile. "It's nothing. I was just thinking."

James spoke up: "About John and Kate? For me, it feels strange not having them here."

Daniel nodded at James. "It feels strange for me too."

He glanced back at Sarah. She narrowed her eyes as she studied his face, then curtly shook her head. "You seem nervous."

Ever since he'd told Sarah about his family's dark secret, she'd become a proverbial sleuth. If she sensed he was hiding anything, she'd keep probing and prodding until she uncovered the truth. He didn't want to lie. He just wanted to get through one family dinner without talk of tragedy.

He shook his head and forced a smile. "It's nothing."

Sarah shrugged and began eating again, giving him a momentary reprieve from further questioning.

He picked up his fork with a shaking hand, then lowered it before anyone at the table noticed. *Sarah's right. I am nervous.* In the past, when he was anxious, he'd smoke one cigarette after another. After cleansing the house, he promised Sarah he'd start taking better care of himself. He couldn't commit to getting a physical, but he did promise to quit smoking. A promise he'd kept. Now, with the nervous tension spreading through every part of his body, he craved a cigarette.

He kept silent throughout dinner, offering smiles as he listened to his sons' lighthearted banter. Then, as Sarah began to clear her dinner plate, he reached for her hand. "We need to talk."

Daniel turned towards James and joked, "Guess that's our cue to leave."

"No." He held his hand up, signaling for them to remain at the table. "I want you two to stay. There's something we need to talk about as a family."

A knowing look washed over Sarah's face. She leaned back and studied his face. "I knew something was wrong."

He tried to keep his voice calm. "I'm sorry. I just wanted to get through dinner. I don't know quite how to say this, so I'll just say it. I believe the demon is coming back."

Sarah's face paled. "Why? Why do you think that?"

Before he could respond, Daniel's voice raised. "But you said burning the book might have destroyed it."

I wish it were that simple—burn the book, kill the evil. He shook his head. "I'm sorry. I think I was wrong. I drove near the field this afternoon. There are hundreds of crows on the fences."

He watched as the color drained from James' face. "I remember the crows," he whispered.

"Do you think the crows are tied to the demon?" Daniel asked.

"I've wondered about it. They've always shown up about a week before I performed the summoning spell. So I didn't know if there was a connection or just here for the corn. But they're back, and there's no corn in the field, so yes, I feel they are somehow connected."

James' eyes widened, and a bead of sweat broke out on his brow. "Did you say a week? Are you saying you think it'll come back *this* week?" he asked in a hushed voice.

Daniel slowly shook his head and whispered, "This doesn't seem real."

He looked at the three of them. He wished he could tell them it wasn't real, that they were spectators and not the central characters in a real-life horror story.

Sarah straightened her shoulders and took a deep breath. "This week? You're fairly certain?"

"Yes, by next weekend. There'll be a new moon."

"New moon?"

"No moonlight."

"I know what a new moon is, Tobias. What does it mean?"

He sensed her irritation. He looked down at his plate, then at the small window above the sink. Each time he thought of the summoning ritual, a pang of guilt shook his soul. *You have to tell them.* Finally, he turned and looked into their faces. "I hate talking about this, but you should know— I've always performed the summoning ritual close to the new moon. If I performed the ritual this year, the best day would be Friday."

Sarah straightened her shoulders. "Pastor Cummings cleansed our home, and I've prayed every day since that God will continue to protect our home from evil."

The fullness in his chest returned, and a squeezing pain stole his breath. It was the same discomfort he'd felt earlier in the day. It wasn't sadness. He was feeling this way because he hadn't fully repented. But there was more. Pastor Cummings instructed him to pray over his house and land. He faithfully prayed for God's protection over his home and family. But praying over the field where his forefathers cast spells and he planted corn? He'd tried but couldn't do it. He couldn't walk more than a few steps without looking over his shoulder, expecting to find the demon right behind him. Then, seeing nothing, he'd quickly looked back at the ground, sure the demon would reach out and grab him at any moment. Unable to spend more than a few moments on the land, he'd begun avoiding it at all costs. Had his disobedience and lack of repentance placed his family in danger?

Daniel's voice interrupted his thoughts. "Our home is protected. But what about the houses in the subdivision. The fences we put up will keep people from coming onto our property. But there's nothing to keep the demon from going to those homes."

His blood turned cold. "If it comes back, it'll come for me," he exclaimed out loud. "It'll be angry because I've turned my back on it."

It was only wishful thinking. But he hoped it was true. It was naïve to think the demon wouldn't attack families in the subdivision. But each time the notion crossed his mind, he'd flick it away like a nasty bug crawling on his skin. He'd rather die than allow another innocent victim to be hurt on his account.

"We'll be right beside you," Daniel said.

He shook his head. "Sarah, I want you to pack a bag and call your sister. You'll be safe there. James, Daniel, you can go with your mom or stay with your brother in Tucson."

"No! Absolutely not." James pushed back his chair and stood. "That's not what we all agreed." He pointed to Sarah. "Yes, to Mom leaving. But, me, Daniel, Charles, and John—we all said we'd fight this with you."

He'd hoped by burning the book and cleansing the house, there'd be a chance the demon wouldn't come back, and if it did, it wouldn't return for years. That was the only reason he'd welcomed their help. Once faced with the realization the evil could come back this week, he wanted his family as far away as possible. Unfortunately, Daniel and Charles weren't young boys anymore; they were grown men. They wouldn't leave willingly.

✴ ✴ ✴

Compared to Sundays, the church parking lot on Monday mornings was as bare as a tree in the middle of winter. Ted knew he'd find only one car in the lot, Bernice's. She arrived early every morning and started the coffee pot. By the time he showed up, she'd have a steaming cup of coffee on his desk.

Driving to church and pulling into his parking space was a routine so mundane he did it almost without thinking. It was no different than brushing his teeth or tying his shoes.

The usual sense of calmness he experienced when he parked his car was shattered once he glanced up at the sign above his parking space. Perched on the sign was a crow. He'd been pastor at Desert Springs for over a year. In all that time, he'd never once seen a bird perched on the sign. Let alone a crow. *What are the odds there'd be one today?* He didn't need to do the math. In his heart, he knew—*zero chance.*

The piercing eyes of the crow stared down at him, sending a chilling wave through his body. He couldn't shake the feeling the crow had thrown down a spiritual gauntlet, challenging him to enter the fight. A warm calmness fell upon him, pushing the chill aside. *We've already won the battle through Christ.* He stepped out of the car, stared back at the crow, and in a voice of conviction, said, "We'll win!"

✳ ✳ ✳

Monday morning. Despite the fitful sleep, Tobias woke early and headed downstairs. Pastor Cummings phoned soon after breakfast. "Good morning, Tobias. When's a good time for me to come over?"

"I'm sorry, Pastor, today's not a good day for me."

"It's really important, Tobias."

Only one thing would be significant enough to bring the pastor out to the farm. *He's calling about the demon.* Did he also sense its return? "I think we should talk over the phone."

After a brief pause, the pastor spoke again. "Okay, I'm calling about the secret you and Sarah shared with me last fall."

Engulfed in shame, he closed his eyes for a moment. The layer of dirt and sweat covering his skin at the end of a long day could be washed away with soap and water. Unfortunately, there wasn't a soap strong enough to cleanse the dark stain from his soul.

"Tobias? You still there?"

"Sorry. Yes, Pastor. Still here."

"It's about the demon, Tobias. I think it's coming back."

"I do too, Pastor. I think it'll come back this weekend."

"Then, I insist on coming to the farm. You'll need my help, Tobias. There's another pastor—"

"No!" A wave of anger washed over him. There was no way he'd put more lives at risk. "I'm sorry, Pastor. I don't want anyone else involved in this. I know you're trying to help, and I appreciate everything you've done for us. But this is my problem. I'll take care of it."

"Tobias, please reconsider. I'm offering to help you!"

"There is something you can do for me, Pastor."

"Anything. Name it."

"You can pray for us. And, if something happens and I'm unable to rid my family of this demon, I need to know you'll help my sons."

There was a gasp on the other end of the line—followed by silence.

"Pastor? I'm serious. I need you to promise you'll help my sons."

"Tobias, I will always help you and your family. But I'm worried about the way you're talking. I can't help thinking you'll do something reckless, something that will put your life in danger."

He would have laughed if the situation were not so grave. Instead, an eerie calmness washed over him. He'd do whatever it took to rid his family of the demon forever.

"Thank you, Pastor, for everything you've done. I've got it from here."

"Tobias…wait. You need me. When the demon comes back, I need to know you'll call me. I can help you."

He closed his eyes and slightly shook his head. Despite the pastor's insistence, his mind was made up. He'd never knowingly put another life in danger. By the tone in the pastor's voice, he feared he'd show up on the farm anyway. He had to say something to appease him. "Okay, I promise to give you a call."

"You will?"

"Yes."

He wondered if lying to the pastor in the hopes of saving the pastor's life still counted as a sin. Even if it did, he hoped God would forgive it.

CHAPTER 37

Eager to keep people away from the farm for the rest of the week, Tobias spent the next day going through a mental checklist. Ensure no deliveries in or out of the farm till the end of the month —check. Secure the gates and fences surrounding their property— check. By nightfall, the farm was secure and temporarily closed.

He hoped it wouldn't be a permanent closure. Because if it was, it meant he hadn't survived. Running the farm was difficult. With two of his sons living elsewhere, Sarah would have to sell the farm if something happened to him.

He brushed his teeth and crawled into bed. As he closed his eyes, the sound of an auctioneer's voice passed through his head. "Next on the auction block, this 1959 John Deere 630 Mounted Corn Picker. Isn't she a beauty? Hardly used, not a spot of rust. Let's start the bidding at..." He shuddered, then silently prayed God would help him.

Within a few moments, he was in the midst of the most vivid dream of his life. In his dream, he stood in the field where he planted corn. It was also the place where his forefathers performed spells and sacrifices. He looked on the ground around him. Once he realized he was in the circular clearing where he'd found Susan's purse and keys, he shuddered.

In the distance, a bright figure appeared. His heart raced within his chest. Slowly, the figure continued to advance. With each step, it consolidated, growing into focus. By the time the figure reached him, he had realized it was an angel of the Lord.

Like a warm blanket on a cold night, a comforting sensation spread through his body. He took deep breaths, slowing his racing heart.

The angel looked around at the field, then into his eyes. "There is no corn in this field."

"I'll never plant it again."

"And the ritual?"

"I'll never perform it again."

"You sense the evil returning, and now you're afraid...."

Afraid? He wasn't just scared; he was terrified. The demon enacted his vengeance on his great uncle, Jonas, by taking his children. What would it do to him and his family?

Movement on the ground caught his eye. He glanced down. All around him, wisps of smoky mist rose from the earth. It churned and grew thicker as it pumped out of the ground at a frenzied pace.

"This is what you fear." The angel pointed to the smoke churning out of the ground.

Within seconds, the mist engulfed him. He couldn't see more than a few inches from his face. *Run!* His mind screamed as his heart raced to a fevered pitch. Finally, he chose a direction and began running as fast as he could. Unfortunately, he only made it a few yards before stumbling and crashing onto the cold hard earth. The mist pressed down on him, choking the breath from his lungs and chilling his body.

"Be strong. Fear not." The angel's voice rang out. It broke through the mist and pulled him upright. Slowly the mist receded. The angel continued holding onto his arm. The warmth in his body slowly returned, and his racing heart calmed.

"Do not be anxious. This battle belongs to the Lord."

This battle belongs to the Lord. This was the same thing Pastor Cummings said when he cleansed his home. Outwardly, he nodded in agreement. Sarah and his sons were innocents; surely, God would fight for them.

But, inwardly, he doubted God would grant him the same favor. He'd summoned the demon, lied to his family, and withheld vital evidence in Susan's disappearance. No matter how much Pastor Cummings and Sarah reminded him, Christ paid for everyone's sins when he died on the cross; he struggled to believe he was worthy of God's love and forgiveness.

The angel spoke as if he'd read his thoughts. "As far as the east is from the west, so far has He removed our transgressions from us."

Pastor Cummings said something similar in the aftermath of cleansing their home. *He also told me the old me passed away and that I was a new creation in Christ!* Pastor Cummings warned that demons try to keep people from accepting the Word of God.

Angrily, he shook his head. *I've allowed this demon to sow seeds of doubt in my mind.* Convinced he deserved eternal punishment, he'd persuaded himself the only way he could atone for his family's darkness was to sacrifice himself to destroy the evil. *But there's no condemnation in Christ!* He had to let go of guilt and rise above his doubts. He needed to believe he was worthy of God's love.

"As the Lord has forgiven you, so you also must forgive."

I do forgive others. I just haven't forgiven myself! That realization sent tears flowing down his face. He fell to his knees and prayed for forgiveness. Then he thanked the Lord for sending him the angel and for His continued mercy, grace, and protection.

His thoughts turned to the demon's return. He looked up at the angel. "How do we defeat the demon?"

"You've already won the battle through Christ."

Pastor Cummings told him this was a spiritual fight, not a physical one. His faith was the weapon that would destroy the demon and his family's curse. Having worked with his hands his entire life, he struggled to wrap his mind around that concept.

Pastor's right. This is a spiritual fight. His sons would be there at his side.

Again, as if reading his mind, the angel pointed to four figures standing in the distance. Although their images were blurred, he was confident the figures represented his four sons. Then, one of the figures turned and walked away. *He's leaving! But which one? John? Charles?* His heart raced again.

"You are afraid your sons will abandon you," the angel said. Then the angel pointed in the opposite direction. "Do not worry. God is raising up an army to come along side you."

He looked in the direction where the angel pointed. A tall, gray-haired man wearing glasses approached. A wave of relief washed over him.

"I recognize him from church. That's Mary's husband, Norm."

CHAPTER 38

The following morning Tobias rose out of bed and dressed. By the time he entered the kitchen, Sarah had breakfast on the table. She looked into his face. "You overslept. Are you feeling alright?"

He nodded. Last night's dream played again in his head. A vision of white smoke seeping up from the field flashed through his mind. *The evil is coming.* He shuddered. *I'm not sure I know how to fight it!* The shudder was followed by a warm feeling of peace as a comforting voice in his head whispered, *Remember, this battle belongs to the Lord. You are not alone!* His shoulders relaxed. *I'm not alone.* He remembered the dream and the promise to send a man of faith. *He'll know what to do.*

"You look worried. Are you sure you're okay?" Sarah asked as she approached and wrapped her arms around him.

He nodded, then softly kissed her forehead. "I want you to call Peggy and let her know you're coming today."

She shook her head. "I'm packed and ready to leave. But I'm not going to my sister's until I'm certain I have to. You said if the evil returned, you thought there'd be a storm. You said there's always a storm on the night you perform the spell, right?" She leaned forward and looked out the window. "It's a beautiful day, Tobias. Not a cloud in the sky. I've checked the news; the forecast said clear skies all week. So maybe burning the book worked."

A slight twinge of hope rose in his chest. It disappeared once he thought about the crows and remembered the dream. He also sensed a growing wave of static electricity in the air. The kind of energy that made you think twice before touching something metal. It was the same electricity that hung in the air after every summoning. The weather forecaster got it wrong. A storm was headed their way.

* * *

After a few bites of scrambled eggs and toast, the sound of gravel being crushed under the wheels of a truck captured his attention. He took another bite of toast and a sip of his coffee before putting the cup on the table. "That's Daniel. I'd better get moving."

"Here…let me put your coffee in a travel mug and take the rest of the toast. Then, I'll walk out front with you."

Together they strolled to the front porch. Sarah reached for his hand. It was such a comforting gesture. He squeezed her fingers gently, relishing the softness. His mind desperately sought to catalog every detail of Sarah. He was prepared to die, prepared to face judgment. He only hoped he'd take the memory of her with him.

He climbed into the front seat of Daniel's truck. Sarah moved to the driver's side and leaned in. "Good morning. Daniel."

A smile spread over Daniel's face. "Hey, Mom."

Of all his sons, Daniel resembled Sarah most. He shared the same olive complexion and dark hair. He'd also inherited her quick wit and patience.

"What time did you wake up this morning?" Sarah asked.

"Honestly, neither James nor I got to sleep much last night. He's already at the barn."

He turned to Daniel. "Did you double-check all the fences and gates as I asked?"

Daniel nodded. "Yep. All the gates are chained and padlocked, except the one you said to leave chained but unlocked."

"That's good."

Yesterday afternoon, he'd asked Daniel to secure all the gates except one, leaving an indiscreet way for Charles and John to get onto the farm. And if last night's dream were prophetic, Mary's husband, Norm, would join them. He'd also need a way onto their property.

Sarah stepped away and waved. "I'll see you all at lunch."

Daniel hit the accelerator, sending bits of gravel into the air. He grabbed onto the small bar above the door while holding the travel mug full of coffee out in front of him with the other hand. The truck bounced and swayed as Daniel sped down the dirt road towards the barn. There was an unspoken agreement between the two of them; he stopped asking Daniel to drive slower, and Daniel stopped asking him to wear a seatbelt.

Within a few moments, they pulled up to the barn. Corrals with various animals dotted the barn's perimeter. James was inside feeding their horses. He smiled and raised his hand. "Morning."

"Good morning, James. Your brother said neither of you got much sleep."

"We didn't…we were talking most of the night. We think you should call Pastor Cummings. He knows about the demon. He'll be able to help us."

Unbeknownst to them, he almost phoned Pastor Cummings as soon as he woke. He'd scrolled through the contact list on his phone, clicked onto his name, but hung up just before the call went through. *It was Norm in the dream, not Pastor Cummings.* Phoning the pastor would bring him straight to the farm and likely put his life in danger. He'd watched Sarah and his sons grieve the loss of Pastor Cummings' predecessor. It took over a year for the congregation to heal. So he'd only call him as a last resort.

"I spoke with Pastor Cummings yesterday. I don't want to put him in harm's way. But I'm willing to call him if there's no other option."

Daniel shook his head "No, dad. I know you're trying to protect him, but he wants to help us. He should be here now, telling us what we need to do."

They both think I'm leading them into a fight without a plan. *I have to tell them about the dream. Knowing Norm would be there to help would ease their mind.* "Come, sit down. I need to tell you about the dream I had last night."

✳ ✳ ✳

For the past two hours, Sarah stared out the window, watching dark gray clouds gather on the horizon. *Tobias was right. There's a storm headed our way.* Behind her, the kitchen door creaked open and slammed shut, jarring her out of her daydream state. She glanced up. Tobias led her sons into the house. One look at their faces said it all. *They'd seen the clouds.*

256

Before she could utter a word, Tobias spoke up: "It's coming, Sarah. I can feel it."

Tears filled her eyes. She felt it too—like an invisible current was running through the air, raising the hairs on her arms. It grew stronger as the gray clouds moved closer. She quietly nodded as tears slid down her face.

He gently held onto her arms and looked into her eyes. Then, in a soft voice, he whispered, "Grab your suitcase. Daniel is taking you to Peggy's house. It's time for you to go."

She opened her mouth to protest, then quickly closed it. There was no sense in arguing. Tobias was under the misguided impression leaving the farm would keep her safe. She'd tried to tell him demons could spiritually attack them anywhere. But he was convinced it was safer at her sister's house. Finally, she relented. If staying with her sister offered Tobias a moment's peace, she'd leave. No matter how far away she was from the farm, God would hear her prayers.

"I'll pack our lunches while you get your bag," Daniel offered.

"Thank you, Daniel," she said.

Once she came back downstairs, Tobias pulled her close. She fell against his chest and gently sobbed.

"I know you're worried, but I will protect our sons at all costs," he whispered into her ear.

She shuddered and whispered back, "That's why I'm worried. I can't help thinking one of you will do something reckless to save the others. But, don't forget, this battle belongs to God. You have to put your trust in him."

She felt him nod as he stroked the hair down her back with his calloused hands. More than anything, she wanted to stay in the moment, safe within his arms. But she and Daniel needed to get on the road. If they left now, he'd make it back by sunset.

She pulled away and then hugged James, kissing him on the cheek. "Be careful and listen to your father. I love you. I'll see you soon."

Then she looked back at Tobias. "Call Pastor Cummings. He needs to come now."

The shake of Tobias' head sent her heart plummeting downward. *They can't do this alone!*

Tobias must have seen a look on her face because he quickly spoke up, saying, "Don't worry, Sarah. We won't be alone. God is sending someone to help us." Then he turned to Daniel. "You two need to get on the road. Tell your mom about the dream I had last night on the drive to Peggy's."

Daniel nodded.

Dream? What dream? Who's coming to help? Before she could ask those questions, Daniel wrapped his arm around her shoulder. "Come on, Mom, we better go."

✳ ✳ ✳

Tobias watched Daniel and Sarah as they pulled away from the house. Then, in a surprising move he hadn't seen since high school, Sarah leaned her upper body out the passenger window and waved her arms in the air. Her long black hair cascaded around her face. He raised his hand in response, fighting back the tears. This was the first time in twenty-two years of marriage they'd spend the night apart. Sarah was more than his lover and lifelong friend; she was his rock. No matter how much he wanted her at his side, he had to send her away. There was no way he'd forgive himself if anything happened to her.

Once Daniel's truck was out of sight, he returned to the kitchen. James was hanging up his cell phone.

"I called Charles and John. Unfortunately, both phones went to voicemail, but I've left messages. Charles will come. I'm sure of it. I know John and Kate just got to Texas, but I think he might come too."

He smiled and nodded. When he told James and Daniel about his dream, he'd left out the part about one of the four figures stepping away. *Some things are better left unsaid.* There was no need to sow discourse among his sons when he didn't know to whom the angel was referring.

They ate their lunch in silence. Afterward, Tobias stepped onto the back porch. The scent of imminent rain filled the air. He looked towards the horizon. The clouds hadn't moved closer to the farm, but they'd consolidated into one giant, dark mass along the top of the mountain range.

The kitchen door creaked open and slammed shut behind him. "What do we do now?" James asked as he stepped onto the porch.

"Let's secure everything at the barn. The storm will be here by sundown."

* * *

The afternoon traffic delayed Daniel's return home. By the time he'd pulled up to the main gate, black clouds were thick in the sky, shrouding the farm in darkness. He leaped from the truck, then fought gusts of wind as he unlocked the main gate. *This must be how Dorothy felt just before the tornado carried her away.*

After resecuring the gate, he continued down the gravel road. The darkness was disorienting. He glanced at the clock on the radio; 7:27 p.m. In the distance, the home's lights beckoned him forward.

As he pulled in front of the house, the first drops of rain struck the windshield. He stepped from the truck and wrapped his arms around himself. Thick, cold air filled his lungs. It was likely his imagination, but the air seemed to wrap itself around him, squeezing the breath from his lungs and holding him in place. Finally, he closed his eyes and called out, "Please, God, protect me!"

The squeezing pressure abated. He sprinted to the back porch, entering the house through the kitchen. The door slammed shut in his wake.

James and his dad were sitting at the kitchen table. Upon his haphazard arrival, they both leaped from their chairs.

"Are you alright?" his father asked.

James's eyes widened. "You look like you've seen a ghost."

He shook his head and raised his hand, "I'm...I'll be okay. It's so dark outside, like it's the middle of the night, dark. And it's cold. It just freaked me out, that's all."

He poured him a cup of coffee. "Here...sit down."

He wrapped his hands around the warm mug. "Mom's safe and sound at Aunt Peggy's."

His dad breathed a sigh of relief. "Thank you for taking her, Daniel."

Then he looked around the room, then at his father. "Where's Norm?" There were only three of them in the room. The storm was barreling down on them. So, where was the help God promised he'd send?

James looked up at his father. "I think we should call him."

Before his dad could respond, the storm increased in intensity. Raindrops pelted the house, while the wind shook the windows and moved patio furniture around the porch like small chest pieces.

"We'd better secure the furniture," James said as he leaped from the table.

He nodded. "Good idea."

The wind rose in fury just as James opened the back door. A gust of wind yanked the doorknob from his grasp. The kitchen door slammed against the house. Sounds of water cascading in sheets off the porch echoed through the kitchen.

He followed James through the doorway and onto the porch.

Rocking chairs and tables lay strewn in shattered heaps over the porch. There was nothing left to secure. He grabbed onto James's arm and pointed to the house, signaling for them to return inside. James nodded and followed.

As they stepped into the kitchen, a crash of lightning and a thunderous boom shook the home's foundation. The wave of energy it generated propelled them forward onto the cold kitchen floor. A wave of pain went through his body. *Did lightning just strike us?* After a moment, he felt a gentle shaking of his arm, followed by the sound of his brother's voice: "Danny…Danny…are you okay?"

"Don't…call…me…Danny," he whispered.

"Oh, thank God…he's okay," James said.

The brief fogginess and pain of the fall faded, replaced with the horrifying knowledge he was lying on the cold kitchen floor awaiting the attack of an evil enemy. "What happened?" he asked as he turned onto his side and then sat upright.

"Lightning struck and sent you two boys flying back through the door." His dad helped him off the floor. "are you okay?"

"Just sore." Then he looked up at James. "So, let me guess, I broke your fall."

"I'm sorry. Are you sure you're alright?"

He nodded.

James turned and stepped out the backdoor. Instead of one long steady gust, the wind came in short intermittent bursts, each a little less potent than before. The rhythmic tapping of the rain continued, but, just like the wind, the intensity lessened.

He and his dad followed James outside and to the other side of the porch. James pointed at the twenty-foot-tall tree standing beside their home. "That strike took out the tree."

A momentary wave of sadness filled his chest. The tree had been a constant presence on the farm throughout his life. It was split directly down the middle. The half of the tree, which housed a makeshift swing, lay on the ground. As the youngest boy in the family, he'd been pushed in the swing by each of his brothers. With half of the tree branches missing, the once beautiful tree stood disfigured and bare. He stared at the place where lightning struck the tree. Despite the deluge of rain, smoldering embers still threatened to ignite.

James pointed again, this time at the main phone line. Its wooden pole and phone wires all lay in a heap beneath the branch. "It's also knocked out all the phones on the property."

They all turned and looked at the storm. It hovered over the north field, the summoning field. In the distance, another bolt of lightning struck, followed nearly simultaneously by booming thunder. The subdivision and farm plunged into utter darkness.

They all jumped. "Damn!" he yelled, then quickly covered his mouth with his hand. It was too late; the word had already escaped his lips. Then he pictured his mom shaking her head. She hated cursing.

"Good thing Mom's at Aunt Peggy's," James chuckled.

His dad smiled slightly; then, a serious look crossed his face. "Could you grab the flashlights Daniel?"

He nodded and ran back into the kitchen. The flashlights, matches, and candles were in a small cabinet near the back door. He fumbled inside the cabinet until he located two flashlights. He handed one to his dad and kept the other for himself. James reached for the one in his hand. He playfully pulled it back. "Get one for yourself. This one's mine."

James shook his head, then fumbled through the cabinet. "Hey, there are only candles left in here." He held a candle to his nose, inhaled, then gagged. "Pine. Gross."

"Take those candles out from the cabinet. We'll need them when we get back," his dad said.

"Get back from where?" he asked.

"I want to drive out to the field to see what's going on."

"I'll drive." He held up his keys. With a flashlight in hand, he led the way along the covered porch to the front of the house. James and his dad climbed into the truck alongside him. The road was water-sodden.

"I'm not sure we can make it without getting stuck in the mud," James stated from the back seat.

His dad nodded his head in agreement. "Do your best to stay on the higher ground."

The headlights of his truck provided the only means to navigate the gravel road. As they made their way to the field, the rain slowed to a slight drizzle. The truck bobbed and weaved like a fighter in the boxing ring. It dipped up and down on the road, jarring them around the cab. He drove slowly, avoiding the water-filled pockets on the road. The layer of gravel thinned as they grew closer to the field. Thick mud puddles covered the ground.

"Stop the truck, Daniel," his dad called out. "Otherwise, we'll get stuck."

He stopped just short of the irrigation canal. He could tell by the feel of the steering wheel; his tires were bogged down into the mud. "I think we might be stuck already."

They climbed out of the truck. His dad shined a flashlight onto the wheels; the front two tires were wedged deep within the earth. "You're right. We'll have to walk back to the house tonight. We can come back tomorrow to pick up your truck."

James grabbed the flashlight he'd left in the truck. He held it up to his chin as he walked by, shining the light upon his face. "Nice driving there, Danny boy."

Daniel shuddered. For a brief second, James looked like a boy in a horror movie. That thought was quickly followed by the realization he and his family were trapped in their own horror story. His stomach clenched. He pushed the thought from his mind and reached for the flashlight.

"Oh, no, you don't." James laughed as he pulled his arm back. "It's my flashlight now."

The edge in his dad's voice captured his attention. "Come on…let's get a look at the field."

They navigated the muddy ground and small footbridge over the irrigation canal. Within minutes, they stood at the edge of the field. James and his dad raised their flashlights in unison, pushing back the darkness.

The pungent odor of sulfur filled the chilled air. He wrapped his arms around his body to ward off the cold, then took a step forward.

His dad grabbed his shoulder and pulled him back. "Stay off the ground."

"But—"

His dad aimed the flashlight on the ground in front of him. "There."

He looked. Swirling wisps of a smoke-like mist rose from the ground. *It's moving.* His stomach clenched. "Is that what I think it is?"

"Yes, I'm afraid it is," his dad answered.

He kept watching the ground. The wispy smoke continued to rise at a rapid pace. Within minutes, the entire field looked like it was consumed in an invisible fire.

James cleared his throat and spoke. "It's happening—isn't it? Burning the book didn't matter. It's still coming back!"

His dad nodded. "It's what I feared would happen. Let's get back home."

✳ ✳ ✳

Tobias looked on as his two sons led the way home. They looked defeated, shoulders slumped forward, and heads hung low. A sullen quiet replaced their typical lively banter. His stomach twisted and turned as if tying itself into knots. The pain in his stomach spread up through his chest. His legs felt heavy as his boots squelched through the deep mud. An unwelcomed thought passed through his mind. *I'm forty-three years old. There's a good chance I won't see forty-four.*

What would have taken five minutes by truck took over twenty minutes by foot. They skirted the cemetery and walked up the gentle slope of water-sodden grass towards the large farmhouse. The grass beneath his boots was a welcomed reprieve. He glanced up at the large tree that once stood proudly next to his home. The lightning had split the trunk into two pieces. The bulk of the tree lay on the ground; its branches were strewn out in all directions. What remained standing couldn't be saved. Tears welled in his eyes. He swallowed. *No time for self-pity.* He glanced at the back porch of the house and abruptly stopped. His mouth fell open, and a dizzying sensation washed over him. Even in the darkness, he could see a dark shadow move along the back porch. He screamed out, trying to stop Daniel and James, but his vocal cords were paralyzed with fear, leaving his voice no higher than a whisper. *It's here!* His legs moved freely, powered by the adrenaline coursing through his veins. He ran, catching up with his sons. By the time he reached them, his voice had returned. "Stop! There's something on the porch!"

They both stopped and turned. Daniel grabbed and held onto his arm. "Are you sure?"

He nodded and pointed towards the house, then bent forward and tried to catch his breath. The pounding of his heart drowned out all other sounds.

"Dad's right. I see movement," James said.

He glanced back up. The shadow on the porch started running towards them. A wave of relief washed over him. *It's a man.*

"Is it Norm?" he asked.

"No, I think it's Charles," exclaimed James. He started running towards the man. After a few yards, he turned back. "It's Charles!"

He closed his eyes. The tightness in his lungs lessened, and his heartbeat slowed. He quietly prayed, thanking God for bringing Charles to them.

Charles hugged each of them tightly. He was crying. "I saw the back porch and the tree. I called out, but no one answered. I thought something happened to you." He shook his head as if to clear away evil thoughts. "I'm…I'm just so happy to see you!"

"My truck is stuck…out at the field," Daniel said.

"You went to the field? Was there anything there?" Charles asked.

James nodded. "Dad's right…it's coming back."

A look of sadness filled Charles' eyes, and his mouth fell slightly open. For a second, it looked like he would say something, but he didn't. Instead, he closed his mouth and quietly nodded.

CHAPTER 39

Before heading into the office, Ted watched the news, paying close attention to the blond weather girl and her forecast. He'd felt a sense of relief when she confidently announced sunny skies over Phoenix for the next five days. *Both Tobias and Norm mentioned the demon arose with a storm.*

The church recently bought a projector and two screens. Instead of printed flyers, the congregation could follow the service by watching the screens bordering the altar. With the help of online videos, he was quickly becoming an expert in PowerPoint.

Safe in the knowledge of a storm-free day, he planned to stay late at the office, creating the PowerPoint slides for an upcoming sermon. He was deep in thought when his phone rang. He glanced down at the phone: Mercy Hospital.

The hospital had a full-time day chaplain. To provide pastoral support for the hospital in the evenings and on weekends, the pastors at the local churches took turns being on call. It was his turn to be on call. He answered the phone.

"Good evening, pastor. It's Bethany Holloway from the Emergency Room. An ambulance brought in a patient in full cardiac arrest. We couldn't save him. I was hoping you'd be able to come in to comfort the family."

These unexpected calls for help were one of the reasons he began working on sermons weeks in advance. Preparing sermons and conducting worship were only a part of his duties. He enjoyed those aspects of his position, but they weren't the driving force that sent him to seminary school. What drove him, day after day, was his role of comforter and counselor. Helping those in need filled his metaphoric cup.

It was only a fifteen-minute drive from church to Mercy. He placed his laptop into his shoulder bag, then turned out the office light. There was a grieving family who needed support. He'd finish the sermon at home later tonight. "I'm on my way."

* * *

Pulling a last-minute order at the hardware store kept Norm at work for an extra hour. By the time he arrived home, the skies were darker than usual. He apologized for being late, kissed Mary on the cheek, then pulled back the curtains covering the sliding glass door. Nervous energy settled in his stomach. Thick, dark storm clouds hung over the nearby mountain range.

Throughout dinner, Mary made attempts at small talk while he kept glancing out the back window.

"Is there something wrong with the food?" she asked.

The thought of an impending storm stole his appetite. He forced a smile and shook his head. "No, just not feeling very hungry tonight."

"Maybe you're getting sick? You look a bit pale."

"It looks like we might get a storm tonight."

She glanced out the family room window. "Those clouds are still ways out. Perhaps it'll pass us by."

"But what if it doesn't, Mary? First, the crows. Then my dream. Now a storm. I don't think it's a coincidence."

Her eyes widened. Then a look of quiet determination crossed over her face. "If it comes, we'll be alright. God is with us."

For the next hour, they watched and prayed as the storm rolled in.

"Whoa! The sky has gotten dark!" Mary exclaimed.

A storm was headed their way. As he and Mary stepped out into the backyard, they were met with the sweet smell of rain. Static electricity permeated the air, raising the hairs on his arms.

"Do you feel that?" Mary asked.

"Uh-huh. It feels like I've just rubbed my feet on our carpet."

"That storm looks like it can do some damage. Let's get back inside the house. There's a few candles in our bathroom. I'll get the candles and matches just in case the power goes out."

He stood by the window as Mary gathered the candles and matches. Lightning cracked across the sky, followed by booming thunder. The wind, a breeze at first, rapidly increased in intensity, rattling the windowpanes. It was followed by rain that fell sideways, pelting the sliding glass door.

As Mary lit the candles, she glanced in his direction, "maybe you shouldn't stand so close to the glass."

He didn't acknowledge the comment. Instead, he continued staring out the window, focusing his eyes on the center of the approaching storm.

With the last candle lit, Mary ignored her own warning and joined him at the window. She pointed out towards the field. "Do you see that, Norm? It's a funnel cloud!"

He saw it. Strangely, he wished she were right. Somehow the thought of a tornado barreling down upon their home seemed less ominous than what it was; the demon that wreaked havoc on his life and caused Susan to run away.

"It's not a tornado."

"Are you sure?"

Before he could answer, another bolt of lightning streaked across the sky. The simultaneous crash of thunder plunged their home into a near dark, eerie silence. The only light they had was from the small flickering candles.

Mary wrapped her arms around his waist. "But the cloud…it was dark and swirly. You're sure it wasn't a tornado?"

He took a deep breath, bent down, and kissed the top of her head. "I am," he whispered.

Just as fast and furious as the storm came, it quickly lowered in its intensity. It was as though the driving force behind the wheel had stepped out of the car. Then, with no driver pushing down on the gas pedal, the storm rolled into a stalling stop. The rain lowered to a drizzle, and the timing between lightning strikes and thunder had also grown wider apart.

"Norm…look at the ground. Is it what you meant when you said you saw smoke in the field?"

His blood turned ice-cold. Despite the darkness, he could see white smoke seeping up from the ground. "Yes, Mary. It's happening all over again. The demon is coming back."

CHAPTER 40

L ooking out the sliding glass door, Norm pulled Mary closer and pointed to the field. Even in the darkness, he could see the mist rising from the ground. "See how the mist is twisting and turning?"

"Like the field is on fire."

"Yes, Mary! Exactly! Like the field is on fire! That's what I saw when I came home from Susan's house. I want to get a closer look at that mist."

"Where's your flashlight?" she asked.

He hadn't held the flashlight since last summer. Afraid holding it would send his mind flashing back to the night of the storm and the two red eyes, he'd tossed it into one of the garage cabinets.

He needed it now to get a closer look at the field behind their home. "It's in the garage. I'll go get it."

Going through the cabinets by feel alone was both exhausting and terrifying at the same time. Every few minutes, the wind would intensify, rattling the garage door. Then, just as he was about to give up the search, he felt the cold, cylinder-shaped metal in his hand. He flicked on the flashlight. A beam of light extended out from the flashlight, casting oddly shaped shadows on the garage walls.

For a split second, he imagined the demon, standing there, hidden in the shadows of the garage with him. He waved the flashlight through the air like a novice swordsman. Then fell back into the cabinets, trying to escape the imagined shadow.

No! His mind angrily screamed as he straightened his shoulders and stood fiercely, ready to fight. No demon, either imagined or real, would have power over him. *Greater is He that is in me than in the world.*

He returned to the family room. In just a few minutes, the temperature in the room had dropped by ten degrees. Mary was wearing her coat. She handed him his jacket. Together, they opened the sliding glass door, then stepped outside. The smell of sulfur filled the air. The crows which lined the fence lines of nearby homes began raucously cawing. Mary stood beside him and gently squeezed his hand. He looked down at her and smiled. The last time he'd faced the fog, he was alone and afraid, separated from God. With Mary at his side and Christ front and center in their marriage again, they were a cord of three strands; strong, not easily broken.

He closed his eyes and bowed his head. "Lord, you placed me here for a purpose. I know the plans you have for me. I pray for peace and protection over the people living in the subdivision and on the Smith farm."

Mary added, "I pray the blood of Jesus over this calling." Then she aimed her voice towards the field. "You have no power here, Satan! We bind and rebuke you!. You cannot destroy the plans God has for us!"

He opened his eyes and shined the flashlight into the mist, moving it back and forth along the perimeter. Despite its brightness, the light only penetrated a few feet.

"Do you remember when I stood next to the fog the morning after the storm?"

"Uh-huh. I remember thinking you were going to get stuck in the mud."

He remembered the difficulty he'd had navigating the mud after the storm and sheepishly smiled. "I almost did." He paused for a moment, then continued. "When I was standing next to the fog, I felt something. Honestly, Mary, it felt like there was something on the other side of the fog, reaching out, trying to pull me through."

She widened her eyes and covered her mouth with her free hand.

"And the way the fog stopped right along the row of corn? Do you remember that?" he asked.

"Now that you mention it, I do."

"On the night of that storm, Mary, it seemed as though the smoke hit some kind of invisible wall and shot straight up." He paused for a moment. "I've wondered about the fog and the demon. I know demons can move freely. But what if the fog acts as a barrier, at least temporarily?"

270

"Then wherever the fog goes?"

"The demon goes."

He aimed the flashlight onto the ground. In rippling waves, the misty border extended halfway onto the dirt road behind their fence. At the rate it moved, it would cover a large portion of the subdivision within the hour. He held onto Mary's hand tighter. Together their reiterated their prayers for the protection of the subdivision.

He'd pictured coming face to face with the demon on the field. But now, with the evil barreling down on them, it didn't feel right. In his heart, he knew this wasn't the place he'd take his stand. *Tobias' home!* That's where they needed to go.

He led the way back into the house. "Let's grab our Bibles. We need to get to Tobias and Sarah's home. We'll call Ted on the way."

✳ ✳ ✳

After comforting the grieving family, Ted stepped into the crowded emergency-room waiting area. At one side of the room sat a guy with a bloody towel wrapped around his hand. Quietly, he wondered if the guy's gray and clammy skin was from blood loss or pain? At the other end of the room, two parents struggled to comfort their toddler, who had a feverish red face, runny nose, and cough. Sandwiched between the two were at least fifteen other patients suffering from a menagerie of ailments and injuries. None of the people sitting out here looked like they'd be asking to see him. He'd make one round through the ED before heading home. *It's better to stay a bit longer than getting called to come back a few hours from now.*

As he approached the ED charge nurse desk, Bethany looked up and smiled. "Thank you for spending time with that family. I know they appreciated you being here."

He smiled back. "It was my privilege to help." He paused for a moment, then added, "I was just wondering if there was anyone you thought I should see before calling it a night."

"Actually, Pastor, there's a Jane Doe the ambulance brought in while you were working with that family. You might want to check with her nurse."

Jane Doe? Was she suffering from homelessness or mental health disorders? He'd never been asked to see a Jane Doe. As he contemplated how he might help, Bethany's voice broke through his thoughts.

"She was in pretty bad shape when they found her."

"Where was she?"

"Lying on the side of the road, near the highway. Our attending placed a psych consult. She'll probably stay in the hospital overnight. Then once she's stabilized, she'll likely transfer to Behavioral Health. I know she's not a patient I'd typically ask you to see. But I think this might be a God thing."

He furrowed his brow and leaned over the desk. "God thing?"

"She wasn't coherent when they first brought her in—dehydrated and malnourished. But after getting some fluids in her, she started talking. She just told her nurse she's had a demon inside her for months and that it finally left her body."

He pushed back from the desk. "Demon?"

"I know it sounds crazy. That's why our attending physician is asking for psych. But you're here. So, I'm wondering if you think this is a person you might want to see."

This couldn't be a coincidence. "Yes. I want to see her. Which room is she in?"

Bethany smiled and pointed down the hall. "Bay three, third curtain on your right. Her nurse is Cheryl."

Cheryl stepped out from the curtain just as he approached. She smiled. "Hello, Pastor."

"Bethany said you might be able to use my help."

Cheryl nodded, then turned and slid back the curtain. As he started to follow, his phone vibrated in his pocket. He glanced down at the caller ID: Norm.

Cheryl popped her head back through the curtain. "I've given her sedation. I'm not sure how long she'll stay awake, Pastor."

He nodded. Instead of answering, he declined the call. Norm would understand. He needed to talk to the woman behind the curtain.

✳ ✳ ✳

272

As Norm pulled out of their driveway with Mary, he left a message on Ted's phone. Since the pastor lived on the other side of town, there was a good chance he didn't know about the storm.

For the past few months, the Smith farm had installed a series of chain link fences. The first fence began at the end of his and Mary's property and extended north. It kept people from wandering through the wash onto the Smith farm, something he surmised Susan did on the day she disappeared. A similar fence extended out at the south end of the subdivision.

As he and Mary kept driving, they ran into one chain link fence after the other. Unable to find a way onto the Tobias' property, they exited the subdivision and went south, turning onto the first gravel road they saw. It looked like an access road, perhaps for the canals. When the road became muddy, Norm stopped the truck and turned to Mary. "I don't want to get us stuck. Stay here. I'll be right back."

"Nope. I'm not letting you out of my sight."

"But-."

She held her hand up and shook her head, projecting a look of unwavering resolve.

There was no sense arguing. Besides, they were stronger together. He nodded and smiled. "You're right."

She smiled back. "Okay. Let's go."

He led the way along the edge of the muddy road, careful to avoid large puddles of water. With each step, the crisp, cold air grew thick and musty. At the end of the road, they ran into another chain-link fence. They couldn't physically move past it, but they could see past it.. He held the flashlight up and aimed it at the canal. Based on last year's cornfield location, he expected the bulk of the fog to end a few feet north of the canal. It didn't. The fog extended at least one hundred feet south of the canal. Faint lights, similar to tiny bolts of lightning, flickered within the misty fog. Even in the darkness, he could see how the leading edge of the mist rolled and churned as it glided over the ground. He sensed an intelligence within the fog—an angry intelligence, hellbent on destruction.

"Do you feel that, Norm?"

"Yes." The tiny hairs on his arms stood erect. He glanced down at Mary. The ends of her hair stuck straight out. "The air is full of static

273

electricity."

CHAPTER 41

As Norm climbed back in the truck, he remembered the only conversation he'd had with Tobias. It was a Saturday afternoon just a few weeks earlier. He was seated at the diner's counter, watching college football. Tobias sat next to him and ordered lunch.

In his periphery, Tobias extended his hand. "Hi, I'm Tobias Smith. I saw you at church last weekend. You're Mary's husband— aren't you?"

He looked away. Could he shake the hand of the man he deemed responsible for Susan's disappearance? Then he glanced into Tobias' eyes. Hidden beneath the farmer's outwardly stoic and business-like manner, he sensed a vulnerability and sadness. A Bible verse passed through his head. *If you forgive others, your Heavenly Father will also forgive you. But if you do not forgive their trespasses, neither will your Father forgive your trespasses.*

Just a few weeks earlier, he asked for Mary's forgiveness, and she gave it to him. That act of kindness saved their marriage and changed his life. Now it was his turn to offer grace to another person. *I need to forgive him; otherwise, I'll never fully heal.*

He took a deep breath and forced a smile, "Norm…Norm Keller," he said as he grasped Tobias' hand and gave it a firm shake. A look of relief washed over Tobias' face, followed by a smile.

They'd only shared a few words in the diner. After that, it was a welcoming nod or brief smile at church, nothing more. How would Tobias react when he showed up at the farm and told him there was a demon headed his way. Did he already know? If so, would he deny it and ask him to leave. They didn't have time for confrontations or denials. He felt confident the victory would be theirs if they worked together. He prayed God would give him the words needed to gain Tobias' confidence.

They drove to the farm's main gate. It was chained and padlocked. There was no way he'd get onto the property through this gate.

"We passed a gravel road. Maybe that will be open?" Mary offered.

He nodded, then headed back the way they'd come. At the first gravel road, he turned. Their path soon blocked by a chain-link gate, secured shut by a metal chain and padlock. He shook his head and put the truck in reverse. He began to drive back, but Mary's excited voice stopped him.

"Look, Norm, the gate isn't locked. It's *staged* to look locked at first glance."

He looked again and smiled. She's right. He parked, opened the gate, drove through, then resecured it. He left the padlock as he'd found it. *Ted will need a way onto the property.*

He recognized the car at the end of the road. *Charles is here.* He pulled behind Charles' car and parked. Then he phoned Ted. The call went to voicemail again. So he left a message with directions to the road. The rest of their journey would have to be on foot. He turned on his flashlight. Then both he and Mary prayed God would get them safely to the front door.

With each hurried step, the gravel road crunched beneath their feet. Near the end of the road, the gravel thinned, and they found themselves trudging through the mud again. Once they reached a treeline, he glanced back at Mary. Her face had a look of quiet determination. It didn't falter even as they passed by the small cemetery behind Tobias' home.

"Well, that's something you don't see every day," Mary pointed to the cemetery. "Feels a bit ominous, though, given what we're doing tonight."

He wasn't someone who looked at cemeteries as frightening. On the contrary, they were a place of reverence. A place where families celebrated the lives of lost love ones. But something Mary said rang true. There was an ominous feel to *this* cemetery.

Soon, they'd reached the wet grass. He glanced up at the house. "They've lost power here too, Mary. But it looks like someone's home. I see flickering lights coming from some of the rooms on the lower floor.."

Directly in front of him was a large branch, cleaved away from the tree. A telephone pole next to the house was snapped in two and lying beneath fallen tree. "That tree took out their phone lines. It sure looks like their property took the brunt of the storm."

"It really does."

He led Mary past the tree towards the front of the house. For a home built nearly a century ago, its sheer size was impressive. The porch roof and wooden beams looked newly replaced. In the wake of the rain, they glistened as if freshly painted. They stepped onto the porch, which wrapped most of the house. The old wood creaked beneath their feet.

At the front door, he paused, smiled down at Mary, and knocked. From inside the house, an approaching light grew brighter. It illuminated a set of stain-glass windows bordering the door.

Tobias answered. A warm smile spread over his face as he extended his hand. "Welcome, Norm. I'm so happy to see you."

Then he looked down at Mary. A look of surprise crossed his face. "Mary?" Tobias gave a quick shake of his head. While his presence almost seemed expected, Tobias seemed concerned that he'd brought her along. But he couldn't imagine being here without her; she was his partner and fellow prayer warrior.

"May we come in?"

"I'm sorry, of course," Tobias said as he opened the door widely and stepped aside.

He stepped through the doorway and looked upon the massive staircase squarely in front of him.

"That's quite impressive," Mary said.

"My great-uncle and my grandfather spared no expense when they built this home," Tobias said. He paused, then pointed to a room on the right. "That's where they welcomed guests."

The light from Norm's flashlight fell onto a large fireplace. *Is that the fireplace where the farmworker found Tobias?*

"When Sarah and I took over the house, we got rid of most of the furnishings. We prefer a simpler life. Come—I'll show you the table my sons helped me build. It's in the kitchen."

Tobias led the way towards the back of the home and into the kitchen. The spacious room looked as if it had undergone multiple small renovations. Newer, stainless-steel appliances contrasted with 1950s style white cabinets covered the walls on his right. *No dishwasher. With a family this large? Mary and I use ours all the time, and there are only two of us.* In the dishwasher's place stood a farm sink, large enough to double as Mary's bathtub. He smiled. A large picture window facing east provided picturesque views for the person washing dishes. He glanced down at the wooden floor, aged and worn. It reminded him of the wooden floors in his and Mary's first home. On his left, filling the rest of the space, stood a large wooden table. Simple in style and wonderfully made.

Mary stepped forward and ran her hands over the table. "You made this with your sons?"

Tobias smiled and nodded.

"It's beautiful."

Eight wooden chairs surrounded the table, and a large white pendant lamp hung over the center. An unlit battery-operated lantern and two flashlights rested on the counter. Four large candles bathed the room in a warm, soft glow.

Tobias pointed to one of the wooden chairs. "Go ahead and take a seat. My boys will be back soon. Can I get you both a glass of water?"

They both nodded.

He wasn't sure if it was the walk from the truck or the impending threat that left his mouth feeling like it was full of dry cotton. He took the water, leaned back with his eyes closed, and basked in momentarily calmness. Adrenaline had coursed through his veins since the storm arrived. As he allowed himself to relax, the adrenaline lowered. *Be calm. Be still.* Mary squeezed his hand. He opened his eyes and looked into her loving face.

"You okay?" she asked.

He nodded. It felt right having Mary at his side. Then he glanced up at Tobias. Where were his sons? Where was Sarah?

As if reading his mind, Tobias spoke up. "My sons are checking on the subdivision. Sarah is at her sister's house."

"Sarah's not here?" Mary asked.

Before Tobias could answer, the floorboards on the back porch creaked. He quickly raised his hand. "It's my sons."

The back door flung open. One by one, Tobias's sons stepped through: Charles, James, and Daniel.

"The mist is spreading out everywhere. Towards the subdivision and our—" Charles abruptly stopped as he turned towards the table.

They know the evil is coming.

Tobias' face became pale. He took a step towards Charles. "Did you say it was spreading out towards the subdivision?"

Charles nodded. "It's strange, though. It's extended up the washes alongside the subdivision, and it's covering the dirt road next to the field. But it seems to stop right at the fences."

He smiled at Mary. God heard their prayers and was protecting the homes in the subdivision.

James interjected, "It's mostly moving towards us. It was at least three hundred feet south of the canal."

Three hundred feet. It was about one hundred feet past the canal when Mary and I first arrived. He interjected again: "Then it's moved about two hundred feet in this direction over the last hour."

A little color returned to Tobias' face. "At least it seems to be moving this way and not towards the subdivision."

"So, if it keeps this speed, the fog will cover us?" Daniel asked.

"Within a few hours," Charles answered.

Charles's estimation sounded right. He nodded his head and then looked at the men's faces. Even in the candlelight, he could see the fear in their eyes. He silently prayed God would bring them comfort. Then he thought of Ecclesiastes 4:12. "And if one can overpower him who is alone, two can resist him. A cord of three strands is not quickly torn." He recited the verse during wedding ceremonies as a reminder of the strength of a marriage that included God. It was perfect for this moment as well. Six people of faith were in the room. Once Ted joined them, there would be seven. Seven people who, with God, made an eight-cord strand. A metaphoric cable strong enough to send the demon back to hell.

Tobias, Charles, and James took seats near Mary. Daniel sat in the chair next to him, smiled, and extended his hand. "Our dad said you'd come to help us. He told us to leave a gate unlocked so you and my brothers could get onto the property."

Mary sat straight up and looked around the table. "How did you know we'd be here?"

Tobias smiled. "I had a dream Norm would come help us."

Now it was his turn to sit fully upright. *No wonder they weren't surprised to see me.* Knowing Tobias had a dream he'd come to the farm further affirmed this was indeed God's plan for him. A warm, comforting sensation washed over him. *I'm not the only one having dreams.*

James interrupted, "Will Pastor Cummings be here tonight?"

Tobias shook his head. "I didn't call him."

He leaned forward. "Mary and I called and left him a message. We told him about the gravel road and the gate."

"Did Pastor Cummings tell you we needed help?"

He shook his head. "God showed me the demon in a dream. I know God has placed Mary and I here to help you fight it."

Tobias' mouth fell open. "You dreamt about the demon?"

"I've also seen it."

Daniel gasped, and the color drained from James' face.

"When?" Tobias asked.

He slowly looked around the room, then continued, "Last summer, there was a storm, much like the one tonight. And, the misty fog moving towards us, it was also here last summer. It hovered over the field behind my home. I saw the demon's red eyes in the mist. But, even though I saw it, I wouldn't allow myself to believe it was real. It's one of the biggest regrets in my life."

"Regrets?" Tobias asked.

His shoulders fell with the weight of his guilt. "It's a long story. But, here's the bottom line. Our neighbor, Susan, vanished because I denied what I saw. If I'd only acted differently, she'd still be here today. I'm sure of it." Tears filled his eyes. He took a deep breath and wiped them away.

Tobias leaned forward. His eyes also welled with tears. "You know…about Susan…and you still came to help us?"

His stomach clenched. Tobias just confirmed his suspicions: the evil force had taken Susan. He glanced around the room. His sons weren't shocked. They all knew it'd taken her, and they'd remained quiet. Then, warmth spread over his neck and face, and his hands began to tremble. A voice in his head cried out. *Satan is the enemy! Not these men!* He squeezed his eyes shut to hold back the onslaught of tears. When he reopened them, he studied their faces, each filled with remorse.

* * *

They'll abandon us! Cold terror raced through Tobias' veins as he watched Norm's face grow red. His body trembled in response, and his eyes once again filled with tears. For a moment, it appeared the man God sent to help him would soon bolt from the room in disgust. *Will he call Pastor Cummings and tell him not to come as well? After all, I lied right to his face.*

With each passing moment, the look on Norm's face softened. Eventually, his face returned to a pale pink color.

"I'm so sorry. I honestly don't know what happened to Susan. But I did find her purse and keys in the field," he said.

"So, it's true. Norm was right all along. That demon attacked Susan!" Mary exclaimed.

Tobias raised his hand and quickly shook his head. "I think you might have misunderstood." He paused for a moment as if to gather the courage to continue. "I did find her purse and keys in the field. I know I should have turned them into the sheriff. When I first discovered them, I was in shock. Then I was too ashamed. But I swear—I never found *her*. I believe the sheriff is right; she ran away."

"You mean she was frightened away," Norm added.

He nodded.

Norm's eyes filled with tears. Then he looked away and gave a slight smile. "Then there's a chance she's still alive," he whispered.

"We keep Susan in our daily prayers. We've asked the Lord to bring her back safely."

Norm's smile widened, and then he nodded. After a moment, his look turned serious. He smiled, nodded, then leaned forward and interrupted, "We don't have much time. But I need you to tell me everything you know about that demon. We're looking for a weakness."

He took a deep breath. *God sent Norm to help us; I have to tell him everything I know.*

"This all started with my great-grandfather when he performed a spell."

"A spell? Like from a spell book?" Mary asked.

"Yes. It's a summoning spell. My family performed it in a hidden room next to the staircase. My great-grandfather covered the walls of that room in the strange symbols from the book. It was Pastor Cummings who told us the true nature of those symbols and that what I'd summoned was a demon."

Both Norm and Mary's eyes widened in surprise. A wave of gratitude washed over him. *It looks like Pastor Cummings kept his word when he promised not to tell anyone else.*

"The field? The corn? Does that have something to do with the spell?" Norm asked.

He nodded. "It's where my great-grandfather began offering sacrifices to the demon. It was my father who started planting the cornfield. He couldn't bear to perform the sacrifices his forefathers did—you know— right there in the open. He'd lead animals to the edge of the cornfield. The demon drew them into the corn. After every harvest, my father buried any evidence of the sacrifices in our cemetery. I do the same thing my father did. Over time, I realized it was better to leave an empty area in the middle of the field, like a snare. It also made it easier to find and clean up the evidence."

Mary's face paled. Norm's eyes narrowed. "You found Susan's purse in the snare?"

A heaviness fell over him. He held Norm's gaze. "But there wasn't a body. I swear."

Norm's eyes softened slightly, but they were still laser-focused on him. "What else can you tell me about the demon?"

"We know its name!" Daniel interjected. "Atvaras."

Norm looked at Daniel. "Knowing its name could help us defeat it. But, demons lie, so you may not have the right name after all." Then he turned back to him. "Pastor Cummings knows everything you just told me?"

He shook his head.. "I told him most of what I just told you. He doesn't know I found Susan's things in the field."

Norm nodded. "I know how hard it was for you to tell us. But I'm glad you did. So, that's it? You've told us everything?"

"There's something else you should know about my great uncle Jonas and grandfather Lukas. They were truly horrible men. My father told me stories about them and their friends. They'd formed some sort of—"

"Coven?" Norm interrupted.

Coven. Just the thought of the word sent a shiver down his spine. Years ago, Sarah used the word "witchcraft" to describe the spell book and summoning ritual. She'd struck a nerve, and he responded with anger. Although he denied it at the time, his father's words flashed through his head. Sarah was right. His grandfather and their powerful friends were witches.

"Yes. I believe coven would be the proper word. My father was dying of cancer that spread to his brain. So, I'm still not sure how much of what he told me was true. But for the sake of argument, let's say he told me the truth. If he did, then you probably need to know Jonas and Lukas performed rituals in that field all the time. There's also a chance some of the rituals involved human sacrifices."

There was an audible gasp in the room. It was the same response he had when his father told him. Given the burgundy-colored soil that was found nowhere else in the area, he believed him. He looked at his sons. "I'm sorry. I wish I could have died with that secret." Then he looked back at Norm. "I've told you everything I know about my family and that piece of land."

Norm didn't look as shocked as he'd expected. After a moment, he spoke: "This all makes sense to me. I believe your great-grandfather opened a doorway to hell in that field. And, if his sons performed rituals there…" He looked off in the distance for a moment. "In my dream, God told me the land I stood on was tainted with evil. He said, 'Take back what is mine.'"

His shoulders fell. *A doorway to hell?* Pastor Cummings told him months ago he needed to pray over the field. But he'd allowed his fear to get in the way. No more! Tonight, they'd send that demon back through the door, straight to hell! Then he and his sons would keep it shut through prayers.

Norm held his gaze for a moment, as if studying him. Then in a soft voice, he asked, "Why did you continue this practice? You, your sons, Sarah—you are all Christians."

Nearly in unison, his sons all began shaking their heads in protest. "We didn't know any of this was going on, neither did our mom." Charles' voice rose above his brothers.

His shoulders slumped as he once again faced the truth; he'd failed his family. "I never had any intentions of passing this down to my sons."

Norm nodded, then looked at him. "Even if you hadn't, I'm sure Pastor Cummings explained your actions perpetuated a generational curse."

"Yes," he whispered. "But we're trying to break it, as a family. So after I told Sarah everything, I chopped and burned the things from the room while Sarah painted over the symbols. And later, when the symbols returned, darker than before, we called Pastor Cummings."

A pensive look crossed Mary's face as she leaned forward. "It had no intention of going quietly."

Norm nodded. "Mary's right. This spirit has had control over your family for many generations. You did the right thing by destroying the demonic items and bringing in Pastor Cummings. But it's only a start. You also need ongoing repentance, prayers, and fasting to truly break it's stronghold."

"Pastor Cummings helped us get rid of the symbols and cleanse it properly. Since then, Sarah and I pray over our home every day."

He glanced at each of them, smiling and nodding. *Norm and Mary must think I've been evil since birth. How can I make them understand? I wasn't given any other choice!* He looked at them. "I need you to understand something. I didn't know any of this until growing up. And when I told my father I wouldn't continue doing what he had done, he told me what happened to my great-uncle, Jonas, when he tried to stop the summonings."

"What happened?" Mary whispered.

"The demon took his three children."

"What?" Mary's face paled.

"Yes. On a stormy night like tonight, a fog fell over the house. My great-uncle and grandfather couldn't see more than a few inches in front of them. When it cleared, the children were gone. Everyone in town were told the children died of the flu."

Norm spoke up: "I heard the flu story last year from two of my friends. It sounded like some conspiracies were going around about the children's death. Up till tonight, I didn't believe three children could disappear without an inquiry. But after hearing your great-uncle and grandfather were part of a coven of powerful men, I now see how they could have gotten away with it."

After a moment's pause in the conversation, James and Charles began whispering, then they stood and walked to the kitchen door.

"Where are you two going?" he asked.

"We're going down to the road to see if John is here."

"Wait!"

He looked at his three sons. It was time to tell them the rest of his dream. One brother would turn away, leaving the other three to fight. He glanced into his sons' faces and shook his head. "John's not coming."

A look of disbelief spread over their faces.

James asked, "Did he tell you he wasn't coming?"

Tobias shook his head. "I just…know…that's all."

James continued, "How do you know John won't come?"

"The same way I knew Norm would. I didn't want to say anything earlier, but that was also part of my dream."

His comment was met with heavy sighs and looks of sadness.

After a moment, Charles opened the door. "I'm going to see how close the mist is to our house."

Both he and Norm stood to protest, but it was no use. Charles and James both bolted through the door.

CHAPTER 42

Norm glanced around the room. Mary, Daniel, and Tobias all had stunned looks on their faces. If he could see his face, it would likely resemble theirs.

As if realizing his sons' recklessness, Tobias' eyes narrowed, and his face reddened. "What are they thinking! We have to stay united!" he yelled as he grabbed a flashlight and followed his sons out the door.

"Go, follow him," Mary said as she nudged his arm. "I'll stay here and pray for everyone's safety."

He kissed her on the cheek and ran. Close behind was Daniel, carrying a flashlight.

"There he is!" Daniel shouted, shining the flashlight on the back of Tobias.

They both ran down the wet, sloping grass to his side.

"Charles! James!" Tobias yelled as he moved his head back and forth. He took the flashlight from Daniel and began scanning the area.

For a moment, there was no response. He knew the anguish he'd felt after losing Rose. His heart went out to Tobias. *Please, God, let them be alright.*

Tobias began running into the cemetery, frantically calling out a second time.

James and Charles called back in unison, "We're down here."

Thank you, God, for protecting them! He whispered.

Tobias aimed the flashlight in the direction of their voices. Within the flashlight's beam, he spotted them waving their arms in the air. Tobias and Daniel ran towards them. He ran close behind. At the back of the cemetery, Tobias and his sons fell into each other's arms.

"Sons, you have to understand—this demon is powerful. He will try to divide us, have us fight among ourselves and not against it! We must work together as a family!"

"You're right. I'm sorry," Charles said.

Then Tobias closed his eyes and raised his head towards the sky. "Thank you, God, for keeping my sons safe."

A frigid wave of air cascaded through the cemetery. He shivered and hugged his arms around his body.

Charles pointed towards the field. "It's moving faster than we thought. At this rate, it'll cover the house within an hour."

"What?" Tobias aimed the flashlight in the direction of the field. After a few seconds, the flashlight fell from his hand. He grabbed his head and fell onto his knees.

Charles picked up the flashlight and shined it on Tobias. His head was cradled within his hands. His eyes were squeezed tightly shut, and his face wore a pained expression.

James knelt beside Tobias and wrapped his arm around his shoulder. "Dad, what's wrong?"

Tobias didn't answer. Instead, his body shook violently, and he fell onto his side. Once on the ground, he writhed in pain and thrashed about, moaning loudly.

What's happening to him? He knelt beside Tobias. As he reached out to touch him, a searing pain went through his head. It felt as though all of the headaches he'd ever experienced had returned at the same time. He grabbed his head and squeezed his eyes shut. Everything went black.

✳ ✳ ✳

Daniel pointed the flashlight beam onto his father and Norm. Both men lay on the ground, writhing in pain. He yelled out to his brothers, "What's happening to them?"

"I don't know! Let's get them inside the house!" Charles exclaimed. He pulled on Norm's arm. Norm responded with screams of pain. Like a contortionist, Norm's back arched, his arms twisted inward, and his fingers bent in an odd position. Charles released him. Once he let go, the screams stopped. Charles grabbed onto his arm again. Norm's screaming resumed, and his body made the same strange movement.

At the same time, James was trying to pull their father upright. "Dad, it's me. We have to get into the house." His dad screamed in pain, and he began writhing on the ground. Once James let go, his dad's screaming stopped, and his body fell limp onto the ground.

"Stop! You're hurting them," he yelled.

Both James and Charles stepped back. Norm and his dad lay on the ground, on their sides, tucked into a fetal position. They held onto their heads; eyes closed. They both writhed and moaned, clearly in pain. Thankfully, without James and Charles touching them, they'd stopped screaming.

Charles looked up. His face had a look of despair. "But we can't just leave them here. We have to get them into the house!"

He shook his head. Not at the cost of hurting them.

✳ ✳ ✳

In Norm's mind, the darkness fell away, taking all thoughts of the cornfield, Tobias, and the evil with it. Instead, he found himself in his living room, sitting in his recliner. Mary stood beside him, looking out the sliding glass door.

"We'd better get a move on, or we'll be late to church," she said as she glanced back and extended her hand in his direction.

He nodded. "I'm coming."

He reached for the lever at the side of the recliner to lower his legs but was unable to move his arms. He looked down. His wrists were shackled to the recliner's arms, and his ankles were shackled to the footrest. His heart raced, and his palms became sweaty. He fought to lift his arms but could only raise them a few inches before he met resistance. The more he struggled, the tighter the restraints dug into his skin.

Mary stood over him, seemingly oblivious to his predicament. "Mary, look at me. I want to go to church with you. But I can't move!" he yelled.

Finally, she looked down, staring into his eyes. "I'll see you when I get home," she said. Then, in that split second, as she turned to walk away, a glint of red filled her blue irises.

The fear in his body escalated, sending his already racing heart pounding in his chest.

* * *

In Tobias' mind, after the blinding pain seared through his head, everything went black. As his darkness fell away, he found himself standing upstairs in a bedroom, staring at an empty crib. A dizzying wave of questions passed through his head. *John and Kate had the baby? Did they leave the baby here for me to watch?* Panic gripped his heart. He ran through all the upstairs room. With no sign of the baby, he ran downstairs. *Please, I can't let John down again! I must find their baby!* His heart began to race, and his palms broke out in a sweat. He continued searching through the downstairs, crossing in front of the alcove. The panels covering the hidden room stood slightly ajar.

The hairs on his arms stood on end as he walked to the panel and pushed it open. One glance into the room and he tried to scream, but no sound passed his lips.

In the center of the room stood the dark shadowy spirit he'd summoned three times in his life. Wrapped in a blanket and held against its pitted skin was his newborn grandbaby. The demon's red eyes challenged him. Then, through gnashed teeth, it hissed. "I'm disappointed in you, Tobias. Despite all the generational *blessings* I've given your family, you've chosen to turn your back on me." He pulled the baby in closer. "I will start over again with this one!"

* * *

In Norm's mind, he sat, trapped in the chair and unable to move. Finally, he closed his eyes and prayed God would set him free.

The family room and the recliner faded from view as a new image formed in his mind. He found himself sitting on a barstool. He looked around the room and realized he was sitting at the bar in Tucson, where he had drowned his sorrows after Rose died. Bottles of various vodkas covered the bar wall. Tim, the bartender, removed one of the bottles off the shelf. He poured vodka into a glass of ice and added a splash of tonic and lime. He pushed the glass across the bar. "Here's to your health, Norm."

He stared at the drink for a moment as his mouth watered. Then he picked it up and slowly stroked the cool glass with his thumb. After a moment, he brought the glass to his lips, then hesitated.

Tim smiled at him from the other side of the bar. "Go ahead, take a sip."

He lowered the glass, thinking of the promise he'd made to Mary to stop drinking. "I don't know, Tim. I'd better not."

"It's just one drink. Aww, come on. I made it, just the way you like it."

He rolled the glass in his hand, caressing it. After a few minutes, the craving for alcohol overpowered him. *One drink isn't going to hurt.* He brought the glass to his lips and took a sip. The cold refreshing taste of the liquor quenched his thirst and settled his nerves. His shoulders relaxed.

"There's more where that came from, buddy," Tim said. "I'm here all night. Just say the word, and I'll line them up for you on the bar."

※ ※ ※

Tobias stood in the middle of the hidden room, facing the demon. His heart pounded within his chest, and his breath came in quick short gulps.

"You're a liar!" he yelled.

"Liar?" The demon hissed.

"You said you blessed my family. But I know the truth. We're breaking free from you! And neither me, nor my sons, or their sons will bend. Jesus is our protector, our provider. He is the one from whom blessings flow." He rushed forward to grab the baby from the demon's arms. "In the name of Jesus, set my grandchild free!"

The demon, the baby, the room—they all vanished into a puff of smoke. He fell onto his knees. He looked around and realized he was kneeling in the cemetery at the spot where he'd buried Susan's purse.

※ ※ ※

While Norm and his dad lay on the ground, writhing and moaning, Daniel glanced up toward the field. His already racing heart began beating faster. The wall of misty fog was barreling down upon them, growing closer by the minute. Tiny sparks of light rippled through the mist. He pointed in its direction. "I think the demon is attacking their minds, trying to keep them here on the ground. We can't move dad or Norm without hurting them! We need help! "I'm going back to the house to Mary. She'll know what to do!"

* * *

In Norm's mind, he drained the glass and pushed it across the bar to Tim.

Tim smiled. "Would you like another?"

His mouth watered at the thought of another drink—a pang of guilt spread through his belly. *I shouldn't be here. I told Mary I'd stop drinking.* Vacillating, he shrugged his shoulders.

Tim leaned over the bar. "Another won't hurt. Why not stay awhile?"

A voice echoed through his head. *Another drink, yes...take another drink. Stay here with me forever! You've already walked away from your friends. You don't need Mary. You can have all the booze you want right here.*

Then came a louder voice in his head. *Look around. This isn't real!* He shook his head, trying to clear his thoughts. The bar seemed authentic, right down to the smell of beer permeating the air and the tacky feel of the old bar counter. He scrutinized the scene in front of him. Only he and Tim were in the bar, and the only alcohol on the shelf was vodka.

Tim's lips curled up into a crooked smile. A hint of red filled his irises. "So, what's it going to be, Norm? Are you staying with me?"

His heart pounded in his chest.

"Lord, help me!" he yelled.

His vision blurred, and the bar slowly faded from view. Slowly, another image came into view. He lay on the ground in the cemetery. Behind the gravestones, moving in his direction, he spied a wall of gray fog. A young woman stood in front of the fog. He shook his head and rubbed his eyes. *Susan! The sheriff was right. She ran away, and now she's back!*

"Susan! You're okay!" Tears streamed down his face. He pushed himself off the ground and began to run towards her.

✳ ✳ ✳

Tobias knelt in the cemetery, digging a hole in the ground with his bare hands. Handful after handful, he scooped cool earth from the center of the hole. Amid a pile of animal remains and pet collars, Susan's purse and keys lay on the ground next to him. He glanced down in the hole, only six inches deep. *This hole needs to be deeper than any I've dug before. I must hide the purse and keys before Sarah sees me.* Beads of sweat lined his forehead; he brushed them away with the back of his forearm. He glanced down into the hole. It had refilled with dirt. His heartbeat quickened, and his hands shook. He began scooping the cool earth again, this time with more force. *My family will be home soon! I must get this buried.*

A twig snapped behind him. His body jerked in a startled manner, and he whipped his head in the direction of the sound. *Susan!* He recognized her from the missing person posters; the image of her face burned forever in his mind. She stood in the distance, in front of a dark gray wall of fog. She raised her arm and pointed. "That's my purse. Those are my keys. Please bring them to me," she called out.

His heart raced in his chest. "But...you..."

"I'm what? I'm here! Please come to me. I want to talk to you."

"Susan...I'm so sorry!"

"If you are truly sorry, come to me. Bring me my purse and keys. We can talk."

✳ ✳ ✳

Daniel burst into the kitchen, jarring Mary from her prayers. She could tell by his widened eyes and anxious stance something had gone wrong. Her heart fluttered. She quietly prayed God would calm her nerves.

"What's wrong, Daniel?"

"It's my dad and Norm...the demon is attacking them!" he stammered.

Her heart sank. *Please, Lord, protect them from evil!*

"Take me to them!" she instructed.

He nodded and turned, running back through the door. She followed him down the slight hill towards the bottom of the cemetery.

CHAPTER 43

Ted followed Cheryl behind the curtain. The lighting in the bay was lowered. Lying on a gurney in front of him was a woman in her twenties. Her eyes were closed, and she lay curled up like a scared, wounded animal. Dirty, matted, brown hair lay over half her unwashed face. Her lips were dry and parched. A clear bag of fluids hung from a nearby pole and infused through the IV in her arm. A thin sheet and blanket lay over her body. One foot, covered in a layer of dirt, extended out from beneath the sheet. The woman had told her nurse a demon had possessed her body. Whether it was true or not, one thing was sure: she'd appeared to have suffered both physical and emotional trauma.

"Looks like the sedative is already working. I'm sorry, Pastor, I don't know if she'll wake up enough to talk to you."

The woman on the gurney opened her eyes and raised her head. Then, in a soft voice, she whispered, "How long?"

He leaned in closer. "How long?" *What's she asking me?* He glanced over at Cheryl. She shrugged her shoulders and shook her head. Then he looked back at the woman on the gurney. "I'm sorry. I don't understand your question."

The woman pushed back a piece of matted hair covering her eye and raised her voice: "How long have I been missing?"

Missing? Every fiber in his being went on high alert. Was the woman in front of him trying to tell him that she was a missing person?

"What's your name?" he asked.

"Susan," she whispered.

His heart skipped an entire beat as his mind wrestled with two emotions, overwhelming thankfulness, and fear. The woman before him was Susan Green. Although she hardly looked like the woman in the flyers last summer, he could tell it was her. *Her parents, Norm and Mary—they'll all be so happy she's alive!* His fear came from the realization she was telling the truth. She had been possessed by the demon tormenting Tobias, and it had returned tonight.

He glanced down into her pleading eyes. Then, in his mind, he counted the months she'd been missing. "Just over six months. You've been missing since the Fourth of July."

He saw the look of recognition on Cheryl's face when he mentioned Fourth of July. "Oh! Pastor, can you keep an eye on her for a minute? I must tell Bethany who she is. She needs to call the sheriff!"

One by one, tears rolled down Susan's eyes. Finally, she nodded, then fell back onto her pillow.

"Susan, my name is Pastor Ted Cummings. I know your friend, Mary."

A flash of recognition crossed Susan's face. A small smile followed it. "You...do?" she asked as her eyes closed.

She was drifting off to sleep. He needed more answers.

"Pastor Cummings?" she whispered.

She paused, stopping mid-sentence. For a moment, it looked as though the sedation had worked, and she'd fallen asleep.

He took a step forward, hoping to keep her talking. "Yes. I'm Pastor Cummings. Did Mary tell you about me?"

She opened her eyes. Her face became pale.

"Mary didn't tell me about you. He did."

A cold chill went up his spine. His heart began to race. "He?"

She nodded. He could tell she was fighting to keep her eyes open. "Atvaras. He laughed when he heard you told the crow you'd win."

His already racing heart fell straight down into his stomach. Norm was right. The crows were the demon's spies! How long had they spied on Norm? Had they also spied on Tobias? If so, what information had they shared with the demon?

Susan's eyes fully closed. Then, just as she slipped into sleep, she whispered, "It's coming for them tonight. They won't be ready."

Tonight? His forehead broke out in a cold sweat. Her comments confirmed his worse fears. After months away, the demon had reappeared, hellbent on destroying Tobias and his family.

He glanced up as Cheryl and Bethany entered the bay.

"She just fell asleep. I'm sorry, but I've got to leave."

He tried not to make a commotion as he navigated the hall full of gurneys and pieces of equipment. But, once he made it outside, he bolted to his car. Once there, he pulled out his phone. *Crap!* Another missed call from Norm. *I was too distracted to feel the phone.*

He returned Norm's call as he pulled out of the hospital parking lot. Beep, beep, beep, followed by a message that all circuits were busy. *Is Norm's phone off, or is something interfering with the signal?* At the first red light, he dialed Tobias' number. Same thing. *Something is interfering with the signal!*

✳ ✳ ✳

As he drove to the farm, he relistened to Norm's last message, telling him how to get onto the farm. Once he'd made it through town, he pushed the accelerator down towards the floorboard and prayed he wouldn't be too late. He drove past the subdivision and shuddered. With no electricity and barely any moon in the sky, the subdivision was shrouded in an eerie dark silence.

Once he drove past the subdivision, he lifted his foot off the accelerator to slow the car. He turned right onto the second gravel road. He saw the chain-link fence gates, but they were open, not closed as Norm said he'd find them. *Someone's come through the gate.* He sat straight up and glanced at his surroundings. His heartbeat quickened as his senses went on high alert.

Slowly, he drove down the road, guided only by headlights. Within a hundred yards, he came upon three vehicles. He recognized the first two cars. They belonged to Charles and Norm. Parked behind Norm's truck was a small red compact he'd never seen before. He grabbed his cellphone and Bible and climbed out of the car.

The red compact was empty. He placed his hand on the hood of the car; it was warm. *Someone just parked here.* Are they here to help? Or will more innocent people be in harm's way?

He jogged towards the farm. Up ahead, about twenty yards in the distance, he spied movement. He quickly glanced around. There was nowhere to hide. His forehead broke out in a cold sweat.

"Who's there?" a man's voice whispered.

The voice sounded familiar. "John? Is that you?"

"Yes. Pastor Cummings?"

He breathed a sigh of relief and ran towards John.

John extended his hand. "It's so good to see you, Pastor. Was it my mother or father who called you?"

He shook his head. "Neither...Norm Keller...he phoned me."

"Mr. Keller? Does he know what's happening on our farm?"

"He knows about the demon. He's here to help us."

John paused, then nodded. "I'm glad he knows, and I'm happy you're both here. I tried to call my brothers and my father, but I can't through to any of them."

"I tried to call Norm and your father to let them know I was on my way. Same thing."

Even in the darkness, he could see John's eyes widen. "I hope they're okay. Follow me. I'll show you the fastest way to the house. It's through the cemetery."

✳ ✳ ✳

Mary followed Daniel down the slightly sloping hill and into the cemetery. Just past the treeline and to her left, sparks of flickering light shot out from the center of a giant wall of rolling fog. Straight ahead were the shadowy outlines of four men.

He could tell from their voices James was trying to hold back Norm. "Stop, Norm! Susan's not there!" Charles was trying to hold back Tobias. Charlie's voice also rang out: "Dad, stop!" It looked like Norm and Tobias were trying to walk into the fog. Daniel bolted towards Norm, who had just pushed past James. She followed. Together, they each grabbed one of his arms.

Like a ragdoll, Mary was tossed about as Norm violently shook his arm, trying to break her hold. "Norm! Norm!" she screamed. It was no use. He seemed oblivious to her presence.

* * *

Ted followed John as he ran deeper into the farm. Just beyond the treeline, yelling and screaming filled the night air. John stopped, turned, and raised a finger to his lips. Together, they glanced around the base of a large tree.

Daniel and Mary were tugging Norm's arms while James was pushing on Norm's chest, holding him in place. Next to them, Charles had his hands on Tobias' chest, trying to hold him back. At that moment, Tobias shoved Charles aside and took a few steps forward. John bolted from the tree line and grabbed onto one of Tobias' arms.

"John! I knew you'd come!" Charles yelled as he scrambled up and grabbed onto Tobias' other arm.

He stood there, hidden in the tree line, quickly assessing the situation. Daniel, James, and Mary were holding Norm back. Charles and John were holding Tobias back. *But back from what?*

To his right loomed a large wall of fog. Bursts of light danced through the fog like tiny sparks of electricity. Both men kept fighting to move in its direction. *The demon is playing tricks on their minds!* Finally, he burst from the tree line and yelled in the direction of the fog, "In the name of Jesus Christ, I command you, demon…leave their minds alone!"

An ear-piercing shriek rang out. He fell to his knees and covered his ears. When the shrieking stopped, he looked around. Tobias's sons and Mary were also on their knees, covering their ears. Norm and Tobias both staggered, then fell backward.

"Thank you, Jesus! Thank you for your protection!" he cried out as he ran in the direction of the cemetery. "We must bring Norm and Tobias inside the house! The Lord's mercy will protect us. Focus on the word of God."

Once in the house, Norm and Tobias collapsed onto the kitchen table chairs. Even in the dim candlelight, he could see both men were soaked in sweat, and their faces were pale.

John closed the blinds and locked the door while James and Daniel huddled around the kitchen table. Daniel glanced up at his brother. "That won't keep it out, John."

John's mouth fell open, then closed. He quietly nodded.

"I don't know what would have happened if you two hadn't shown up when you did," Charles said.

He nodded. He wasn't sure what would have happened. He was just grateful they were all safe. "Let us sit together and praise God. He is our Rescuer and our Refuge. Let our prayers focus on removing this demon's stronghold on your family, keeping it out of this home and out of your life."

A worried look passed over James's face. "Pastor Cummings, there's something you should know. When you cleansed the house, my father didn't fully confess. He did so tonight. He told Norm everything before the demon attacked his mind. Can you help us cleanse the house again?"

"Rest assured God heard your father's confession. He knows his heart and knows he is truly repentant."

A chill fell over the house. It was as if someone had shrouded it in a wet, icy blanket. A dull pressure spread over his chest, stealing the breath from his lungs. He looked around the table. The men adjusted uncomfortably in their seats. *They sense it, too, right outside the house.*

He led them in prayer. After that, everyone around the table called out to the Lord on their own, offering praises, praying, and reciting scripture.

The light above the table dimly flickered on and off.

"Is the power back on?" James asked.

"I don't think so," Daniel said.

The light above the table flickered on once more. Slowly, it grew brighter. "Keep praising God. Keep praying," he said. With each passing second, the light grew brighter, and a warm sensation washed over him as if someone wrapped a heavy warm blanket around his shoulders. "Do you feel that?" he asked. "Do you feel the sense of comfort I do?"

He glanced into the faces of the everyone sitting around the table. Seeing the color had returned to Norm and Tobias' faces filled him with relief.

John whispered, "I feel...peace."

"It's the presence of God," Norm said. "His angels are surrounding us."

In his mind, he envisioned tall, muscular angels standing behind them. Fine warriors, protecting them with their unfurled wings. "They are protecting us. Pray for continued protection. Pray that the Lord will strike down this evil."

A long screeching sound resonated through the kitchen. It was followed by a loud bang that shook the windows and walls. It sounded as though pieces of the overturned patio furniture were sliding across the porch and slamming into the house. In his mind, he pictured additional angels outside fighting the demon.

"The evil bounced off the wall. But it didn't come through!" he exclaimed.

The porch creaked and groaned. "Keep praying!" he yelled. "It's prowling around like a roaring lion, trying to find a way back into the house. But the Lord is strengthening and protecting us. We're keeping it out! So keep the prayers coming!" A constant murmur of prayer filled the room.

With each passing second, the creaking and groaning grew. The evil continued to reverberate against the walls rhythmically. Finally, the spirit made a guttural, near frantic howl.

"Tune out the demon! Focus on prayer!" he encouraged.

The light above the kitchen table grew brighter. He squeezed his eyes shut, blocking out the light.

In a soft voice, he heard James whisper, "Atvaras."

He shielded his eyes from the light overhead and looked at James. "What? What did you say?"

"Atvaras. I think that's the demon's name."

That's the name Susan said at the hospital.

His gaze moved from James to Tobias. Tobias' eyes grew bright and clear. He nodded. "We know its name."

With sure fast faith, he yelled, "Atvaras! In the name of Jesus Christ, we command you to leave this family alone! You have no power here! Lord, we pray you to reach down into this family's generations, remove this demon by its roots, and throw it into the lake of fire. We pray in your Son's Holy Name, Jesus."

Everyone repeated his prayer and commanded Atvaras to leave the family alone. Then, the sound of repeated banging against the wall changed. It sounded like someone or something was being tossed from one side of the porch to the other. Then, another ear-piercing shriek filled the air, louder than the one in the cemetery.

He covered his ears with his forearms and laid his face near the table. The shriek shattered the kitchen windows, sending shards of glass flying. Then the shrieking abruptly stopped. The cool pressure surrounding the house lifted.

"Is it over?" Charles asked in a voice of disbelief.

"I believe it is…thanks be to God, who gives us the victory through our Lord Jesus Christ!" Norm said.

He watched as the men closed their eyes and quietly offered prayers of thanksgiving. Tears rolled down their faces. Then they began hugging each other. It was clear the ordeal had strengthened their faith in the Lord and brought their family closer.

"Did anyone get hurt from the glass?" he asked. They all shook their heads no. He rose and walked to the back door of the kitchen, swinging it wide open. The fog was nothing more than an ever-fading mist. Everyone followed him outside. He descended the backyard stairs, took deep breaths of the crisp night air, then looked back.

Daniel, James, and Charles stood arm in arm along the porch rail, looking out over the backyard. Next to them, were Norm and Mary, their arms wrapped around each other. John and Tobias followed him down the stairs.

At the bottom of the stairs, John embraced Tobias. "You followed through on your promise. You told us you would break our family's curse."

Then he focused on him. "Thank you for being here, Pastor Cummings. We couldn't have done this without you."

He shook his head and pointed his finger up towards the sky. "The honor and praise belong to him."

CHAPTER 44

I mages of the night flashed through Ted's mind in a dizzying fashion. After graduation, he asked God to place him where he was most needed. He never imagined it would be here, helping a family fight a demon.

Tobias pulled out his cellphone. "My cellphone is working again. I need to call Sarah and tell her what happened."

John pulled out his cellphone to call Kate. Seeing everyone so happy reminded him of seeing Susan at the hospital.

"With everything happening so quickly, I never told you, they found Susan tonight! She's alive and at the hospital!"

The revelation was met with looks of stunned silence, followed by smiles of joy and prayers of thanksgiving.

"Is she okay?" Norm asked as a huge smile spread over his face, and tears streamed from his eyes.

"She's been through quite an ordeal, looks disheveled and dehydrated." He paused for a moment. "There's something else. The demon possessed her body."

"Oh no!" Mary exclaimed. "When can we see her?"

* * *

In the early morning hours, Ted met Norm and Mary in the hospital lobby. Then, together they went to Susan's room. From the doorway, he could tell the nurses had bathed her. A man and a woman were at the bedside. Judging by the way they hovered over her, it was her parents.

Norm and Mary stepped into the room.

"Hello, Susan," Mary said in a cracking voice. Tears flowed from her eyes.

Susan glanced up and gave a smile. "Hi, Mary." Then she raised her hand and looked past Mary. "Hi, Norm. Hi, Pastor Cummings."

Not only does she remember me, she remembered my name. Based on the way she looked last night, it seemed like a pretty remarkable feat.

He stepped forward and smiled. "Hello, Susan. You look well-rested. How are you feeling today?"

"Better."

While Norm and Mary stood at Susan's bed, he extended his hand towards the couple hovering nearby. "Are you Susan's parents?"

The man nodded and shook his hand. "I'm Steve." He pointed to the woman. "This is my wife, Anne."

He shook their hands. "I'm pleased to meet you both. What a tremendous blessing to have your daughter back."

They both nodded, then turned their attention to Norm and Mary. While the four of them spoke, he stood back and watched Susan. She was staring out the window. A few seconds later, a large crow landed on the windowsill. Susan's face lit up and her lips curled up into a rather odd-looking smirk.

The crow tipped its head side to side. Susan continued to stare at the crow. The unblinking manner at which she stared at the crow turned his blood ice cold.

Anne asked a question that drew Susan's attention away from the window. A small conversation ensued, but in all honesty, he couldn't remember anything they said. Instead, he couldn't shake the image of Susan smiling at the crow from his mind.

Norm followed him into the hallway. Mary remained in the room talking with Anne and Steve.

Norm narrowed his eyes. "You're awful quiet. Is something wrong?"

He took a step further into the hallway, then whispered, "Did you see the crow on the windowsill?"

Norm's eyes widened. He quickly glanced back into the room, towards the window, then shook his head. "There was a crow?"

"It flew away. But it was there while you were talking with Susan's parents."

"And?"

"Susan was staring at the crow and smiling."

Norm's face fell. "I'm pretty sure she doesn't like birds."

"She didn't seem bothered by the crow. In fact, if I didn't know better, I'd say they were communicating with each other."

Norm's face went pale. "Do you think we're dealing with another demon?"

"I don't know. Tobias said there were powerful men in this town who practiced witchcraft alongside his grandfather and great-uncle. So doesn't it make sense they'd be large demonic activity lingering within this community?"

Norm nodded. "We'll pray that God reveals these strongholds and prepares us for the next battle!"

THE END

Visit Author's Website
Shariweise.com

Blog, Short Stories, and Updates on Upcoming Books

Book Playlist

Whenever I hear these songs, I picture images from the book. I've listed them below with the corresponding book chapters. I hope these songs touch your heart the same way they've touched mine.

Chapter 26
Song: What a Beautiful Name Artist: Hillsong Worship

Chapter 27
Song: Never Too Far Gone Artist: Jordan Feliz

Chapter 30
Song: Alive and Breathing Artist: Matt Maher

Chapter 31
Song: Keep on Hoping Artist: Riley Clemmons

Chapter 43
Song: Rescue Artist: Lauren Daigle

Chapter 43
Song: Battle Belongs Artist: Phil Wickman

Made in the USA
Las Vegas, NV
24 July 2021